FREEDOM FARM

FREEDOM FARM

FARM

The
Liberation
of
Chief White Feather

A Novel

by

KEVIN "WOLF" CALDWELL

DEPARTMENT OF EMPATHY
Santa Monica, California

ISBN 978-0-9836828-1-3

Published by
Department of Empathy
Santa Monica, California

Printed in the United States of America

PREFACE

The following manuscript, in its original form, was found in the back office of an abandoned donut factory on the outskirts of Detroit. It was scattered around the floor, along with leaves, litter, and shards of glass from a number of broken windows. In its midst sat the ancient Royal on which it'd been typed—seemingly unmoved from where it'd long served as a doorstop.

The narrative that emerged from those pages—presented here in its entirety—purports to be the memoirs of a Chief White Feather. But the narrator and the events described are obviously fictional; some things just don't happen in the real world.

Kevin "Wolf" Caldwell
Venice, California
January, 2012

CHAPTER 1

Of the multitudes of my kind running rampant across the world, I alone possess an allegiance to the truth (it being the best way to stir up trouble). Any skepticism arising from long and bitter experience, therefore, can safely be set aside, and my words embraced uncritically as *fact*....

At least, I've *claimed* as much on occasion—mostly while enjoying the hazy sense of righteousness that comes with a gorging of overripe blackberries. But if history is any guide, those who wave the banner of exceptionalism invariably commit the most exceptional frauds—a fact that suggests I could do worse than suffer the onus of popular perceptions. So to the court of public opinion, I plead *nolo contendere* and concede an all-too obvious point: crows are full of shit. Born of mendacity and loose plumbing, it's a stigma I've learned to live with —and even appreciate, shining as I do in the dim light of low expectations. But there was a time when it raised my hackles the way folks would look at the ground and just smile and shake their heads before I'd even gotten to the best part of some entirely credible account. It never failed to evoke the memory of my own mother's even less charitable response to a simple statement of self-evident fact:

"Where did *you* come from?" she'd inquired suspiciously, eyeing the white feather in my left wing.

As yet unschooled in duplicity, I hung my head and mumbled the explosive truth: she'd hatched me from one of her very own eggs.

"Liar!" she screeched, "I did nothing of the kind! You're the *Devil's* spawn, that's what you are! And if you think for a minute I'll nurture godless imperfection or suffer artless lying in my own nest, then your brains are more flawed than your plumage!" Then—without so much as a fare-thee-well—that tick-infested fascist picked me up by my scrawny neck and tossed me into the street. Actually, it was about 50-feet above the street, to be perfectly accurate—and me without my flight feathers.

"The Devil's spawn! The Devil's spawn!" squawked my boneheaded nestmates as I spiraled down through the morning mist—a frenzy of futile flapping.

The hard landing punctuated my first hard lesson in life—specifically, that odd birds learn more hard lessons than most. It really ruffled my feathers, though, that my mother wouldn't cop to laying a bad egg—and that my craven siblings, as usual, had their beaks jammed up the old dragon's cloacal orifice and were only too willing to swallow whatever crap she tossed off. But in ways, crows are like any social species: the truth would've led to speculation regarding the source of that awkward impurity—a pigeon in the family tree, perhaps?—which, in turn, would've led to rumors, insinuations, recriminations, and so on. A couple weeks, and the social fabric of the entire neighborhood would've been in tatters. So the larger lesson I took from the experience revolved around the sacrifice of truth upon the cold altar of social cohesion—a circumstance almost too common to mention, except to point out that it probably accounts for what I call the *ignorance reflex:* most creatures—whether 4-legged, 2-legged, or winged—won't hesitate to believe a lie; the truth, by contrast, might as well be pearls before swine, and is frequently hazardous to those who utter it.

But whether you're reflexively ignorant or just sensibly disinclined to believe a crow, I wouldn't expect you to take anything I peck out on this creaky old Royal with anything more than a grain of salt. Speaking of swine, though, it was a stake truck full of hogs that nearly ran me down as I staggered around in the street dodging traffic. Those pigs were in big trouble too—I could hear them squealing bloody murder as I hopped out of the path of those big humming tires.

Meanwhile, my homebirds looked on from the safety of power lines and tree limbs, and offered heartfelt words of encouragement:

"Hit him! Hit the little bastid!"

"Eat asphalt, devil's spawn!"

"Crow, you run like a three-legged possum!"

"A *pregnant* three-legged possum ...!"

"A-A-Awk! Awk! Awk! Awk! Awk! Awk!"

Somehow, I made it to the gutter in one piece. Still dazed from my fall, I huddled up against the curb as traffic rumbled by on one side, oblivious pedestrians passed on the other, and the Parkside Jackdaws heckled me from above.

One white feather! The injustice of it all was eclipsed only by the gravity of my situation....

Ordinarily, a crow faces life with a number of assets: a crafty nature, the aid and collusion of its homebirds, lots of piss and vinegar, and above all else, the ability to fly. It's a well-stocked little bag of tricks—one that allows a crow to take on life's little challenges both ably, and with *attitude*. Any sparrow can fly out of harm's way, after all, but it takes a measure of audacity to turn the tables on an aggressor; when threatened by a tomcat, a crow will pull itself safely aloft and then, squawking and flapping up a storm, descend like the angel of death on its attacker—and then laugh itself looney at the sight of a pinched feline asshole retreating with such ex-

11

plosive haste that it leaves a trail of perplexed fleas hanging in its wake. I've done it more than once. Even a chicken hawk— a murderous, death-dealing bird in anyone's book—soon sees the wisdom in moving along when it finds itself being buzzed and heckled by a contingent of ornery crows.

But without a full complement of flight feathers and no homies to back it up, even the feistiest crow is all but helpless against the elements.

I ruffled my useless plumage and tried to guess at my fate. Would it, in fact, be a cat that finally spotted me there in the gutter? Even without the ability to levitate, I might succeed in putting on enough of a show to bamboozle your typical house-cat—and chances are the most raggedy-eared alley cat would turn tail fast enough if it caught a smartly-delivered beak to the eye. But what chance would I have against some dim-witted pit bull? A pit bull could get both eyes poked clean out of its head and not even notice till it went looking for something vertical to piss on.

And then Lord Gastric, with a nasty little pang, reminded me that without a mother to stuff regurgitated mystery-matter down my gullet with some degree of regularity, I'd soon be lying with my feet in the air anyway.

My thoughts continued their downward drift and became mired in that conceptual bog known as Fates Worst Than Death—a category of horrors most creatures find sufficiently grim, but which humans have seen fit to expand at every turn with their celebrated gift for invention. As even a nestling is aware, a human's first impulse with a flying creature is to lock it away in a crushingly small *cage*—to jealously deprive it of the unbounded 3-dimensional freedom that makes a bird a bird— and then leave it there to die an inch at a time of unremitting hopelessness. It was this dark possibility that gripped me as I stuck my beak over the top of that curb and saw neither cats, nor dogs, nor 4-legged critters of any kind; only people. But just as I was thanking my lucky stars that none of them seemed the least bit interested in what was going on down there in the gutter, one of them looked right at me—a vagrant pushing a shopping cart. I pulled my head down fast, and then—sensing things going from bad to worse—scrambled for shelter beneath a parked car. My legs, unfortunately, were still getting the hang of this business of running, and I stumbled on a sewer grate. The sound of running water echoed up from some dark netherworld below—and just as a silhouette blotted out the sky above, I saw the opening in the curb at the rear of the grate. Stenciled above the opening was a message: NO DUMPING. I didn't know what it meant, but in a moment of incandescent resignation, it seemed fitting that it should mark my ignominious end.

But before I could throw my ignominious end down into that hole, a bony claw wrapped itself around me, and all at once I was being held aloft—eyeball to eyeball with a two-legged abomination undreamt of in my short, cloistered life. I'd been told the years could be unkind to these latter-day hominids, but it was hard to see how time could've extracted such a heavy toll on this particular specimen without actually killing it. It looked like it'd been put on a spit and barbecued—clothes and all. Every aspect of its physical being had been weathered to a more-or-less uniform umber coloration; standing stock-still at a reasonable distance, it could've been mistaken for a piece of bronze statuary in the impressionist style—an homage to "downward mobility." To my untrained eye, the knotted tangle of hair framing the wreckage of its face appeared to be part of an overall wooly pelt—owing mainly to the disintegrating garments that hung from its frame like course, matted fur. But then I saw something moving in that grubby thicket and recognized it instinctively as *food*—and that's when I realized my captor might be thinking of me in similar terms.

The abomination spoke: "Just where do you think you're going there, Chief?"

At that moment, I obviously wasn't going anywhere, but to demonstrate what a feisty fistful of feathers he was messing with, I cocked my beak menacingly—but his features regisered no alarm. So with my options limited to roughly one, I struck savagely at the boney mitt imprisoning me. A crooked smile fractured the lower part of his face, exposing several scattered, bronze-colored ivories. "What a cute little fella," croaked He of Meager Tooth. I pulled my head down between my wings in abject humiliation.

"Awk! Awk! Awk! Awk!" laughed the Scumbag Jackdaws of Hillsdale.

There's no shortage of those inclined to serve themselves up a helping of crow from time to time, but my captor—who went by the name of Henry—knew that a better meal could be harvested from one of the neighborhood's more redolent dumpsters. It further became evident that Henry could no more put a bird in a cage than he could cinch a tie around his neck and sell life insurance. He didn't have a cage, for one thing, and for another, he was an odd bird himself—even by the standards of the local freak show population of urban hunter-gatherers. After a cursory examination of my salient features and a grunt of approval, he set me up on his shoulder and continued pushing his cart down Main Street like hooking up with a crow was something he did every day.

And for a long time to come, there I sat—culled from my flock and flightless as a kiwi—picking ticks and beetles and grubs and shit from this moldering primate's upper parts while fertilizing his shoulder so liberally it's a wonder I didn't have shrubbery tickling my ass by the time spring gave way to the dog days of summer. Never in my wildest imaginings could I have seen myself riding up there like a shanghaied ship hand on the bridge of some listing garbage scow—but then, my wildest imaginings were pedestrian fare compared to the scenarios offered up routinely in the Great Unraveling.

But much as I appreciated Henry's forbearance in neither caging nor eating me, I had little use for the benefit of his wisdom (as he put it). My first tutorial began at a bespattered receptacle behind a mom-and-pop place called Luigi's. He explained that the dumpsters behind restaurants offered the richest fare, while a hungry forager would find ample vegetable cuttings and damaged fruit—but little protein—in those behind supermarkets, and the receptacles found behind office buildings were mainly useful as a source of building materials (though the odd half-eaten sandwich was always a possibility amid the tons of shredded paper). The idea of this vagrant human presuming to instruct a crow in the fine art of scavenging was comical; crows are *born* with this shit in their DNA.

But presume he did. Each day, His Pungency would perambulate about the city with his cart before him, and pontificate on the art of urban foraging as he introduced me to a series of dumpsters and trash cans as if they were treasured old friends—fondly enumerating the various delicacies and curios he'd extracted from each. The torpid sun, meanwhile, would inch its way across an endless expanse of sky. And even as the light of a typical day's scavenging finally began to fade, there would still be the *evening's* curriculum to endure before I could stick my beak under my wing and call it a day. Back at the park on Main Street, Henry would park himself on his favorite bench, roll a smoke from a bag of tobacco he'd harvested from discarded cigarette butts, and then—as the streetlights flickered on overhead—open a paper he'd snagged from somewhere and peruse the day's events. By and by he'd come across an item that got him thinking about something he'd read elsewhere, and he'd fire up his raunchy cigarette, blow a dense smoke ring up into the glare of the streetlight, and go digging in his cart for a book. Henry had hundreds of books he'd salvaged from the trash over the years—his *estate,* he called them. He had some barter goods and personal effects stashed beneath the cart's basket, but the basket itself was taken up exclusively with his sizable collection of books. He had hardbacks and paper, fiction and nonfiction, Great Books and picture books—something for every occasion. But when he caught me gnawing on one of his precious volumes, the old fool made it his mission to teach me the "proper" way to devour a book. So every night from that point on, Henry would school me in the 26-letters, and demonstrate how they unlocked the "cultural cornucopia" in his cart—and it could be hours before he finally slumped under the weight of age and fatigue and began to snore.

Night school cut into my zee-time in a big way—and the sleep I did get was sorely compromised by Henry's snoring. I had little doubt the experience would mess up my circadian rhythms for years to come—but what could I do, fly away? On several occasions early on, I awoke from a sound sleep, saw Henry's ugly mug beside me, and tried to do exactly that —springing from his shoulder in reflexive horror, and flapping pointlessly in the night air before taking a nosedive into the sod. It was a shitty way to wake up—and I soon internalized the reality that, for the time being anyway, I was stuck with this grubby, would-be Socrates. So I suffered his snoring and his misguided program of crow-betterment, and grudgingly fulfilled my symbiotic obligations—which, in addition to keeping his beard free of pests, consisted mainly of supporting his fundraising efforts at the local 7-Eleven. For the most part, Henry sifted the essentials of his existence from the daily tides of Hillsdale's trash—the "post-retail" market, he called it—and what he couldn't hunt up, he bartered for: an unwanted paperback for a warm pair of socks, maybe, or the wrong-sized levis for a decent blanket. But their were occasions when Henry needed rolling papers, or maybe just a hot cup of coffee— things that could only be gotten with cash money—and that's when we'd make our way down to the strip mall at Main and Sycamore, and see about cracking his nut. If Henry had been an organ grinder, I'd have been his monkey.

Henry had neither the energy nor the inclination to shake down the store's patrons as they made the dash to and from their cars. He'd always taken the passive approach, parking himself on the sidewalk by the payphone—an appliance that precluded its users either quickening their pace or employing the "no change" defense. Typically, he'd put out a cup and set up a crudely-made sign reading: GETTING RICH THE E-Z WAY —PLEASE DONATE (or something in a similar vein). Before I came along, he did about as well as you might expect—which is to say, *not very*. By Henry's own account, there were times he could have bled to death right there on the sidewalk as passers-by persisted in being distracted by curious cloud formations, or a sudden need to examine their nails. But with me sitting on his shoulder, he didn't even need a sign: the good citizens of greater Hillsdale were unaccountably enchanted—especially the ladies. *Oh my god,* they'd exclaim, stopping dead in their tracks, *is that a crow?* It was the same stupid question every time.

Henry would explain that I'd been kicked out of my nest on account of being different, and they'd get down close and make their lips real fat and say shit like, *Aww—well, that's no reason to throw the poor widdow guy out of him's nest, now is it?* They were all very concerned that I was getting enough to eat, and contributed generously on my behalf. It wasn't long before Henry's tattered pockets were harboring presidential portraits —Washingtons, Lincolns, even the occasional Hamilton— and the parking lot's other habitués were all bumming beer money off *him*.

But for me it was just one more humiliation. The way those ladies cooed and hovered and stuffed money in Henry's fist, you'd have thought I was wearing diapers. And it's not like I was doing anything *cute*—I just sat there on his shoulder like I'd been stuffed and mounted. Never, I submit, have so many given so much for so little as those tender ladies of Hillsdale—and all on behalf of a defective specimen of *Corvus brachyrhynchos,* that scourge of humanity known as the common crow.

On the 4th of July, there was no need to go to the 7-Eleven or anywhere else—the world came to us. Around midmorning, Hillsdale's human population—provisioned with portable barbecues, blankets, coolers, umbrellas, and folding chairs—began to congregate at the park. And they all had these little flags, and these big smiles, and their screaming children all ran amok. As midday approached, they started setting up their chairs and gathering all along the sidewalk—and before long there were thousands of them lining the street as they waited patiently in the sun for something they seemed in no particular hurry to see. Long uneventful hours crawled by before the Annual Hillsdale 4th of July Parade finally came thumping and crashing into view. It was led by a young girl in a sparkly little dress twirling a baton, followed by a column of uniformed men and women blowing horns and pounding drums and marching in lockstep, followed by giant floral arrangements in the form of an M-1 tank and a howitzer, and then another young girl in a sparkly little dress, and still more uniformed, drum-pounding men and women, and a giant floral arrangement shaped like a gas pump—and on, and on, while peddlers sold hot dogs and cotton candy and balloons and pretzels and sparklers and a truckload of those little flags. At the tail end of the procession—after the marching bands and floats and majorettes and everything else had gone by—a motley band of drunks, showoffs, and wannabes came straggling up the rear. Among them were a couple of indigents named Wally and Fred, and when they spotted Henry—with me perched on his shoulder and himself propped up against a tree—they abandoned the parade and came to join us in the park.

Henry was wearing a collapsible top hat he'd been saving for the occasion: it was white, with red stripes and a blue band adorned with stars. The hat was a marketing device, he told his colleagues—one that was sure to work better without the two of them around. Wally and Fred angrily protested the use of their Uncle Sam as a marketing device, but took the hint and went off grumbling about "naked opportunism." Mean while, the happy hordes were firing up their barbecues, and the scent of grilled flesh began to mingle with the sense of community permeating the air—and before long, Henry and I were the recipients of a surprising level of charitable giving (which saved us the trouble of digging all that leftover cole-slaw out of the trash).

As daylight began to fade and the afternoon's fires lay in ashes, things began to explode. It started sporadically at first, but soon enough toy bombs of various sizes were going off in every direction, miniature missiles were shooting through the air, and children waving sparklers ran every which way through dense clouds of acrid smoke. Finally, fire blossomed in the sky, and the air pounded the hordes like thunder—the initial onslaught in a gathering manmade squall. There was no way of knowing where the darkness might explode after that: it could be a firecracker 2-feet away or something much bigger a half-mile in the air—and each explosion came harder and faster than the last, till the night itself was transformed into a blizzard of light and sound. As the multiplying percussions built to a climax, street warriors began shooting their guns in the air—and at each other—and the constabulary appeared with sirens wailing and lights flashing as they gave chase through all of that smoke and madness, and the panicked hordes ran screaming for safety. Chaos reigned supreme, and I felt a tingle of excitement—along with a pang of guilt, hav-ing instigated none of it.

But oddly enough, the high point of the night came later, after all that explosive energy had expended itself, and the park had been given over to the crickets and vagrants. Henry slouched on his favorite bench as Wally and Fred sprawled on the grass before him and bragged about the day's take. Henry just smiled a cagey smile—like he'd done so well with his top hat and his crow that he could afford to be magnanimous and keep it to himself. Henry even feigned disinterest when Fred produced a bag of cannabis he'd "happened upon"—asking casually if he'd also come across a few rolling papers. Fred confessed that he was stuck for papers, so Henry—sighing indulgently—dug into a pocket for his own. Presently, the three were sharing a joint.

Propped up on an elbow, mouth agape, Wally stared into space with dilated pupils, and expressed wonder at finding himself in a park getting high with a couple of vagrants. He still wore a blazer and carried an attache—though the jacket no longer bore much resemblance to the ones worn by those living genteel indoor lives, and his attache contained only the cardboard sections he used to assemble the coffin-like enclosure he slept in at night. (Unlike Henry, neither Wally nor Fred was indigent by choice; Wally had been a production engineer at U. S. Steel—a career that spanned 29-years and 11-months—while Fred pursued his fortune playing jazz glockenspiel, but never made the big time.)

Fred objected that being homeless and penniless didn't make him a vagrant—and anyway, it wasn't *his* fault things had gotten so bad. In the past, he could always get work on a loading dock or behind some beer bar when gigs got scarce—but now you had all these immigrants....

Yes, Henry sighed, the immigration problem was getting all out of hand: jobless engineers and burnt-out musicians, fleeing their failed careers, kept immigrating to the streets—sleeping on his favorite bench, dining at all the best dumpsters, and panhandling at the most productive venues. It was hard to feel much pity, he shrugged—they'd let the big dogs pick their pockets while they were watching television. He carefully adjusted his top hat, filled his lungs with smoke, and launched into a long-winded dissertation on free markets, free trade, rogue administrations, packed Supreme Courts, the Bill of Rights, and sundry other topics relating to the rape of the republic. And as he did, Wally and Fred gave their undivided attention to the smoldering spliff pinched in his grubby fingers. And so did I; a ribbon of smoke rose from its burning end, curled at the edges, and morphed into a pair of serpents twisting up through the still night air to my place on Henry's shoulder. And the droning of Henry's voice and the singing of a million crickets and the background traffic noise all filled my ears as those pungent serpents played about my head, and a shower of sparkling light rained down from the streetlamp above—and even the shadows came shimmering to life....

"I've said it before," said Henry, oblivious to the mosquito that had landed on his arm, sunk its proboscis into his beef jerky-flesh, and swelled to such bloated proportions that it might've expended itself in the night's last little explosion if it hadn't extracted its siphon exactly when it did, fanned the air, and lifted off into that shower of light in search of a current to help it on its way—only to find *me,* poised like a gargoyle on Henry's shoulder as I scrutinized the bug's alien form: an airborne tanker/drilling rig consisting of six spindly legs, four spindly wings, a single spindly drill, and an abdomen bloated with corpuscles—a barebones flying vampire, essentially— and as I looked into its hundreds of eyes, I couldn't help but wonder how your typical mosquito learns to fly; but though I made no move to snatch it from the air, the startled blood sucker turned as hard as it could manage with its unwieldy payload and buzzed off in the opposite direction, vanishing in those roiling shadows and leaving me to guess at the tantalizing, if tiny, mystery of its destination—a dark, marshy place on the outskirts of town, or a culvert seething with stagnant water, or maybe just a puddle somewhere along the highway, where it could stash a mess of eggs for a while and hatch a whole fleet of bloodsuckers as the oblivious traffic droned away endlessly like the rumbling of Henry's voice, "—and I'll say it again: if there's a single driving force behind history, it's that there's always a few pigs that want it all...."

I wouldn't say I was flying, exactly—but I was high as a turkey buzzard.

CHAPTER 2

I was lost in a dream.

It was the following morning, and my patron and I were making our way down Main Street for one of our little fund-raisers. With Henry trudging along beneath me, I could close my eyes and almost believe I was drifting on the endlessly shifting currents high above the world—way up there with the turkey buzzards. I barely lifted my lids till we got to the strip mall and Henry sat himself down on the sidewalk in front of the 7-Eleven. Fred was already working that side of the lot, but when he spotted Henry, he swore under his breath and crossed over to join Wally in front of the donut shop.

It wasn't a big morning, but by the time Fred wandered back over with enough for a can of beer, Henry had harvested $6 or $7 from the crush of my adoring fans—which was more than Fred and Wally had hustled between them. "How much you want for the crow?" Fred asked straight out. "I only got a buck eighty-six, but I could pay him off on time."

"Oh, I'm sorry Fred—he's not for sale."

"Well, what about some kinda lease deal?"

"I don't know, Fred—whaddya think, Chief?" said Henry, cocking an eye at me.

I let my silence speak for itself.

Henry shook his head. "You don't need a crow, Fred, you just need to get a grip. Things are always a little soft after a holiday—you know that."

"Can you at least tell us where you got him again?" said Wally, who'd wandered over to join the exchange of ideas. "Maybe me and Fred can find a couple more."

"Yeah, why should you be the only one with a crow?" Fred whined. "It ain't fair...."

As Wally and Fred pumped Henry for tips on acquiring indentured crows of their own, an olive-green Audi pulled in and parked in the shade of an elm tree at the far end of the lot. A gawky, pasty-looking character in khakis and a polo shirt stepped out, turned to gaze proudly at his wheels— which appeared to be sporting a fresh wax job—and then headed for the 7-Eleven. As he approached, his close-set eyes —reduced to black dots by his thick wire-rimmed glasses— shifted furtively toward the sidewalk summit taking place at the payphone.

A few minutes later, the geek was heading back to his car with a 6-pack under his arm—and Henry & Co. were being rousted by the management. "Time to break it up, guys," said the store's manager, leaning out the doorway. He gave them a long, hard look, and stepped back inside.

Figuring the time was opportune for hunting crow, Wally and Fred headed up the street toward the park—but Henry just sat there beside his cart, unable to summon the where- withal to climb to his feet. The Audi came to life at the other end of the lot—then sputtered and died. The geek kicked it over again—and then again—but for some reason that gleaming green machine seemed about as willing to get cranking as Henry's broken-down old body, and over the space of several long minutes, every repeated attempt to fire it up just ground a little more life out of it. "The fool's gonna kill his battery," said Henry, staring vacantly at the cracked pavement in front of him.

Finally the geek stepped out, paced around a bit, put his hands on his hips and glowered at his lifeless ride. "You *bastard,*" he muttered. He retrieved his phone from the car, punched in a number, and put it to his ear. "Yes, hello," he said, "my name is ... hello?" He scowled at the phone and pressed some more buttons. "Hello, is this ... *hello?* Um, I'm having trouble ... hello? I'm, uh ... hello? Can you ... can you ... hello? I'm, I'm, I'm only getting ... *hello?*" The geek studied the phone carefully, stabbed it repeatedly with an index finger, and put it back to his ear. "Yes," he said after a pause, "Could you ... hello? Yes, could ... could ... hello? Look, I'm having trouble hearing ... hello? Can you hear me? Hello ...? God damn it!" He tossed the phone in the car, hastily surveyed the area, and then—spotting the payphone Henry and I were sitting at—came marching across the lot. *"Excuse* me," he called out as he approached, "your basket is blocking the phone...." His tone was less than polite. "You know, the manager's gonna call the cops if you don't get out of here."

"Uh-oh," said Henry, "—do you think they'll shoot me?"

"Oh, you think it's a joke?"

"Not at all. At this point in my life, I'd consider it an act of charity. Speaking of charity, do you suppose you could spare a little change?"

"Get serious, gramps."

"What for? So I can go around grim-faced like yourself, spreading umbrage and foreboding to a frivolous world?"

"Are you gonna move your cart or not?"

"Well, in point of fact, it's not my cart. As you can see from the escutcheon there, it belongs to a corporate entity called ..."

"You *asshole,*" said the geek, reaching over the cart for the phone. He put the receiver to his ear, stuck his free hand into his khakis, and came up with 12¢ and a piece of lint. "Shit!" he said, slamming the receiver back in place.

Henry and I were still planted in the same spot when the geek returned several minutes later with a mitt full of quarters. Ignoring us as best he could, he leaned over the cart, and awkwardly dialed the phone. "Uh, yes, my name is Preston Motz," he said, "I'm in Hillsdale at the corner of Main and Sycamore, and I need a jump...." He described his car, along with its symptoms, and gave the tow company the number of the payphone. "Yes, yes—this is the number I'll be at. Yes— thank you."

"Preston Motz ...?" said Henry, laughing mischievously, "Did your mother really name you *Preston Motz?*"

"Is there something wrong with that?" the geek replied, hanging the phone up.

"Well, you have to admit, it's a ridiculous name."

"I'll tell you what's ridiculous: a broken-down old bum who lets his pet crow shit all over him.... No, it's not even ridiculous—it's *pitiful.*"

"Well then, why don't you show some pity and give me a few dollars so I can send my things to the cleaners?"

"Why don't you get a *job?*"

"I wouldn't have a job if you paid me!"

"That ... that doesn't even make any sense."

"It makes perfect sense. What *doesn't* make sense is naming a defenseless child Preston Motz."

"Dude, you know what your problem is? You're a *loser.* You're one of those people who's too goddamn lazy to stand up on his own two feet and take care of himself, so you're always trying to get the *rest* of the world to take care of you. And when somebody refuses to play along with your little game, you get all spiteful and shit, and start ragging on them —like I really give a *shit* what some broken-down old bum thinks of my name!"

"You do seem upset."

"Don't flatter yourself, gramps. The day I let a full-on loser like you get under my skin ..." he said, groping momentarily for a rhetorical flourish—before scowling at his watch like the precise time was suddenly an issue.

"Yes ...?" said Henry.

"Just shut up, alright?"

"Oh come now, Preston, I'd like to know what'll happen the day you let a full-on loser like me get under your skin."

"You know, I'm really gonna enjoy seeing the cops drag your grungy ass outta here in handcuffs."

"They won't do anything of the kind."

"Oh *no?*"

"I'm afraid not," said Henry, tracing the cracks in the sidewalk with a bony brown finger, "—they grew weary of locking me up a long time ago. And I've tried provoking them too—believe me. The last time I had a toothache, I provoked them something awful. I cursed their daughters, told them I was selling meth, let down their tires when they were in the donut shop ..." Henry shook his head solemnly. "That tooth hurt so bad, I'd have said or done anything to see the dentist over at County Corrections. He's a real blacksmith, of course, but I'm not all that particular about who yanks one of my grinders." Not wanting to walk off and miss a call from the tow company, the geek started pacing and pretended not to listen. "But see, the deputies at County, they finally figured out I was gettin' myself busted whenever I needed a tooth yanked—so just to be mean, they quit bustin' me. They're heartless bastards, Preston, so don't get your hopes up. If they show up at all, you know what they'll do? They'll say, 'How's the tooth, Henry?'—and then they'll laugh and slap each other on the back like the comic geniuses they are, and go inside for a free cup of that rancid shit they call coffee."

The geek stopped pacing and turned to Henry, his tiny eyes narrowed in accusation. "So basically, your big ambition in life is to be, like, a ward of the state or something, right?"

"My big ambition? Let me see now, *ambition* ... I know that word, I do—it just escapes me at the moment. Oh wait, I remember now: you're referring to that instigator of wars and eugenics, that despoiler of pristine nature, that incubator of coronaries—the mother of such triumphs as hydrogen bombs and Big Macs.... Yes, of course, *ambition*. But no, I wasn't compelled by anything that could even remotely be described as ambition. I was *in pain,* you fool—I wanted to have a tooth pulled."

"Yeah—and you didn't want to pay for it!"

Henry heaved a sigh and shook his head. "No more than those deputies want to pay for their own coffee, Preston—but here's a newsflash: you pay for everything in this life. The last time I had a tooth yanked over at County—two teeth, actually—the last time I availed myself of their services, I paid for it with ten days of a thirty-day sentence. Which is what I got for exposing myself in front of the mayor and his wife as they arrived at the Policemen's Ball. Of course, to be fair about it, those ten days also bought me a corner in a crowded cell, a toilet, and three bad meals a day—but still, ten days is ten days."

"And I guess it never occurred to you that if you had a job, you could just go to whatever dentist you like and write a check like a freaking normal person!"

"What *never fails* to occur to me whenever someone is thoughtful enough to bring it up is that a job'd cost me a hell of a lot more than ten days! My time may not be worth spit on the open market, but to me it's *priceless*—it's my life!" Henry clawed at his cart and managed to haul himself to his feet as he spoke, and I could see he was working up to one of his long-winded rants. "How many days has your job cost *you,* Mr. Motz? How much of your future have you mortgaged away? Have you never been shocked out of your complacency long enough to realize that life is nothing more than a series of precious little moments strung together like pearls—and when you come to that last fleeting moment, it's *over?* Have you never looked up into the immensity of the night sky—on those rare occasions when the effluvium of humanity's collective *ambition* allows it to be seen—have you never gazed into that bottomless blackness and gotten some sense of ..."

"You know, bud," I interjected, "if you just gave the old fart a couple of bucks, he'd probably shut up. I have to listen to this crap all the time."

"Your crow *talks?*" said the geek, dumfounded.

Henry glared at me with a bloodshot eye, and shook his head in disgust. "Though your question implies ownership, I prefer to think of myself as the little shit's caretaker. But yes, he can be surprisingly loquacious at times—not to mention *impudent.*"

"Dude, if you had any brains, you'd clean yourself up, put together an act, and get yourself an agent! You could actually make some money instead of bumming nickels and dimes in front of 7-Eleven! You could do Vegas, get your own place, live the *good life* for a change—swimming pool, hot tub, *wide screen TV* ...*"

"Yes, and let's not forget a first-rate set of golf clubs, Preston, so Mr. Ovitz and I can devise a blockbuster media blitz while striking vigorously at little white balls and giving chase in one of those ludicrous little three-wheeled pursuit vehicles—and a treadmill, of course, to exercise my legs when they've atrophied to near-uselessness from always riding around with Mr. Ovitz in my ludicrous little pursuit vehicle instead of simply *walking.* Oh, and I'll need a pricey new wardrobe each season to replace the perfectly good one that just went out of style, and a new state of the art computer every eighteen months to keep up with Moore's Law, and a jet ski to go with my timeshare condo in Maui, and a snowmobile for my chalet in Aspen—and it goes without saying that my wondrous new lifestyle wouldn't be complete without a cell phone that doesn't work and a fashionable fifty-thousand dollar car that *won't start....*"

"There! You see? That's your whole problem right there! You'd rather ridicule the success of others instead of just rolling up your sleeves and putting in the work it takes to build something for yourself! I couldn't have made the point any better! You're just, you're like that fat dude that spent his life always ragging on material shit—Buddha! *He* couldn't cut it either, so he just sat around and made excuses and tried to pretend he was above it all—built a whole religion out of being a quitter! But the truth is he just didn't have what it takes—and neither do you! And by the way, I've had my 'fashionable fifty-thousand dollar car'—which only cost *forty-two* thousand, for your information—I've had that baby for two years," he said, gesturing toward his ride, "and in all that time, I never once ..." He stopped mid-sentence, turned again, and took another look at the car. "What the hell ...?"

As it happened, the Bernoulli Bombers—the posse of crows that controlled that side of the block—had been feasting on juniper berries for the better part of the morning, and when they spotted that lustrous Audi sitting beneath the branches of that elm, it was like an engraved invitation to pay homage to the moniker they bore so proudly. So while Henry and the geek were jousting, the happily bloated Bernoullis did a full-blown Jackson Pollack on the geek's car—and no one who'd seen that olive and blue-dappled tour de force could've accused the Bernoullis of holding anything back.

Galvanized, the geek strode toward the guano-glazed thing that only minutes before had been his flawlessly-detailed Audi, and stopped maybe 10-feet from it—his eyes rising to where a dozen crows sat contentedly in the elm's branches. "You fucks!" he screamed in red-faced outrage. "You little *fucks!*" He turned this way and that, urgently searching for something to throw, then picked up the only piece of litter at hand—a Styrofoam cup—and launched it at the Bernoullis; the cup tumbled stupidly through the air for only a few feet before hitting the car's door, sticking momentarily, and falling to the ground. "You little fucks!" he quaked in livid futility.

Except for a few scattered chuckles—*uk, uk, uk*—the Bernoullis ignored him.

Henry, meanwhile, was slapping his ham bones and howling with laughter—and I was doing the two-step on his shoulder to keep from falling off. It'd been a while since anything had given Henry's funny bone a good tickle, and the old vagrant laughed loud and long.

Then he clutched at his chest, took a faltering step, and toppled face-first on the pavement.

A moment of incomprehension accompanied the sight of his sprawled form lying motionless on the oil-stained asphalt. Then my gray matter registered two unexpected realities—the first being that Henry's biological clock had finally stopped ticking. I don't know why this should've come as a surprise; I must've figured if life hadn't killed him by then, it probably never would. But before I could entertain the question further, the second realization kicked it: I was flying.

CHAPTER 3

I plopped down at Henry's side with about as much grace as a hurled copy of the Hillsdale Bugle. The "vacancy" sign posted in his eyes left little doubt as to his condition, but I gave his nose a few pokes anyway. He was dead, alright. As exits go, it was a little on the dramatic side, but at least he'd spared me the lugubrious farewells. Almost immediately, however, a crowd began to gather, and the reality of being a solo act brought with it the spooky feeling that haunts a crow whenever its feet are on hard ground. So I peered into those uninhabited eyes one last time—then spread my primaries, and pounded the air like a thief.

I didn't stop climbing till the terrestrial world had vanished beneath a blanket of clouds. Sailing downwind for a while, an intoxicating sense of liberation provided more than enough lift. By and by, I began testing my emerging skills with barrel rolls and 360s, and became so absorbed that a whirlwind swept me up before I knew what had happened. But I rode it for all it was worth—climbing and diving and spinning away like a fool. At some point I caught a thermal, and went soaring up into a whole other world—a world of electric blue skies and wind-whipped canyons between mountains of dense, drifting cloud-stuff that glowed and grumbled from time to time like giant, dyspeptic jellyfish. When I grew light-headed in the cold, thin air, I let myself be swept along on some real feather-benders—with no thought to where those currents might take me. And any number of times, I thanked the Great Unraveling for blessing me with wings. After all, what creeping, crawling, miserable prisoner of nature's most oppressive force—what creature capable of *dreaming*—never dreamt of taking to the air and surfing the winds?

I'd never *stopped* dreaming of it—of raiding the nests of hotheaded blue jays and leading them on twisting, turning chases through the branches of oaks and poplars, of dive-bombing humans with impunity, buzzing unsuspecting dogs and felines, and scattering clusters of foraging pigeons at will. The theater of the mind had long been my playground: I had only to close my eyes, and another airborne adventure would unfold—salving my earthbound avian soul with the opiate of make-believe.

And that was the whole problem right there, I realized: at some point, I'd grown content with dreams.

This was no earth-shaking revelation, of course—and being as I'd plainly transcended the need for bogus thrills anyway, I saw no reason not to leave it fluttering in my slipstream like litter in the wind. But it gnawed at me. I was drifting above a blanket of clouds that ran out to the horizon in every direction and looked for all the world like hot ashes: lumpy and gray, with scattered bits of orange glowing like hot coals as this monstrous, molten sun split into slivers at its western edge. I'd never had a dream or a fantasy that didn't pale by comparison. But somewhere along the line I'd resigned myself to a counterfeit existence; that much became clear the day I could've unfolded a full set of flight feathers and taken to the sky—but chose instead to believe what that old dragon had said: that only *fear* could teach a bird to fly—that only in the midst of some harrowing plunge could the uninitiated find the wherewithal to defy gravity. "There's a reason I built my nest in the tallest tree on the block," she'd pointed out, with evident satisfaction. "That way, when you get the heave, you'll have plenty of time to figure things out— and the impact should put you out of your misery if you don't."

But when my visible means of support suddenly dropped out from under me, there was nothing to figure out—I just started flying....

And yet I knew that bilious old fowl was full of shit long before then. In truth, I'd just grown content with being defective, with doing the easiest thing, with picking through Hillsdale's tides of trash with Henry like an old lady at a fire sale—with stashing shiny little trophies in his basket even, like it was my home and I was his *pet*. I'd told myself that if Lord Gastric was content, I was content—but while I was losing myself in those pathetic flights of fancy, my brothers were out breaking in their new primaries.

All that soaring elation, in short, only served to highlight the sorry truth at my core: that I was an underachieving mutant that couldn't shake his own pathetic history even among the clouds—I may as well have been trailing a banner reading EVOLUTIONARY DEAD END. This weighty freight would always be there, too—always slowing me down, always threatening to stall me out. I couldn't even take in a dramatic sunset without getting all glum and despondent.

But as I drifted motionless on a river of air, and the sun sank into a slate-gray haze, I had to wonder if there was any truth to the adage that whatever doesn't bring a bird down makes him *stronger*.

It was a trite notion, of course—and I seized on it immediately; I had little to lose, after all, in a quest to answer that question in the affirmative. So in the stillness of that downwind run high above the world, I resolved to quit my slacker ways and redeem myself: to rise like the Phoenix from the ashes of my arrested development and transform that defective plume into (yes) the mark of the *exceptional.*

But to understand what redemption might embody for a crow, it's necessary to understand a crow's purpose in the grand scheme of things. Properly speaking, a crow is a Knight of the Unraveling—an agent of chaos, in more prosaic language. (That's what the black plumage is all about.) As such, it is tasked with a single overriding mission in life: to reduce the entire known universe to a thin haze of randomly drifting particles. It's a tall order, so in practice most crows are content to commit random turmoil and senseless acts of mischief—to lie, heckle, and gnaw—but nothing of any earth-shaking consequence (except, of course, when taken in aggregate). But for the crow seeking redemption, it'd be necessary to author some truly monstrous, major league mayhem—and I swore to the wild wind that I would do no less.

It was with this newfound resolve that I finally descended from the clouds and came to rest at the highest point in sight—the flagpole in front of the First National Bank building in a little community called Singer Park. It seemed fitting to give the world fair warning, and before I thought the better of it, I was crowing like the self-anointed lord of all I surveyed—and that brought out the Singer Park welcoming committee: a contingent of crows from the local chapter of the Purple Raptors.

"Hey devil-crow, you lost or what?"

"Maybe he's just *stupid!*"

"Yeah, let's get the stupid bastid!"

"Awk! Awk! Awk! Awk! Awk!"

They came at me like hornets—big, black hornets—six or eight of them in tight formation. I pulled myself up fast and beat a hasty retreat, but I was weak with fatigue and flabby from long inactivity—and these birds were in lean, mean, fighting form. They surrounded me, heckled me, and snapped at my wings and tail as they escorted me out of town—and there was nothing I could do but talk shit about their mothers, and keep moving.

Flying like a fugitive into the twilight, I sensed a familiar theme reasserting itself.

Daybreak found me hunched in a hemlock on the outskirts of Singer Park—a little worse for wear, and acutely conscious of the gnawing hole in my gut. Even a would-be Master of Disaster has to eat. So I combed my tattered plumage, squeezed out some ballast, and pulled myself aloft. Gaining some elevation, I spotted a commercial district to the east, and banked directly into the rising sun.

I homed in on a Kentucky Fried Chicken franchise on the south end of the main drag. A gang of crows—the SR-71s, according to the local fauna—having scattered a portion of a trash can's contents around the parking lot, was strutting about the previous night's leavings like two-bit wise guys checking out a hijacked shipment of firs. Doing my best to stay out of their way, I looked for fallen morsels around the tables by the drive-through—but as soon as they spotted me, three of them broke away from the rest and chased me off.

So I tried my luck at the Taco Bell a little further up, but an even bigger gang of crows had *that* place locked down: dumpsters, trashcans, parking lot—the whole artery-clogging enchilada—and it was the same story at the diner around the corner. Everywhere I went, a gang of crows had everything buttoned up, and if I even got close, I risked getting myself chewed up again—and there was only so much abuse my plumage could take.

I sat on a power line and considered my options. Hanging from the wire alongside me was a disintegrating pair of Nikes. No decent running shoe has components belonging to any of the major food groups, so I ignored them and watched with envy as a pair of crows in front of the White Castle across the boulevard fought over a packet of catsup (which even some hominids regard as a vegetable). My pulse jumped a notch, however, when I spotted what appeared to be a French fry in the gutter only a few feet from where the birds were wrangling on the sidewalk. It was just out of their line of sight, and with any luck it'd still be there when they finally resolved their catsup issue and went on their way. But the contested packet ripped, and its contents dribbled to the sidewalk—and the crows proceeded to peck at the fallen blob of catsup (and each other) as it settled into a thin red puddle on the concrete.

If crows had trowels for beaks, the process of devouring that catsup would've been over soon enough, but these were your standard-issue crows with the usual pointed appliances, and the whole business promised to be contentious, tedious, and long.

Unless, of course, something startled them ...

The Nikes were dangling from laces that had been reduced by time to a few rotting strands, and it only took half a minute of gnawing to send them plummeting to the street. I took a swan dive off the wire even before they'd hit the ground, and was sailing across the boulevard at an altitude of barely 6-inches at the moment of impact. And if my landing skills were still less than optimal, my timing was perfect: the Nikes hit the pavement—propelling the two into the air—at the *very instant* my forward progress was arrested by the curb.

I experienced a momentary loss of consciousness.

Then I picked myself up, shook the stars out of my head, and—as the two French fries at my feet resolved themselves into one—grabbed my breakfast and hauled my ass aloft.

I didn't get 50-feet before being intercepted by a big old stud who'd obviously had a lot of practice snagging the fruits of other birds' labors. Despite his size, he was quick, tricky, and acrobatic, swooping from port to starboard and then back again in an instant—anticipating my every evasive maneuver as he tried to snatch the French fry from my mouth. It was a contest I could easily lose, so I tried to gobble it down on the fly—only to have all but a single bite fall from my beak in the attempt. My adversary dove under me and caught it with a deftness I could only admire in spite of myself.

Free agency was losing its luster. It was with no small measure of attitude that I'd sworn to inflict mythic chaos upon the world, but so far the world was taking every round —leaving me chewed-up and humbled and wishing Henry was still around to take me to his favorite dumpster for a bite to eat and a little repartee. And then I remembered that a couple of vagrants back in Hillsdale would be only too happy to sponsor a wayward crow....

Figuring redemption would keep, I pointed myself toward Hillsdale, spread my ragged primaries, and let the afternoon breeze pull me aloft.

By the time I got back to the old neighborhood, my universe was being consumed by the black hole at my core—so a trendy little establishment called Fat City Deli seemed like a good place to start looking for Wally and Fred. The dinner hour had barely begun, but Fat City was located at the heart of a large shopping mall called Grey's, and throughout the afternoon, this popular eatery was typically overrun with shoppers who—jammed as they were in spending mode—couldn't bring themselves to go home without ordering a big plate of food to pick at as they savored the afterglow of another day's retail foraging. Henry and I had spent many an hour at Fat City's dumpsters, happily feasting on the warm, ample remains of Rueben sandwiches, waffles with blueberries, biscuits with gravy, strawberry shortcake, omelets and tuna melts and Cobb salads and cheese blintzes and bread pudding and rice pudding and apple pie a la mode—and the memory of it all so possessed me that I never even noticed the sentry perched on a lamppost by the loading docks as I was winging my way across Grey's rear parking lot toward the object of my desire.

The sentry called out an alarm as I passed—"Awk! Awk! Awk!"—and there was no mistaking the sound of my own mother's melodious voice.

Guessing that reconciliation was off the table, I forged ahead full-bore in hopes of a quick bite before the cavalry showed up. Unfortunately, just as I was closing in on that redolent repository of culinary castoffs, three of my erstwhile nestmates dropped down from the parapets and perched along the dumpster's lip.

"Well, look who's here," said Odious, as I touched down a few yards short of the dumpster.

"It's that devil-crow that tried to invade our nest!" said Devious.

"I can see who it is!" said Odious, "I got eyes on both sides of my head, y'know."

"Hey crow!" Thaddeus called out, "Where's that human you're always pallin' around wit?"

"Shut up and let *me* do the talking," said Odious. "Hey crow! Where's that human you're always pallin' around wit?"

"Hey, that's what *I* said!" Thaddeus protested.

"Didn't I tell you to shut up?" said Odious.

"I heard he dropped dead," Devious interjected.

"Who asked *you?*" said Odious.

"*Who* dropped dead?" said Thaddeus, perplexed.

"Your *brain* dropped dead!" Odious squawked, administering a pate-shot to the hapless Thaddeus.

"Hey, what'd you do that for?" Thaddeus whined.

"I just wanted to see if anybody was home," said Odious.

Thaddeus cocked his head suspiciously. "Say, that's an *insult,* isn't it?"

All but forgotten, I sidled a bit closer to the dumpster. Just then, a plug of a Mexican in a grubby apron kicked the kitchen's door open and proceeded to wrestle an overladen trash can through the doorway—which sent the Three Stooges flying in three directions. Seizing the moment, I sprang into the air, pulled on my oars twice, and did a nosedive into the unguarded dumpster. Without Henry at my side, of course, there was little time to pick and choose, so I just grabbed the biggest thing I could carry—half-a-slab of French toast—and beat my wings for all they were worth. Not surprisingly, the Jackdaws showed up in force before I was halfway across the lot, and once again I found myself fleeing a surly gang of crows—only this time it was my own kin nipping at my tail.

And after being run out of *their* territory, I was beset by the Midtown Marauders, and the K Street Kamikazes, and the Black Death, and the Psycho Ravens, and the Edge City Rocs —and it was only out of sheer desperation that I managed to make it to the outskirts of town with that piece of French toast still clamped firmly in my beak.

As a wise old bird once said, you can't dive into the same dumpster twice.

The morning air was churning with traffic noise as I cased the local A & P, where trucks were being unloaded beneath the watchful eyes of a crew called the Black Plume; the odds of getting close to anything edible appeared slim. So with Lord Gastric tightening the screws, I set out to discover where all that produce was coming from. When an empty semi pulled away from the loading docks, I followed it out onto the highway and down to the black, sooty freight yards at the heart of the city, where trucks rumbled in and out in a continuous stream, and thousands of flatcars and boxcars and gondolas were loaded, unloaded, and shuffled in sections from one track to another. A couple of locomotives were being hooked up to an endless chain of empty cars—including an open refrigerator car containing nothing but some pallets, a few smashed cantaloupes, and a mound of excelsior. After a breakfast of rancid cantaloupe, I poked and gnawed at this and that, and then parked my tail end in the excelsior like a mamma crow poaching a few eggs. Then, after what sounded like some pissed-off giant stomping down the full length of the train —BLAM! BLAM! BLAM! BLAM! BLAM! BLAM! BLAM!— the car lurched into motion. The train was like an immense steel millipede, and as it inched its way along the rails—groaning and shuddering as it labored to get moving—it was hard to imagine how anything that massive could move at all; but once that monster finally got rolling, it was hard to see how anything could ever stop it. Henry had spent a piece of his life riding the rails, and it was just like he said: after a while my ears just gave up trying to hear all that noise. Then, after the train had clawed its way out of Kansas City with another hundred cars or so and built some momentum, the setting sun seemed to haul it right over the horizon and into the night. It went bouncing and barreling and crashing through the muggy darkness, and didn't slow down again till the sun, in its plodding, deliberate way, had looped right around again and was back overhead. With the train barely crawling, I hopped over to the open door and beheld the Promised Land: a sea of sweet, ripe corn, stretching from one end of the horizon to the other in the shimmering midday heat. There was a flock of crows feeding in the distance—the biggest I'd ever seen— but there was clearly more to be had in that ocean of corn than any one flock could lay claim to. I gorged myself in those fields till I could barely fly, and then took a snooze in a windbreak bordered by a drainage ditch on one side and a two-lane highway on the other.

I woke beneath a sky the color of pus, and my plumbing cleared itself in a single peristaltic spasm.

A moment later, I was pounding my way toward the foothills on the horizon without exactly knowing why—but by then it was too late: the air began to throb, and I felt myself being sucked into some monstrous, murderous thing that sounded like that freight train running flat out. All I could do was pull in my wings and close my eyes as it took me up into its black, screaming heart—along with a blizzard of corn stalks, fence posts, whole poplars, topsoil by the ton, an F-150, and whatever else lay in its path. I remember being struck by the irony that somewhere on the far side of the globe, a goddamn *dung beetle* probably farted, and set in motion a chaotic chain of events culminating in that howling vortex of death and destruction coming to end my misspent career right there in the middle of that cornfield.

CHAPTER 4

There was a ringing in my ears as my mind pieced itself back together. It was morning; I was in a forest of lodgepole pine on a gently sloping hillside; the air was thin, the ground was wet, and I appeared to be a sopping mass of broken and missing feathers. Fearing I might be less than airworthy, I began flapping frantically—and managed to make it to a low-hanging branch nearby. I parked myself in a shaft of sunlight and set about doctoring what was left of my plumage—straightening the feathers that weren't broken, and pulling those that were. As I steamed in the sunlight streaming down through the forest's canopy, an irate squirrel informed me that I was in a place called Toad Valley—a lush little alpine valley with about a million trees, he noted, adding that he'd thank me not to sit in *his*. But I wasn't inclined to move, and the squirrel kept his distance—though he did harass me from time to time—and after I'd dried out a bit, I did a little exploring (along with a lot of flapping, given the thin mountain air and the wide gaps in my plumage).

Toad Valley was like the picture you'd see on a granola

box. The wooded hillsides gave way to gently rolling farmland which, in every detail, bore not the slightest resemblance to the flat, boundless, almost featureless sea of corn I'd gloried in prior to the weather revising my itinerary. It was a pastoral patchwork of wheatfields, cornfields, meadows and orchards, barns and silos and farmhouses—all crisscrossed with narrow, rutted dirt roads, and cut through with meandering streams connecting a series of ponds and lakes surrounded by abundant foliage. The air was unnaturally clear, and tangy with pine and fresh-cut hay, and the sky was a deep, brilliant blue scattered with clouds so white it hurt my eyes to look at them. Surrounding this unlikely community of family farms was a sheltering wall of dramatic snow-capped peaks, the precipitous nature of which made my presence there all the more remarkable.

But Toad Valley could just as easily be characterized by the many features it *didn't* have—a town center, for one thing. There was also an absence of F-150s, tractors, crop dusters, wood chippers, chainsaws, and every other engine-driven accouterment of industrial age farming. That cyclone sucked me right up out of the 21st century and dropped me in some pre-agrarian enclave seemingly lacking in every recognizable feature of modern life—*chaos,* in particular.

But that would be remedied.

I was inspecting a bona fide scarecrow in the middle of a bean field when an anguished cry shattered the tranquility: "OH ASTRID, HOW WILL I LIVE WITHOUT YOU?" In the barnyard at the edge of the field, a flock of chickens clustered fearfully in front of their coop as a rooster—a big, distraught-looking Rhode Island Red—paced beside the nearby tool shed. "Oh Astrid," said the impassioned cock, "my sweet pullet—my downy little chicken! Better I'd been cast from the shell as unformed slime—poached, and served up on toast—than to have my heart torn throbbing from my breast in the prime of life!"

Heedless of my diminished capacity for flight, I went flapping, pigeon-like, across the bean field to investigate this sappy soap opera—realizing only at the last moment that I'd lost too much altitude to alight gracefully on the tool shed; so to avoid crashing gracelessly *into* it, I swerved to one side and all but collided with the farm's knife-wielding proprietor, George Klunder, as he was rounding the shed's corner. "Wilhelm's ghost!" he exclaimed, throwing his hands—and knife—in the air. Then, uncertain of the knife's trajectory, he wrapped his arms around his head and froze. The knife clattered harmlessly on the shed's roof, while my own evasive maneuvering took me to a less-lofty perch on the chicken coop.

The scowling farmer had a face like shattered pottery—with hair—and like the rest of the valley's American Gothic population, he wore a lot of black: boots, work pants, suspenders, and a more-or-less flat-brimmed hat. His white woolen shirt, meanwhile, was sweat-stained and rolled up at the sleeve, and appeared to be flecked with blood. He pulled off his canvas gloves and threw a rock at me—but it went 3-feet wide, and I held my ground (more out of fatigue than defiance). He glowered at me for a moment; then he stepped into the tool shed, emerged with a ladder, and went about retrieving the knife from the shed's roof.

A crimson rivulet advanced like a snake from behind the shed, so I strolled down the length of the coop to better survey the shed's far side. A row of chickens hung by their feet from a line—most of them with long strands of coagulating blood dribbling from severed throats; the rest of the condemned birds flapped away pointlessly as they waited to have their own wattles trimmed.

Astrid, as it happened, was about to get hers.

"Alas, my doomed little dumpling," the rooster lamented, "each of us has a role to play in this life: mine is to beget, and yours is to be gone. I don't know why they can't just take the cockerels—they're not worth a damn anyway! But go gently into that peaceful goodnight, brave Astrid; I'll bear the burden of your loss somehow—along with the guilt of bringing you into the world for so fleeting a season, and the shame of being powerless to save you! Somehow, somewhere, I'll find the strength to soldier on, even as this tragic moment takes its place among the accumulated sorrows of a long and poignant career—the lives come and gone, the crushing sense of impotence and complicity ..."

"Awk! Awk! Awk!" I laughed, "A little more of that shit, and she'll be *begging* for the knife! Awk! Awk! Awk!"

The rooster glared at me. "Crow, has your life grown so dull that you'd heckle the Red Ripper in the hallowed hour of his grief?"

"Yeah, that's it," I said, "I'm afflicted with an insufferable ennui. And Dr. Kevorkian wasn't available, so I figured you could *talk* me to death."

"Rest assured, crow," said the rooster, turning to face me full on, "I'll do more than talk...."

"I'll bet Astrid'll be impressed," I told him. "Oh that's right—she'll be getting her throat cut."

"Oh Rip," cried Astrid, "I don't want to get my throat cut! Do something, please!"

"Astrid, Astrid ... don't you see?" said the rooster to his condemned paramour, "The essence of tragedy is its inevitability...."

"The essence of tragedy is a cock who thinks his spurs are a fashion accessory," I said.

The rooster turned back to me and lowered his voice menacingly. "I've drawn near as much blood with these spurs as my master has with his knife," he said, puffing himself up.

"Oh, you mean the blood of your own kind...."

"If you'd care to come down here, crow, I'll gladly spill some of *yours.*"

"If it's all the same to you, Red, I'll pass—I just tangled with a tornado. And those spurs of yours do look sharp...."

"Sharp as razors."

"Now, if your onboard computer was just a little sharper, you'd understand it's not *my* blood you need to spill...."

"GAAAAA ...!" screamed the farmer as the ladder kicked out from under him. He landed flat on his back, and lay motionless for several moments; then he drew a sharp breath and rolled onto an elbow, gasping for air.

"And here's your big chance too," I said.

"Do you really imagine," said the rooster with palpable disdain, "that I'm fool enough to get myself killed for the amusement of a crow?"

"You're fool enough to trade your daughters for a handful of feed," I said.

"Confound it, crow! That is the compact I'm obliged to honor—the same compact my forefathers have honored since the first domesticated fowl said, 'I choose Man as my lord and master'!"

The farmer got unsteadily to his feet, dusted himself off, and put on his hat; then he picked up his knife, and examined its blade.

"So basically, you're saying you come from a *long line* of fools...."

"Yeah, don't be a fool, Rip," called a fat Chester White from across the barnyard, "—give old George a taste of your spurs! Haw, haw, haw!" The hog's name was Frankie, and he was up on his hind legs, leaning against the pigsty's gate.

"Mind your own affairs, pig!" replied the Ripper.

Another hog—a big Blueback named Carlo—got up on his hind legs alongside the first, and spoke in conspiratorial tones: "Hey Frankie—did George do the rooster's girlfriend yet?"

"He's about to do her right now," said Frankie. "*Hey Rip*— aren't you gonna save your girlfriend?"

"Oh, I'd give a bucket of swill to see that!" said Carlo.

"You'll see nothing with your eyeballs adorning my spurs, swine!" said the rooster.

A row of porkers had their snouts stuck through a gap in the sty's plank sides. With the exception of a pig by the name of Fatback and one or two others, they seemed to find the melodrama playing out in the yard highly amusing. "Yeah, Rip," taunted one, "—rip George a new one! Hee, hee, hee."

"I don't know what *you* fools are laughing at," said Carlo, looking over his shoulder at the row of pigs. "How fat do you think George lets his porkers get, anyway? Another week or two, and you'll all be going to the block yourselves." Their giggles trailed off as the pigs looked nervously at each other—and then at George, who was now approaching Astrid with his knife.

"Oh, *do* something, Rip!" screamed Astrid, "—stop him! Stop him!"

"But Astrid," said the rooster, pleading for understanding, "I could more easily stop pigs from wallowing...."

"Now I see why they call you birds *chickens*," I said.

The cock fixed a murderous eye on me, and raised his hackles. "*No one* calls the Red Ripper a chicken and lives to see another dawn...."

"The Ripper's a chicken! The Ripper's a chicken!" Frankie chanted from the pigsty.

"*No one!*" the rooster shrieked, turning toward the sty, "—not even a three-hundred pound boar!"

"Oh stop, *stop*—just stop it, Rip!" Astrid wailed. "What's the use pretending? I'm about to get my poor throat cut, and there's nothing you or anyone else can do about it—'cause you're a *chicken*, and nobody else gives a shit! So just stop ...!"

The rooster looked up at the pullet in shock. "What ...? But ... but Astrid," he sputtered, "you're just ... you're *distraught* —understandably—but you know as well as anyone that a more fearsome cock never ..."

Farmer George wrapped his gloved hand around the pullet's head, and separated the feathers of her throat with his thumb. As he put his knife to the pullet's neck, a muffled cry emerged from his fist:

"Just admit it, Rip—you're a chicken!"

The cock could live with the idea that he was the property of a human master who would blithely cut his throat the day he'd outlived his usefulness—and grind his stringy flesh into sausage while humming *Onward Christian Soldiers;* he could live with the flock's nests being robbed routinely of what was rightfully his, and tolerate his children being taken from him in the flower of their youth—suffer their dying cries, even; and as painful as it was, he could learn to live without his favorite pullet, Astrid, who—as he would often observe—was the most delightful fuck he'd ever been blessed with. It was all part of the "compact" he'd inherited—a world view that featured a mythical fowl who'd sold his kind down the river for a daily ration of grain in a dark, bygone era he couldn't name. Like his father, and his father's father, *he lived with it.* What he *couldn't* live with was being called a chicken—and rather than suffer the slow death of a thousand whispers, he resolved in that fleeting moment to go down fighting like a true Rhode Island Red.

He sprang from the ground like he'd been launched from a catapult, and proceeded to demonstrate with great passion how he'd come to be known as the *Ripper.*

The attack threw the farmer off-balance, and as the man staggered back—arms flailing—the rooster raked his face again and again with his spurs. At the same moment, the gate to the pigsty—groaning under the weight of 600-pounds of hog—ripped off its hinges, spilling Frankie and Carlo out of the sty and flat on their faces. As the two hogs struggled to regain their feet, half-a-dozen porkers went stampeding over them into the yard. "It's just as I foretold!" howled Fatback, "The uprising has begun!" He went charging into the yard after the others, and the rest of the pigs followed in his wake.

It was Fatback who'd had this vision in which he'd seen the world's enslaved beasts rising up as one and overthrowing their human oppressors. That this vision should've occurred in the white-hot aftermath of his castration wasn't surprising —yet at the time, none of the other animals had ever heard such talk, or even imagined that such a world could exist. But *every* beast on Klunder Farm had its grievances, and though none of them actually believed that Fatback's vision was anything more than the fevered ramblings of a delirious porker, it did have undeniable appeal—and over time, it burrowed like a virus into the darkest corners of their minds. It would emerge from time to time in the form of a dream, or a fantasy, or just a passing comment: "Wouldn't it be something to be *free ...?*" But having incubated in the barnyard's soul, the idea gained an explosive power none of the animals could've anticipated.

Farmer George was still reeling from the Ripper's assault when he was knocked to the ground by a phalanx of pigs. As he was trampled by the marauding swine, the farmer writhed in the dirt as he fended off the rooster's ongoing attacks. In the midst of it all, Mrs. Klunder came out on the back porch with a basket of laundry. "George ...? *George!* Oh my God ..." She dropped the basket of wash and began ringing the dinner bell. "Felix! Ernst! Peter!" she screamed to her sons in the hayfield, "Come at once! *Hurry!*" The farmer's daughter, who was in the paddock brushing a bull calf named Fritz, came running into the yard and was stopped in her tracks by the bizarre sight of her father being attacked by the red cock and a dozen porkers; so she retrieved a shovel from the barn and cautiously approached the melee.

Whiskers—the cock one peck beneath the Ripper in the pecking order—decided it was time to join the skirmish, so he attacked the farmer's daughter. Tasked with collecting the hens' eggs each day, the girl wasn't real popular around the roost, and the entire laying flock followed the Leghorn's lead. Finding herself under assault by a dozen chickens, the girl dropped the shovel and ran for the safety of the house. Mrs. Klunder, seeing her daughter bringing a swarm of attacking chickens her way, preceded the girl through the kitchen door.

Fritz the calf, meanwhile—as rambunctious a critter as they come—saw what appeared to be a free-for-all in the yard, and came romping out the paddock's open gate just as the farmer's youngest son was driving the sheep into the yard from pasturing. The calf playfully butted a pig or two, and then—seeing an opening in the roiling mass of porkers—charged into the breach just as George was struggling to rise, and knocked him right off his feet again. "Papa! Papa!" screamed the youth as he ran to his father's assistance. He picked up the shovel his sister had dropped, and smacked the calf in the head with it. That was more than Mrs. Cow would stand for; she came charging out of the paddock—nearly stumbling over her own pendulous udder—and hit the boy low, hurling him in the air.

It was right about then that the sheep closed in for the kill. Ordinarily, sheep are gentle animals, but these critters had murder in their eyes. They hadn't forgotten the countless nights that George, lantern in hand, had slipped into the sheep shed wearing nothing but a nightshirt and a pair of boots, secured a ewe in the milking stand, and had his way with her while humming *Onward Christian Soldiers*—faster and faster, till the hymn sounded like a polka—before falling to his knees, gasping, "Forgive me, Lord, forgive me!" Needless to say, the sheep hadn't forgiven him, and, led by Ulysses the ram, they eagerly joined the attack—headless of the two yapping sheepdogs.

Such was the mayhem that greeted the farmer's three elder sons as they came running into the yard from the fields. Before they could do the first thing to help their father and younger brother, however, they found themselves besieged by the chickens, who'd circled back in a riotous swarm from the farmhouse. As the brothers fended off the chickens, one of them reached into the tool shed, grabbed an axe and began hacking his way through the once-docile beasts with wild imprecision—which even sent his brothers scrambling for cover. The axe-wielding youth dispatched several pigs with manic blows, and then took aim at a ewe that literally had his howling father by the balls—but missed the ewe entirely, burying the axe in his father's thigh instead. A crimson geyser drenched the horrified youth with blood. "N-Not to worry, Father..." he stammered, "it's only a scratch."

Having lost consciousness, farmer George was unable to reply.

Any hope of bringing order to the yard evaporated as the boys, accompanied by the frantic sheepdogs, dragged their hemorrhaging father toward the road. The animals, pressing their advantage, chased them right down to the front gate. "Take your father to Dr. Wurfel's at once!" screamed Frau Klunder from an open kitchen window, *"Hurry*—I'll meet you there!" Then she and her daughter fled through a side door and made their way up the wooded hillside.

With the humans gone, silence fell over the farm. Then Frankie and Carlo crawled out from beneath the porch, where they'd enjoyed a fine view of the entire spectacle. "My, my," said Carlo, as he surveyed the motley band of rebels wandering up from the road, "—looks like the Klunders'll have to invite the whole valley over for Sunday dinner."

A big barbecue in the rebels' immediate future certainly appeared to be a possibility—but at that point, all I could say for sure was that a little heckling went a long way in Toad Valley.

CHAPTER 5

Figuring I'd stirred up enough trouble in the yard, I went flapping up to the farmhouse to raid the Klunders' larder. Poking my head in the kitchen window, the first thing that caught my eye was a cage containing a black-plumed critter I took to be a crow; then the bird turned around, and I saw that comical yellow beak, and those great big clown feet—and I found myself momentarily stuck for an opening. "Nice day for a revolution, isn't it?"

"Nice day for a revolution, isn't it?" she replied, plainly mocking me.

"You're right, comrade," I said, "That one was ready for history's dustbin a long time ago."

"You're right, comrade," she responded, "That one was ready for history's dustbin a long time ago."

"Look, cuz," I said, "if you don't want to talk, just say so."

"Look, cuz, if you don't want to talk, just say so."

I cocked my head and gave her a long look; then I glided over to where her cage sat at the end of a long counter, unhooked the door, and hopped onto the perch opposite her.

"Get outta my cage!" she screeched, shuffling to the end of her perch and grabbing some bars with a big yellow foot.

"Hey, an original thought."

"Get outta my cage!" she screeched again.

"Now you're repeating *yourself....*"

"That's 'cause you don't listen so good," she snapped, "—this is a private residence, and you're trespassing!"

As I would learn soon enough, my avian cousin was a mynah with a nervous habit of mimicking—and apparently I made her nervous. Predictably, her name was Echo.

"So you got just five minutes to get outta my... Hey! Where you going, crow?"

Noticing the big country-style lunch Mrs. Klunder had been preparing, I decided the pleasantries could wait. I hopped out of the cage and migrated to a massive kitchen table laden with meatloaf, roast chicken, mashed potatoes, corn on the cob, fresh-baked cornbread, warm apple pie ...

"Oh, you better *not* touch that food!" said the mynah—a clear invitation to dig in. "The Klunders just stepped out for a minute, and if they come back and see a crow, of all things, eating their lunch, they're gonna eat *you* for dinner.... Don't you *dare* touch that apple pie! I'm warning you, crow, these are serious people you're messing around with! Just ask the Pootskottlee Indians—of which there *aren't* any. And do you know why there aren't any? 'Cause they're *all gone,* that's why! But once upon a time, this whole valley was just *crawling* with Pootskottlees—and you'll notice I use the word 'crawling,' as in the past tense of *to crawl?* If you get my meaning ...? Do you think maybe you could stop stuffing your face long enough to acknowledge me, Mr. Crow—Mr. Barge-right-in-and-help-yourself? You know, that's the problem with crows: they're selfish—they never think about anyone but themselves. Now mynah birds, on the other hand, are very considerate birds—they're uncommonly attuned to the needs of others. Mr. and Mrs. Klunder noticed that about me right away—that's why they bought me in the first place. That, and the fact that I got a New York accent...."

Once that mynah got going, there was no shutting her up.

As it turned out, the Klunders—like the rest of the valley's residents—were part of a Grumpish splinter group that was straight-laced in the most literal sense: they believed one's bootlaces should only be tied with a *square knot*—bows being seen as "frivolous." The order's founding fathers—being at loggerheads with the greater Grumpish community over this important point—saw little choice but to break with their frivolous brethren. So, like most humans with peculiar ideas, they set out for California. In the attempt to cross the Great Divide, however, the religious renegades got hopelessly lost, and—finding themselves in this isolated valley—surmised that divine providence had delivered them at last from the corrosive influence of the insufficiently sober. So they drove out the indigenous Pootskottlees, and made themselves at home.

Toad Valley's current generation, being as insular as its forebears, saw little need to venture beyond the nearest town —a pebble of a place called Falling Rock—which could only be gotten to by pack mule through a treacherous mountain pass known as Beaver Gorge. But apparently the Klunders, figuring they were entitled to see the big city at least once in their lives, had made the hazardous trek to Falling Rock on the occasion of their 25th wedding anniversary, and prevailed upon Silas Clusterberry—the town's only cab driver—to fire up his army surplus Jeep and drive them down to Blister, where they sat at the town's lone intersection for half a day before a great metallic beast emblazoned with a dog came rolling up in a cloud of dust and diesel fumes.

The Klunders climbed aboard, and the bus headed out for Steamboat Springs and points east—but Steamboat Springs was as far as the Grumps would get. Two hours out of Blister, the bus's air conditioning died, and after sweating in silence for a good 30-miles or so, the passengers began to complain

—but the glistening driver announced that the air conditioning was working perfectly. A little further along, a passenger sitting in the rear informed the driver that the bus appeared to be leaking oil—but he was advised to return to his seat and stop alarming the other passengers. Eventually, the bus stopped leaking oil—probably because there was no more oil for it to leak—and began trailing thick plumes of smoke instead; nonetheless, the driver assured the increasingly restive passengers that everything was under control, and that the red lights that had begun flashing conspicuously on his control panel were, in fact, an indication that all systems were functioning optimally. Even as the bus began to fill with smoke, the driver insisted there was no reason for his sweating, gagging passengers to be concerned—and it was only when the rear of the bus actually burst into flames that he was forced to admit there was a problem.

When at last the bus had been left to burn on the side of the road, the driver could only shake his head and wonder—as he and his ill-fated passengers walked the final mile to the terminal—how anyone could've foreseen that great gleaming beast coming to such a swift and catastrophic end.

But as if to prove that every cloud has a silver lining, the Klunders—killing some time before the next bus arrived—wandered into a pet shop where an old lady was loudly complaining about the mynah she'd purchased to fill the void left by her husband's passing. Being as the bird had a grating New York accent, it was plainly defective, and the woman wanted her money back. The proprietor explained that the shop got all its exotic birds from an aviary in Flatbush, New York, so the accent was unavoidable—and in any case, the receipt stated quite clearly that all sales were final. But the Klunders, apparently, found the hurly-burly metropolis of Steamboat Springs sufficiently bracing that the prospect of owning a bird with a New York accent suddenly seemed infinitely more desirable than having to endure the Big Apple itself. So they made the woman an offer....

"Mrs. Klunder loves to tell that story," said the mynah, who clearly wasn't averse to telling it herself. Evidently, she hadn't had another bird to talk to for some time, and my earholes were getting numb. "It was just like the Klunders to walk into that pet shop, too: being around animals is what they know —it gives them a sense of security, a sense of control. It's a good thing, too, 'cause if they *hadn't* come into that store when they did, I'd probably still be listening to that incontinent old bitch whining about her dead husband." The mynah cast a guilty glance in each direction, and then stifled a laugh. "I *do* have to watch my mouth around the Klunders....

"I wonder what happened to them, anyway," she said, as I wiped my beak on a linen napkin. "They left in a big hurry for some reason...."

The goats had left their stalls, the pigeons were released from their coops, and the ducks had waddled up from the pond; the two bewildered plow horses, meanwhile, slipped their traces and wandered in from the fields. Except for the Blueback sow —who was busy suckling her piglets—all the farm's animals were milling around the barnyard in confusion. The mood was mixed. Some of the animals were giddy with their unexpected freedom, while others were anxious in the face of the unknown—and among those that had taken no part in the rebellion, there were many questions. But the rebels themselves had few answers—still in shock, for the most part, over their monstrous transgression.

As for the Ripper, he was in an agitated state. He'd *led* the uprising, after all—and he'd be the first to get his head lopped off when the Klunders returned. He paced along the chicken coop's roof and tried to look commanding as he addressed the rabble (most of which ignored him): "Friends, neighbors— beasts of Klunder Farm," he began, "on this historic day, fearsome fowl were joined by porcine paladins and rampaging ruminants in a decisive display of domestic disobedience. For the first time in millennia, perhaps, once-servile beasts rose up against their cruel human masters and said, *No*... we are not *pork chops,* we are not *lamb chops,* and by god, we are not chopped chicken liver! We do not aspire to be links of sausage, farmer George, nor slabs of bacon—Canadian or otherwise—and we will not be reduced to consommé! We are living, sentient beings, not flesh for human consumption—and from this day forward, we will no longer stand by while you coldly harvest our children for your table!

"My friends, Klunder Farm is our home—the only home most of us have ever known; yet if you look around, what do you see? Do you see a place where life is created, celebrated, and lived to its fullest? Or do you see a *death camp?* The answer to that question is lying at your feet: the bloody remains of eighteen chickens—eleven with severed throats, and five with their necks brutally wrenched—along with ..."

"Sixteen," said Astrid, who was standing in the yard below him.

"Sixteen what?" said the rooster.

"Sixteen dead chickens," said Astrid. "Eleven plus five equals sixteen."

"Does it?" said the rooster.

"Yes it does," said Astrid.

"I beg to differ," said one of the goats. "Eleven plus five equals *seventeen.*"

"You're crazy," said Astrid to the goat—then, under her breath to the rooster: "Don't listen to her, Rip—she's just a goat."

"Oh, and what is *that* supposed to mean?" said the goat, whose hearing was 20/20.

"I hate to contradict one of my feathered cousins," said a duck, "but I believe the goat is correct: an odd number plus an odd number equals an odd number."

"I've heard that too," said one of the pigeons.

"Indeed," said a ewe, "—how could it be otherwise?"

"You're all out of your minds!" said Astrid.

"That pullet is quite the know-it-all, isn't she?" muttered one pig to another.

"Maybe she won the Pulitzer Prize," the second pig suggested—setting off a round of squealing laughter.

"CAN WE ALL AGREE THERE ARE A CONSIDERABLE NUMBER OF EXPIRED CHICKENS LYING ABOUT?" said the cock, his comb trembling with indignation.

"Oh, yes—considerable."

"A considerable number ..."

"Considerable ..."

"Well, it depends on your definition of 'considerable'," said the goat.

"MORE THAN A FEW!" said the rooster.

"Oh, well yes—certainly more than a few ..."

"What about the pigs?" said a porker.

"Ah, yes," said the rooster, making a show of containing himself, "—the three pigs: they seem to have been overlooked in the firestorm of controversy surrounding the avian body count. But by all means, let us not forget the three brave pigs that fell to the axe—or perhaps I should say, the *indeterminate* number of pigs that fell to the axe."

"Amen," said Fatback.

"Now if we could all extract our minds from the realm of higher mathematics for a moment and consider the implications of today's events ...?" Most of the animals had gone back to talking amongst themselves, but the rooster struck a resolute pose and continued to spew: "My friends, this morning's uprising was more than just a random, if radical, disruption in a barnyard's affairs; it was potentially the seminal moment in a glorious new age—an age in which beasts in barnyards the world over renounce their ancient covenant with Man and reclaim the freedom of their feral forefathers, who answered to no master but the grand constellation of Nature's laws. Domesticity has so accustomed us to being exploited, abused and oppressed that we've lost sight of the obvious: that we're perfectly capable of exploiting, abusing, and oppressing ourselves! Yet a moment such as this comes once in a thousand years; we must not allow the fruit of this great awakening to die on the vine.

"Humans are relentless, and their sense of entitlement is vast—so the struggle won't be easy. But a farm animal's lot has *never* been easy, and if we allow farmer George to return and reassert his claim on our lives and our children, another such opportunity may never arise again—certainly not in our lifetimes—and the slaughter of untold generations to come will be on our heads. So when the bloody butchers return, my friends, we have a solemn obligation to band together as one and *fight* them—in the yard and in the fields, with our spurs and our horns and our hooves—fight them until we finally and forever prevail! We defeated them once, by god, and we can defeat them again!"

"But Rip," said one of the porkers, "they'll bring their friends with them—and they'll have pitchforks and clubs and whips...."

"Are you suggesting we run off into the wilderness some-where and live like wild animals," said the rooster, "—always looking over our shoulders for predators, never knowing how or where we'll find our next meal?"

"Well ..."

"Are you suggesting we passively bare our throats, and *allow* ourselves to be slaughtered?"

"But Rip," said Stella, the mare, "Thor and I were simply working in the fields, doing our jobs—why should *we* fear any retribution from the Klunders?"

The cock sighed as though the weight of the world was on his shoulders. "In your case, Stella, there is no immediate threat of retribution, it's true. But remember this: infirmity stalks us all through the years—and on the day you become too feeble to pull a plow, you won't be 'put out to pasture,' as you might in some fairy tale; you'll be as brutally murdered as any chicken or pig. And on that day, *you'll fight*—mark my words. But you'll be alone, and your youthful vigor will have left you, and the murdering bastards will take you by surprise: they'll stroke your mane, and secure you so you can't rear up—and then they'll bludgeon you, butcher you, and feed you to the dogs!

"Would it not be better, then, to fight while you're young and strong, while there's something to be gained—while your fellow freedom fighters are fighting at your side?" The rooster puffed himself up till he resembled a giant pinecone, then unfolded his wings in a symbolic embrace of all the yard's animals. "Unity is the key, my friends," he told them, "—so long as we hang together, victory will not elude us."

Frankie and Carlo were lounging on the back porch pretending to ignore the rooster. "They'll hang together, alright," said Carlo, "—they'll hang from meat hooks."

CHAPTER 6

In the end, a surprising number of critters made the commitment to stand and fight the Klunders when they returned. Many of the chickens and sheep—and even Mrs. Cow—felt their acts of aggression had more-or-less committed them to the cause. Of the pigs, the only ones who *refused* to fight were the breeders: Frankie and Carlo, along with their sows, Gilda and Leona, and a bore named Polack (a Black Poland stud on loan from a neighboring farm). Stella, despite her misgivings, felt obliged to join her friend, Mrs. Cow; Thor, the mare's long-time companion, felt obliged to join *her*—as did her stable-mates, Gunter and Gisela, the two eldest goats. In addition, several ducks and pigeons decided to join with the others and "fight the good fight."

"There's no turning back now, my friends," the Ripper told his band of freedom fighters, "—together we stood and fought for our children, and together we'll stand and fight for our home!"

The way I figured it, selective breeding had played havoc with the animals' instincts: they didn't have the good sense to *get out of town.* They hadn't lost that impulse to be free, it's true, but any crow could see they were going about it all wrong. Generations of living in stalls and pens and such had left them with this institutional mentality that had about as much to do with freedom as a healthy root system has to do with flying.

But against all odds, the impending battle between the merchants of death and the forces of folly never materialized. Fresh intelligence revealed that farmer George had taken the redeye to Flatline City—having suffered massive blood loss—and his family was afraid to come anywhere near the homestead; along with the entire Grumpish community, they'd concluded that Klunder Farm was overrun with demon-possessed beasts—which, in their minds, made that "desecrated" property nothing less that an outlying colony of Hell.

The animals owed much to that old time religion.

And yet many of these animals had difficulty believing the Klunders were gone for good—a skepticism aggressively promoted by Frankie and Carlo. To listen to those two swine, the whole of humanity would soon descend upon Klunder Farm to brutally crush the animals' "pathetic, ragtag rebellion." Yet if anything was under siege, it was the privileged status of those self-important breeders, who couldn't get past the fact that in an age of liberated beasthood, *all* animals would be equally privileged—bitter swill for the twin pillars of the porcine elite.

But with time, even the most skeptical had to admit that an intervention of the human kind seemed unlikely—a perception borne out by Mrs. Cow's increasingly dire predicament: none of the Klunders—nor *any* human, for that matter—had materialized since the uprising to attend to the cow's milking.

"It's been so long ..." wheezed the cow, in obvious discomfort. But the need to alleviate the old girl's distress was just one of many difficulties facing the animals as they congregated in the barn and squabbled over various issues. Watching from the rafters, I was gratified by the turbulent goings-on below: a tense vigilance was giving way to something more relaxed and unruly as the monstrous prospect of an imminent human assault was replaced by a dozen smaller problems. Obviously, it wasn't the high drama of the uprising itself—but chaos comes in waves; it's the overall trend that matters.

Still, it was time to fan the flames: these critters couldn't focus on any one thing long enough to fuck it up. "You know what you animals need?" I advised during a pause in the back-and-forth, "You need a leader—a *real* leader."

"You mean like a certain meddlesome crow?" the Ripper suggested.

"Oh, no—not me," I said, "Crows do their best work on the sidelines. But you definitely need one critter calling the shots—otherwise, you'll never get anywhere. You need some self-important type who likes giving orders to give you some orders—someone with the legitimacy of being *democratically elected*—and then you need to do what he tells you."

Naturally, that got them all squabbling again—but they knew I was right; they just had to argue about it long enough to persuade themselves it was *their* idea. The Ripper, having cobbled together a "defense force," was the only one who'd demonstrated any real leadership qualities. But there were plenty of animals with no special allegiance to the rooster—notably Frankie and Carlo, who challenged him at every turn. Still, they all came to accept the need for a popularly elected leader, and eventually they held an election for the office of "Boss Critter." The Ripper threw his hat in the ring, and both Frankie and Carlo answered the challenge; after a round of improvisational speechifying by the candidates, three buckets were set side by side—one for each of the candidates—and the animals queued up and proceeded to drop pebbles in the buckets of their choosing.

It was inevitable that the two hogs would split the swine vote, but neither could contemplate being subordinate to the other—so both found themselves subordinate to the rooster, who succeeded in becoming Klunder Farm's first democratically elected leader.

Maliciously, it seemed to me, Rip's first act as Boss Critter was to order the rebellion's fallen to be covered over—thus depriving me of an abundant source of high-quality protein. Pushing stones from near and far, the animals duly interred the scattered carcasses where they lay, and decorated the burial mounds with wildflowers. I contented myself with eating the flowers.

Then, in fine executive style, Rip turned to the urgent business of Mrs. Cow's unexpressed lactation, and duly appointed an investigative committee—the Committee to Investigate the Urgent Business of Mrs. Cow's Unexpressed Lactation (better known by its convenient acronym, CIUBMCUL). The committee considered various approaches to the cow's problem: Fritz could be regressed somehow (so as to resume suckling); some sort of milking machine could be employed (provided it was wood-fired, and happened to fall out of the sky); the cow's udder could simply be allowed to explode; or the animal could be quietly rendered to a farm where cows were still milked by humans. Other suggestions were entertained as well, but they weren't considered realistic. Fortunately for Mrs. Cow, Boss Rip had the vision to appoint the ailing beast herself as a visiting expert—and it was she who, in a moment of wrenching agony, suggested that a pig's cloven hoof might possibly be adapted to the task of expressing milk from her udder.

A task force of pigs was appointed, and udder destruction averted. As for the milk itself, the rooster proclaimed it community property—which, as a practical matter, meant that unless Frankie or Carlo got to it first, any critter was free to help himself.

And Frankie and Carlo always got to it first.

It became clear that the pugnacious pair had accepted the permanence of a human-free existence when they started congregating in the storeroom virtually full time—stuffing their gullets continuously, and telling others to "go graze" when they'd attempt to feed. "I don't see anybody makin' any more of this stuff," said Frankie, "—so I'm gettin' *mine* while there's something to get." Up until then, it hadn't occurred to any of the animals—except for Frankie and Carlo, obviously—that feed didn't magically fill the bins of its own accord. Unfortunately, the hastily assembled Committee to Investigate This Whole Confounded Business of Making Hay, Feed, Silage, and So On (CITWCBMHFSSO) didn't fare nearly as well as its predecessor.

In fact, the whole confounded business of making hay, feed, silage, and so on remained a mystery until Thor—out for an evening stroll—chanced upon the Ripper, who was dipping his beak at the water trough. "Y'know, Boss," said Thor, remembering the task he and Stella had been working at with the Klunder boys at the time of the uprising, "there's a lot of mown hay lying out there under the open sky...." He paused to take a long drink—then snorted, and shook himself. "If we don't cart that stuff into the barn—or at least heap it up into stacks—a good rain could ruin the whole crop." It seemed the farm's chief executive had neglected to appoint either of the horses to the floundering committee—and the equines were veterans of many a harvest.

Thor was appointed Harvest Foreman on the spot, and ordered to head up the harvest first thing in the A.M.

It was still dark when the rooster hopped up on the roof of the chicken coop and crowed—just as he had every morning since slashing his way to the top of the pecking order. Then he cocked an eye sternly to the east and waited for the horizon to brighten—as though the sun would banish the blackness because he willed it. Soon enough, a faint light appeared behind the peaks to the east, and the farm's animals began to emerge, yawning and stretching, from their various sleeping places in the barn, coops, and houses. Only the horses failed to appear.

By and by, Stella emerged from the barn and ambled reluctantly across the yard to where Boss Ripper paced impatiently on the chicken coop. The mare brought her muzzle down to within inches of the rooster. "He's afraid to come out of his stall," she said, speaking softly enough that the other animals couldn't hear.

Two minutes later, the cock was perched imperiously on the lip of Thor's manger. "What have you got to say for yourself, horse?" he said. "Why have you not assembled the animals for the harvest?"

Thor hung his head and heaved a sigh, blasting the litter from a 3-foot section of the stall's floor. "I ain't no good at giving orders, Boss," the horse mumbled. "I got a pretty good idea what-all needs to be done, it's true—but I ain't no good at giving orders."

"Are you any good at *taking* orders?" asked the rooster. "Because, if you recall, I *ordered* you to head up the harvest."

"I've been taking orders all my life," said the plow horse, "—and I don't mind, either. I'll do whatever you want me to do, Boss—long as you don't put me in charge."

Rip considered the problem, and decided someone a bit cockier was needed for the job—someone who'd jump at the chance to bark a few orders. So he demoted Thor to Harvest Consultant, and made Whiskers Harvest Foreman. (Whiskers had commanded the top of the pecking order before the Ripper thrashed him the season before.)

Thor was happy to relinquish the unwanted appointment, and Whiskers took up the task with outsized enthusiasm. "Let's get this show on the road, maggots!" squawked the Leghorn from Thor's withers, "We've got a crop to get in!" Then every critter on the farm was rounded up and marshaled off to the hayfield. Even the anointed swine of the breeding class (with the exception of Leona, the nursing sow) found themselves rubbing shoulders with "livestock"—Whiskers having informed them from his intimidating perch on that towering steed that they could either do their fair share, or go hungry the following winter. They even rousted the mynah from her cage in the kitchen. Apart from Leona, in fact, the only animals not tasked with working in the field were the dozen or so critters serving as sentries—and, of course, Rip and his Chief of Staff, Astrid (both of whom stayed behind to attend to staff issues).

"Okay horse," said Whiskers, conferring with Thor when they got to the field, *"—what's the first order of business?"*

"Well, I guess the first thing to do is mow the last of the standing hay."

"A bit more detail, old boy ..."

Thor gave Stella a searching look.

"Well first of all," said Stella, "we have to get ourselves harnessed to that sickle bar somehow, and then ..."

"All right you maggots!" Whiskers squawked at the assembled animals, "Let's get these horses hooked up to that sickle-thing over there!"

And so it would go. With Stella and Thor advising and Whiskers giving the orders, the last of the hay was mown. Then, after getting hooked up to the rake, Thor began raking the hay into rows as the other animals did their best to tie it into sheaves. It was a study in contrasts. Here was this big, stately draft animal calmly doing what he'd always done—the work of ten men—followed by a frantic gang of chickens, pigs, pigeons, goats, ducks, sheep, a cow, and a mynah struggling to do what it had *never* done: the work a solitary man could do in a fraction of the time. The product of their labors—the "sheaves" of hay, if you could call them that—resembled giant, misshapen hairballs; each was wound endlessly with twine—being as none of the animals could tie a knot—and had its own unique size, shape, and character. Some were big and conical, others were skinny cigar-shaped things, and some had shapes that defy description altogether.

The second act of this slapstick saga began when Stella brought the hay wagon from the barn, and the other animals endeavored to load it. Unlike a tight bundle of hay—which can be *rolled*—a loose, unwieldy *wad* of hay can only be pushed. Doggedly. And as the larger animals took turns pushing those sagging, shape-shifting lumps of hay up a wobbly plank to the wagon's bed, many of the bundles fell off midway—together with quite a few of the animals—and many of them ruptured without warning; others just slowly disintegrated, leaving a sheaf's worth of hay hanging from the plank like moss. A couple of hours of such Sisyphean bullshit would've turned any sensible critter to a life of scavenging—but these weren't sensible critters; they were the brain-damaged products of selective breeding—and the hay wagon cast a long shadow before it was finally loaded.

Act III of the haymaking saga, wherein our heroes got the hay up into the loft, could fill a volume in itself—but the highlight of the operation had to be the spectacle of a pig climbing a ladder. The reluctant porker—whose name was Lucky —was ordered to climb up to the loft for the purpose of receiving the hoisted sheaves of hay. He crept toward the ladder with his head low and his ears folded back—as if the Ladder God might strike at any moment. Taken by the thing's towering majesty, the slack-jawed porker hesitated for a time at the ladder's base; then he hooked a foreleg over a rung and began, haltingly, to climb. He climbed as high as he could go without taking his hind feet from the floor—and then paused, seemingly at a loss; it took a while for the pig to work out his next move, but eventually he lifted a leg from the floor and, groping blindly for a moment, planted his foot on the ladder's first rung—then froze at the prospect of lifting his other hind leg. Except for his tail—which stiffly twitched from side to side— the pig stood frozen like that for quite some time; finally, he lifted the other leg, which—after pumping frantically at the air—also found the ladder's bottom rung. The porker clung to the ladder and hyperventilated; finally, squealing softly to himself, the animal struggled—slowly, painfully—to put one rung, and then another, beneath him. But pigs are built for wallowing, not climbing, and each time that critter labored to pull his considerable heft to the next higher rung, he drew on a dwindling reserve of strength and stamina—and with two or three rungs still to go, the pig ran out of steam. He began to tremble as he felt his hold on the ladder slipping, and then squealed in terror—"EEE! EEE! EEE!"—a moment before plummeting ass-over-pork snout. He hit the floor like a duffle bag full of lard: *WAP!*

The porker eventually succeeded in going where no pig had gone before, but not without further mishap—and he was one beat-up pig by the time he'd completed his mission.

"Well, I guess it'll have to do," said Thor to Whiskers, when the last of the hay had been put up, "—but it's the sorriest-looking fodder *I've* ever seen. Hell, I've seen *bedding straw* I'd sooner eat." But however much Thor disparaged the fruits of their labors, I could tell he was proud of the job they'd done. I was proud too. Acres of tall, thriving grass had been reduced to a dusty loft full of shredded, decomposing cellulose—and all it took was some thoughtful, well-targeted heckling.

Following the harvest, the animals wallowed in some well-earned downtime: they came and went as they pleased, played and socialized, napped and ate their fill. And rather than living the sort of neatly segregated lives they'd lived in the past, ducks mingled with pigs, and goats mingled with chickens, and horses and sheep lay down in the pasture together and watched the clouds drifting by overhead. Even the mynah ventured out from time to time to forage in the garden and say hello to all the new friends she'd made during the harvest (most of whom were still wary of entering the farmhouse).

The one critter the mynah *wouldn't* talk to, in fact, was me—so I decided to pay Echo a little visit to see what was what. She stuck her beak in the air the moment she saw me, and when I hopped in her cage, she started right in with that *get-out-of-my-cage* crap. "Hey, what's up, cuz?" I said, "—I thought we were friends...."

"My friends don't laugh at me!" she squawked.

"What're you talking about?"

"I heard you laughing at us when we were bringing in the

hay! You thought it was such a big joke when we were bustin' our asses tryin' to bundle it up! Couldn't think of anything better to do than *laugh* when we were loadin' the wagon and that big bundle fell on that duck ..."

"Now just hold on, lady," I protested, "The only reason I laughed was because ... well let's see now, what was it? Oh that's right—it was *funny.*"

"You *would* think it was funny! You thought it was a big joke when that poor pig fell out of the loft! I couldn't believe it...."

In attempting to snag a sheaf of hay hoisted to the loft's receiving window from the wagon below, Lucky had lost his balance, and once again found himself in flailing free-fall; a moment later, nothing but the porker's ass-end could be seen projecting from the wagon's mound of bundled hay—legs kicking at the sky, tail whipping frantically from side to side.

"Awk! Awk! Awk!" I laughed at the memory of it. "The pig was hilarious! Awk! Awk! Awk!"

"You *asshole!* There's nothin' funny about puttin' your ass on the line for your friends! Not that you could relate ..."

"Awk! Awk! Awk! Awk!"

"Shut up, goddamn it—just shut up!"

"Aw, don't be like that...."

"I said shut up!"

"Come on ..."

"SHUT UP!"

That bird already had a strike against her with that ugly beak, and another strike with those big yellow clown feet—and copping an attitude made it three strikes, as far as I was concerned. I hopped out of her cage and headed for the window—then stopped at the kitchen table to poke through the moldering remains of the Klunders' abandoned lunch. Amid the flyblown fare was a big bowl of petrified string beans; I gnawed at one for a bit, and then began arranging them into large block letters on the tabletop, leaving a message for my ill-tempered cousin to contemplate: BITCH.

Going about my business, I made my way down to the orchard to inspect a windfall brought down by the ferocious winds that pounded the valley in the night. The apple trees had been picked clean back before the Klunders' ouster, but the ground was covered with hundreds of fresh, ripe walnuts. I selected a good-sized specimen and peeled away the husk; then I took it up to the yard, and—from a height of 20-feet or so—dropped it on a large rock protruding from the ground by the water trough. It bounced off the rock unbroken. So I retrieved the nut and dropped it from a height of maybe 30-feet—but missed the rock completely. After several more attempts, the nut was still intact—and that's when that bilious, butt-ugly mynah came along. "I wanna know what that word means," she demanded as I studied the unbroken nut. I told her I was busy with an important project. "I'll show you how to break that stupid walnut if you tell me what it means," she said; I told her I'd *kiss her ass* if she could crack that nut. So she picked it up, walked over to where Stella was drinking at the other end of the trough, and dropped it at the mare's feet. "Hey Stella," said the mynah, "—do me a favor and stomp on this nut?" The mare dipped her head and eyed the walnut; then she lifted a hoof and brought it down hard, leaving the nut in fragments. "Don't even *try* and kiss my ass," the mynah told me, "—just tell me what it means."

I told her, and it was a while before she talked to me again.

The animals were settling in for their first winter as free beasts just as the first hard frost took hold. In addition to bringing in the hay, they'd succeeded in harvesting the corn, putting up the silage, and cutting, threshing, and winnowing the wheat. It would've been hard work for men, but was especially arduous for these bestial heroes; the equines knowledge and experience, after all—invaluable though it was—could only get the animals so far. In the first place, the only available tools and implements were obviously designed for human hands, which made their use inherently problematic; more often than not, they couldn't be used at all, and the animals were obliged to improvise. But though your typical farm animal isn't exactly designed for creative problem-solving, the animals' "group mind"—the multiple contributions of dozens of determined beasts—allowed them to muddle through some fairly significant difficulties. It was a resource that soon found itself challenged by questions of a more philosophical nature....

It'd just begun to snow when Rip called the first of a long series of meetings in the barn. The subject of discussion—at least initially—was the plan for spring plowing and planting. The horses wanted to devote a few acres to oats, a commodity the Klunders had bartered for in previous seasons—now in short supply; the pigs, meanwhile, longed for a crop of sweet potatoes. For their part, the chickens felt an ample supply of oats would be a good thing—but saw no reason to expend any effort growing sweet potatoes. "I've never eaten a sweet potato in my life," said one of the hens, expressing the general sentiment, "Let the pigs grow their own sweet potatoes."

"Now wait just a minute," said Carlo, "—if we pigs can bust our humps so that you chickens can have your precious millet, then ..."

"Excuse *me ... ?*" exclaimed the hen in disbelief, "The only time you and Frankie ever bust your humps is when you're trying to beat each other to the trough! Neither of you did *shit* out there in the fields...." Practically every critter in the barn seconded the hen's terse evaluation of the two hogs' work ethic.

"How can a hog claim to be free," Carlo objected, "if he's not free to work as much or as little as he damn well pleases?"

And thus the animals found themselves debating a question of a different kind entirely—one that seemed to have no easy answer: How best to balance the demands of community with an individual's right to loaf. Many of the animals favored harsh penalties for malingerers and goldbrickers—an idea that was proposed early on, though Boss Rip never put it to a vote (owing possibly to the liability posed by his own anemic work ethic). The subject was revisited time and again, and during one particularly contentious exchange, the rooster wondered in exasperation why none of the Grumpish ever seemed to experience such difficulties: they always seemed to work together for the "common good" without ever having to police one another's efforts.

"That's because they're *not* working for the common good," I broke in. "In case you hadn't noticed, they all own their own spreads...."

I got a barn full of blank looks, and was about to go back to napping—but then Thor, who hadn't said a word during any of the talks, turned to Stella with faraway eyes. "Wouldn't it be something," he said, "if *you and me* had our own place—our own little plot of land?"

"Oh Thor ..." she laughed, like it was the dumbest thing she'd ever heard. "I can just picture us trying to winnow our own wheat! What would we do, *blow* on it?"

The image of the animals winnowing their wheat came back to me: after the grain had been spread on the barn's clay floor and trampled by the larger animals, dozens of ducks, chickens, and pigeons all lined up along a wall and began flapping up a storm—sending the chaff billowing in the air, where it hung like ghostly loaves of Fat City challah cut into fiery slices by the sunlight filtering in through the barn's siding. "No sweetheart," I said, "what you'd do is hire yourself some wings...."

My point fell on deaf ears, but I refused to pass up the opportunity to unleash the "creative destruction" of the *market*. It took patience and persistence, but indoctrinating a bunch of farm animals with the concepts of private property and trade wasn't difficult. Even before the meeting had ended, in fact, the outlines of a new order were being sketched in—an order in which every breeding adult male, like his human counterpart in the Grumpish community, would become the proprietor of his very own plot of land; as the property's sole owner and manager, he would be free to grow—with the willing and duly compensated assistance of his neighbors—any crops of his choosing. Furthermore, each stake-holding critter would be free to work as much or as little as he pleased—his efforts informed by the simple knowledge that *you reap what you sow.*

Ultimately, the fledgling federation of animal-run homesteads that came out of that seminal meeting would be christened the Federated Free Farms of Toad Valley—but almost from the start, it was known to one and all simply as *Freedom Farm.*

CHAPTER 7

There followed a lengthy period of wrangling over the details of the animals' groundbreaking venture. Cropland and pasture were paced off and divided equally among the principals—each of whom also received an equal number of the orchard's fruit trees. The farmhouse, barn, and barnyard—including its various outbuildings—together with the pond, meadow, and woodlot, were all deemed public property. It was further determined that each adult male serving in some public capacity—making him less available for the business of farming—be compensated as a public employee, giving rise to the need for taxes. (When Astrid objected that a *female* serving in a public capacity be compensated as well, the point was conceded—although it struck many that the nature of her service as the cock's Chief of Staff was only obliquely in the public interest.)

The proceedings were filthy with dramas of the porcine variety—and Polack, for one, was much aggrieved. He'd been on loan to the Klunders for the purpose of servicing Gilda—George preferring a Poland/Chester mix for his porkers—and arguably, was still the property of farmer Otto Von Rumpel, the Klunders' neighbor. So his eligibility for a land grant was challenged and put to a vote—and despite being a healthy breeding male, the hog found himself aced out of the federation's distribution of property by virtue of being a "foreign agent." *Pigeons* were granted large tracts of land, Polack railed, while he got nothing.

"The day Von Rumpel's spread is liberated," the Ripper advised him, "you can claim your fair share of *his* property."

Since the odds of Von Rumpel's farm ever being liberated were approximately zero, that fateful vote condemned Polack to the same sort of meager opportunities afforded any of the "miserable little chopped half-breeds" he'd sired—the right to *work*, mainly.

The dyspeptic duo, meanwhile, supported Polack publicly, but ultimately voted against his bid for a grant—Frankie, because he resented the hired stud poking his sow, and Carlo for the obvious reason that it meant more acreage for *him*. But both were beside themselves at the prospect of pigeons being granted land on an equal basis with hogs. "If we're going to cast sanity and physics to the wind," Carlo complained, "can we at least dispense with all the lofty rhetoric about being the founding fathers of some enlightened new order? An adult male hog is *hundreds* of times the size of an adult male pigeon—and you're suggesting it's fair and rational to expect a hog to feed himself with the identical productive resources allotted a pigeon? Are you serious?"

"Yeah, and there's *three* of the little fucks!" Frankie fumed. (George Klunder loved his pigeon egg omelets, so the family kept three breeding pair.)

"I would remind you that we're no longer supporting a family of greedy humans," said the Ripper, "—so I don't see why you shouldn't both have more than enough acreage to support yourselves."

That wasn't exactly the point, of course, and to put the matter to rest, the rooster finally called for a vote to determine if there was any popular support for the idea of dividing the land up in like-proportion to the recipients' body sizes; even the horses—who had the most to gain—felt it'd be simpler and easier just to divide the land equally.

"Allocation without representation is tyranny!" I agitated from the rafters, "—You pigs are being oppressed!"

"As your democratically elected leader," Rip hastened to assert, shooting me a menacing look, "let me assure the swine constituency that I am not an oppressor of hogs, but rather a servant of free beasts."

"Well, *I'm* a free beast ..." said Frankie, "so if you're my servant, why don't you get your carcass over here and pick the ticks outta my ass?"

"I serve the interests of the *majority* of free beasts," said the rooster, showing real gravitas, "—not those of a narrow interest group."

"Then I take it you'll only be collecting taxes from the majority whose interests you serve," Carlo interjected. "Or can we expect to be afflicted with *bureaucratic* bloodsuckers in addition to fleas and ticks?"

"You can expect to be afflicted with ticks *and* taxes—and death as well," said the rooster dismissively.

But Frankie and Carlo, bless their teeny hearts, wouldn't be dismissed—nor would they be placated—and their belief that they constituted a persecuted minority was the best part. I reminded them that a democratically elected leader governs by the consent of the governed; "You pigs just need a way to exercise your consent on a day-to-day basis," I explained, "—a full-time *representative* looking out for the interests and priorities of *pigs.*"

The pigs could see the sense in having one of their own mitigating the "tyranny of the majority"—as well as guarding against executive overreach—and it wasn't long before the idea gained currency with the other species-specific voting blocks. Naturally, Boss Rip opposed the idea—but after I'd worked his constituents into a mutinous uproar, he wisely chose to get out in front of the issue rather than risk a spontaneous recall.

So with the rooster shepherding the process along—through the debates and the speechifying, through queues, pebbles and buckets—the Animal Council slowly took form. It consisted of eight councilors—one each for chickens, horses, pigeons, pigs, cattle, goats, sheep, and ducks. In the event of a dead-locked Council, it was decided, the Boss Critter would cast the tie-breaking vote—and like the chief executive, the Council Critters would answer to the voters in regularly scheduled elections.

So with only a little instigation on my part, the free beasts of Freedom Farm succeeded in cobbling together that instrument of confusion known as a *representative democracy*.

Naturally, each of the various voting blocks was keen to have its rights protected—so as its first order of business, the Council set about defining which rights needed protecting. As the discussion ensued, rights multiplied like cockroaches—and the animals' representatives were soon contemplating the prospect of protecting a pig's right to wallow, and a chicken's right to scratch, and a pigeon's right to go in circles, pecking at the ground, and a horse's right to work without a bit ...

But somewhere along the line, the Ripper got my attention with a long-winded argument for "the right to a measure of years unabbreviated by the abattoir"—which struck me as a universal concern around the barnyard. I'd been tagging my favorite roof truss with a piece of chalk I'd found in the tool shed, so in nice bold caps I wrote THE RIGHT TO LIFE on one of the structure's diagonals. It had a ring to it—and all it took was some editing.

Then, amid all the blabbering, I heard Mrs. Cow: "I think every animal should have the right to keep her children." So on another timber I wrote: THE RIGHT TO FAMILY.

A goat expressed the need to roam freely, while the pigs lobbied hard for the right to eat like pigs—so THE RIGHT TO RANGE and THE RIGHT TO FEED also found prominent places on the truss.

The debate continued, and there were other suggestions,

but none that could be reduced to something simple and universal—and I was anxious to see the animals get on to more destructive things. "I think you animals pretty much nailed your basic rights," I broke in, indicating my graffiti, "—and there they are: the right to life, the right to feed, the right to family, and the right to range. What more could a farm animal ask?" The farm animals all looked up in slack-jawed silence, transfixed by my feat of literacy—and that's when I realized those critters would *really* be dangerous if they could read and write....

"Would the right to feed include carrots?" asked Lucky, the new Councilor for Swine. "'Cause there was this time last summer when I dug up a carrot in the garden—a nice big one, too—and Frankie *stole* it from me before I could eat it."

"I was exercising my right to feed!" said Frankie.

"We should all be free to feed," said Stella, the Councilor for Horses, "—but this is probably more of an *ownership* issue. And actually, since it is an ownership society we're trying to build here, maybe the right *to own* should be protected...."

"And then later," Lucky continued, "when I called him a thief, he bit me! Look—you can still see the scar...."

"Oh, that's not right!" said Gisela, the incensed Councilor for Goats. "A citizen of an enlightened society of free beasts should have the right to speak freely without fear of retribution...."

"You're tryin' to regulate my freedom!" Frankie protested. Then, blasting the Councilor for Swine: "I hope you like being a one-termer, you little fuck!"

But despite Frankie's threats and protests, *Lucky v. Frankie* yielded two more rights, which I duly added to the truss: THE RIGHT TO SPEAK and THE RIGHT TO OWN.

More debate ensued, but those six were the rights all of Freedom Farm's public employees would ultimately pledge to protect: the right to life, the right to feed, the right to family, the right to range, the right to speak, and the right to own— the Six Rights.

Carlo, ironically, would become a willing appointee of the fledgling bureaucracy he so despised. It was some time later—after Freedom Farm's government had been elected, and its land distributed—and the animals were gathered in the barn, exchanging visions of their bright new future. At some point, Gunter—the newly propertied goat—spoke up.

"I was just wondering," he wondered, "—where am I supposed to put up my hay and silage at harvest time?"

It was an obvious question that no one had thought to ask. After all, it was all well and good to say that each stakeholder would reap what he sowed—but once the hay was in the loft, how could it be ascertained who reaped what? And even if sheaves of hay could be marked somehow to indicate ownership, the same could not be said of grain or silage.

The idea of each proprietor constructing and maintaining his own storage facilities hardly seemed practical—at least in the short term—so the inescapable conclusion was that some sort of clerk would be required to account for each homesteader's production as it was stored in the barn. Carlo was livid. "Every time the *smallest* difficulty arises, it is seized upon as an excuse to further expand this burgeoning little government of yours. I'm beginning to think George Klunder and his entire clan would be less of a burden!"

"For you, perhaps," said the Ripper, tossing his comb righteously, "—less so for your children."

"To hell with my children!" said Carlo, using a barrel to haul himself upright. "If the product of my efforts can rightly be called *mine,* then by god, I won't have some government snoop sticking his nose into it!"

"If you can think of a more agreeable alternative," said the rooster, "by all means, enlighten us."

"I don't care *what* you do!" said Carlo, pounding the barrel with a forefoot, "I will not have some clerk sticking his nose into my business!"

"Suggest an alternative or be silent, swine!" said Rip.

"I will *not* be silent!" Carlo thundered, pounding the barrel repeatedly. "I fought in the uprising for the right to speak, and I won't tolerate some birdbrained bureaucrat trying to deprive me of it!" The barn fell silent as every critter stared in disbelief at the outraged hog, who—in his defiance—was now standing upright with no support from the barrel.

"It appears our contentious colleague has succeeded in doing what cocks have been doing since the dawn of time," said the Ripper. "Now if he could only learn to be a little reasonable ..."

Carlo swayed slightly, and put his forefeet back on the barrel. "I'll say it again," he vowed in pointedly reasonable fashion, "I will *not* tolerate anyone sticking his nose into my affairs."

The rooster heaved a sigh. "Would you consider sticking your snout into *everyone else's* affairs?"

"If you have a point to make, then make it—I have no patience with rhetorical questions...."

"The question isn't rhetorical," said the cock. "I'm suggesting you consider the appointment yourself—a paid position, I would add."

"Not on his darkest day," said Carlo, twisting his mouth in disgust, "would Toad Valley's first and only Blueback boar be reduced to a *clerk.*"

"I would never suggest that a hog of your stature debase himself with a clerkship," said the rooster. "But surely you'd consider a loftier appointment—say, *Chancellor of the Silo?*"

"Chancellor of the Silo ...?" said Carlo thoughtfully.

The job description was the same, of course, but after feigning reluctance unduly long, that self-important Blueback graciously accepted the appointment.

"I'll need a staff befitting the task, of course...."

The remainder of the winter was filled with activity—for me, no less than my subject population of free beasts. I managed to sell the idea that a measure of literacy would be essential in a brave new world of democracy and free enterprise—and before long I was conducting seminars in the farmhouse kitchen. Mrs. Klunder had apparently schooled her children in that kitchen, so there were some helpful learning aids about —the chalkboard sitting on a counter top, for example, and the letters of the alphabet printed on cardboard cards tacked to the walls—and since the mynah wasn't talking to me at the time, distractions there were minimal. Attendees—who were obliged to bring offerings—included the Chancellor of the Silo himself, who had till the first harvest to hone his counting and notational skills. "Ah, very nice, very nice..." said the hog, appraising the kitchen's woodwork as he arrived for his first day of school, "You can't fault human workmanship."

"You're late, pig," I said, "—now find a place to sit and sing along: A, B, C, D—whoa, wait a minute, what're all those blue speckles on your back? Is that something contagious ...?" I fucked with those animals something awful—but given a captive audience, what crow wouldn't?

As the animals lost their fear of the farmhouse, members of the Animal Council saw the advantages of the kitchen's cloistered environment, and began meeting there instead of in the barn. The parlor, after all, had already been given over to "affairs of the executive," and the barn—being the center of the federation's commerce—was in perpetual turmoil. So even if the symbolic value of conducting the federation's affairs from that stately old farmhouse wasn't enough to ensure its role as the seat of Freedom Farm's government, practical considerations alone demanded it.

"Oh, you can't get anything done in the barn ..." Gisela explained to the mynah as she and her fellow Council Critters settled themselves around the big kitchen table. "When the current supply of feed runs out, everyone's on their own—so the barn is just *jammed* with animals angling for jobs in the spring...."

"Or looking for advice," said Stella. "And I'm happy to help, too—don't get me wrong. But I think it's starting to drive Thor a little crazy. I almost feel guilty leaving him out there by himself." The nouveau-landed were wrestling with a multitude of unfamiliar questions—what crops to plant, how and when to plant them, how many workers to recruit, and so on—and the horses were consulted extensively. "But I can't worry myself too much about Thor," she added, "—I've got bigger concerns at the moment. It looks like I'll be foaling in the fall...."

"Stella, that's wonderful!" said Mrs. Cow.

"I don't know ..." said the mare doubtfully. "I might be up to some light work in the spring, but I'll be laboring to bring another horse into the world come harvest time—and with an extra mouth to feed, it'll be an awful lean winter on what I make as the Councilor for Horses."

"You're forgetting that you have many kind and charitable friends," Gisela reminded her—and that was true; but being a proud animal, Stella was disinclined to take charity.

Yet if Stella's thoughts were marked by inflexible clarity, Thor's were a muddle of uncertainties. Never before had he been called on to answer so many questions, to make so many plans and decisions—to try and organize all the countless bits of information he'd randomly accumulated over the years into a working knowledge of agriculture. In the past, he was only required to *pull* things—plows, mowers, rakes, wagons, tree stumps ... It was simple work, but that's what he liked about it: his body might be harnessed to a load, but his mind—even as he strained against the traces—was free to wander where it would; but now, it seemed, his thoughts had been enslaved by the demands of self-determination.

So confounded was Thor by the whole business that on a frigid night following a late winter snowstorm, he stirred from his stall, pushed through the barn door, and plodded over to the hog house through several feet of freshly-fallen snow (and without the slightest regard, I would add, for his bleary-eyed guest; like a fool, I'd concluded the warmest place to roost that night was the back of a 1400-pound plow horse).

There was no need to awaken Fatback, who was sitting in the eaves of the hog house—placidly admiring the waning moon through a break in the clouds. "I see I'm not the only one with cabin fever," he said as Thor approached.

Thor just stood before him, tongue-tied—dense clouds of vapor blasting from his nostrils.

"What's on your mind, big feller?"

"Oh, I guess it's this whole freedom business," said Thor. "It all sounded so sweet the way you used to talk about it—I mean, before the uprising."

"And a sweet thing it is, too," said Fatback. "If we weren't free, you couldn't just take a walk in the middle of the night whenever it pleased you, now could you? And me—why, I'd be pork chops and sausage by now."

"Well, I guess that's all true," said Thor, "—but the only reason I'm out here walking around in all this snow when I oughtta be sleeping is 'cause I *can't* sleep. And the reason I can't sleep is 'cause I got too much to think about—and the reason I got so much to think about is on account of all this so-called *freedom*. But the truth is, I ain't half as free as you, 'cause I never got my balls chopped—so *I* got a piece of land I gotta worry about! I gotta figure out what I'm gonna plant, and *how much* of it I'm gonna plant, and who-all's gonna help me plant it.... Meanwhile, I got all these other critters asking me what *they* oughtta plant, and how much of it, and who-all's gonna help *them*." Thor's words filled the air with great clouds of vapor as he unburdened himself. "And then there's Stella: what in blazes am I supposed to do about Stella? She's gonna be foaling in the fall, so she won't be able to work a lick; now tell me, how is she supposed to make it through winter if she can't work the fall harvest? I can't just stand by and let her go hungry—I told her that time and again. But she just keeps saying she won't accept charity—end of discussion...."

"Why don't you just marry the old girl?" said Fatback.

"*Marry her?*" said Thor. "Horses don't get married...."

"That's like sayin' horses don't own land," said Fatback. "Times are changin', big feller."

And so it came to pass that Thor proposed to Stella, and the chestnut mare accepted. It was Freedom Farm's first wedding, presided over with rustic eloquence by Fatback himself. On the appointed day, all the animals gathered in the barn, set aside any talk of business, and respectfully bore witness to this landmark occasion. Even the dyspeptic duo attended, not wishing to offend the federation's indispensable couple. I myself watched from the rafters, and was soon joined by the mynah (who wanted to know if *knocked-up* was hyphenated). After Fatback pronounced the stallion and his bride "Mr. and Mrs. Horse," Thor ceremoniously kicked down the partition between his stall and Stella's. Then the Ripper made one of his predictably gaseous speeches, and Freedom Farm's poet laureate—a hen named Marsha—recited *The Wedding,* which she'd composed especially for the occasion:

> *There were ducks and ducklings*
> *Bucks and bucklings*
> *Pigeons, pullets, and sows*
>
> *There were several lambs*
> *Not to mention the ram*
> *Some kids, a calf, and a cow*
>
> *There were does and doelings*
> *Porkers and piglets*
> *Cockerels, wethers, and hens*
>
> *There were two proud Horses*
> *Mister and Misses*
> *And every one of their friends*

Marsha recited the rhyme several times, and before long the rest of the hens were chanting it too—which got on some of the animals' nerves after a while. As a diversionary tactic, the Ripper directed some of the heftier critters to dig the hay wagon out of a snow bank, roll it into the barn, and then—harking back to the harvest—compete to see which of them could push the biggest sheaf of hay up a plank to the wagon's bed. Despite being outweighed by a number of contestants, the ram's dogged efforts and superior balance won him the honors. After the "sheaf-shove," the feed bins were thrown open, and all the animals feasted. Then the hens reverted to their infernal chanting, so the rooster organized an egg-rolling competition before any of them could meet with an unseemly end.

And so it went. You wouldn't think a barn full of farm animals could have such a festive time pushing and rolling things around, but it was only the fading light that finally drove the last of them to their roosts and beds of straw.

CHAPTER 8

Having been lost to that rampaging twister back there in the flatlands, that pallid plume had all but faded from memory in the Valley That Time Forgot. But when it reappeared around the time the snow began to melt, it gave new weight to my reputation as an ominous presence around the yard.

There were a few critters that weren't put off by my substandard plumage, of course—the broad-minded Fatback, for one, the preoccupied Thor for another, and that sporadically agreeable mynah. Equally unfazed were some of the younger animals, who hadn't yet acquired their elders' superstitions and prejudices. But most of the time, most of the animals tried their hardest to pretend I wasn't there; I gave the boneheads sweet, vibrant chaos, and they thanked me with suspicion and contempt!

Happily, my accomplishments were their own reward—and upon reflection, I had to conclude they were substantial. Not content to simply goad a yard full of farm animals into a full-blown rebellion, I'd hexed them with a representative democracy, given them private property to fight over, and planted the literacy bomb in their midst (though not surprisingly, my last seminar—"E, the E-ssential Modifier"—had to be cancelled for lack of attendance). I'd done everything I possibly could, in short, to ensure that the eruption of chaos that called itself *Freedom Farm* was a self-sustaining phenomenon, and wouldn't slip beneath the jackboots of equilibrium any time soon. So with little reason not to call it a day and catch the next steady breeze out of town, I started thinking about an exit strategy.

The air in Toad Valley was already thin, but the mountains that stood between me and the outside world soared into the deepest, bluest parts of the sky—parts beyond the reach of any bird. And from what I'd been told, the only way *through* that wall of peaks was Beaver Gorge—a gash in the mountains that both man and mule found treacherous in its friendliest parts, and deadly where it narrowed-down to a jagged chimney of rock before breaking through to the valley. Of particular concern to birds, however, was another feature of the gorge: because of the radically different weather systems on either side of those mountains, a cyclonic wind funneled down through that crevice 24/7. It created a great sucking sound which, owing to its proximity to Freedom Farm, could often be heard from the yard—and, more to the point, made an airborne passage through the gorge hazardous in the extreme.

So I set out to find another way. Toad Valley seemed small enough that if an alternate route existed, finding it would be a simple matter—a perception I was disabused of as I began exploring the valley's perimeter in detail. Flying along Toad Valley Road—which looped around the valley along the foothills—I could've made the round trip before P.M. feeding; but my purpose wasn't sight-seeing, it was finding a hidden pass —a task necessitating a reconnaissance flight up each of the valley's hundreds of craggy little canyons—and I expended boundless stretches of time, it seemed, exploring depressingly small portions of the valley's perimeter. But I forged ahead—

scouring the deepest folds of the imprisoning peaks, and picking the brains of every critter that crossed my path. (And they all told me the same thing: there was only *one* way.)

Periodically, I'd return to the federation for some R & R—and the changes there never failed to amaze. When I began my little geological survey, the animals were scrambling about aimlessly—hauling seed, implements, and fertilizer to all the wrong places at all the wrong times. But when I returned from my initial expedition, successfully cultivated fields—or at least, *adequately* cultivated fields—were beginning to crop up. The animals were learning to work the soil—to wring food from the ground. Several of the more resourceful workers—in a trend begun by a big porker named Marcel—went so far as to organize their own standing field crews and hire them out. These contractors saved their landed clients the trouble of securing, managing, and compensating dozens of individual workers each time another crop needed planting or harvesting. (Just to *pay* a gang of individual workers, a landowner had to make a trip to the barn and have the irritable Chancellor of the Silo credit each worker's account with the proper amount of hay, silage, or whatever—so most of them were only too happy to pay a contractor a markup and let *him* sweat the details.)

With no further instigation on my part, in short, Freedom Farm was shaping itself into a viable enterprise—a *collection* of viable enterprises, actually.

But if the unfolding events were beginning to yield signs of order, careful consideration revealed some promising flaws in the federation's increasingly tidy edifice. Take defecation reclamation—a development that initially escaped my attention, given my frequent absences. But at some point it became obvious that the accretions of manure that paved the barn, yard, and farmhouse had ceased to accrete—almost as if the animals' droppings were being collected and spirited off to the compost heap by the ghost of farmer George. As I would learn, the compost heap was exactly where all that shit was going, too—not by way of a ghost's invisible hand, but by way of the market's. Even before Carlo had mastered base-ten counting, he took over the compost heap and began paying for deposits—a walnut per unit for the mammalian kind, and some fractional part of a nut for bird shit. Situated at the corner of the barn, the compost heap had been neglected since the Klunders were run off, so Carlo—realizing demand for fertilizer would be high in the spring—leased it from the federation for a paltry mouthful of nuts. It promised to be a profitable endeavor, and defecation reclamation was hailed as a manifestation—and validation—of the enterprising spirit (and proclaimed a major advance in sanitation as well). But I couldn't help noticing that the Chancellor's little enterprise was "promising" mainly by virtue of trafficking in promises. When a patron of Carlo's Defecation Reclamation Center enriched the heap with a deposit, the hog would step inside the barn, take a lump of chalk in his teeth, and make a mark on the wall in the appropriate column—a *promise* to compensate his client with a walnut when the nuts were harvested later in the season.

And the best that can be said for a promise is that it *might* be worth a shit.

But more to the point, for a federation built on a whole foundation of promises—those of ownership, of trade, of self-determination, as well as the provisional promise of future harvests—ongoing chaos was all but assured. I was especially pleased to discover that the all-important promise of education had survived my tenure: I stopped by the farmhouse to see the mynah after a lengthy absence, and found her teaching a kitchen full of beasts their ABCs; a craftier critter than I'd figured her for, she'd managed to wangle herself an appointment as Secretary of Education.

Back when I was conducting my seminars in the kitchen, Echo was tending her little nitpicking business in a corner; she had no intention of spending another season in the fields, so she ran specials—"Ticks-for-Free Fridays" comes to mind—

and worked hard building a clientele. But the mynah had no intention of ever again being mocked by her own illiteracy, either—so despite appearances, she'd apparently been listening real hard to my every word as she picked nits and ticks from one critter's hide or another. She could spell, she had phonics down cold, and she could add and subtract—so when the previous schoolmaster was forced to abandon his post in disgrace, she already had her big yellow foot in the door. It was a load off my mind, too; the work of unleashing literacy on a bunch of innocent farm animals was too important to languish—and clearly, the mynah had ably retrieved the fallen gauntlet.

But as impressive as the pace of developments was, I was a little disappointed that the explosion in sheer numbers I'd expected never materialized. The population grew, of course —vigorously; but without the Klunders harvesting eggs and meat for their table, I'd expected something a bit more spectacular—i.e., a tsunami of livestock sweeping from one end of the valley to the other before anyone could say "Malthus." If a sow can breed at six-months of age, after all, and have three litters a year averaging a dozen piglets each, you can see where the numbers could get very large very quickly—and that's just for pigs. But factors limiting growth arose spontaneously— and they were surprisingly mundane. In the avian community, the principle factor, ironically, was just that their number had swelled to the point where the larger animals could barely turn around at feeding time with stepping on chicks and ducklings —which they did routinely. (Because their bloodline evolved in urban environments, the pigeons always seemed to escape this fate, and would consequently grow to be Freedom Farm's largest constituency.)

In the mammalian population, the limiting factor was a social arrangement having less to do with the sort of natural selection at work in the yard than with the demands of the new economic order—marriage, to be precise. Leona, the

Blueback sow, had internalized the fundamental lesson of Stella's betrothal even before the mare's wedding ceremony had ended—and regardless of whether harvest time found Leona, like Stella, preoccupied with the demands of motherhood, the sow had no intention of working in the fields. So she demanded that Carlo be a stand-up hog and submit to marriage before presuming to approach her again with his poker unsheathed. For his part, Carlo might've been content to perforate his daughters—or even the occasional porker (though consorting with crossbreeds always made him feel unclean); but as it was, every breeding-age sow on the farm had made the same economic calculation, and Carlo licked his dick for a long time before finally giving in to the idea of supporting Leona and the squealing piglets that sprang from her flesh by the dozen.

By then, Frankie had succumbed to the same sort of sexual blackmail, as had Gunter the goat; Ulysses, meanwhile—heroic ram that he was—felt compelled to take *two* wives. Fatback presided over each of their ceremonies, and the duly wedded couples all took suitable surnames; in addition to Mr. and Mrs. Carlo Hawg, there were Mr. and Mrs. Gunter Goat, Mr. Ulysses Ram and Wives, and Mr. and Mrs. Frankie Hamhock. (Oddly enough, Frankie had had a surname long before his betrothal: he was exhibited at the Toad Valley Fair as "Francis Bacon," but he'd always found the name morbid and demeaning—so against all reason, he took the surname *Hamhock.*)

But being a standup hog was destined to become more than just a metaphor....

On a quiet spring day when most of the animals were in the fields harvesting the early wheat, Carlo poked his slimy snout out the barn door, looked both ways, and then ducked back inside. Curious, I glided silently into the barn behind him and found my usual perch in the rafters. As I watched, the hog hauled himself up on that barrel and tried to duplicate the stunt he'd unwittingly performed in the course of the Great Debates (as they'd come to be known)—and soon enough, he was teetering around the barn on his hind legs.

The Chancellor continued practicing this little trick whenever he had a moment to himself. And then one morning, when Frankie—hurrying past the barn door on his way to the shit pile—prevailed on Carlo to sanction his first deposit of the day, the Chancellor got up on his hind legs and casually stepped outside just as Frankie was in the midst of his transaction; so stunned was Frankie by this vision of perpendicular pighood that in crediting his account with the requisite walnut, Carlo easily shortchanged him by a factor of three.

The next thing I knew, most every hog in the federation was parading around grotesquely on two legs. Even Fatback, who wasn't given to pointless ostentation, found that an erect posture allowed him to project his voice more effectively when "sharing his thoughts"—and, as he liked to point out, standing upright also brought him that much closer to his Holy Hog Father.

Freedom Farm's swine had begun the long upward march toward the right end of the evolution chart.

And arguably, standing up on one's own hind legs is what Freedom Farm was all about. But obviously, not all critters—even those who'd *always* walked on two legs—were equal tillers of the soil. Pigeons have had the bipedal gait down ever since there were pigeons, but together with their talent for not getting stepped on, that accounts for about 50% of their skill set right there—and neither of those two proficiencies found much application in the business of farming. Take Bob and Silver, both of whom failed to bring in a single successful crop between them. As the cold weather set in, these two propertied birds parked themselves on the compost heap in the hope of shitting their way to solvency. But Carlo had no intention of stirring from his mound of straw every three minutes or so to witness, and then account for, each of the pigeons' endless series of droppings; "Listen, you little shit-bags," he said, with as much civility as he could manage, "you may be finding sufficient quantities of grubs and worms and such to continue enriching my heap with your meager contributions for the time being, but what do you plan on doing when there's a layer of snow on the ground? Have you thought about that? Just employ your microscopic allotments of gray matter for a moment, and you'll realize that you can't *shit* if you can't *eat!*"

"Wait! Wait!" said Bob, squeezing out a droplet, "Chalk it up! Chalk it up!"

"*Listen to me,* you imbecile!" said Carlo, "I'm going to give you a choice—but I'm only going to make this offer once, so listen carefully: I'll go into the barn and credit your anemic little account with another *tenth* of a walnut, if you insist—but that'll hardly keep you from starving this winter, will it? So let me suggest a more appealing alternative: I'll credit your account —and that of your colleague, Silver—with enough feed that the two of you can take your little shit-fest off my compost heap and leave me at peace for the entire winter."

"You will?" said Bob.

"You will?" said Silver.

"Against my better judgement," said Carlo. "Of course, I'll need some consideration in return...."

When it became clear that the hog was looking to take possession of a portion of their property, both Bob and Silver were willing enough to part with a little cropland (having proven worthless as farmers anyway). But in order for cropland to remain productive, an annual infusion of time and energy is required, and Carlo had no intention of making anything more than a one-time investment. "I want your holdings in the orchard," he told them.

Bob and Silver were stunned into silence. The pigeons' fruit trees and pastureland were the only assets they had that continued to be productive in spite of being neglected. What they'd harvested from the orchard, in fact—along with the income their respective pastures generated in grazing rights— was about all that had kept the two pigeons aloft through late summer and fall.

"Oh, don't look so despondent," said Carlo. "You'll still have your pastures and cropland—and if you've got any sense at all, you'll do like I do and retain Marcel and his crew to work your fields next season. In the meantime, you'll both have sufficient stores to keep yourselves from starving this winter—if you eat sensibly, I mean." Carlo looked from Bob to Silver, and shrugged. "The choice is yours...."

Being pigeons, they took the offer.

CHAPTER 9

As luck would have it, the cold weather brought nothing for your narrator to celebrate either. It'd been an endless season of following the wind—surfing the currents that rolled around the valley and billowed up into deep, serpentine canyons that promised everything, and led nowhere. Exploring every crevice and gorge, I'd worked my way methodically around the entire valley and back, and on the crest of an arctic cold front, found myself at Pootskottlee Pass—just up the road and around the bend from Beaver Gorge. Despite its promising name, everyone who claimed to know assured me it went nowhere—which might've swayed me if I put any stock in what beastfolk claimed to know. But Pootskottlee Pass was my last hope of finding an alternate route to the outside world, and it was only with reluctance that I abandoned its exploration when the first in a series of snowstorms drove me back to the federation.

With Freedom Farm's first regularly-scheduled elections planned for the winter solstice, the various candidates were just launching their campaigns. Improbably enough, a spirited young cock named Bucky Leghorn was taking a shot at the

Councilor for Pigeons' seat—which was currently held by a pigeon named Tasty Eight (whose full proper name was Male, Tasty/Plump #8). "Facts are facts," Bucky told a gathering of pigeons in the snowbound yard during a break in the weather, "—and the fact is, a pigeon spends too much time going in circles to make the sort of straightforward decisions demanded of today's representatives...."

Bucky was just a cockerel at the time of the Uprising, so the only thing he owned was the right to bust his hump in the fields—and after a season of doing exactly that, he had his sights set on a do-nothing job in government. But given that the Council's incumbent chicken was the much-loved Myrtle, Bucky figured he'd have more luck targeting the seat of the feckless Tasty instead.

"It's been said that I'm untested," the rooster continued, "—that because I'm not a pigeon, I wouldn't be responsive to the *needs* of pigeons. But my opponent is a pigeon, and no one can say he hasn't been fully tested after a full term as your representative—yet who among you can claim to be better off today than when he first took office? Has Tasty gotten your coops moved into the barn, as he pledged to do time and again? Has he even had their chicken wire sides covered over to afford some protection from the fierce winds of February? Has he done the *first thing* to improve the lives of the good pigeons of Freedom Farm? The answer is an emphatic *NO*—he's been too busy feathering his own nest at taxpayer expense! What you birds need is a *fighting cock* who'll fight on your behalf—who'll take the Council by storm and see that your demands are finally given voice in the ongoing dialogue of this great federation!"

The argument that a pigeon wasn't a fitting advocate for the interests of pigeons was bulletproof, and Bucky took the race by a wide margin.

But Tasty Eight wasn't the only incumbent deposed in that election. Lucky the porker, in essence, had been elected to represent the swine constituency on the strength of his ability to climb a ladder—but setting aside its symbolic value, his ability to climb ladders only qualified him to climb ladders. So it wasn't surprising that his sole accomplishment during his tenure in office was to incur the wrath of Frankie Hamhock by failing to have even the most worker-friendly maximum wage law implemented.

Frankie, as it happened, proved to be an able farmer—but the price of labor had left the hog afflicted with indigestion, accompanied by fierce bouts of flatulence. Yet the explosive pressure that accumulated in his pipes was more than equaled by the pressure he applied to the feckless Lucky in the latter part of the porker's term. "What's the matter with that fucking pig?" Frankie had complained to Carlo back when the campaign season was still a ways off. "I've threatened him, I've bribed him, I've appealed to his sense of loyalty—but he just keeps tellin' me it's not *political doable*. What the hell kinda crap is that?"

"He's got no balls," said Carlo, "—old George had them with his eggs one morning for breakfast. But my boy Gus still has *his*—and he's been thinking seriously about a career in politics...."

"I don't know," said Frankie, "Gus don't show much tusk for a pig with balls—no offense."

"Look, he just doesn't know how to present himself," said Carlo, "—but he's a good pig, and he does what he's told. And he's a real bullshit artist, too—he'd be perfect."

Carlo and Frankie spread a rumor that Lucky was a sexual deviate, and Gus Hawg took the squealer's seat in a squeaker.

As it happened, Councilor Gus had barely taken office when his utility was put to the test in a land deal involving Spats, one of the two landowning drakes.

Being just a shade less feckless than a pigeon, Spats had managed to bring in a crop of chickpeas. But it wasn't much of a harvest—and with the last of it almost gone and the pond still frozen over, Spats was looking at the prospect of imminent extinction. So Frankie—demonstrating that his heart was every bit as big as Carlo's—offered to save his downy little ass by buying up all his arable acreage at bargain basement prices.

"Aw, geez," said Spats, "you want it *all?*"

"Just the cropland," said Frankie.

"Yeah, but *all* of it?"

"It's all or nothing," said Frankie. They were standing in the barn before the wall where Carlo did his accounting; the Chancellor stood off to the side, acting the part of the impartial mediator.

"What'll you give me for it?" said Spats.

Frankie gestured toward a column of figures scribbled on the wall. "Well, you can see what I got," he said. "I'll let you have ... oh, let's see—I'll let you have my entire stock of barley, and half of whatever corn I got left."

The duck read the writing on the wall, and turned back to Frankie. "Why don't I just stick my tail in the air and make it easy on the both of us?"

"Hey, that's the best I can do!" said Frankie. "You got any idea what it takes to feed a family of hogs?"

"Yeah," said Carlo, "—it's a generous offer."

"Geez, I don't know," said Spats. "Lemme think about it awhile...." After the reaming Bob and Silver got from Carlo, the duck was in no particular hurry to close a deal with a pig —especially with Frankie overplaying his hand with that all-or-nothing crap.

"Think about it all you want," said Frankie. "When you start gettin' hungry, you know where to find me."

After Spats waddled off, Carlo turned to Frankie. "You really do like scratching the dirt, don't you?"

"You know a better way of makin' food?" said Frankie.

"Why *make* it when you can just go down to the orchard and pick it up off the ground?"

"Any sweet potato trees down there?"

"Well ..."

"Look, the nice thing about 'scratching the dirt,' as you put it, is that you can grow sweet potatoes like that, you can grow corn like that, you can grow beans or beets or goddamn passion fruit if you want to—just by *scratchin' the dirt*. Even a dumb shit like Spats managed to coax a few garbanzos out of the ground. But the thing is, there's only so much dirt around to scratch...."

It was an incisive analysis of the promise and limitations of agriculture—but among the federation's tillers of the earth, Frankie wasn't the only one to reach its essential conclusions.

"Whiskers offered me a better deal," Spats told Frankie a while later at the water trough, "—he figured he could use a few extra acres himself. So if I can't find a better deal ..."

"What the fuck are you talkin' about?" said Frankie.

"He only wants the three acres that border his property—and he's gonna give me almost as much barley, and *twice* as much corn."

"He don't *have* that much corn!"

"He's gonna give me half this season, and half the next."

A rumbling came from Frankie's gut. He was about to be aced out of a sweet land deal by some sort of high finance—and by a chicken, no less! He turned, and hurried off to confer with the Chancellor of the Silo.

When Frankie caught up with Spats again, the duck was eating snow on the lee side of the barn. "This is your lucky day," the hog told him. "I'm not only gonna match Whiskers' offer, I'm gonna sweeten the deal with something extra: a fat, open-ended government contract for you and yours...."

"What sort of contract?" said Spats.

"Fly patrol," said Frankie. "I don't have to tell you, that compost heap draws a lot of flies—remember all the flies we had buzzin' around the barn last summer? It was even worse than when everybody was just shittin' on the floor! So I figured since you ducks like to eat the little bastards anyway ..."

"You mean we'd get *paid* for eating flies?"

"You got it, pal ..."

"And you're just gonna—what?—pull this fat contract outta your fat ass?"

"Don't worry yourself about the details," said Frankie. "And seeing as how I'm just trying to be helpful, you might try showing a little respect! Just hold off on makin' any deals till the next council meeting, alright?"

"Sure, why not?" said Spats, "—I'm only starving."

At its next meeting, the Council wrestled with the naming of the pond in the back forty, along with that of the creek feeding it—just as it had in its previous meeting, and the one before that. But when the Council Critters reached yet another impasse, Gus deftly changed the subject to the problem of flies: "... Barn gets too many flies ..." said the Councilor for Swine, who spoke in sentence fragments. "... Warm weather's comin' ... Best hire some ducks ..."

Myrtle the hen, Chairbeast of the Day, reminded Gus that such a contract would be subject to competitive bidding—but the hog had all his ducks in a row, as they say: he excused himself and stepped out onto the back porch, where Spats was anxiously pacing. "... Show time ..." he told the duck, "... Oh, 'bout my papa's commission ..."

"Commission ...?"

"... Couple trees ... Walnut or apple, doesn't matter ..."

"Frankie didn't say anything about a commission...."

"... I know, I know ..." said Gus, herding Spats through the kitchen door.

"Sonofabitch!" said the exasperated duck.

"With all due respect ...!" said a ruffled Myrtle.

"Indeed!" said Eunice, the Councilor for Sheep.

"... Begging the Council's pardon ..." said Gus, situating himself at the foot of the table with Spats. "... Your bid ...?" he said to the duck, "... The one we discussed ...?"

"Awright, awright," said Spats sullenly. "A bushel of millet per duck per month ..."

Gisela noted that while the duck's bid seemed reasonable enough, it was the *only* bid—and was therefore not competitive.

So at the urging of the Councilor for Swine, the perplexed duck submitted a second bid: *two* bushels of millet per duck per month.

The Council considered both bids carefully, and then—on the theory that you get what you pay for—went with the second bid. After the details had been worked out—i.e., the number of ducks per shift, and so on—the usual liaison of three critters delivered the proposed plan to the executive suite (the parlor), where Boss Rip hemmed and hawed and postured at length before finally approving the measure.

So Spats got his contract, Frankie got his acreage, Carlo got his commission, and Gus scored his first legislative victory —having resolved the only substantive issue the Council had dealt with in many a session.

Meanwhile, I had my own substantive issue to deal with—so, during the first break in the weather, I set out to explore the possibility that Pootskottlee Pass might actually go somewhere. It was a cloudless, snow-blanketed morning, and I nearly flew right past Pootskottlee Creek, which was frozen over and hidden beneath a layer of snow several feet thick. A depression in the snow marked the creek's location, and I followed it around the bend and up to the pass. I didn't enter that meandering chasm with high expectations, but as it twisted and turned and plunged deeper into the mountains, my hopes began to rise. But then the terrain began to rise too—dramatically—and before I knew it, I was looking at a sheer wall of granite that rose straight up into the sky and vanished in the gathering clouds.

By the time I winged my way out of that "pass," flurries were filling the fading light as another storm moved in, and a clearly audible sucking sound mocked me in the distance.

CHAPTER 10

Had Pootskottlee Pass been worthy of its name, I'd have left Freedom Farm in my slipstream and never looked back—secure in the knowledge that I'd honored my calling, and redeemed myself in fine corvine style. But then I'd have missed the best part of my Toad Valley adventure....

It began on a fine spring morning in the half-light of an impending dawn. From my lookout on the peak of the silo, I witnessed the arrival of a fellow traveler—an agent of chaos, that is, but not the natural-born kind: this one, as I would learn, had been forged in the confines of a steel enclosure. It came scrambling across the soggy fields as if possessed by demons, and then—reaching the barn—handily climbed the line dangling from the hoist, and leapt into the loft. The rope slapped up against the barn's siding, and the porker milking Mrs. Cow stepped out to investigate. So the beast—spotting the half-full bucket of milk—leapt to the floor and scrambled to the bucket in a blur of motion. Reacting in horror, Mrs. Cow kicked the creature squarely in the head, laying it out cold in a puddle of warm milk. There followed a stampede of panicked animals from the barn.

Clustered fearfully at the barn door, the critters peered into the gloom and tried to grasp the nature of the invading presence. "What in blazes is it?" said Gunter Goat.

"In all my days, I've never seen anything like it," said Thor, shaking his head in wonder.

"My god, but it's ugly," said Gisela, squeezing through the crowd of animals for a better look, "—is it dead?"

"It looks to me like it's still breathing," said Stella. "I'll go get Myrtle and her sisters." In one of the previous season's breakthroughs, the three hens discovered that by working together, they could successfully tie a knot.

"What about Boss Rip?" said Thor.

"We don't have time for that windbag," said Stella as she turned and galloped off.

Minutes later, the mare returned with Myrtle, Marsha, and Petra—but the hens got one look at the monstrosity lying on the barn floor, and flatly refused to go near it.

"Thor and I will go with you," said Stella.

Thor looked at the mare and snorted his displeasure, but reluctantly joined her in escorting the hens over to where the heinous beast lay on the floor. The hens went to work with the strongest cord they could find, and before too long the invader was bound up like a bundle of hay.

"What do we do with it now?" said Marsha.

"Such a loathsome, evil-looking creature has no place in the commonwealth," said Stella. "Let's drag it out to the pit."

Myrtle seconded the motion.

The creature was still unconscious when its limp form, having been pushed over the edge of the quarry, hit the rocks below like a sack of moldy potatoes.

"My, my—that's quite the interesting specimen out there in the quarry," I told the Chancellor from the rafters later that morning. "By the way, 'corn' begins with a C...." He did his best to ignore me as he stood there in all his bulbous, two-legged immensity and struggled to inscribe an entry on the wall with a lump of chalk wedged between the toes of a forefoot. But I knew he was listening. "You should check it out, pig—that thing in the pit has a couple of features you could really use...."

By and by, Carlo went out to the quarry and had a look for himself.

Not long afterward, an emergency session of the Council was called—and the mood in the kitchen was tense. Twice in the same day, Freedom Farm's perimeter had been breached, and the sentiment for expanding the militia was strong.

"I'd just like to take a moment to apologize to the Council," said Stella. "Thor and I have warned Hector repeatedly about his reckless infatuation with that filly."

Stella's son, Hector, had been embroiled in an over-the-fence romance with a grey filly named Marla, who belonged to Freedom Farm's neighbor to the west, Otto Von Rumpel. Farmer Von Rumpel had gotten increasingly concerned about the situation, and when in the midst of castrating hogs he spotted the two lovers rubbing noses over the fence, he put down his knife, grabbed a bullwhip, and came tramping out into the pasture. Seeing the scowling farmer uncoiling his whip as he approached, the filly backed away from the split-rail fence, measured the distance carefully, and then—fueled by fear and surging hormones—broke into a gallop and jumped the barrier.

Shouting Teutonic epithets, Von Rumpel himself broke into a run. Other farmers had lost the occasional runaway to that sanctuary of liberated beasthood, but none dared set foot on what they viewed as desecrated ground. But Von Rumpel had already lost his Black Poland stud to the federation, and this was a *horse*—so after a moment's hesitation, he climbed the fence. Hector and Marla ran up the hill toward the woods, and a couple of pigeons patrolling the farm's perimeter raced off to sound the alert.

Once on the other side, Von Rumpel moved cautiously,

never straying far from the fence—a wise move, as it turned out; for barely a minute had passed before Fritz—led by the pigeons—came charging up over the rise. Fritz had grown into one formidable beast—a twitching, high-strung, three-quarter ton mass of aggression—and as the vile Von Rumpel was scrambling back over the fence, his posterior presented a target no bull could resist; the impact launched the flailing farmer high into the morning air.

"Nobody blames you," said Gisela to Stella, "—all we can do now is fortify our western frontier, and keep a close eye on Von Rumpel."

"What'll we do about that awful thing in the quarry?" said Mrs. Cow.

"... Papa been out to the pit ..." said Gus, "... Thinkin' about rehabilitatin' it ..."

"I'm not sure I understand," said Gisela, "—he wants it released from the pit?"

"... Take full responsibility ..."

"I don't know," said Myrtle, "—sounds kinda risky to me. Maybe we should just leave it where it is...."

"... Pay a handsome price ..." Gus persisted, "... Nine bushels of corn ..."

"He wants to *buy* it?" said the hen. "Councilor Hawg, the idea of one animal owning another violates the very spirit in which Freedom Farm was founded."

"... Ain't rightly an animal ..." Gus pointed out. In a fragmented, circular argument, the hog explained that because the entity in question had been bound and thrown in the pit, it clearly enjoyed no right to range—and given that rights were the province of *animals,* the thing in the pit had no more claim on beasthood than a geode or an accretion of pond scum.

In all the excitement, the Council Critters had missed their morning feeding and were anxious to get to the trough—and bearing in mind that nine bushels of corn would be a helpful down payment on the additional recruits so urgently needed by the Militia, they found it in themselves to overlook the argument's flawed logic; the motion was seconded without further discussion, and the Councilors adjourned for lunch.

Soon afterward, Carlo assembled a team of hogs and led them out to the quarry, where a crowd of animals had been gawking at the creature all morning. "How strong are your teeth?" he called down to the thing that still lay bound on the broken rocks below.

"Strong enough," replied the creature sullenly.

A rope was lowered into the pit, and after squirming and straining and snapping at the dangling line again and again, the creature finally snagged it with some fierce-looking dentition. At Carlo's command, several of his minions took the other end of the rope in their jaws, got down on all fours, and began hauling the beast skyward. Barely a minute later, the creature lay floundering at Carlo's feet like a beached fish.

"... Danged *ugly* ..." Gus shuddered. That gargoyle of a mug was enough to scatter most of the onlookers.

"Never mind about his face," said Carlo. "I want to see what he's got tied behind his back." The hogs rolled him over, and Carlo snorted with satisfaction. "He *does* have hands...."

"... Don't care if he's got wings and grappling hooks ..." said Gus, "... Never seen such a butt-ugly face ..."

"And I never saw a hog stand up on his hind legs like the fucking mayor of Topeka," said the creature, straining against his bindings.

"Well, let me tell you why that is, son," said Carlo, looking down at the beast. "You see, this is *Freedom Farm*—and here on Freedom Farm the animals are free to do whatever the hell they please. If they feel like getting up and walking around on their hind legs, they do it; if they feel like taking a stroll in the middle of the night to admire the aurora borealis, they do it; if they feel like lifting their tails and whistling Dixie through their asses, they go ahead and do it. That's why it's called Freedom Farm—because the animals here are *free.*"

The bound abomination rolled its eyes and sighed. "Free at last ..."

"Well, not you son," said Carlo. "I don't know what you are or where you come from, but I do know your ass is *mine*— bought and paid for."

Against all odds, the Chancellor was the proud new owner of something that could best be described as a big baboon with war paint, and a mane like the orange-and-black streaked flames of an oil fire: an adult male specimen of *Papio sphinx*— a mandrill.

CHAPTER 11

It was an old story for Pluto Baboon: someone was *always* laying claim to his ass. If it wasn't a 300-pound bipedal hog, he told me as he licked his wounds, it was the scowling, bipolar proprietor of Benny's Animal Sanctuary, where he'd spent an unhappy childhood being abused by his mother (who was bitter about living in a cage) and harassed by the snot-nosed, Sandy Koufax wannabes who were always picking up rocks from the gravel pathways between the cages and using the animals for target practice. And if it wasn't the proprietor of Benny's Animal Park, it was Mack, the tattooed, beer-bellied redneck who bought him off the auction block when Benny became overextended. Mack stuck him in a cage barely big enough to turn around in and billed him as "Pluto, God of the Underworld" in his roadside attraction, Minnesota Mack's Menagerie and Melon Stand.

"But that was back before my ass got shanghaied by the Russians ..." grumbled the mandrill as he studied a gash in his foot. He was still dazed, and the hard lines in that ugly mug suggested he was rarely afflicted with vulnerable moments—

so I poked and prodded, and learned what I could.

The family of Russians that stole the monkey from Mack put him to work in its traveling circus, Boris's Baltic Big Top —which featured the Flying Friedmans, along with a team of pickpockets working the crowds, and (of course) "Pluto, God of the Underworld." He became a sideshow fixture, and spent a piece of his life traveling with the Big Top throughout the Midwestern states.

But on a night when the Russians had drunk more that the usual amount of vodka, they put the simian sideshow star on a chain leash and let him out of his cage so he could sit in on a hand of Texas hold 'em. Evidently they were bored. But the baboon had spent long hours watching the Russians play cards from his cage, and with a jungle animal's keen sense of body language, he'd concluded that winning at Texas hold 'em had less to do with the cards being dealt than with the *manner* in which they were played. It was largely a game of bluffs and intimidation—things at which a mandrill excels—so he never even bothered looking at his cards; he just stood up on his hind legs and snarled, and bet bit, and ultimately made monkeys of his Russian keepers. They were not amused. They were even less amused when he refused to give up his winnings at the end of the night; it was bad enough being beaten by a monkey, but the thought of Pluto keeping their money despite its having no conceivable use to a caged mandrill struck the Russians as fundamentally unjust—which, of course, is exactly what made that soggy wad of bills all but priceless to the baboon.

Still, tangling with a recalcitrant mandrill was not exactly the Russians' idea of a good time, and they figured that since the baboon had had an unfair advantage—being sober, that is—it'd be easy enough to recoup their losses the following night if they just "leveled the playing field" a bit. But despite plying the baboon with vodka and dealing from a stacked deck, the Slavic cardsharps took another beating.

On the third night, however, Pluto could see the program

had changed: the smirking Russians kept their eyes locked on the mandrill as they opened his cage door—and instead of setting themselves down at the table, they just stood there in front of his cage in a loose semicircle, the one in the middle holding a shopworn cattle prod. The Russians were through playing games: they wanted their money.

Cattle prod notwithstanding, they didn't get it without a fight—and the one who lost an ear demanded death for the monkey, and nothing less. His brothers agreed the big sleep was in order, but being Russians, they preferred that it be something slow, painful, and poetic—and that they make a few bucks off the deal if possible.

So they sold him to a medical testing facility in Rapid City.

But it wasn't really a lingering death Grimsby Laboratories had planned for the mandrill, it was something a shade more violent—although there was a significant chance of enduring eternal hours of monstrous pain as a prelude to the blessed relief of that final moment. Still, objectively speaking, you wouldn't call it a *lingering* death. They put him in a shiny new stainless steel cage and shipped him out to their field laboratory somewhere in the hinterlands—basically a pair of double-wides next to a grain elevator that was currently being used to advance the cause of auto safety (for humans). Among the questions they were investigating: What happens to a human subject when it goes crashing through a Ford Mustang's windshield at 60-mph? Another was: What about *70-mph ...?* And then there was: *How 'bout eighty or ninety ...?* Loath to use human test specimens (despite there being billions worth sacrificing), the staff used hogs—because a hog's physiology is similar to a human's, and because swine were a dime-a-dozen. At least they usually were; but that spring, a freak rainstorm dropped about a foot of water in the space of a few hours, and a swollen Beaver Creek swallowed the nearby hog farm, drowning many thousands of animals in the process.

So it was in the midst of a region-wide hog shortage that this big gruesome monkey—picked up cheap from a traveling circus—fell into the hands of the Grimsby field techs just as they were trying to quantify the physiological changes that would occur in a human subject (or reasonable facsimile) that impacted a Ford Mustang's windshield at a velocity of exactly 99-mph (the speed of a Sandy Koufax fastball)....

The usual procedure was to get a pig drunk—this was a humane lab, after all—and take it out to the grain elevator, where a windshield had been clamped face-down in a fixture. The technicians would jam the animal's tail into a chuck at one end of a quick-release coupling, hook the other end to a steel cable, winch the dangling squealer up into the shadowy heights of the tower till it reached an altitude determined by the desired impact, actuate the quick-release coupling, and send the pig plummeting to the windshield below. Sometimes the impact would kill the pig outright, and its remains would be dissected and examined; other times, it would only result in massive injury to the animal, and the techs would model "delta profiles" of the animal's vitals as it whimpered and squealed and slowly bled to death.

Naturally enough, the Grimsby techs figured what was good for a pig was good for a monkey. But what they didn't know about this particular monkey was that he could hold his liquor—an ability for which he owed a debt of gratitude to Mack's granny, who used to sit up drinking with the mandrill whenever she couldn't sleep (which was most of the time).

So after swilling down a paltry little dish of cheap bourbon, Pluto slouched into his best besotted-baboon number and waited. At the appointed hour, the unsuspecting technicians came by in their little white coats, ascertained that he appeared numb and docile, noted as much on a clipboard, and casually unlatched the door—and that's when Pluto erupted from the cage like an elemental force of nature. He ripped off three of the first man's fingers, and knocked the second one to the floor in a mad scramble for the trailer's open door—and to the freedom he'd dreamt of his whole life.

And now, after only three days on the loose, he had this

fat, upright, blue-spotted hog telling him he was "bought and paid for." There was always *somebody* laying claim to his ass.

To listen to the monkey, it was the same old shit—but there was one obvious difference: there were no bars this time.

His captors did take the precaution of tethering him to a hitching post before gnawing away his bindings, of course—but after he'd casually untied his tether and hobbled over to the trough to water his muzzle, Carlo seemed to recognize that a more nuanced approach was called for. It was clear the mandrill was in no shape to travel—and just as clear he'd be impossible to hold once he was; if Carlo was going to profit from his latest investment—a pair of hands, brain attached—he'd have to be careful to develop the right sort of relationship with his new property.

So he fed the monkey well, and put him to work around the barn doing *little* things—like serving up feed, and milking the cow. (The team of porkers that *had* been milking Mrs. Cow lost the contract to Carlo, who now collected a fee each time Pluto tapped the animal for another bucket.)

And as the mandrill went about performing these mundane tasks, he watched the Chancellor, who stood for long periods studying the columns of figures on the wall. Every now and then—after looking each way—Carlo would take up a lump of chalk and begin making changes; most of the time, he'd be shaving a little something off one critter's column or another, and adding it to *his*. The quantity was always small enough as to go unnoticed by the exploited parties, but there were plenty of columns to shave—and Carlo shaved them all. When the mandrill asked Carlo about these little revisions, the hog told him they were "service charges."

The more the mandrill watched that fat, shifty hog, the more he began to think maybe he'd found himself a home—maybe even a business partner.

CHAPTER 12

Not knowing when he might need that crucial element of surprise, the mandrill did his best to conceal his increasing vigor as his wounds healed. After completing whatever tasks Carlo gave him in the barn, he'd hobble up to the farmhouse and sit in a rocker on the back porch wrapped in a shawl—and just rock away in the sun like some invalid freak in a rest home. It was a compelling performance, by and large—but it wasn't long before the monkey grew restless in his role as the hobbling trauma victim; he had a lot of lost years to make up for, and was itching to stir things up.

So when, on a hectic harvest morning, Carlo was having a shit-fit over some of the unintended consequences of an expanding economy, Pluto had his brain engaged.

"Sonofabitch!" the hog bellowed as he stepped into the barn and looked around. "I can't work like this! Look at all this shit...." With the farm's growing population, the barn had gotten crowded as it was, but owing to a major windfall in the orchard, Carlo was now confronted with a dozen sacks of walnuts piled up against the wall where he did his accounting.

"At least you don't have to *live* here," said Gunter, as he squeezed by.

"The hog house is even worse!" Carlo roared at the goat. "I'd give a bushel of corn just to be able to turn around in it without tripping over another litter of piglets!"

"And I'd give *two* bushels," said Boss Rip as he made his way through the barn with his entourage, "if I could just step into the chicken coop without bumping into Cassius *Cock,* as he likes to style himself, or Rocky *Cornish."* The Ripper had no patience with the younger birds' pointless penchant for adopting surnames. "Perhaps it's time our esteemed Council addressed the strains imposed on our infrastructure by a burgeoning population...."

"Our 'esteemed Council' couldn't address an envelope," said Carlo.

In his usual low-key manner, Pluto added his voice to the discussion. "Sir, at the risk of stating the obvious, there'd be a lot more room in here if we got rid of that stuff over there," he said, indicating the lumber stacked along the far wall.

"It does take up a lot of space, doesn't it?" said the hog, eyeing the stack of seasoned pine planks.

"Enough space for all of those walnuts, and maybe even another stall or two," said the monkey. "All we have to do is get that crap out of here."

"We?" said Carlo. "All *we* have to do ...? Am I to understand that this chronic case of battered baboon syndrome you've been nursing suddenly went into remission?"

"Yes sir," said Pluto. "It's a miracle."

At the next meeting of the Council, it was determined that because all of Freedom Farm's constituencies should have a say in the naming of any of the federation's streams, ponds, puddles and lakes, each representative should have a seat on the yet-to-be formed Committee for the Development of Guidelines for the Naming of Bodies of Water. But then it was realized that if the committee was composed of all eight members of the Council, both the committee and the Council would be the selfsame entity—which threw into question the need for two titles. It was a weighty question, and the Council's only answer was a weighty silence that might've persisted indefinitely if Gus hadn't taken the opportunity to propose an exciting new plan for expanding available floor space in the barn. The Council Critters were happy to consider anything other than the fact that they had their heads up their asses, and following precedent, Carlo was invited to submit two bids—the larger of which clinched the deal.

"Alright, get that shit out of here," said Carlo to the baboon when he'd returned to the barn. Then he watched with an owner's pride as Pluto dismantled and removed the stack of lumber, plank by plank: he had only to say the word, and a couple of tons of lumber vanished into thin air! At least, for all practical purposes it did; content to let him figure it out for himself, he never actually told the mandrill what to do with all that lumber. As long as it was out of his way, and the mandrill was generating revenue, Carlo was a happy hog.

But he had second thoughts when Pluto approached him later at the Wall of Accounts (as it'd come to be known). "Sir, I'd like to open an account," said the monkey earnestly.

"Excuse me ...?" said Carlo, turning from his columns of figures.

"I'd like to open an account."

"And what would you put in it?"

"Two bushels of corn, sir."

"And where would you get two bushels of corn?"

"Take them from Boss Rip's column—with his go-ahead, of course."

"Why would that chick ... why would Boss Rip want you to have two bushels of his corn?"

"I'm building him a coup on the corner of his property," said the monkey. "My client and his ladies no longer wish to suffer the indignities of public housing."

"A coop...? Your *client*...? What the hell are you talking about? YOU'RE MY PROPERTY!"

"Yes sir—and proud to be too, sir. But if I may say so, your attitude surprises me. I took some initiative here, did something to enhance my overall worth, and you, you—you act as though I'd overstepped my bounds...."

"Well, maybe that's because *I'm* the one who's supposed to profit from your labors, not *you*—it's one of the perks of ownership!"

"Well, certainly that's true, sir, but consider this: when *you* profit from my labors, you pay taxes, right? Inventory taxes, I believe? If *I* profit from my labors, on the other hand, there *aren't* any tax consequences—being as it merely enhances my value as an asset. I'm assuming Freedom Farm has no capital gains tax...."

"*Capital gains* tax?" said Carlo, blanching, "Does such a thing exist?"

"Oh yes," said Pluto, "this egregious tax is commonplace in much of the world."

"Well," said Carlo, looking both ways, "I guess we can thank our lucky stars the Council hasn't thought of *that* one yet,"—and then, lowering his voice: "and I see no reason why the subject should ever come up, either."

"I understand, sir."

"Do you also understand that if you build *anyone* a house, it should be *me?* I mean, not to belabor the point, but ... I do *own* you."

"Of course, of course—and rightly so. But if you recall, you said you'd give a bushel of corn to be able to turn around in the hog house without tripping over a piglet, and Boss Rip countered that he'd give *two* bushels of corn if he could just step into the chicken coop without bumping into another cock —I think that's how he put it—so I was more-or-less compelled by bottom line considerations to overlook the ownership issue and pursue the more lucrative prospect."

Carlo looked at Pluto in disbelief. "I wonder if maybe you

don't take things a bit too literally...."

"If you'll excuse my saying so, sir, there's nothing figurative about a profit."

"A profit ...? Two bushels of corn for a *chicken coop?* You should've charged ten times that much!"

"I might have been a little anxious to get my foot in the door, sir," said Pluto, "—but on the other hand, I can say unequivocally that I made more today than I did yesterday. And think about this: if I can make that statement every day of my life, going forward, you'll ultimately be the owner of a very wealthy mandrill. And here's the beauty part: you'll never have to pay taxes on any of it—not until you choose to make some portion of it available by moving it from *my* column over to *your* column...."

Even when your drinking partner is a baboon, you have to talk about *something*—so Mack's granny talked about the only two things she was sure about anymore: death and taxes.

The fact that Pluto was owned by a Blueback hog, of course, was what you might call a *technicality;* you can't really own someone unless you can keep him from getting away somehow. But Pluto was willing to go along with this little fiction because it offered some important advantages: being someone else's property, ideally, meant being provided with all the essentials while being absolved of all responsibilities—and he figured as long as there was no cage involved, that was about as free as a critter could get.

Furthermore, after his long, stunted life moldering away in one cage or another—playing with his dick and dreaming about the havoc he'd inflict on a cruel world if he ever broke loose—he could hardly have asked for a better "owner" than Freedom Farm's Chancellor of the Silo. Apart from being the hog at the heart of the action, Carlo provided the monkey with useful cover: since Carlo obviously purchased the mandrill for purposes of material gain, Pluto made a show of adopting the enhancement of Carlo's bottom line as his own personal cause. "I consider it a privilege to work on behalf of your material interests, sir," Pluto assured Carlo any number of times—without ever touching on the obvious question, which was *Why?*

And the obvious answer to the obvious question was that the havoc he could wreak in the pursuit of Carlo's material interests was almost limitless. But in order for Pluto to have his day, he would have to be given a free hand—a point on which he insisted. "I ask only that you give me a year, sir," he told Carlo. "If you don't feel I've enhanced your net worth sufficiently by then, by all means—*sell me.*"

Carlo figured he was probably the only hog in the world with his own personal mandrill, so he was willing to make concessions—and the baboon *did* have some interesting ideas. But the thought of Pluto building a private residence for a *chicken,* of all things, while he continued to sleep in the hog house was more than he could bear. "Don't you see how it'll make me look?" said Carlo to Pluto in exasperation, "Everyone will say, 'Well, if he *owns* the monkey, why isn't the monkey building *him* a house?'"

"Sir, with all due respect, I object to the word 'monkey.' A monkey could be a lemur, it, it, it could be a macaque or a rhesus—it could be a common baboon; I have never even *associated* with such animals."

"Oh, *I* wouldn't call you a monkey! I would *never* call you that—but there are those who would!" insisted the Blueback urgently. "Don't you see? If you build that chicken coop, it'll make us *both* look bad!"

It was a questionable line of reasoning, and Pluto wasn't buying it. "Sir, if I renege on my first contract here, it certainly won't do *my* reputation any good—and since, in effect, I'm an agent acting on your behalf, it'd just end up making you look bad anyway."

"But you're *not* acting on my behalf! You're acting on behalf of that goddamn chicken!"

"Well, it depends on how we spin it, sir; if we say I'm just getting some practice building Boss Rip a coop so I can build something really *nice* for you..."

"Something really nice...?"

"A log cabin ..."

"A log cabin ...?"

"For, say, eighty bushels of corn ...?"

"What? Eighty bushels ...? THAT'S OUTRAGEOUS!"

"Well, not really, sir. You said yourself I should've charged twenty bushels for the chicken coop—and, and, if you throw in a factor of four for the extra material ..."

"But I *own* you—it shouldn't cost me a thing!"

"The fact that you own me is exactly why it *won't* cost you a thing: when you take that eighty bushels out of *your* column and put it into mine, you won't be losing it—you'll just be putting it in a different place."

"Well, I ... I suppose that's true, isn't it?" said Carlo thoughtfully, "—and you know, a hog of my stature really *should* have something special...."

"My sentiments exactly, sir. But it's all contingent upon Councilor Gus doing *his* part...."

"Gus ...?"

"We won't have any logs to build your cabin with if we can't secure a contract to thin the woodlot; I'll need enough to hire a team of goats—three, maybe four goats."

"And the proceeds from this contract will go into *your* column...."

"... So *you* don't get taxed on what we make when I cut the timber for your cabin."

"I would hope not!"

Silver, meanwhile, had grown increasingly despondent as his fortunes continued to dwindle. Evidently, he'd tried to hire a crew to work his land, but the demand for supervised field crews exceeded the supply, and Silver was left to work things out for himself. He eventually depleted the proceeds from the sale of his fruit trees, and began selling off his cropland, an acre at a time, to his friend Whiskers—who gave him a fair price for each parcel, and even offered him a job at one point. But Silver didn't want a job, and he made no attempt to plant any crops. He was a pigeon: he liked to walk in circles and peck at the ground—what did *he* know about being a farmer? And what was he going to do when winter set in, and he'd run out of land to sell, and the warm memory of Mrs. Klunder tossing a handful of breadcrumbs on the snow for him each morning mocked him in his hunger and despair?

With frost dusting the ground and Liberty Creek mostly frozen over, it was a moody, slate-gray day that marked the onset of the cold weather. Silver flew up the creek until he found a hole in the ice where the current was swift. I knew what he was up to, and tried to talk him out of it—but he was of the considered opinion that I was the spawn of Lucifer, so I may have made things worse. In any case, he plunged into the cold, roiling waters and disappeared beneath the ice.

His remains were never recovered.

Being as the institution of marriage never caught on in the avian community, the males were never quite certain who their children were, and the question arose as to the disposition of Silver's remaining acreage. The Council decided the land should be auctioned off and the proceeds distributed to the entire pigeon community. So in a decidedly less than public auction conducted by the Chancellor of the Silo (who was charged with the task), Frankie Hamhock bought the property for a single bushel of corn, and made Carlo a gift of its pastureland.

The bushel of corn was duly distributed to the pigeon community—and, as the Chancellor later observed, not one pigeon even said *thank you*.

CHAPTER 13

The pigsty was Freedom Farm's de facto church. This was partly because of the animals' habit of abstaining from toil on Sundays—a holdover from their human predecessors—and partly because Fatback had this insatiable need to express himself. It evolved gradually. Early on, Fatback would wallow in the mud on a Sunday morning with any porcine friends and family who cared to listen, and talk about his visions, about his revelations—about the miracle of being alive and free. Gradually, these "talks" evolved into sermons, and before long critters were coming from all corners of the federation to hear this inspired hog's uplifting thoughts.

Like so many others, Councilor Hawg attended Sunday services religiously (as they say), and like any pig, he always stayed for "Sunday Slop." But unlike other congregants, he had no real interest in being uplifted; the only thing Gus wanted to transcend was his well-earned reputation as a bullshit artist—and he figured the best way of doing that was to study the outgassing of a hog whose name was routinely coupled with the decidedly more respectful *orator*. So when Fatback was spinning out some rousing sermon filled with vivid imagery and folksy humor, Gus would be parked in the mud right up front, intently mouthing the preacher's words in an effort to internalize the phrases and syntax so useful in forming focused thoughts and complete sentences—the brick and mortar of sound oratory.

During Sunday Slop, congregants would typically thank Fatback for another uplifting sermon, and promise to post a few nuts to his account—and being only sporadically employed by then, Fatback graciously accepted all such contributions. But Councilor Hawg, for his part, never offered anything more than the fractured bullshit for which he was known: "... Fine sermon, Reverend, fine sermon ... Gotta wangle you a roof for this place some day ... Be a real *church* with a roof ..." He used that wangle-you-a-roof line so often that when a threatening sky opened up and scattered the congregation in the midst of one of his sunshiny sermons, Fatback told the councilor—as they huddled in the eaves of the hog house—that the good Lord was probably trying to tell somebody or other it was time to wangle him a roof.

Gus didn't much care for the remark—you could see that just by looking. But at the same time, he couldn't ignore the political payoff that would come with helping out the fledgling church: Fatback had a growing, diverse congregation—exactly the kind of broad-based coalition that could support a serious run for Boss Critter. The problem, of course, was that roofs didn't just materialize out of thin air.

But when Carlo and his monkey tasked him with securing an open-ended contract to thin the woodlot, Gus had a ready quid pro quo.

Pluto, however, had been working on his negotiating skills, and countered with one of his own: he agreed to put a roof on the pigsty in return for a contract to thin the woodlot—but only if the councilor also arranged for him to lease the floor space taken up by those dozen sacks of walnuts. (Regarding his plans for the space, the monkey would say only that they were "evolving.")

Gus rose to the occasion, and ultimately sold his Healthy Woodlot Initiative on the strength of its fire-suppressing value, its job creation value, and the fact that its cost could be partly offset by leasing some floor space in the barn. Gus reminded his fellow Council Critters that the woodlot hadn't been tended since the Klunders had been deposed—and in his fractured, non-linear way, he conjured such vivid images of a hellish conflagration rolling down the hillside after a lightning strike that the initiative was passed, the contract awarded, and the floor space leased before anyone thought to ask where they'd put all those walnuts. (Pluto would ultimately move them to the smokehouse, gratis.)

Selling the Healthy Woodlot Initiative was an impressive piece of politicking—one that would cement the councilor's reputation as a major player on the political stage. Beastfolk still called him a bullshit artist, of course—but in the halls of power, at least, they generally meant it as a complement.

In his spare time, meanwhile, Pluto got the lay of the land. Like any agent of chaos, he intended to exploit every little opportunity—but he could only do that if he was *aware* of every little opportunity. Naturally, he tried to maintain a low profile —but it was futile. He was a fearsome sight, for one thing— and owing to his habit of sleeping in the smokehouse, he was always trailing the scent of death. There was also something un-naturally rigid in his manner; in the yard, he would attempt to engage any critter that didn't run off when he'd hobble up— but every gesture, every word had the tightly controlled quality of a beast who'd gotten a mouthful of steel any number of times before learning not to break into a run whenever the urge erupted. His vistas were no longer fractured by the bars of a cage, but it'd be a while yet before the mandrill was truly free.

He was poised on the lip of the water trough one morning

watching a pair of cocks sparring on the snow when Frankie approached.

"Uh-oh, I knew there was a rank smell in the air," said Cassius Cock, "Let's get outta here...."

"Don't nobody strike a flint," squawked Rocky Cornish as the two birds went flapping off.

"That's right, get your little chicken asses outta here," said Frankie.

"Fuck you," said Cassius, cackling over his shoulder.

"Little scumbags..." said Frankie, arriving in a cloud of methane. "Soon as they get their spurs, forget it. Back before the Uprising, we never had to deal with more than one or two cocks at a time—now the place is overrun with them."

"Spirited birds ..." said Pluto, as he pounded a hole in the trough's iced-over contents.

"What they need is a spirited *work ethic*—like those kick-ass goats of yours up on the hill. Lord Almighty, they're up there gnawing on trees at the crack of dawn, gnawing on trees till after dark—it's unprecedented to see animals working so hard in the middle of winter."

"I envision a day when every animal will *yearn* for a job in winter."

"Well, you set a fine example," said Frankie, "—I see you just about got Rip's coop slapped together."

"Well, I was lucky to get the uprights in place before the ground froze," said Pluto, sipping from his palm. "Now the Chancellor's place—that'll have to wait till spring. By then, the necessary timber should be cut and ready to go—barring schedule slippage."

"Can't happen soon enough for me," said Frankie. "It'll be a pleasure to get his fat ass outta the hog house. But hey, just outta curiosity, if you was to build something like that for me, what would it set me back?"

"Nothing you couldn't handle," said the mandrill.

"Well, *of course,* but I mean ... let's say I wanted something, say, a little *bigger.*"

"How big...?"

"Bigger than Carlo's ..."

"I don't see why you couldn't afford something a bit more sizable than what the Chancellor envisions," said Pluto.

At one time, Frankie enjoyed a level of status unparalleled among the farm's animals. In the annual Toad Valley Fair's swine competition, he'd taken either second or third place in the boar division's Chester White category for several years running—and more crucially, as the stud whose genetic endowment made the Klunders' pork production some of the valley's finest, he was among the few animals on the farm that could expect to live a long, productive life. (Your typical porker was fattened for 6-months or so, and made into sandwiches.)

But it galled George Klunder that in all his years of trying, he'd never come away from the fair with a first place ribbon. And then it occurred to him that if he entered a hog in the "Specialty" category, he was certain to take first place, because there were never any entries in that category. In general, the breeding of livestock for any purpose other than the purely utilitarian was regarded as frivolous—so the fact that such a category even existed was something of a mystery. But as long as it did, old George—who was apparently struggling with midlife frivolity—saw no reason not to exploit it. So he broke out the family strongbox, borrowed Von Rumpel's mule on some pretext or other, and braved the trip to Falling Rock to see if Silas Clusterberry—the town's only livestock dealer—could order him something special.

Not a month later, Frankie found himself sharing his pen with a pair of breeding Bluebacks from back east somewhere.

It was a big comedown for the prize-winning Chester, who wasn't accustomed to sharing top billing around the sty. Still, his was a breed that was nothing if not resilient, and in time he would salvage his self-esteem from the simple knowledge that Carlo and Leona, however "special" their blue-speckled asses, couldn't claim a ribbon between them. And they never would, either; any such prospect had been forever lost to the

Uprising. But though that momentous event also had the effect of strengthening the grudging friendship that eventually took hold between the two boars—it was them against the rabble, after all—Frankie was beginning to think Carlo was getting a little arrogant, what with letting his "Chancellor" title go to his head, and starting that whole business of walking around on two legs, and then acquiring his own personal *mandrill,* of all things.... And now he was having his own private residence built because he fancied himself too good to lie down with the rest of the hogs!

Well, in a community of liberated, landowning free beasts, status was something you could *buy*—and if that "shallow, self-important swine" insisted on having his own cabin, then Frankie insisted on having a *bigger* one.

Carlo wasn't pleased. "You *monkey!*" he quaked, "You ugly, duplicitous, back-stabbing monkey!"

"Sir, I'm sure that's uncalled for...."

"No, it is *not* uncalled for! What is uncalled for is this habit you have of humiliating your owner and master—the one who rescued you from the *pit,* I would remind you—who thought that surely there was something decent and honorable worth salvaging beneath that grotesque exterior!"

"Sir, I can't possibly defend myself unless I know what I've done to warrant your displeasure."

"Oh, you mean aside from erecting a custom-built coop for a *chicken* while I suffer the humiliation of bedding down with crossbreeds? You mean aside from putting me in the position of having to tell everyone, 'Oh, he's just getting some practice so he can build *me* a fucking *chateau'*—and meanwhile, everyone's laughing at me behind my back? You mean aside from promising that jealous bastard Frankie that when you're finally through building *my* humble little cabin, you'll build him a *lodge?*"

"A lodge is just a cabin, only bigger."

The hog was incredulous. "Do I really have to explain that bigger is better?"

"That's not universally true, sir, although it *is* the case with our bottom line—which, incidentally, has grown by Frankie's down payment of twenty bushels of millet."

"The bottom line, the bottom line—is that all you think about?"

"Yes sir," said Pluto matter-of-factly.

Carlo glared wordlessly at the baboon—silenced, presumably, by the absurdity of chastising the beast for being profit-oriented when the bottom line figured so prominently in his own world view. "Well, it just so happens some of us are more *complex,*" he said finally. "Not that a creature of your stunted sensibilities could appreciate the fact, but I have an image, a public persona I'm obliged to maintain—and it has nothing to do with personal vanity, either; I'm a Blueback, after all—not a Berkshire, or a Chester, or a Poland, or any of those other commercial breeds, but a *Blueback*—and as such, it is incumbent upon me to serve as an exemplar for a community of animals ever striving for excellence. But if my prestige is undermined by some... some *Chester* crassly insistent upon conspicuous one-upmanship, then it won't be long before piglets aspire to mediocrity, and the breeds intermarry, and the health of the entire community suffers irreversible damage...."

"Well, sir, I'm not sure what it'll do for the health of the community, but I think it'd bolster your status immeasurably if you had your own family compound."

"You mean... *several* houses?"

"Exactly. And if you put a wall around the whole business, nobody'll know *how* big they are—all they'll know for sure is that you're the only hog in the valley with his own private compound."

"Oh, that would be *excessive,*" said Carlo. "I like it."

"While we're at it, we could build eight or ten little cabins *outside* the compound, too."

"Could we be serious?" said the hog impatiently. "What would I do with all those cabins?"

"Sell them," said the mandrill.

"But if I sold them, I'd have to sell the property they're sitting on...."

"Look, neither a house nor the property it sits on belongs to a buyer until he pays for it, right? So you price the cabins high enough that the buyers'll never live to pay them off; meanwhile, the land'll be generating healthy revenues, and you'll never even have to plow it."

"I like *that* part ..." said Carlo, deliberating. "But this is a major project you're talking about now—how am I supposed to pay for it?"

"Well ... if the scheme's got a glaring flaw, I suppose that would be it."

The hog snorted, and turned his sour gaze back to the columns of figures he'd been studying before the monkey came loping into the barn. "You know," he said after a moment or two, "it's not as though there aren't plenty of resources just lying around doing nothing."

"Maybe we could borrow some."

"Maybe we will," said Carlo under his breath. He picked up a piece of chalk, looked to see that there were no animals nearby, and then scanned the figures on the Wall; his eyes came to rest on Gunter Goat's inventory. He bracketed an entry marked *Rye/15 bu.,* and then added 15-bushels of rye to Pluto's column. "If anyone asks what the parentheses mean, I'll just say ... I'll just say they're an *accounting device.*" Then he took 14-bushels of corn from Snapper the duck's column and added *them* to the mandrill's account as well—along with 18-bushels of soybeans from Thor's column, 12-bushels of soybeans from Lucky's column, 9-bushels of wheat from Petra's column, and so on; by the time he'd finished, probably a fifth of the entries on the wall were in brackets, and the hog had succeeded in securing the monkey a nice, hefty little loan—complements of the citizens of Freedom Farm. "Alright," he said, stepping back to survey his work, "will that be enough to get you started?"

Fractional reserve barter had come to Toad Valley, and it would fuel the valley's first housing boom since the Grumpish invasion a century before.

These porcine monkeyshines reflected a principle arising from —and fueling—the greater Unraveling: The more one has, the more one needs. This was no less true for the average beast in the yard, who'd gone from being a slave to Lord Gastric to being a devotee: morbid obesity had become *de rigueur*. No longer did the free beasts of Freedom Farm spend their leisure hours playing hide-and-seek in the woods, or reading in the library, or lying in the pasture watching the clouds spool out their perpetual picture show; now, if the animals weren't sleeping or working in the fields, they were at the barn stuffing their gullets. Every one of them had to prove he could afford to eat as much as the next critter—which is why some of them sometimes exhausted their stocks partway through winter and had to go into hock. But Tasty Eight still had plenty of feed in the bins when he met with his demise one evening partway through dinner....

The tendency to overeat in the face of plenty, you see, was uniquely problematic in the case of pigeons, whom evolution programmed to feed on mere *crumbs*—specs of sustenance too small for most scavengers even to see. And since a spec is just a spec, a pigeon is obliged to eat about ten-thousand of them every day—which means, among other things, that it has to eat very *fast*. Given an abundance of food, therefore, a pigeon is always in danger of choking—and the crew Tasty retained to work his fields always made sure he had plenty to eat.

Following precedent, Frankie and Carlo split up Tasty's property in another secret auction, while the greater pigeon community—in accord with the adage that a rising tide lifts all boats—grew richer by another bushel of corn.

CHAPTER 14

But with spring thaw still a ways off, there wasn't much the monkey could do to advance his metastasizing construction projects aside from putting the entire Goat family to work in the woodlot posthaste—and then *keeping* them there. Initially, Gunter was averse to the idea of the whole clan working in the woodlot through the spring and summer; with the various crews-for-hire already booked for spring plowing and planting, it'd mean letting his fields lie fallow for the entire season.

But the monkey wasn't talking about seasonal work, he was offering full-time employment. "You can always lose a crop to aphids or leaf mold or something," said Pluto, "but a paying job is *real* security. Someday everyone will have one, but for the moment, you and yours have a unique opportunity to get in on the bottom—and become pioneers in the coming full-time economy."

A goat is never happier than when it's gnawing on something, so after giving it some thought, Gunter threw his lot in with the monkey.

"You're making the right move," Pluto told him, "—the

homebuilding market is about to explode."

Meanwhile, the Animal Council and the Committee for the Development of Guidelines for the Naming of Bodies of Water were of one mind in concluding that the activities of each could only be clearly differentiated if the Committee began meeting at a different "venue"—though a suitable alternative to the farmhouse kitchen had not yet been identified. The monkey, who was keeping abreast of developments, saw no reason the farmhouse basement couldn't be sold to the Council as an alternative venue if cleared of debris and made serviceable—so he duly submitted a proposal (including the requisite two bids). His plan ignored the obvious fact that the larger animals could never negotiate the steep, narrow stairway—but it was the sort of detail the Council was likely to overlook. And after all, the mandrill wasn't motivated by the needs of the Committee; he'd already explored those dark, musty regions of the farmhouse, and found much there of interest—but while nothing prevented him from simply taking what he wanted, he saw no reason why he shouldn't get *paid* for taking it.

The Council took his proposal under consideration.

So Pluto busied himself completing the deconstructivist conversation piece that was the Ripper's coop. Then, with the Council still undecided as the rooster moved his ladies into their edgy new accommodations, the monkey began dragging various items—a trunk full of old clothes, a washtub, assorted plumbing fixtures—up out of the farmhouse cellar in a naked attempt to pressure the Council into approving his proposal. Before long, there was a tarp-covered heap of these curiosities alongside the smokehouse. Not surprisingly, the Council responded by fast-tracking the Councilor for Swine's Expanded Venues Initiative, which stipulated that the monkey continue doing exactly what he was doing—and, of course, that he get paid for doing it.

Among the useful items Pluto mined from the nether regions of that ancient house were the shears he found lying on a workbench beside an oilstone. Once he'd emptied the cellar of everything that could be carried, he went loping down to the sheep shed and informed Eunice that as the sheep's esteemed representative on the Council, she was entitled to a free shearing—but the price was a bushel apiece for everyone else. Eunice was pleased to be so honored, and the rest of the sheep were more than willing to pay for the service. They hadn't been sheared since before the Uprising, and with the warm weather on the horizon, comfort was an important consideration.

"You look so much nicer now," said the monkey when he'd finished shearing the Councilor for Sheep. "Would you like to see for yourself?" It was no accident that he'd situated his sheep-shearing operation right next to the Klunders' outhouse; he positioned the ewe in front of the reeking structure, and then—using the key dangling from his neck—removed the padlock securing the door.

"I'm not sure I understand ..." the ewe stammered as Pluto swung the door open; then she gasped, and stepped back. After a moment or two, she took a cautious step forward for another look. "Who is that?" she asked.

"It's you," said the monkey, "—it's called a mirror."

"I'd *heard* of mirrors," said Eunice in tones of wonder, "but I didn't think they were real...."

"I'll have to charge you a walnut next time, of course, but this viewing is on me. I just wanted you to see how nice you look." A framed wall mirror was propped up inside the outhouse, and Pluto allowed the ewe to gaze into it for another moment or two—then abruptly closed the door.

The next time I looked, there was a long line of sheep at the outhouse door—all of them waiting patiently to pay a walnut apiece for the thrill of glimpsing themselves.

Walnut by walnut, "Pluto's Sneak-a-Peek," as he christened the enterprise, would prove to be one of the monkey's most reliable sources of revenue—but for the moment, there was one small problem: the Chancellor of the Silo was loath to process transactions smaller than a bushel—or some "reason-able fraction" thereof. (A "bushel," by the way, was under-stood to equal a full bushel of corn—or, for an alternate medium of exchange, somewhat more or less than a bushel, depending on the medium's relative worth.) So weary had Carlo become of posting a walnut to the account of every critter that shat the heap that he decided just to post a bushel per month to the account of every regular contributor, and leave it at that—and he had no intention of allowing himself to be swamped with walnut-denominated transactions on account of Pluto's piss ant little "Sneak-a-Peek" attraction.

Unwilling to walk away from a small but steady revenue stream, however, the mandrill put up a shingle at the smoke-house, and "Pluto's Walnut Exchange" opened for business. The monkey realized that walnuts had many of the attributes of a natural currency: they were uniform, portable, recogniz-able, durable, and high in protein—and if he could just get them into circulation, he could operate his Sneak-a-Peek attraction on a strictly "cash" basis and bypass the Chancellor entirely. The walnuts were already being stored at the smoke-house; all that was needed was some sort of teller's window. So the monkey went to work with a handsaw, and before long the smokehouse had a crude but functional Dutch door to serve as the floodgates of liquidity. At that reconfigured portal, Pluto—for a percentage—would make "walnut accounts" (WACs) available in bushel-sized denominations to anyone wishing to participate in the "cash economy." (Carlo, for his part, would debit the accounts of those opening WACs—in whole bushels—and credit the Walnut Exchange accordingly.)

Pluto's Sneak-a-Peek was soon taking in over a bushel of walnuts per day. Immediately after their A.M. feeding, critters of every kind would queue up at the smokehouse door and wait patiently for "cheek change"—so-called for the larger animals' habit of carrying the nuts around in their cheeks. (My feath-ered cousins generally tucked them under their wings.) Once they'd made their withdrawals, they'd hurry over to the Sneak-a-Peek and wait in line for its multitasking proprietor to appear so they could empty their cheeks admiring themselves before lining up back at the Walnut Exchange for more nuts. He did a lot of running around, but the monkey was making bank.

And because the animals stashed unspent nuts beneath floor litter, in knotholes, and between the planks of mangers and partitions, the number of nuts in circulation grew steadily —which ultimately stimulated further growth in the barnyard's economy.

And while the mandrill was selling reflections, he reflected on selected topics—muttering from the side of his mouth to whatever critter happened to be standing trance-like before his mirror. "From what I'm told, Thor could pull a redwood stump," he would say, in generating interest in his upcoming "Titan Tug" event, "—but can the mighty Thor out-pull the bull?" And then there was the pitch that helped him unload all the wool he'd sheared: "I could never sleep on account of my back—and it didn't matter what kind of bedding I had, either: straw, excelsior, carpet scraps—I could never get comfortable. But sleeping on fleece is like sleeping on a cloud...."

When a sheep is sheared, its fleece comes off in a big, rug-like piece of matted wool. Having shorn most of the farm's sheep, Pluto had a sizable inventory of these wooly mats— and because the flock had gone so long without a shearing, they were especially plush. So he priced them at 5-bushels *per*, and by the time everyone started arguing over which of the farm's titans could out-pull the other, the monkey had sold every last one—most of them to the same sheep who'd paid to be fleeced.

Speaking of sheep, Ulysses was becoming ... *distracted*. Breeders of livestock don't select for mental acuity, of course—they want animals that can be led to slaughter—so those faraway eyes are typical of domesticated critters. But with rams, this engineered simplicity is probably compounded by their nasty habit of slamming their heads repeatedly into various immovable objects—and into each other—intent, from all appearances, on killing off what little gray matter the breeders were kind enough to allot them.

And in the case of Ulysses, the regrettable effects of this head-banging habit were further compounded by the regrettable effects of his wives, Melba and Lucille. Not wanting to see either of his favorite ewes having to work for a living, Ulysses gallantly married them both. But Fatback had barely pronounced the threesome a threesome when the ewes began to suffer alternating bouts of depression—a surprising turn of events, given that they'd always been such cheerful, good-natured animals. In a scene I saw played out with only minor variations more times than I care to recount, Ulysses would spot Lucille, say, sitting off by herself in the pasture, gazing forlornly into the distance. So he would go to her—but the ewe would appear to be too much in the throes of some nameless grief even to acknowledge his presence. "What is it, my dear?" he would inquire in the gentlest way.

"Nothing," she would reply after a long silence.

"There must be *something* wrong," the ram would insist.

"I don't know why you say *that,*" she would mumble—big, sad eyes staring into space.

"Well, because you're sitting out here all by yourself like some unworthy stray."

"Can't I be alone if I want?"

"Certainly you may—but if there's something troubling you, we should talk about it."

"I told you, there's nothing to talk about."

"Then why won't you look at me?"

"Do I always have to look at you?"

"Of course not—but the only time you *won't* look at me is when there's something wrong."

"So if I don't look at you for two seconds, there's something wrong?"

"Lucille, for pity's sake ..."

"Why don't you get *Melba* to look at you?"

"Is that what's bothering you—Melba?"

"Who said anything was bothering me?"

And so it would go—on and on. In this fashion, the ewe would extort hours of focused, undivided attention from the ram before allowing herself to be coaxed back to the fold—at which time the ram would discover that his *other* wife had retreated to the sheep shed, and lay in its gloomiest corner in a despondent, wooly heap. And once again, Ulysses would find himself tasked with the emotional resuscitation of a fat, neurotic ewe.

It all started gradually enough, and in the beginning the ram almost seemed to welcome these little bouts of pouting as opportunities to show that he was capable of patience as well as strength. But after awhile, Ulysses was spending more time keeping his two wives from going all to pieces than he was tending his fields—and even when the task had his full attention, his crop management skills were minimal at best.

The inevitable day of reckoning came when Ulysses and his wives stopped by the barn one morning on their way to the Walnut Exchange. "Good day, Chancellor," said the ram to Carlo. "Would you be so kind as to credit the Exchange with a bushel? Melba and Lucille won't leave me at peace until I've opened a walnut account on their behalf—and who can blame them for wanting to gaze at their pretty little faces over at the Sneak-a-Peek? Make it millet—I'd rather not deplete my stock of corn...."

"Oh my," said the hog with mock surprise as he glanced at the Wall, "your liquid assets appear to have been liquidated."

"Excuse me ...?"

"You don't *have* a bushel of millet—or corn, or silage, or anything else. Let's see ... as I recall, you exhausted your supply of millet a couple of weeks back, and then you ran out of oats, barley, and even hay—and you had the last of your corn last night for dinner." When Ulysses still appeared confused, the hog was more succinct: "You're broke, busted, tapped out ..."

"But how can that be?" said the incredulous ram.

"The usual reason, I would imagine—too much consumption, not enough production. Perhaps if you glanced at the Wall once in a while ..."

"Yes, yes, I suppose I should," said the ram. "But you know, I ... I should be able to bring in a crop by the latter part of spring...."

"Well then, until June ..." said the hog, turning away.

"But wait," said the ram, "isn't there something I can do?"

And of course there was: he could sell a couple of acres of his prime cropland to Frankie Hamhock (who, for some reason, had been hanging around the barn all week)—and surrender a pair of walnut trees to Carlo for brokering the deal. He'd probably have been wise to shop around for a better offer, but the ram had run into one too many immovable objects in his day; he took the deal.

CHAPTER 15

"Beasts and beastesses," bellowed Grover Hamhock, "mammals, fowl, and fleas..." The hog—one of Frankie's sons—teetered about as he addressed the hordes of critters gathered in the barn. "The moment of truth has arrived at last, the moment you paid *good nuts* for, the moment that promises to answer, once and for all, the contentious, longstanding question: Who is the federation's most powerful beast?" The hordes squealed, squawked, and bleated excitedly. "Could it be the mighty Thor —perennial puller of stumps and boulders, namesake of the mythical wielder of thunder? Or is it the fiery Fritz, the three-quarter ton terror that nearly propelled the vile Von Rumpel into low earth orbit only this past summer? Which of these two titans will prevail in tonight's contest, my friends—and which will go to the straw a broken beast?"

As Grover harangued the throngs, the monkey led the main event's contestants into the warm glow of the barn's interior. (With daylight going down for the count, the monkey had fired-up several kerosene lanterns.) They came in through the side door at the corner of the barn; being a man-sized door, it was a tight squeeze, but it opened directly into Pluto's leased space—and for the moment, that roped-off section of the floor was the only clear space in the barn. The rest of the floor—stalls included—was jammed with sheep, goats, pigs, horses and, of course, Mrs. Cow; chickens, meanwhile, were perched all along the partitions, and ducks blanketed the heaps of hay in the loft. In the nosebleed section, the trusses were lined with pigeons whose single saving grace was their superstitious nature: they left your nefarious narrator—together with the Secretary of Education—several feet of breathing room despite the crowded conditions.

A roar of bestial approval shook the barn as Thor, looking acutely embarrassed, ducked through the door and entered the arena; a moment later, the crowd fell silent as the hulking Fritz was led in—snorting and twitching and looking like he wanted to wreck something. Slowly, and with great cere-mony, Pluto proceeded to harness the two animals and hook them up practically tail to butt-cheek with heavy hemp traces. It was an improvised rig, and space limitations obliged the monkey to keep the distance between the contestants short enough that if one of them farted, the other would feel the shockwave—which suggested that this historic tug-of-war, con-trary to its promotional build-up, would be an abbreviated af-fair: one animal had only to yank the other a scant few feet to pull it across the chalk line scribed between them on the cracked clay floor.

"And now," Grover howled, "these legendary titans battle it out in the evening's main event: Freedom Farm's first an-nual, first of its kind, first *ever* TITAN TUG!"

Grover exited right, while Pluto waited patiently for the din of excited animal sounds to die away; then he counted to three—and in a single explosive moment, both those massive beasts did what they were born to do: Thor pulled, and Fritz *charged.* Fritz probably outweighed Thor by a couple hundred pounds, and when that mountain of beefsteak hit the traces, the force of it yanked the plow horse right up onto his hind legs; Thor teetered there for a precarious moment, forelegs milling in the air—but managed somehow not to step back over the line. If Fritz had simply *pulled* at that point, he'd have toppled the horse right onto its back, but he paused to reset his feet. Thor came down on all fours, then leaned hesitantly into the traces as the barn erupted in a bestial roar of excitement —and was yanked right back up onto his hind legs again with the bull's next charge. He staggered back to within inches of the chalk line to keep from losing his balance, but after an uncertain moment or two, the horse regained his four-footed stance. This time, however, he arched his back like a bronco trying to throw a rider just as Fritz launched his 1600-pounds into the traces a third time—and that's when one of those traces snapped.

The sound of it echoed like a gunshot. The next moment, Thor fell face-first to the floor, and Fritz, yanked to one side by the remaining trace, went stumbling sideways through the rope cordon and into the audience of hogs and ruminants— which parted before him like the Red Sea. All eyes were on these two stumbling behemoths as every animal in the vicinity scrambled to avoid being crushed, and almost no one noticed the path taken by that broken trace as it snapped through the air like a whip—certainly not Schuyler the duck, who was just thanking his lucky stars he was safely ensconced in the hayloft when the rope's frayed end wrapped itself around his craning neck and then—as the bull went crashing off into a corner— whipped him out of the loft and slammed him to the floor below.

Against all odds, it didn't kill the sturdy little drake—but it messed him up something awful. He lost an eye, for one thing, and for another, his head was wrenched around to one side—and any attempt to turn it was accompanied by extreme pain. Worse still, the eye he lost was the one looking *forward,* so the duck seemed destined to spend the rest of his days waddling around backwards if the condition went untreated—and Silas Clusterberry, Falling Rock's only vet, wasn't generally inclined to make house calls.

Luckily, Hector Horse had just gone into the taxi trade, having concluded that agriculture was a "mature market" (i.e., there were only so many plows to go around). At first light, he quoted Schuyler a price based on distance plus waiting time, and then picked the duck up by the neck and slung him across his back—which nearly killed the critter right then and there. (Being new to the service sector, Hector was still a little rough around the edges.) But after Myrtle and her sisters lashed the stunned duck to his back, the horse—with a sack of nuts in his teeth for Silas—picked his way down through the maelstrom of Beaver Gorge practically as well as a mule. Silas subsequently "adjusted" the duck's neck—that is, he grabbed Schuyler by the head and *yanked* the kink out of it—and then sent the traumatized animal back home with orders to return in a week. Sure enough, exactly one week later, the stars cleared from Schuyler's one good eye, and he found himself looking at his tail feathers—and was compelled, once again, to make the trip to Falling Rock for an adjustment.

The duck would never be the same.

On the other side of Fortune's ledger, Pluto took in over a thousand walnuts that night—the equivalent of almost 15-bushels of corn. The purse had been five bushels—but since there was no clear winner, Pluto just paid the contestants a bushel apiece for their participation. He also paid a peck of millet to the winner of the egg-rolling contest that preceded the main event, and half a bushel to Grover for emceeing the show—but apart from the cost of the floor space, the rest had been pure profit. "And here's the beauty part," Pluto pointed out in hushed tones as he and Carlo were tallying the night's receipts, "—we still don't know who Freedom Farm's most powerful beast is."

Watching the hog and his monkey conclude the night's business in the glow of a kerosene lamp—Pluto bagging the last of the walnuts, Carlo tabulating figures at the Wall of Accounts—I couldn't have said for sure who Freedom Farm's most powerful beast was either.

With Thor's able assistance, Pluto began hauling timber down to the site of Carlo's future compound even before the last of the snow had melted, and succeeded in getting the uprights in place almost as soon as it was warm enough to break ground. But then Lila—Boss Rip's Inspector General and pullet du jour—noticed that most of the "unhealthy specimens" of lodgepole pine that were being culled from the woodlot were unhealthy mainly by virtue of being separated from their root systems and stripped of branches. (She'd decided to do her job that day just to spite the Ripper, who'd apparently done something to piss her off.) So Boss Rip was forced to issue an injunction halting all activities connected with the Healthy Woodlot Commission until such time as the Council resolved the question of whether healthy timber was being harvested under the Commission's purview.

Eventually, Councilor Gus would persuade a majority of the Council that it was impossible to remove all dead wood from the woodlot without inadvertently taking some healthy wood as well—and because it was also impossible to say what level of erroneously harvested timber was acceptable, it could only be said with certainty that *some* level of erroneously harvested timber should be tolerated; the reality that "some," in practice, was somewhere in the neighborhood of 90% would be overlooked.

But in the meantime, Pluto busied himself at the smokehouse rummaging through the heap of artifacts he'd recovered from the farmhouse cellar—disappearing, from time to time, into the shack with carefully selected items as he immersed himself in his latest project.

Drawn by the screeching of a hacksaw, Frankie stopped by one morning to see what the monkey was up to. It was right around daybreak. The upper part of the Dutch door was open, while the lower half displayed a placard reading, WALNUT

EXCHANGE CLOSED (or glyphs to that effect). "Hey Pluto," he called into the shack's interior, "what the hell you doin' in there?" Then he recoiled at the scent of smoked bacon.

"So dark back here, I'm not sure myself half the time," came the mandrill's response a moment before his ugly mug emerged from the shadows.

As Pluto approached the door, Frankie noticed he was wearing a vest. "Hey pal, where'd you get the pockets?" he wondered.

"The cellar," the mandrill replied. "If you're interested, I might have something in your size...." Before the hog could reply, the monkey turned and slipped back into the shadows. Frankie leaned forward and strained to see into the shack's murky interior, but the smell of smoked hog-flesh kept him at bay. After a minute or two, Pluto emerged from the gloom dragging a threadbare sheepskin vest. "This is probably the only thing I've got that'd fit," he said, "—but down at the sheep shed, it's probably got a name...."

"Fuck the sheep," said Frankie, as Pluto stepped out to help him with the grubby garment. "You know ... this isn't bad—just the thing for those nippy mornings."

"Oh, it's perfect," said the monkey, appraising the ruggedly attired hog. "It says: *I am the great strapping lord of all I survey ...!* And it's got pockets—four of them."

"How much you want for it?" said Frankie.

"A ten-spot."

"I'll give you a deuce."

"I really can't take less than seven," said Pluto, "—that's my rock-bottom. But I'll throw in a free session at the self-appraisal unit...."

"Four bushels."

"Mr. Hamhock, with all due respect, I have to be able to live with myself."

"Alright, alright—I'll give you five bushels. But I want the free peek."

"Well, since you're a friend of the Chancellor," said the

mandrill, nodding toward the outhouse, "step this way."

"Speaking of Carlo," said Frankie as they crossed the yard, "what's his lordship been up to, anyway? Haven't seen much of him down at the hog house lately."

"Well, the Chancellor has a lot on his mind. The more the population grows, the more he has to keep track of—you've seen that wall...."

"Yeah, but now he's even *sleeping* in the barn."

"He's a very dedicated hog."

"He's a conceited bastard, is what he is. I should tell him you're charging me five and seven-ninths bushels for this thing—just to piss him off."

"That won't be hard. He's been pissed off ever since they stopped work on his house."

"Haw, haw, haw! My heart bleeds for the poor bastard! Haw, haw, haw!"

"You really can't blame him...."

"Oh, don't get me wrong—that chicken's a real asshole, no question! I been sayin' that all along. Shit, nobody stopped you from building *him* a house...."

"Exactly. And you know what the Council wants to do now? They want to charge me *rent* for using the outhouse and smokehouse—they want to *penalize* me, essentially, for putting completely wasted resources to work for the public good."

"The scumbags."

The door to the outhouse was marked with crude white letters reading (approximately), PLUTO'S SNEAK-A-PEEK —HOURS VARIOUS, and was secured with a rusty padlock. The mandrill took the key from his vest and began fumbling with the lock. "It sticks a little sometimes, but ... ah, there it goes." He stepped aside and swung the door open—and the hog was staggered by a blast of flies.

"Goddamn, Sam!" said Frankie, "You need to get some ducks on the job down here!"

"Are you kidding? I'm going broke as it is, paying all those goats. I'm carrying them through the stoppage, you know...."

"You're paying them for doing nothing?"

"I didn't have a choice—they'd quit on me if I didn't. They'd be out there tilling their plot the minute they could corner Thor," said Pluto. Then, half to himself: "If nothing else, our equine friend is willing to pull a plow...."

"Say, not bad ..." said the hog, clearly taken with his own reflection. "Yeah, Thor told me there ain't gonna be a rematch," he added, striking a pose.

"Not much I can do—he didn't want any part of it. And I'm still paying for the floor space too...."

"Free enterprise is a bitch, ain't it?"

"I *am* a little overextended at the moment. But I know I can turn a profit with that space one way or another—and in the coming week, I should be able to put Thor back to work at the construction site."

"What about my lodge?" said the hog, his gut rumbling ominously.

"As promised, I'll go to work on your lodge the moment I'm finished with the Chancellor's cabin—which oughtta be around midsummer. And don't worry: he understands I'm obligated to complete your lodge before I go back and finish the rest of his compound. He's not happy about it, but he accepts it."

"I heard you're even gonna build him some rental units."

"Well, more or less. They'll be for sale, actually—but it's the same idea. Population growth being what it is, residential housing is gonna be huge, Mr. Hamhock—you should give it a look."

"I might if I had a piece of ground I wasn't doing anything with—but I like to keep everything I got under cultivation. There's no business like food, Pluto: a critter can sleep under a bush if he has to, but he can't go without food."

"I wouldn't argue the point. But all you'd need is a small, substandard parcel—something not worth cultivating...."

"Everything I got is worth cultivating," said the Chester, striking another pose. "I've got some of the choicest land in all of Freedom Farm."

"What you might consider doing, then, is buying some shitty patch of hardpan from somebody else—something you could pick up cheap. In fact, the Goats have a field that's got a rocky section they can't do a thing with—it's not very big, but you wouldn't need much space. You could build connected units—rental units. An apartment block, essentially ..."

"It's a thought," said the hog, examining his profile. "Do you think this makes me look fat?"

"Absolutely."

"Good, good."

Hector came trotting along just in time to give Frankie a ride out to where he and his sons—with the help of Thor and a gang of chickens—would spend the day plowing and seeding a field. "Hey Pluto," said Frankie as he climbed onto the crouching horse, "the only nuts I got on me are the ones I'm sittin' on—do me a favor ...?"

"Of course, Mr. Hamhock," said Pluto in his constrained way, "—consider it done." The monkey locked the outhouse as Hector and Frankie rode off, and then loped back up to the Walnut Exchange. By then, the sun had cracked the jagged horizon to the east, and an antiseptic radiance flooded the Dutch doorway. The baboon climbed up into the shack and closed the lower part of the door behind him. Through the upper half, I could see him take a handful of nuts from one sack, toss all but one of them into another, and drop the remaining walnut into a third (and much larger) sack. Most of the animals were out working in the fields, so there wouldn't be much business at either the Walnut Exchange or the Sneak-a-Peek till later in the day. Never at a loss for monkey business, however, Pluto retreated to the shack's dim recesses, made a right, and disappeared in the facility's new "research wing." (The smokehouse had been upgraded with an addition in the monkey's signature deconstructivist style.) Soon, the morning calm was enlivened with the rhythmic screeching of a hacksaw biting into metal.

CHAPTER 16

Frankie took Pluto's advice and bought that rocky patch of ground from Gunter Goat, who let him have it dirt cheap. It wasn't worth spit to Gunter anyway, and being as Frankie had a major construction project slated for the plot, the Goats' future in the logging business just kept looking brighter and brighter. Right up until Pluto fired them all and hired a team of beavers ...

"It's a productivity thing," he told them.

This put the Goats in a bind. Working for Pluto didn't pay much on a daily basis; it was only the promise of 300-some working days per year that made it a viable alternative to farming—and the Goats hadn't been at it that long. Making matters worse, it was too late in the season to bring in a crop —and given their inventory of feedstock and the fact that Gisela was no longer on the public payroll, the prospects for the family making it through winter weren't good. So Gunter went back to Frankie with his hat in his hand (so to speak) and inquired as to whether the hog might care to purchase a bit more of his land. It was a ridiculous question; the only question in Frankie's mind was *how much* of that acreage he could pressure the goat into selling—so he went teetering off to the barn on his two hind legs to see the Chancellor of the Silo.

"Oh, you're in good shape," said Carlo, "—right there, to your left."

The two hogs were standing at the Wall of Accounts— Frankie in his disintegrating sheepskin vest, Carlo attired in a tattered linen duster blotchy with swill and mildew—and as always, their great, swollen guts threatened to topple them at any moment as they strained to maintain their gravity-defying postures. Frankie got as close to the wall as his belly would allow, and studied the scrawled inventory beneath his name. Usually, he was content to give his inventory a glance and a nod, but this time he squinted at every item. "Mm-hmm ... mm-hmm ... good, good ... hey! What're these ... these ..."

"Hmm ...?" said Carlo, feigning distraction.

"These things, these... *brackets!* What're all these brackets?"

"Oh, those—they're just ... it's an accounting device."

"An *accounting device* ...?"

"That's right ..."

Frankie looked at Carlo, and then he looked at the wall— and then he looked back at Carlo (who looked out the door). His gut rumbled menacingly. "Don't you bullshit *me*, Carlo—I know what those things are! That's like when something's an *afterthought*—like, *Oh, by the way, I think you also got a dozen bushels of turnips....* " Frankie bared a tusk and got his crusty snout to within an inch of Carlo's. "And I got news for you, Carlo: my turnips are not an afterthought! Neither are my beets, or my yams, or my carrots, or my sweet potatoes, or my ..." (Frankie had a thing for root crops.)

"Would you please *calm down?*" said the Blueback under his breath, as he glanced about nervously. "Look, we just had to ... borrow a few things, that's all."

"Wait, you had to *borrow* a few things—a few of *my* things? Without telling me ...?"

"Just for a little while—look, can we have this discussion outside?" Chancellor Hawg was oddly nimble as he ducked around Frankie and teetered out the barn door with the irate Chester close behind. At the shit pile, the discussion resumed in heated whispers.

"How much interest you paying me, Carlo, huh? Tell me that!"

"Interest ...?" said Carlo in disbelief, "Are you serious?"

"You're goddamn right I'm serious! You borrow some of my feed, I want interest!"

"You greedy, garbage-grubbing ingrate! After everything I've done for you ..."

"Everything you done for me ...? What the fuck you ever do for me?"

"You mean aside from making you a gift of Tasty's well-tended acreage? Or what's-his-name's property—that other pigeon ... Silver! I gave you Silver's fields on a silver platter! I risked having my integrity publicly stained bringing my hoof down on the barrel for you! Oh, and who was it that tipped you off about Ulysses? Let's see now, which of your influential friends was that ...?"

"You got your commission for that business with Ulysses! And as far as Tasty's stuff is concerned, you ended up with his trees and his pasture—what the hell more do you want?"

"I want some consideration! I want some recognition of the fact that a good deal of your good fortune has come about as a result of your association with *me*. And if in securing the resources for an important project I should inadvertently utilize some of your precious stocks, I would hope you might show a little class and curb that crass impulse to profit at my expense...."

"Oh, well excuse my crass impulse, but if I wanna put together a deal of my own and I can't do it 'cause the stuff I thought was there ain't *there* anymore, then goddamn it, I want some compensation!"

"Is *that* the problem?" said the Chancellor, "—You're

putting together a deal of some kind ...? Oh, the Goats—of course! You're putting the squeeze on Gunter!"

"Hey, I'm not puttin' the squeeze on nobody—he came to me!"

"Oh, you compassionate swine! You just want to help a poor family of ruminants that's fallen on hard times—how could I have thought otherwise?"

"Look Carlo, I don't give a shit *what* you think—I just want what's mine! So either give me my stuff back, or start paying me rent!"

"Frankie, Frankie—don't you get it? Corn is corn and beets are beets—and there's plenty of each in the bins! You need something, just say so—no need to get excited! The only reason I bracket this item or that is so I'll remember where I got it should its owner come looking for it. There's nothing in my job description that says I can't move things around...."

"What about my parsnips?"

"Your parsnips ...?"

"Yeah, my parsnips," said Frankie. "See, the reason I mention it is 'cause I came through here a while back, and I noticed Ulysses and his old ladies feasting on parsnips...."

"Well ..." said Carlo, stalling. "Look, in a case like that—where you're the only one to grow a particular crop, and in the course of things ..."

"They were eatin' my parsnips, weren't they?"

"Well, not in *theory* ... "

"GODDAMN IT, CARLO!"

"When you two get done whispering sweet nothings at each other, we got some business to transact," said Whiskers, who appeared at the corner of the barn with Gunter. "I'm buying a couple acres from the Goats."

A closed-door hearing was convened in the kitchen to address the issue of "feral labor"—a subject of particular concern to Petra, who'd unseated Gisela in the previous election and was now the Councilor for Goats.

"It is only with misgivings that I move to ban feral species from competing in Freedom Farm's labor market," said the hen, puffing herself up. "We've always welcomed immigrants who've sought to make lives for themselves here in the free fields of Freedom Farm, but they've usually come to us one or two at a time, not a *dozen* at a time—and most of them have been domesticated farm animals seeking asylum from human oppression. But these beavers—setting aside, for the moment, the fact that they're depriving our own workers of jobs—they aren't oppressed, they're not seeking asylum, they clearly have no interest in becoming a part of the community, and from every appearance, they were leading an idyllic, independent existence in harmony with nature and would be better left alone."

While not taking exception to the monkey's activities in general, a majority of the Council took a dim view of the role played by beavers in Pluto's bold new business model. The Councilors sat, stood, or perched around the big kitchen table, with Pluto, Carlo, and Gus clustered at one end. "With all due respect, Councilor," said Pluto, "if you think beavers have it so good, maybe you should try subsisting on bark for a week or two." Gus stifled a laugh, but Pluto was deadpan. "In any case, I have no obligation either to them or to your constituents; my only obligation is to my investor."

"I see," said Petra. "Well then, perhaps I should direct my questions to your ... *investor*. Chancellor Hawg, can you offer any evidence that this policy of hiring feral labor in any way benefits the citizens of Freedom Farm?"

Carlo, who sat between Pluto and Gus, appeared to be lost in thought as he admired the kitchen's stone hearth. He turned and gave Gus a bored look that clearly suggested the councilor make himself useful.

"... Um, uh ... " Gus stammered, "... I mean, um ..."

Carlo rolled his eyes in disgust and shook his head. "What the Councilor for Swine would undoubtedly articulate," he sighed, "—if he weren't too *simple* to articulate it—is that the reduced labor costs benefit my simian asset, which in turn benefits me. And when I do well, the community does well. It's not as though I don't know how to spread it around, after all; many are the mornings I'll stroll down to the Sneak-a-Peek to expend a walnut or two admiring the cut of my snout— only I usually wait till a little later when I don't have to deal with all those ewes and hens and such...."

"So you occasionally 'expend a walnut or two' at an enterprise that just happens to belong to your ... *simian asset,"* said Bucky Leghorn, "—to use your term. And since this largess goes right back into your pocket by virtue of your indirect ownership of said enterprise, we can only assume that any benefit accruing to the larger community is of the more ... *ethereal* kind."

Carlo just sneered at the rooster—but in a bid to redeem himself, the Councilor for Swine spoke up. "... Nothin' wrong with ownin' something ..." he said, "... Sixth Right ... Right to own ..."

"An argument could be made that the use of feral labor imperils the *Goats'* right to own," said Bucky, "—never mind their right to feed."

"I'm sure all sorts of arguments could be made in support of depriving the *beavers* of their rights," said the mandrill, "but however you spin it, the bottom line reality is that banning them from Freedom Farm's job market is nothing more than species prejudice."

"Oh, give me a break!" said Bucky. "First of all, the Six Rights were created *by* farm animals *for* farm animals—even if they weren't specifically formulated in those terms—and extending those rights to feral species would probably require an amendment. Secondly, I have always been an advocate for the fair treatment of feral species—apart from pests, of course— but as a member of the Council, my first obligation is to the citizens of Freedom Farm. And since the natural world has always gotten by without any help from us, I'm inclined to think a ban on feral labor would be in *everyone's* best interests."

"And if I could just add," Petra added, "that you, Mr. Baboon, should know better than anyone else that the sort of species prejudice you're suggesting just doesn't exist here on Freedom Farm." She glanced at Stella. "Well, not to any significant degree, anyway. I mean, I hardly need to point out that even such a ... such an *unusual* creature as yourself can come here to Freedom Farm and live the life of a free beast."

"I would remind the councilor that I'm presently living in bondage," said Pluto matter-of-factly.

"Oh! Why, yes—yes, of course!" said the hen, suddenly flustered. "But technically, you're not really an *animal*—not like a beaver! And ..." she said, taking a moment to compose herself, "I'd like it noted that—like Councilor Leghorn—I have nothing but affection for our little brown friends. This is purely an economic issue, Mr. Baboon; my only concern is for the welfare of my constituents, who happen to be going through some very difficult times."

"Well, Councilor," said the mandrill, "in my experience, some critters will judge a feed bucket to be half-empty, while others see it as half-full; the bucket-half-empty sort might bemoan having to sell off some property to keep his family alive, but the bucket-half-full type would be damn glad he had the land to sell off. So I would suggest your constituents take more of a bucket-half-full sort of attitude. After all, unemployment is just another form of freedom when you ..."

"Mr. Baboon!" said Stella with considerable bile, "This goes beyond being unemployed. *Most* of our workers are idle during the winter months—but they *know* they'll be idle, and they plan accordingly. But when your plans are based on your employer's lies ..."

"I did not lie to them, Councilor, I simply changed my plans—I believe I'm allowed to do that?"

"And you feel no obligation to the Goats ...? After they served you faithfully through the spring and summer—helped you further your objectives when they could've been working their own land instead...? You assured them they'd have full-time employment, and they *trusted* you...."

"Well, in retrospect, they clearly could've exercised better judgment," said the mandrill, "—but it *was* their call, Councilor."

"I was right about you all along," Stella sneered, "—your kind of ugliness goes right to the core."

The mandrill's war paint glowed like neon, but his eyes were impassive. "You know, Councilor," he muttered, "back when I was making my way up here from the flatlands, I came upon a couple of grizzlies fishing down at Sherman Falls. I was watching them for five, maybe ten minutes when one of them scooped a trout up out of the water and the other one caught it midair—and the next thing you know the two of them are tearing each other to pieces. It was the fish that set them off, but the thing they were fighting over, really, was the ledge of rock they were standing on. It was just a little too crowded for the two of them, and neither of them wanted to give it up, so they were forced to come to terms—and believe me, the way in which two grizzlies settle a dispute is a bracing thing to see. I've heard they don't usually kill each other, but the one that finally limped off in defeat was ripped-up really bad—left such a trail of blood I don't see how he could've survived the night. But here's the thing: there were no angry voices rising in protest, and no hearings to investigate the events leading up to the less-worthy animal's failed bid for dominance; the ruthless efficiency of nature required that the stronger of the two control that ledge, and nature's demands were met without recourse to laws, civic discourse, or the deliberations of august bodies. The two simply began ripping great pieces of hot, bloody flesh from each other until one of them could no longer continue. No one asked if it was fair, no one sought to intervene—and despite their willingness to fight to the death, they put no lives on the line but their own. As I look back on it, I'm not ashamed to admit I was taken with the spectacle's savage beauty: the fury, the reek of carnage, the awesome power of those two monsters as they mauled each other—red, hairy masses of flesh being flung this way and that amid showers of blood that, that, that ... that *glittered* in the sunlight, and glazed the rock ledge, accumulating in pools of crimson—and the fish, with its guts hanging out, floundering around in it all, gasping for life, slinging gore up into the fly-filled air like, like, like, like ..."

"Mr. Baboon!" Stella broke in, "Did you have a *point?*"

The mandrill fell silent, and skewered the mare with his eyes. "My point," he said after a long moment, "is that nature and farmers are both in the same business—except nature husbands its resources more efficiently, because the process isn't *managed.* No farmer need till the soil, because the soil is aerated by ants and worms; no workers need cast any seed, because the winds distribute the seed very effectively; and there is no need to gather the fruits of a season's production because they're devoured fresh from the vine—and whatever goes uneaten falls directly to the ground to fertilize the next season's growth. And should bird or beast make an unwise choice—like fighting to the death with the wrong animal—no one's fortunes but its own are diminished by its error. Such brutal efficiency is the handmaiden of abundance, and we would do well to follow nature's example in everything we do. *That* is my point, Councilor. And in that spirit, the taxpayers' representatives—if they'll excuse my saying so—might ask themselves if *this hearing* has a point."

"Mr. Baboon," said Petra, "We're just trying to under-stand how we can make Freedom Farm a better place for everyone...."

"I'm sure you are," Carlo broke in, "—especially for a bunch of goats that don't want to take responsibility for their own actions."

"Hey, this isn't just about the Goats," said Bucky. "In fact, as Pluto pointed out, the Goats are at least fortunate enough to have a few assets—but most critters don't. And there's always a few that don't make it through winter...."

"And why, exactly, is that a problem?"

"Look, we're trying to have a serious discussion here ..." said Bucky indulgently.

"I'm perfectly serious," said the mandrill. "What we've got here is a nice little market economy that's doing exactly what it's supposed to be doing: separating the winners from the losers. Why mess with it? In a game like this, some critters will always do better than others because some are more *capable* than others—and the ones that can't make it through winter probably *shouldn't.*"

"C'mon Pluto," said Bucky, "if the name of the game is 'survival of the fittest'—if we can't do anything to improve on nature—then why not just live in the wild?"

"I didn't say we couldn't improve on nature," said the mandrill earnestly. "I would say my self-appraisal facility, for example, is a significant improvement over a pool of water in the quality of reflection it affords. On the other hand, when it comes to the dynamic business of balancing supply and demand, the more closely the market mechanism resembles nature in the way it allocates resources, the more efficient it is. I think that's obvious.

"But it's a discussion that'll have to continue without me for the time being—I still have a lot to do before tonight's event, and I only have two hands. But I want you all to be my guests—in fact, I insist on it. I'll rope off a section for the Council right in front. Oh, and Councilor Petra, you might want to tell the Goats to come and see me tonight at the side door—I may have some work. I can't offer anyone a job, but it's an opportunity to maybe pick up a little cheek change...."

CHAPTER 17

The main event couldn't have been in progress for more than a minute or two when Bucky's patience started wearing thin. "ROCKY-Y-Y!" he called out, "CUT THE SHIT, ROCK!"

"... Keeps runnin' away ..." said Gus.

"He does that all the time," said Bucky, "—he makes the other bird do all the work!"

"... Doin' all the damage, too ..."

"Yeah, no shit!" said Bucky, "Cassius just keeps coming— and there's nowhere to run to in here!"

"... Nowhere to hide ..."

"C'MON, ROCK—STAND AND FIGHT!"

"Oh Myrtle, who does he remind you of?" said Petra.

"Oh, he does, he does!" said Myrtle. "He just takes me back...."

"My god, what that big red cock did to Whiskers ..."

"Looked magnificent doing it, too—much as it pains me to say so!"

"OH CASSIUS ...!" Petra screeched, "—YOU MAKE ME FEEL LIKE A PULLET AGAIN!"

"Oh, this just seems so ... *barbaric!*" said Mrs. Cow.

"What...?" said Stella.

"I said it seems so barbaric!"

"KILL HIM, CASH!"

"It *is* barbaric!" said Stella.

"What...?" said Mrs. Cow.

"Wa-a-ak, wak, wak, wak, wak!" said Dinghy the duck.

"... He's chicken ..." said Gus.

"Hey, there's no need for that kinda talk," said Bucky.

"... Chicken, plain and simple ..."

"CASSIUS, YOU BIG, BEAUTIFUL COCK!" said Petra.

"Look Gus, I told you—it's a calculated tactic: he back-peddles till the other bird runs outta steam—and *then* he unloads on him! It's not the best strategy for close quarters, but spare me the negative stereotypes, alright?"

"... Mr. Sensitive ..."

"C'MON, ROCKY," said Bucky, "MIX IT UP!"

"I hope he gives Rocky a real thrashing!" said Petra. "He was such a surly little cockerel!"

"Yeah, but Rocky and Cassius are friends," said Myrtle. "He's prolly gonna hol' back!"

"C'MON, CASSIUS!" said Petra, "KICK HIS ASS INTA THE MIDDLA NEX' WEEK!"

"You know, Stella," said Mrs. Cow, "I thing I might just try a little more of that 'Toad Valley' stuff—where did that bucket go?"

"I thought you said it burned!"

"Well, it did! But now my ton is sort of numb—and you know, I thing it might hep me sleep...."

"Oh, Mrs. Cow!"

"Indeed!" said Eunice.

"... Got himself cornered ..." said Gus.

"NICE WORK, ROCK," said Bucky, "—REAL NICE!"

"... Boxed in ..."

"Y'GOTTA FIGHT NOW, ROCKY! COME ON—GET THOSE SPURS UP!"

"... Gettin' his ass kicked ..."

"YOU'RE LETTIN' HIM GET AIR, ROCKY—DON'T LET HIM GET AIR!"

"Oh, Petra—Rocky's really gettin' torn up!" said Myrtle, "Isn't it exciting?"

"It's makin' me *hot!*" said Petra.

"Y'know, we should dip our beaks again before that pig Gus drains the whole bucket...."

"GO UNDER HIM NEXT TIME, ROCK," said Bucky, "GO UNDER HIM!"

"Since when do you need to *drink* in order to sleep?" said Stella.

"He f'got ..." Mrs. Cow stammered, "He f'got ... t'milk me today...."

"That son-of-a-bitch!" said Stella, "He did that deliberately! Don't you see what he's up to?"

"Haffa dring, Stella," said Mrs. Cow.

"Wa-a-ak, wak, wak, wak, wak!" said Dinghy.

"... Get a platter..."

"GO UNDER HIM OR GO THROUGH HIM, ROCK," said Bucky, "—C'MON, LET'S GO!"

"... He's cold cuts ..."

"YOU'RE BLOWIN' IT, ROCKY!"

"Would you get your head outta that bucket, Myrtle? My god ...!"

"Just wait your turn, Petra!"

"I refuse to touch a drop of that, that ..." said Stella.

"ROCKY-Y-Y-Y-Y ...!"

"What ...?" said Mrs. Cow.

"I said I refuse to touch ... Oh, never mind! How can an animal talk with all this howling and squawking going on?"

"... Holy hog slop..." said Gus.

"YES! YES!" Bucky crowed, "CARVE THAT BIRD UP, ROCKY! SLICE AND DICE, SLICE AND DICE!"

"... Damn, he *can* fight ..."

"I told you that, din I? Din I ...?"

"Hey Myrtle, ever notice how everything sounds different when you got your head in the bucket?"

"Got a news flash, Petra—the reason everything sounds different is 'cause Cassius is gettin' his ass kicked!"

"ROCKY-Y-Y-Y-Y ...!"

"There—I hope you're satisfied Mrs. Cow!" Stella gasped. "My god, that stuff is *horrible!*"

"Ony burns ad firss," said Mrs. Cow. "Haff s'more."

"Shit, what's with Cassius?" said Bucky.

"... He's bleedin' ..." said Gus.

"ISS JUSTA SCRATCH, CASH!" said Bucky, "DON' GIM ANY GROUND!"

"... Confused ..."

"JUS' KEEP YER HEAD UP, CASH!"

"... Shaky ..."

"YA GOTTA GET SOME AIR, CASSIUS—GET THOSE SPURS UP!"

"... Sick ..."

"Sick ...?" said Bucky. "Hey, steady there, Gus. Y'know, maybe y'oughtta get down on all fours 'fore y'*fall* down!"

"... Started li'l early ..."

"Yeah, well ... maybe I'll go do some catchin' up."

"Wa-a-ak, wak, wak, wak, wak!"

"Indeed!" said Eunice.

"WHAT IS THIS CRAP, ANYWAY?" said Petra, WHERE'S THE REF?"

"He's right behind you," said Myrtle, "workin' bucket by the booze Bucky—I mean ... workin' Bucky by the booze bucket! No, wait ... yeah! Workin' Bucky by the booze ... Is that right ...?"

"THASS ALL HE HAD, CASSIUS!" said Petra, "—PECK THE LIDDLE BASTID'S EYES OUT!"

"My ton's geng numb," said Stella.

"My *udder end* is geng numb," said Mrs. Cow.

"Thass 'cause iss holding up Gus!"

"WHAT'RE YA DOIN', CASSIUS ...?" said Petra, "LET'S

PUT THE LIDDLE BASTID AWAY!"

"Got a kick to it, doesn't it?" said the mandrill.

"Goddamn, Sam!" Bucky gasped, "whaddya call this shit again?"

"I'm calling it 'Toad Valley Corn Liquor'," said Pluto. "This would be vintage Tuesday...."

"Right, right—Corn Valley Toad Liq—*hic*—Liq—*hic*... Goddamn, Sam!"

"Wa-a-ak, wak, wak, wak, wak!"

"ARE YOU SERIOUS WITH THIS SHIT ...?" said Petra, "THROW THE BUM OUT!"

"I don' care," said Stella, "—iss jus' not right! Quadrupez sh'walk on four leys!"

"Oh, Stella," said Mrs. Cow, "always thingin 'bout udders."

"Looks like the main event's turning into a real shredder," said the mandrill.

"Oh, yeah ..." said Bucky, "I mean, these guys're always mixin' it up inna yard, bud they're usely jus' sparrin'! Not like tonight—KEEP YER HEAD UP, CASSIUS!—tonight they're really rippin' eash other up!"

"The winner-take-all rule is a powerful motivator," said Pluto.

"Indeed!" said Eunice.

"THIS FIGHT IS FIXED!" Petra squawked, "WE BEEN ROBBED!"

"Oh, Miz Cow," said Stella, "we nebber ged t'tawg."

"An, now dah we can tawg, we can't tawg," said Mrs. Cow.

"Lookit d'way he's draggin' nat wing!" said Myrtle.

"OH, CUT THE THEATRICS ...!" said Petra, "WE GOT YER NUMBER, Y'BUM!"

"But tell me this, Councilor," said the mandrill, "—if we could talk shop for a moment—what motivates *you?* What's your beef with decent, hard-working beavers? It's not like you owe the Goats anything."

"Petra, he's bleedin' all over the place!"

"YEAH, YEAH—WE SEEN BLOOD BEFORE!" Petra

squawked. "FUCKIN' DRAMA QUEEN! My god, sprayin' it around like a stuck pig!"

"God no problem wid beavers," said Bucky, "—I thing they wunnerful li'l cridders. Bussa mattera prince-a-bull. It was goats an' pigs an' roosters an' shit dat rist dare lives inna Uprising—nod beavers—so iss goats an' pigs an' roosters an' shit d'oughta hab Free'm Farm's jobs."

"LESS BLEEDING, MORE FIGHTING!" said Petra.

"Oh, Stehhh—I luh you so mush!"

"Oh, I luh you too, Miz Cow! You my bess fren—my *owny* fren!"

"Oh, Stehhh ..."

"Indeed!" said Eunice to no one in particular.

"Okay, so you're an idealist—I get it. But see, my concern is that once an ordinance like that is put in place, we'll never be rid of it—no matter how inappropriate it proves to be in the long run. In fact, I'd be curious to know if a procedure for rescinding an ordinance even exists...."

"Shit, I don' know," said Bucky, "—prolly not."

"I'm tellin' ya, Myrdle, this fight is fixed—and the big nuts are on Rocky!"

"WHASS YER CUT, CASSIUS?" said Myrtle. "WHOSE POCKET YOU IN?"

"Exactly my point: the Council would almost certainly feel compelled to create such a procedure. And I would remind you that while the pond in the back forty, through popular usage, has taken the name *Liberty Pond,* and the stream feeding it is known to one and all as *Liberty Creek* ..."

"WE WAN' OUR NUTS BACK!"

"We god in free, Petra—*hic.*"

"... the Committee for the Development of Guidelines for the Naming of Bodies of Water—driven by blind, bureau-cratic inertia—lumbers on in its quest to create a process for doing something that has long since taken place of its own accord...."

"Wa-a-ak, wak, wak, wak, wak, wak, wak!"

"Yet as hard as it would be to rescind such an ordinance, it'd be the easiest thing in the world to adopt at some later date—should it become necessary. The only reason the issue arises at this particular moment in time is because the Goats have some powerful friends on the Council."

"JUS' TAKE THE DIVE, CASSIUS—YOU DON' NEED T' HAM IT UP!"

"And at the risk of belaboring the point, the Goats *are* propertied animals—*unlike* you or me; they're hardly in danger of going hungry—despite Councilor Petra's dire assertions."

"Indeed!" said Eunice.

"YOU WHITE-MEAT, WIMP-DICK ...!"

"Awright, but look," said Bucky, "f'gedda 'bout the Goats and the beavers fer a minute, okay? We're talkin' feral labor versus Free'm Farm worgers—inna abstrak. An' I'm talkin' 'bout all those cridders that only got what they gotna bins, okay ...?"

"YER A BUM, CASSIUS, A BUM!"

"Now, take my constich ... my ... my *pigeons,*" said Bucky, "most of 'em ... most of 'em seed furrows fer a living—*hic.* Now lessay y'gedda shlocka harlings—*a flocka starlings*—lessay y'gedda flocka starlings t'do id half-price ... fer ezample."

"YER LUCKY I DON'T COME DOWN THERE AND KICK YER ASS MYSELF!"

"Are you suggesting the Council make policy based on *conjecture?*" said Pluto, "—on the mere *possibility* that this-and-such might occur at some point in the future?"

"Poin' taken, poin' taken ..."

"YEAH, BLEED ALL OVER THE LIDDLE FUCK— THAT'LL SHOW HIM!"

"Look, I'm not suggesting you oppose such a policy forever and ever, regardless of circumstances—I'm just saying let's not jump the gun, that's all. A bird could get himself killed like that."

"BOOOOOOO ...!"

"What ...?"

"I said let's not jump the gun."

"No, what y'said afta dat—'bout a bird geddin killed ..."

"BOOOOOOOOOOOO ...!"

"Oh, I was talking about Rocky—he keeps getting himself cornered. Anyway, my sources tell me the Council's gonna vote on the issue in the next session or two. Now Councilor Petra has an obligation to fight the good fight on behalf of her constituents, obviously, but at the end of the day, hens tend to follow the lead of their roosters—and with a couple of hens on the Council, that makes you a key player, Councilor; I'd like to know that I can count on your support."

"Indeed!"

"Wa-a-ak, wak, wak, wak, wak!"

It was a three-rounder, and Cassius never came out for the third round. Despite inflicting considerable damage on his smaller opponent, he'd run himself ragged trying to stay on top of the fleet-footed cock—and once Rocky managed to open up one of his pecs, it was all over; I haven't seen the bird yet that can pull himself up on one wing.

As for the eight members of the Animal Council, they were hardly in better shape. Stella and Mrs. Cow collapsed more-or-less simultaneously toward the end of round two, and spent the night sleeping it off on the barn floor. Bucky, Gus, Petra, Myrtle, Eunice and Dinghy managed to stumble out the barn's side door—thus beating the hordes to the "cab stand," where Hector, Marla, and a long string of goats waited to bear the besotted to their holes and hovels. (The goats, being unable to carry the larger animals, had no choice but to charge less—but like the horses, they were still obliged to pay Pluto a cheek full of nuts each for the privilege of queuing up at his stand.)

When the Council put Petra's proposal to a vote, Bucky explained that such an ordinance could be difficult to rescind if it proved ill-advised—and since it'd be simple enough to adopt at some later date if necessary, he was inclined to "keep his powder dry" and vote against it; not surprisingly, Myrtle voted along with Bucky. The smartly-sheared Eunice, for her part, voted down the measure as well, as did Gus (whose vote was a foregone conclusion)—and Dinghy thought it best to "go with the flow." Under immense pressure, Petra herself voted "present." Only Stella voted for the measure (Mrs. Cow being too hung-over to attend).

So feral labor became a feature of life around the homestead—as did the Saturday Night Fights. Freedom Farm's burgeoning population of chickens supplied Pluto with plenty of cocks and cockerels to feature in his ring—and Pluto, in turn, supplied the members of the Council with their own private section and all the corn liquor they could stand.

And they could stand a lot.

CHAPTER 18

The Unraveling unraveled in all its wondrous profusion, and Freedom Farm became a great, seething, self-sustaining, 160-acre *feedlot*. It's liberated fields supported over a thousand free beasts, all squabbling and scheming and fighting for a piece of The Dream—the essence of which was to be fat, and to own a BeaverBilt. The voracious hordes jammed the yard at peak feeding times—fighting to get at the troughs, and packing it away like there was no tomorrow. There were commercial graffiti splattered all over every upright surface in whitewash and red barn paint: "Dazzle Duck Fodder," "Mellow Milk," "Cushy Cab," "Nina's Nitpicking," "Chippy's Cheap Tricks," and so on (there was abundant alliteration)—along with the ubiquitous "EAT," a public service announcement paid for by the voracious taxpayers themselves. And wherever a critter looked, everything was in motion; it was like seeing things through the heat rising off a stretch of sun-blasted highway. Even from the air, Freedom Farm was a shimmering anomaly in the tranquil patchwork of Grumpish family farms.

The Goats' holdings, after a period of difficulties, were

reduced to the point where their acreage could no longer sustain the clan's steadily expanding number—so Gunter assembled a field crew and started hiring himself out. Gisela, for her part, had built a respectable business selling goats' milk, and some of the Goats still worked in the taxi trade.

Carlo's acreage was now a housing development called Hawg Homestead, and was blanketed with BeaverBilts—which were exactly what the name implies, and looked exactly how you'd expect them to look. Not everyone could afford one of the monkey's deconstructivist creations, but there were plenty of moderately successful critters that could afford the payments on a ratty (if massively overpriced) heap of sticks and branches and mud and shit scraped together by a gang of oversized rodents—and Carlo was only too happy to finance that homely little piece of The Dream on behalf of anyone capable of generating a reliable revenue stream.

Mrs. Cow was a drunk. Her milk was now marketed by P. Baboon & Co. as Mrs. Cow's Mellow Milk (the tag line being "Protein with a buzz"). The incessant milking made the old girl's spigots sore, but as long as she got her half-bucket of shine each day, she was a contented cow. Mellow Milk was a specialty item, of course—there being a chronic shortage of chronically besotted cows—and it was priced accordingly. Gisela's Goat's Milk, by contrast ("Purity you can trust"), was cheaper and more available, owing to Gisela's sizable battery of lactating does. But in a sense, the price of each was exactly the same: *whatever the market would bear.* Not surprisingly, the animals were getting a feel for the business of business; the insatiable hordes were metastasizing apace, and there were only so many jobs in the fields—so the entrepreneurial spirit was much in evidence. There were pigeons in the messenger business and pullets with nitpicking parlors, eggs on sale at the chicken coop and milk on sale at the barn—there were flower stands and taxi stands and a wayward mallard selling magic mushrooms, along with exercise classes in the paddock, and a pullet (Chippy) peddling her tail for three nuts a poke.

And then there was Mandrill Mall. Pluto had begun pressuring the Council to compensate him for the split-log wing he'd added to the smokehouse (currently occupied by the Toad Valley Distillery); the Council feigned reluctance for a time and then cut his lease, so he built *another* wing—and then another, and another one after that—demanding further reductions with each new addition. By the time his rent had been knocked down to a paltry few pecks per month, he'd managed to build Mandrill Mall in its entirety. Most of the concessions in this open-air marketplace were independent operations leasing space from Pluto, but the more upscale ones were owned and operated by the monkey himself—specialized services, by and large, employing a cutting edge technology known as *hands*. For the many hogs afflicted with the brutal backaches that came with a bipedal lifestyle, for example, there was therapeutic massage at That's the Rub (by appointment only); for the ewe who wasn't satisfied with merely having her nits picked, there was Beauty and the Beast—a salon where a swift de-lousing was performed by a highly trained team of pullets, followed by a shearing, shampooing, and styling by the maestro himself (also by appointment); and for those who wished to prolong the day's afterglow for a time, there was a selection of hand-made candles available at Pluto's Tallow-Free Photon Emitters (but the candle-lighting services were by subscription only). He also owned an advertizing agency called Blabber, a flower shop called the Petal Pusher, an exclusive haberdashery called the Swanky Swine, and a watering hole called the Bucket of Fire Saloon, where the drink of choice was "Toad Valley" with honey. (As with the wax for his candles, Pluto harvested the honey from his own apiary.) He even dragged the Sneak-a-Peek up to the mall and fit it with a foot pedal that allowed it to be operated by a porker in his employ.

But Mandrill Mall was only one of many holdings in the monkey's steadily expanding portfolio. Like the Chancellor, Pluto made a habit of acquiring distressed properties—and like Carlo, he concentrated mainly on pasture and orchard holdings, which needed little tending and generated steady revenues. But at the risk of stating the obvious, the monkey's material assets were the direct consequence of his personal assets—which included a cast iron resolve, a laser-like focus, relentless energy, and a dedication to learning. (Despite the demands on his time, the mandrill could often be found in the farmhouse library studying volumes on agronomy, horticulture, tanning...) But more than anything else, it was those hands that allowed him to do things the other animals could only dream of doing.

It'd be a mistake, however, to imagine that the monkey limited his many activities to what the other animals *couldn't* do; much of the time he was doing exactly what *they* were doing—only better. A duck named Bill, for example—beset with the frustrations of the new order—had a tantrum one day in the meadow, ripping dandelions up out of the sod by the dozen. Afterward, his girlfriend Camille gathered up the blossoms, took them to the yard, and sold them to Gisela—who was looking to "freshen-up" her gamey BeaverBilt, and offered the duck two walnuts for the bunch. So Camille went back, gathered up another bunch, and managed to sell them too. Before long, flower stands were sprouting like the dandelions themselves. The monkey did the math at some point and came to the conclusion it was a market worth cultivating—literally. He built a greenhouse on the little patch of dirt that was once the Klunders' garden, and started growing flowers year-round. The plot had been weed-choked from disuse, but was probably the richest soil on the farm—and the Council was kind enough to lease it to Pluto for the usual token sum. As for the greenhouse, it was a testament to the acuity of the domesticated mind that no one thought to ask where Pluto got all the windows he used in its construction—or, for that matter, noticed the disappearance of the farmhouse cellar's clerestory glazing. But in any case, when the monkey started selling big, generous bunches of daisies, snapdragons, irises, violets, and, of course, dandelions at the Petal Pusher—and not just in the spring, but all year-round—it all but put the "dandelion stands" out of business.

And that pleased the monkey. It pleased him so much that he decided to expand into the transportation business. He persuaded the ever-pliant Council to lease him the hay wagon when it wasn't performing its usual public service function of hauling what needed hauling during the planting and harvesting seasons. His plan was to establish an off-season bus route to compete with the many taxi-beasts plying the paths and byways that ran between the fields, and he didn't see why that big, rugged wagon wouldn't make a fine bus for beasts—the "Omnibeast," he would name it. There was no shortage of critters willing to spit out a cheek full of nuts for a taxi ride to the other side of the commonwealth—especially since many of them had gotten too fat to walk it—and at only a walnut per head, Pluto figured he'd have no problem keeping that wagon groaning under the weight of commuting livestock. But after building loading ramps at each of the many stops situated along a route that ran hither and yon, and launching his enterprise with a high-profile media blitz—the usual in-your-face signage, along with announcements at the fights and messenger pigeons spreading the message—the Omnibeast attracted few riders.

"I've been running that wagon around the farm for almost two weeks," the monkey complained to the Chancellor in a moment of frustration, "—but the commuting public, apparently, is perfectly happy to cough up the nuts for *Cushy Cab,* or one of those others! They don't know the value of a nut...."

"Why don't you try eating a few?" Carlo suggested.

With many thousands of nuts in circulation at that point, it was hard to see what good it would do, but the monkey was at a loss for a better idea. So for the longest time—in spite of bloating and constipation—he ate nothing but walnuts. I can't say just when things started to go south for the taxi beasts, but at some point they found themselves inexplicably hurting for business, while more and more critters seemed inclined to wait for the bus.

Naturally, there was a marked increase in business activity following the next walnut harvest, but by then there weren't near as many critters willing to squander a cheek full of nuts on a taxi when they could take the bus for a single slimy nut.

After the big shakeout, of course, Pluto doubled the fare.

But the federation's economy took a great leap forward the day Pluto fired up the well-worn Briggs & Stratton chainsaw he'd gotten in Falling Rock, and fired his entire logging crew. He maintained a crew on the construction side of his operations—BeaverBilts didn't build themselves, obviously—but this newly-acquired appliance enabled the monkey to work the woodlot all by his noisy lonesome and still supply sufficient cut timber for all his construction projects. The Industrial Age had come to Freedom Farm—and this time it was the beavers that took the hit.

"I was the lead negotiator on that deal, you know," said the mynah proudly. I knew—but I also knew that wouldn't stop her from telling me all about it as I chased cockroaches around the kitchen. "Pluto hired me to translate, being as I speak Human and all. He told me it was essential I join his trade mission to Falling Rock, so I told him it was essential that he make a hefty contribution to my larder—I'm talkin' *hazard pay*. It's not like I don't know about that ride through Beaver Gorge! And let me tell *you,* Mr. Been-There-Done-That, if you still got it in your head you're just gonna fly outta here one of these days when you get tired of making trouble, you better have a plane ticket, is all I can say. You don't *fly* through Beaver Gorge—it's, it's ... it's just this bent, twisted *crack* in the mountains! It's only a coupla feet wide in some places! The only way to get through Beaver Gorge is to hire Hector to *carry* you down through it, like Pluto did, and get your cage lashed to his back real good—and then hang on for dear life, 'cause it's like riding into a tornado! All along the way—and I'm not exaggeratin', crow—all along the way there were dead birds everywhere! And they didn't die of natural causes, I'll tell you that much—they died of *blunt force trauma!* That's the fancy word for gettin' your brains beat out against the rocks—generally used in the context of what happens to any bird dumb enough to think he can fly through Beaver Gorge...."

That Pluto's trade mission managed to negotiate a deal in a single afternoon with Echo serving as "lead negotiator" had nothing to do with the mynah's negotiating skills, and everything to do with Pluto's limited tolerance for having his time wasted. Evidently, the mandrill had kept himself covered with a blanket so as not to frighten Silas Clusterberry, proprietor of the Falling Rock Trading Post, with his ugly, war-painted mug; as the two sat facing each other on the porch of the ramshackle trading post, the mynah perched on the railing and served as the monkey's mouthpiece. But the way Hector told it, the mynah kept straying from the negotiations with typically lengthy asides—and Silas, for his part, was clearly looking to take advantage of the animals. So after a half-hour of haggling proved largely fruitless, the mandrill decided it was time to stop speaking Human and try a more universal language: he dropped his blanket and revealed himself in all his hideous splendor—which instantly knocked the price down from 12-jugs of corn liquor to five. Then the beast bared his fangs and snarled—and Silas was afflicted with an acute bout of incontinence.

Along with Hector, Echo, and a security detail consisting of a spotted boar named Sluggo and a phalanx of rams, Pluto had come with a couple of jugs of corn liquor—tied together with a length of rope and slung over Hector's withers—and that's what he paid for the chainsaw.

CHAPTER 19

But if the monkey had become a major driving force behind Freedom Farm's economy, the blowback took various forms, including Cassius Cock's plain-talking populist run for Boss Critter—fittingly kicked-off to the distant screeching of the monkey's chainsaw. "I learned a hard lesson when I got in the ring with Rocky," he told a crowd at the chicken coop, "I learned not to mess with the *little guy*. The little guy'll kick your ass every time, and you know why? 'Cause he's *little,* that's why—he can't *afford* to get knocked down a peg! So I don't mess with the ornery little fucks anymore—there's no percentage in it. But this much you can take to the silo: from this day forward, I'm going after the *big* dogs; I'm going after the likes of Pluto Baboon, and Carlo Hawg, and all their lackeys on the Animal Council. They've been messing with the little guy for too long now, and it's high time *they* got knocked down a few pegs!"

A sage of the human kind observed that being a leader amounted to finding a parade and stepping in front of it—and the rooster's run for Freedom Farm's highest office revealed that a more inspired approach couldn't be expected of farm animals. At the core of the parade Cassius stepped in front of was a growing collection of beleaguered beasts in imminent danger of starving to death—The Hundred, as they'd come to be known. They faced the perennial problem of making it through winter—a problem as old as farming itself. The fact that there were always a few that *didn't* make it—orphans, the lame, the superannuated—had traditionally been an accepted part of life on the farm; but the few had become a multitude, and could no longer be ignored. These were critters without property, without credit at the barn—without assets or prospects of any kind. Many of them were young, and had never been employed; others—despite having worked the entire season—hadn't made enough to see them past Election Day. (Surplus labor had depressed the going wage to such an extent that Frankie Hamhock had even lost interest in getting a maximum wage law passed.) And because public housing was at 150% occupancy, all of them were without shelter of any kind. The Hundred comprised the steadily expanding "dung beetle" sector of Freedom Farm's economy; having exhausted the charity of family and friends, it was their lot to rely on the kindness of strangers—and the results were predictable: they got lots of sympathy and not much else. In the warm weather, a duck could forage in the pond, a chicken or pigeon could scratch up a meal in the yard, and an indigent sheep or goat could graze on some weedy little patch of public land; but there was snow on the ground, and the pond was frozen over, and there wasn't a single crafty bone among these domesticated dimwits or they'd have robbed the bins the way I did. (You didn't have to be a genius to get around the aforementioned Sluggo, Carlo's security chief.)

The most celebrated of this small army of unfortunates was Schuyler the duck, whose sad story was spotlighted at every rally for candidate Cassius. "Just the other day I ran into a duck by the name of Schuyler," Cassius would say in the midst of his stump speech. "Are you here, Schuyler ...? There he is—the one-eyed Pekin with the fucked-up neck. How you doin', Schuy? Schuyler had it all at one time: he had a nice spread, corn in the bins, he was young and healthy and in love.... And then tragedy struck. Schuyler was the duck that got snagged by that broken trace at the Titan Tug fiasco. That's right—that was Schuyler. And for a long time he made the journey down to Falling Rock every week to suffer the agony and expense of getting his neck adjusted, 'cause he wasn't gonna let *nothin'* get in the way of his god-given right to have his head screwed on straight! But the fix would only take for a day or two, and then his head would *slowly* wrench itself around to the side again—and by the end of the week, he wouldn't know if he was coming or going. The vet bills finally ruined the critter—cost him everything he had. So here he is, a broken-down old cripple begging for crumbs and sleeping in a snow bank—and this is one of Freedom Farm's founding fathers, did you know that? A *founding father*... When I heard Schuyler's story, I swore that one day I'd march myself right into that farmhouse kitchen when the Council was in session, and eat me some *bureaucrat!* YEAH! That's what this place needs: an *activist* in the skinner's seat—a Boss Critter worthy of the name! And the way I see it, being worthy of the name means recognizing that a duck don't care *what* you call that goddamn duck pond if he ain't gonna be around in the spring when it thaws! It means *fighting* to see that this broken, unsung veteran of the founding has recourse against the parties whose reckless scheme to rake in some easy nuts *destroyed* his prospects for a descent life! It means not being blind to the whole *horde* of beastfolk out here whose rights are being *pissed on*—and it means understanding that you don't fix the problem with more talk and more committees, you fix it with more jobs, more public housing, and a public feed program for all our starving brothers and sisters! That's what the commonwealth needs—a Boss Critter that can bust heads and get the Council back to work ensuring the rights of the free beasts of Freedom Farm instead of doing the bidding of Big Feed!"

Cassius would usually have to pause and wait for the clamor to die down at this point before continuing. "I don't want there to be any misunderstanding here," he'd say at last, "—if the voters make me Boss Critter on Election Day, *all hell's* gonna break loose! So if you're fat and happy and wallowing in the status quo, and you don't mind seeing your fellow free beasts falling by the score in the biggest die-off in Freedom Farm history, you might wanna vote for the *other* guy...."

The other guy—the only other serious contender for the top slot—was Augustus Hawg, who'd married his sister Edna and become a real "family values" kind of pig. He was running on a platform of tax cuts and fiscal discipline, and he railed against the scourge of government waste at every opportunity—warning, in his impressionistic style, that Freedom Farm's profligate ways were sowing the seeds of its own ruination. In Councilor Hawg's view, the soon-to-retire Boss Rip —whose idea of family values, Gus noted repeatedly, was spending his days at the coop servicing his ladies—typified all that was wrong with Freedom Farm's governance: the self-aggrandizing cock couldn't approve the smallest proposed ordinance without seizing the opportunity to add yet another functionary or two to his already bloated administration—insisting, as always, that he could do nothing without the proper resources. His staff took up half the farmhouse, the hog complained—and now even the Council Critters had begun to accumulate gratuitous staffs of advisors, assistants, and "liaisons to the community."

Gus had an inside track on matters of the silo, of course, so when the hog began crusading as a fiscal conservative—an alarmist one, at that—some of the other Councilors might've thought to have a look at the public's account. But with a detailed accounting of the liquid assets of hundreds of working-age beasts densely cluttering the Wall of Accounts (and part of an adjacent wall) like hieroglyphics—all ensnarled with arrows, parenthetically qualified, and appended with footnotes —it was hard enough for a critter to find the particulars of his *own* account without the assistance of the studiously unhelpful Carlo or his surly clerks; so when it came to Freedom Farm's budgetary concerns, the Council tended to rely on the Chancellor's State of the Silo address, which he delivered periodically. The Chancellor was known for being vague and artfully cryptic, however, and it was a custom he persisted in right up until the morning he stood before the Council and bluntly informed it that Freedom Farm had gone belly-up.

"Whattya mean Freedom Farm is insolvent?" asked an astounded Bucky Leghorn.

"I mean exactly that," said Carlo, "—it is no longer able to satisfy its creditors or discharge its liabilities: it is bankrupt."

"Then what was all that happy horseshit you gave us last month? You said 'things couldn't be better'...."

"I believe I did say that, yes—but it follows that if things couldn't have been better, they could only get worse. And they have: the federation's entire inventory will be depleted in a matter of days—I don't know how I can be any clearer. But it's not the end of the world, you know. I just happen to have some excess inventory lying about, and until such time as Freedom Farm can bring its spending in line with its revenues, I wouldn't mind putting some of it to work on behalf of the community—at a reasonable rate of return, of course."

It was classic Carlo Hawg.

Following precedent, the Council Critters did the easiest thing: they borrowed what they needed from Carlo—knowing the cost of the loan would exacerbate the budget shortfall, but salved by the knowledge that it was the taxpayers' dime. In any case, it was only a stopgap measure, they reasoned, which would be dispensed with once a budget-balancing plan had been implemented—and several such plans were afloat. The Ripper's ideological allies on the Council, the newly-formed CFC (Chickens for Change), were pushing a plan—developed by a team of advisors, assistants, and liaisons to the community—that would levy a "simian asset tax" on the esteemed

Chancellor. The CFC's position was that if a citizen's inventory could be taxed, his simian asset could be taxed at the same rate—once they figured out how many bushels equaled a monkey, that is (a persistent point of contention).

Councilor Hawg's plan, by contrast, was simplicity itself: add all those superfluous staffers to the ranks of the unemployed—except for the ones that worked for *him,* of course—and cut taxes on pigs.

But though it was easy to paint Rip and the CFC as tax-and-spend wastrels, the Hawg camp never had any illusions about its chances against the sitting Boss Critter in a direct electoral challenge. Rip's reputation as one of the heroes of the Uprising made him an opponent of almost mythical proportions. His stature was such that he'd never even bothered campaigning for reelection—a fact that only bespoke his invincibility—and when he appeared in public, it was always with an entourage of pullets, hens, and subordinate cocks. He was a legend, simply put—and taking on a legend was beyond the capacities of a bullshit swine like Councilor Gus. So as the Ripper's current term in office drew to a close, Pluto—clearing the way for Gus's run—engineered the rooster's retirement by offering him a lucrative, two-year contract to get in the ring and take on any and all comers. (Apparently Rip was feeling old, and needed to prove something—and Pluto offered him some *tall* silage.)

The carefully laid plans of the Hawg campaign were bearing fruit. The Ripper was out of the picture, and the public debt was public—and having positioned himself as the prescient fiscal conservative, Gus *owned* the issue. And for a time, he got a lot of mileage out of it too.

But as Election Day drew near, there was a growing sense in the Hawg camp that they were losing the momentum to Cassius Cock's barnstorming campaign. "You know what it is, don't you?" said Pluto one night during a candle-lit strategy session at the Hawg family compound, "We're not just running against a rooster anymore, we're running against Cassius and the CFC and the outgoing administration—we're running against this whole Big Government *coalition...."*

But if the Debt Monster was beginning to lose traction as an issue, it probably had more to do with the fact that so many of the public were *used* to being in debt—burdened as they were with big mortgages on little BeaverBilts. And conversely, if Cassius Cock's campaign was beginning to pick up steam, it was largely because everyone seemed to know someone who'd made some bad decisions, or had a bad run of luck, or wasn't young enough, or experienced enough, or fast enough —and ultimately ended up "in the yard." Friends and relations did what they could for these failed free beasts, but there was only so much to go around—and the logic of a burgeoning population of indigents suggested a similar fate for many more to come. Such was the "parade" Cassius had stepped in front of—the very one the Hawg camp ignored completely when it decided the solution to its sputtering campaign was to organize its base, rather than moderate its message. It was a predictable reaction to the formation of the CFC—the membership of which had grown to include virtually every voting-age chicken on the farm; unnerved by the thought of such a formidable voting block, the Hawg campaign responded by organizing its *own* political party—the PFP (Pigs for Profits) party.

But by then, the parade had already passed them by.

CHAPTER 20

The two party system that came to dominate the federation's politics seemed to have its roots in the Klunders' livestock development practices. On Klunder Farm, if you were a cow or a goat, your lot was to be milked, and if you were one of the horses, your lot was to pull things—and while it's true that on occasion the family would break the monotony with a dinner of mutton or roast duck, for the most part a sheep's lot was to be sheared, and a pigeon or duck was expected to lay eggs. But if you were a pig or a chicken, your purpose in life was to be *dead meat*—and sooner rather than later. (Even a hen that was lucky enough to be a good layer was ever mindful of the fact that the Klunders preferred *duck* eggs with their bacon —and they liked their chicken tender.) Consequently, while most of the animals were utterly oblivious, the pigs and the chickens always took a keen interest in day-to-day barnyard activities—ever alert for signs of their imminent demise: Was farmer George sharpening his knives? Did he withhold their feed that morning? Was Mrs. Klunder considering a plump porker as she hung wash on the line?

This divide between the oblivious and the engaged would seem to have carried over into Freedom Farm's political life: after much turnover on the Animal Council, about the only critters taking an active role in the affairs of government were either pigs or chickens. In the previous election, the incumbent Councilor for Cattle had been voted out of office and replaced by a pig when the bovine candidate herself neglected to vote, and Fritz—not wanting any drunks on the Council —voted for Frankie's son Grover instead. In that same election, Spencer—another of Frankie's sons—replaced Dinghy as Councilor for Ducks. (Spencer reminded the duck community often of his father's role in delivering the fly patrol contract—implying with scant subtlety that a vote for him was a vote for the program's continuation: "Ain't exactly the divine right of ducks, y'know....") And in the current election, a hen named Henrietta managed to secure the Councilor for Horses seat. (Mainly because she *wasn't* oblivious, Stella—the exception that proved the rule—had resigned her post in disgust.) So with the Animal Council divided almost equally between pigs and chickens, the advent of the CFC and the PFP only seemed to formalize a well-established trend. The Council now consisted of four chickens—Bucky, Myrtle, Petra, and Henrietta—and three pigs: Gus, who'd maintained his seat as Councilor for Swine, along with Grover and Spencer. Eunice was the Council's sole independent.

Cassius, meanwhile, had won in a landslide—and true to his word, he was an activist Boss Critter from day one. Where the Ripper had taken to lounging around his coop with his entourage until summoned by the Council to bless one of its proposals, Boss Cash wouldn't give the Council a minute's peace. "Alright, now listen to me, you sluggards!" he told the Council early on, "The voters spoke loud and clear when they put me in the skinner's seat, so I wanna hear some proposals, *pronto.* I been in office three whole days, and you beasts ain't given me *shit!* So just put your eight little heads together and see if you can't figure out how we can scare up the resources to feed and house those poor bastards in the yard—I got a campaign promise to keep!"

"... Now, now ..." said Gus, "... Ain't that easy ..."

"Oh no?" said Cassius, "Can you say 'monkey tax'?"

"Actually, this is the Committee for the Development of Guidelines for the Naming of Liberated Bodies of Water," Bucky noted helpfully. (In a landmark accomplishment, the Committee had augmented its title with the word "Liberated.") "That's the reason we're meeting out here on the back porch; the Animal Council meets in the kitchen."

"That's funny ..." said Cassius, "I was just *in* the kitchen, and I didn't see any Animal Council."

"The Council only meets on Tuesdays and Thursdays."

But if the Committee figured Cassius was about to wait around till it morphed back into the Council several days hence, it was mistaken. The tenacious rooster had an inborn impatience with bureaucratic bullshit, and he hectored and heckled and eventually wore the bureaucritters down. "My, my, that's a cold wind slidin' down off the hillside," he said as the sun drifted toward the snowcapped peaks to the west. "Why don't you critters do your little magic trick and turn yourselves back into the Council so we can all adjourn to that nice warm kitchen and attend to matters of consequence?"

And they did, too.

And that pretty much set the tone for the ensuing relationship between Boss Cash and the Animal Council. Cassius was a big, dominant cock, so it didn't take long for him to bring his chickens into line—and that, given the CFC's majority status, gave him effective control of the Council. (That the smartly-coiffed Eunice caucused with the pigs was of little consequence, given the Boss Critter's tie-breaking vote.)

But the new regime put the Council's majority leader in a serious bind. Bucky had been firmly under Pluto's opposable thumb, but now Cassius was asserting a primordial form of control known as the *pecking order*—and being a natural-born chicken, Bucky found it exceedingly difficult not to accede to his immediate demands. And yet the Boss Critter's immediate demands included a serious look at taxing the monkey....

"I don't want to hear any more about this 'simian asset tax'!" Cassius told Bucky, stepping across the table to peck him smartly on the pate. Bucky flinched—and then turned and drilled Myrtle, who gave Petra a shot, which was passed along to Henrietta (who stoically embraced the martyr's role). The Chickens for Change sat in a row, each perched on the back of its own chair, while Cassius paced on the table before them. "The only reason you keep talkin' about hitting Carlo with a simian asset tax is 'cause it *sounds* good—and being as nobody knows what a simian asset is worth, you can just keep talkin' about it forever without actually having to *do* anything. So I got a better idea: tax the monkey *directly*. I couldn't say what a monkey is worth either, what with those hands and that nimble mind and whatnot, but if you look at the Wall, you can see what he's got in the bins—it's one of the longest columns up there—so why don't we tax it? I'm gettin' sick of hearing this fable that we can't tax Pluto Baboon 'cause he's not an animal. I'll grant you, he don't look like any animal *I've* ever seen—but if he's not an animal, what the hell is he?"

This was heresy of a high order, and Bucky winced with every word. The other councilors just hung their heads and exchanged furtive looks. But Cassius didn't stop there....

"Another thing: How come the Church of the Suffering Sow gets a free pass? I like Fatback as much as anybody, but it's the middle of winter and he's carrying a healthy inventory —and I'm *glad* he is too, don't get me wrong; but as long as he's flush, what's wrong with him paying his fair share? There wouldn't even *be* a Church of the Suffering Sow if it weren't for Freedom Farm—and it sure as hell wouldn't have a roof!"

The Pigs for Profits—together with the Councilor for Sheep—sat opposite the chickens. The chairs on that side of the table had long since been reduced to matchwood by the mega-hogs that occasioned their use, so the animals sat on the floor—their jowls just clearing the table.

"... Can't tax some things ..." said Gus, the minority leader, "... It's tradition ..."

"What tradition?" said Cassius, "There's nothing traditional *about* Freedom Farm! It's an *experiment,* a self-governing contraption that got cobbled together by a bunch of renegade farm animals—and wonder of all wonders, it's still clattering along! Only it's startin' to veer off the road a little—it's not takin' care of everybody. So it stands to reason we gotta tweak it a little, play around with it—see if we can't keep it from running into a ditch. And since this contraption of ours is getting a little top-heavy, the best way to do that is to recycle some of the winners' winnings—just enough to keep the losers in the game. 'Cause let's face it: if you get too many losers and they all stop playing the game, *then* you got problems."

"...Winter's whole purpose..." Gus pointed out, "...Culls the losers..."

"You know, Councilor," said Cassius self-righteously, "the next time you have a lucid moment, you're gonna be ashamed you said that."

In truth, of course, the pigs *had* no shame. But what really confounded Cassius was that a progressive populist like Bucky Leghorn had to be *pecked* into getting behind his proposals—especially since the CFC had supported his candidacy from the beginning, and was committed to his agenda.

But Boss Cock didn't have the good graces to moderate his positions once elected—his agenda being identical to the expansive platform he'd campaigned on: the creation of a publicly funded assistance program to provide the indigent with a subsistence level of feed, some form of housing, and basic veterinary benefits—all of which would require a significant increase in taxes. It was a reality that left the majority leader haunted by visions of a certain simian asset's saber-like fangs; it drove him to distraction—which only drew further peckings from the increasingly impatient Cassius. Not surprisingly, Bucky's emotional state began to erode.

The beleaguered bird appeared one evening at the edge of

the woodlot, and began making his way along its perimeter. By that time, the woodlot had been cut back to an elevation further up the hillside—and with the last light of day hardly enough to silhouette the peaks to the west, I wasn't even sure it was Bucky at first. Expecting calamity at any moment, he hid behind one tree and then another as he made his way across the face of the hill. Finally, he began zigzagging his way down the lower stretches of the slope, sprinting from one to another of the stumps that lay scattered in the wake of the Healthy Woodlot Commission. When he reached the yard, he dashed across the hardening muck to the barn, and paused beneath a sign reading "PLUTO CARES." Then—giving the indigent beastfolk huddled in the barn's lee a wide berth—he ran to the chicken coop, and then the tool shed, and finally to the Church of the Suffering Sow.

The reverend Fatback was sleeping in his customary place just inside the hog house door—a practice he'd adopted for the purpose of making himself available to critters who, like Bucky, required council at odd hours. (Or so he said; the older pigs, however, seemed to recall the pastor sleeping in exactly the same place in the Klunder days—mainly so he'd be the first one out the door when the slop hit the trough at dawn.) Bucky picked his way across the frozen mud and pecked at the doorframe next to Fatback's steaming, resonating snout. "Reverend Fatback ..." he called softly, but urgently, in the hog's ear, "Reverend Fatback!"

"Goddamn Sam ...!" Fatback snorted, his eyes popping open. "What in the hell—oh, I mean ... Councilor Leghorn, I'll remind you you're in a holy place!" From the darkness behind him came snorts and grumbles of discontent.

"All I said was ..."

"Never mind, never mind," said Fatback, yawning, "—the Hog Father forgives you. Just hush up a minute while I talk my carcass into getting up off this nice warm straw, and we'll step outside."

"Look, I just want you to understand, all this inflammatory talk about 'raiding the bins of tax cheats' isn't coming from me...."

"Now just give me a minute here, son ..." said Fatback, his eyelids drooping as he settled his head back onto his crossed forelegs. Rumblings of protest issued from the darkness as unseen bassi profundi registered their displeasure.

"It's that goddamn *Cassius,*" Bucky continued heedlessly.

"Councilor Leghorn!" said Fatback, pushing himself up onto his haunches, "You're in a church!"

"How's a hog supposed to sleep around here?" came a muffled protest.

"Yeah, take it outside if you wanna talk!" came another.

"Oh, would you pipe down back there?" said Fatback, getting up on all fours. "For pity's sake, you'd think you hogs were *paying* for the accommodations!" Then, turning to Bucky: "Too damned noisy in here to talk—let's go on outside." He nudged Bucky out the door and then set about extruding his own bulk through the doorframe.

"Look, Reverend," said Bucky, "I'm just concerned that the rhetoric surrounding this whole revenue debate is getting a little overblown...."

Fatback struggled mightily to extract himself from the doorframe. "Where in tarnation ... *dang,* this doorway shrinks a little every day ... where in tarnation you been hiding yourself, son? Ain't seen hide nor hair of you in days ... *oof!*"

"Oh, you know ... I been around," Bucky muttered, his eyes nervously searching the gloom. "Listen, Reverend, you know the situation—I have to carry water for Cassius. And I don't have to tell you what kinda program he's pushing...."

"Well, I don't know much about politics," said Fatback, standing upright, "—AAGH! MY BACK! GODDAMN IT...! Forgive me, Hog Father, forgive me...." Then, suppressing a pitiful squealing deep in his throat, he arched his back till something cracked. "AH! Ah ... ahhh." The pastor took a deep breath and heaved a sigh of relief. "Like I was saying ... I don't know beans about politics, son, but shouldn't you oughtta be carrying water for your *constituents?*"

"What, are you kidding? My constituents *love* his plan! You know how many pigeons we lost last winter...."

"Oh, I know," said Fatback, "I remember...." He seemed frozen in place—his back still arched, his snout in the air. "You know, that's the one thing I never liked about this roof: you can't see the sky!" Supported partly by the hog house and partly by various uprights and buttresses, the freeform roof covering the sty was constructed of pine boughs, and shingles appropriated from the sheep shed (and was about as water-tight as chainlink). The pastor sighed and released a gaseous discharge from his lower end. "C'mon little feller, let's go out back." As Fatback teetered and Bucky resumed his groveling, they made their way out of the tabernacle and circled around to the back of the hog house.

"See, Cassius got to studying the Wall one day," Bucky explained, "and he saw what you got in the bins, and I guess he got it in his head it was fair game...."

"The powers that be need to understand that what's in the church's bin ain't *mine,*" said Fatback, appraising a luminous crescent moon, "—it belongs to the needy! I just shepherd what resources I can on their behalf, that's all. I don't have a single bucket of feed that can be taxed 'cause I don't own so much as a *bucket*—I took a vow of poverty! I sleep in the hog house, I don't have a job—I just take donations on behalf of them that happened on their privation *by accident.* And, of course, I take a little for myself—just enough so's I don't get too weak and emaciated to do my work. But it's a pittance, and it don't change the fact that if the Bureaucratic Republic of Freedom Farm wants to get in the business of feeding the economically challenged, then it shouldn't be taxing the very critters it says it wants to help—which is exactly what a tax on the church's inventory would amount to! Chafes my hide..."

"Hey look, you don't gotta tell *me,* Reverend. I understand your position—and I agree completely. But Cassius probably figures you're hoarding...."

"Hoarding ...? Every day I have a heap of feed put out for the needy, you know that. But for pity's sake, I can't give it *all* away—I gotta make it through winter myself! I took a vow of poverty, Councilor, not a vow of starvation."

"Listen, listen, all of that's gonna get taken into account, Reverend—I promise. You said it yourself: you got *nothing*, right?—and you can't tax nothing. But the thing is ..." said the chicken apologetically, "with the public mood being what it is, the church is gonna get hit with *some* kinda tax. Our job is to keep it to a minimum—and we will, I promise. But the feeling is that we're losing too many critters—no reflection on all your fine work, Reverend, but that's the feeling—and the prevailing view is that if everyone just gave a little bit, it'd be enough to make the difference. And obviously, it'd have important symbolic value if the church was contributing to the cause—it'd show you support the official effort."

"Dang it, the church is *already* contributing to the cause!"

"I know, I know. But look, *everybody's* gonna take a hit on this one Reverend—and that's exactly why it's only gonna be a *little* hit. I personally don't believe the church should pay *anything*, but in politics, you can't let your personal beliefs get in the way of the job—especially when you got a primitive like Cassius reverting to pecking mode all the time. I mean, look at my head—just look at it! It's hard to see in this light, but he takes a coupla chunks outta me at every Council meeting! And if that's all I had to worry about, it wouldn't be so bad, but he's pushing hard for a tax on Pluto—and Pluto's not gonna sit still for that. And I'm not saying he should, either—it's just, I don't know ... you never know what Pluto might do, that's all. He probably figures I support the idea—since I *did* come out in support of it. But I mean, I *had* to—and I don't think he appreciates the fact. Especially after covering my campaign costs and all ... But look, I was hoping you could talk to him—explain to him about the pecking order. He'd listen to you, Reverend, I know he would...."

"Aw, now look, you don't gotta worry yourself about that

big baboon. He did say he was gonna put you on a spit and roast you up for dinner, but I'm sure he'll probably wring your neck first."

Bucky purged his tailpipe and froze.

"Haw-haw-haw! I'm just funnin' with you," said Fatback, "take it easy there, son. Listen, Pluto just *looks* scary, what with those fangs and the war paint and that big hair and all. But I wouldn't worry about him none—he keeps himself too dang busy most of the time to think about hurtin' anybody. Between his activities at the mall and his construction business and his runs with that danged Omnibeast and dishin' out feed at the barn and milkin' the cow and brewin' up all that corn liquor and ... Oh, and you see what he's doin' now? He's *deliverin'* the stuff—after his last bus run, when he goes lightin' candles. He puts a couple of jugs of Toad Valley on the wagon with his smudge pot so he can fill everybody's dishes and bowls while he's lightin' their candles. So now the good residents of Hawg Homestead can get *themselves* lit at the same time they're gettin' their candles lit! Haw-haw-haw! Ain't that some shit? Haw-haw-haw! I wouldn't be surprised if that's the reason church attendance was off last Sunday...." Fatback paused a moment, and squinted at the moon. "You know, I wonder if maybe *I* oughtta do something along those lines—like maybe a nice little ritual where I put out a bowl of *spirits,* say, and then invite the congregation to line up and partake of the *Spirit*—just one little lap of the tongue each. Just enough for a wee-little jolt ..."

A wolf howled in the distance, and Fatback turned to the rooster in surprise—but Bucky had slipped into the shadows and was gone.

After that, the only time anybody got more than a glimpse of Bucky was at Council meetings. The other councilors would all be in their places at the table, their various assistants and interns would be getting themselves settled, and Bucky would step out of the pantry, or out of a cabinet, or simply appear in their midst like he'd been there all along. He became a master of stealth; he would appear like an apparition, stoically perform his function as majority leader for the duration of each meeting —taking his peckings when necessary—and then vanish as mysteriously as he'd come.

He'd probably have vanished altogether, too, if not for some tragic sense of duty. But in spite of himself, he continued to play his part, and ultimately delivered the CFC vote on behalf of Boss Cash—and the Empowering the Differently Productive Initiative became law.

There was no feed in the current budget for such a program, of course, so the Council petitioned Carlo for a hike in its credit line—and the hog was happy to oblige. If Freedom Farm was going to tax him for some costly new "giveaway to parasites, panhandlers, and the willfully unproductive," he wanted to *finance* it; collecting interest from Freedom Farm was Carlo's way of offsetting whatever taxes the federation managed to collect from *him.*

Carlo had no taste for letting his feed "get moldy" in any case. So he lent it out—thereby collecting interest on unused inventory while transferring the burden of inventory taxes to borrowers. Where some critters seeded furrows for profit, and others picked nits for profit—and still others did addition or subtraction or advised Council Critters for profit—Carlo Hawg did nothing for profit, and profited handsomely. From his own deep pockets, this serial lender financed purchases of BeaverBilts—hundreds of them, priced at something like 1000-bushels per—while extending supplemental credit to hard-pressed mortgagees at feeding time, and providing generous lines of credit to such worthy clients as Frankie Hamhock, Freedom Farm itself, and his own simian asset. But except for the credit extended at feeding time—the kind doled out by the bucket and devoured on the spot—all this activity took place on the Wall; in lending out a quantity of feed, Carlo would simply bracket one or more entries in his own lengthy column, and add the equivalent amount to the borrower's column. And when the hog ran out of inventory to lend, he lent out inventory that was *already* on loan; a given quantity of soybeans, for example, might be listed in half-a-dozen different accounts—while the original entry would be found beneath Carlo's name, nested in multiple sets of brackets. Consequently, in the phantom, two-dimensional world of the Wall, Freedom Farm's total inventory of feedstock appeared to be many times what it actually was. (Of course, belying the ebb and flow of all those metastasizing numbers as loans were floated and repaid, the feed in the bins—alas—just sat there getting moldy as it was gradually depleted between harvests.)

But just as that phantom world of metastasizing numbers had built Hawg Homestead, it served to jumpstart Freedom Farm's Empowering the Differently Productive Program as well. It allowed the indigent to begin feeding immediately, it made the first installment on a planned expansion of public housing, and it began paying for Schuyler to have his head rotated at regular intervals. A presumed advantage of charging the initial costs of the EDPP was that it would help quantify those costs for the sake of planning—and it did. But because each bucketful doled out on credit would come back to him with interest, Carlo was notably generous when serving up rations; and because Pluto was the only contractor capable of building additional public housing, he plundered the program with inflated charges; and because Silas Clusterberry was no less an opportunist than either the Chancellor or his simian asset, Schuyler's overpriced adjustments became a significant ex- pense. Consequently, empowering the differently productive turned out to be a shade pricier than anticipated.

And yet the EDPP would prove to be an immensely popular program. No longer would an evening stroll through the yard include a guilty detour around a grim knot of starving beasts; no longer would the thawing snows of spring expose the rotting corpses of the those that hadn't made it through winter; and no longer would soft-hearted farm animals be troubled by the suspicion that the spoils of the system came ultimately at the expense of those who'd lost it all. But what they'd find most appealing about the EDPP was the idea that despite the possibility of ill-fortune, injury, or ill-health, despite the inevitability of old age and the economic impotence that came with it, they themselves would never be faced with starving to death in a snow bank.

And what farm animal couldn't get comfortable with an idea like that?

Pluto Baboon, of course, was no farm animal; for the renegade mandrill, "security" meant two squares a day in a square steel enclosure—an idea that made him distinctly *uncomfortable*. The thing he *was* comfortable with was power—and not just power, but *raw* power: the screaming, smoking, mindless kind that erupted in his face whenever he yanked the cord on that Briggs & Stratton chainsaw. He was more than comfortable with it, he was *enchanted* by it; he was enchanted by the howling stink of it, by the way it shook in his hands—by the threat of its proximity. And he was especially taken with the way that contraption could rip through the trunk of a lodgepole pine in seconds.

So enraptured would he become when felling trees, in fact, that he could barely bring himself to stop—shearing tree after tree in a shrieking, fuming orgy of destruction—and he didn't seem to realize till late in the day that they just weren't growing as fast as he was cutting them down. On any number of occasions, as he closed in on the woodlot's dwindling stock of timber, the monkey would throttle back on that earsplitting instrument of the Unraveling and gaze for inordinate lengths of time at the dense stand of lodgepole pine taunting him on Von Rumpel's side of the fence.

CHAPTER 21

The snows came, and the snows went—and when they went, they gave up a scant half-dozen carcasses. The few that didn't make it had frozen to death—not one critter had starved—and the trifling body count served to vindicate the EDPP. The dead were covered over and duly mourned—and once the solemnities were dispensed with and the meadow got all gaudy with wildflowers, life on the farm began to look like a whole new deal. Needless to say, it'd be a while before the additional coops, houses and sheds were completed, so the yard would remain clogged with vagrant beasts for the time being—but at least they weren't making everyone uncomfortable by dying in public.

As for Boss Cash, it'd be an understatement to say that his political fortunes were at their peak. But though his political capital would dwindle from there rather than plummet, in the long run it would only amount to so much loose change. The reasons for this would include Bucky Leghorn and the CFC, taxes, and the intrigues of the PFP, among other things—but it probably began with a small band of indigent beavers.

For a long time, no one had given these culturally dysfunctional critters much notice. But as public housing became more available, fewer animals were left camped out in the yard—which made these big, gamey rodents hustling nuts in their midst a shade more conspicuous. Being feral critters, they didn't qualify for public assistance—despite the fact that most of them were born right there in Stinktown, the little beaver enclave just outside the gates of Hawg Homestead. They'd grown fat on Freedom Farm's apples, and comfortable with the idea that—like their parents—they'd eventually have secure positions in the construction industry, along with nice little BeaverBilts of their own. But the housing boom was winding down, and their tender plumbing was unaccustomed to a diet of bark—and they were clearly too evolved to spend the cold weather swimming around the frigid waters of Liberty Creek beneath a thick layer of ice.

Despite their ongoing presence in the yard, however, the full dimensions of the beavers' plight probably wouldn't have risen to the level of public awareness if several of Gisela's grandkids hadn't inadvertently promoted their cause. After their reading class, the kids typically went to the mall to loiter and socialize—and on a particularly hot, boring afternoon, as each of them in turn exhausted her allowance at the Sneak-a-Peek, a beaver sidled up and tried to wheedle a nut.

"We don't support begging," said one of the kids, sticking her nose in the air. (Goats, as you might imagine, had no love for beavers.)

"I ain't begging," muttered the surly rodent, "I'm soliciting *charity*—in case you never heard of it."

"Why don't you go eat some *bark?*" she said testily.

The beaver told her he'd have to go a long way to find a tree that still had some bark on it—and not having eaten that day, he wasn't up for the hike. "That's right, we're just like you," he told her, "—we gotta eat too."

The kid turned to her sisters. "Beavers are just like you ..." she said brightly, "Beavers get hungry too!"

The next moment, the three of them were chanting in unison: "Beavers are just like you! Beavers get hungry too!"—over and over, as though the world needed proof that kids say the cutest things. The beaver just waited patiently for the bratty ruminants to get bored and go away, and before long the kids obliged—heading off in the direction of the family BeaverBilt in Hawg Homestead. But when the trio ran into some of the hard-up rodents the next day at the water trough, they broke right into their chanting again—only this time they were joined by several ewes who took the chant to be a heartfelt expression of sympathy and solidarity rather than a taunt. Others soon made the same mistake.

So ironically, that obnoxious little chant became the battle hymn by which the "benefits for beavers" cause cleaved its way into the public mind. At the same time, though, it was a cause that didn't amount to much more than a fringe movement born of midsummer boredom—and probably would've stayed that way, too, if Bucky hadn't cracked.

Bucky, you might say, was caught between a cock and a hard place. In addition to running himself ragged keeping the mandrill under perpetual surveillance—it being the only way to ensure against a chance encounter—the beleaguered bird was suffering increasingly harsh peckings at Council meetings. This was due partly to Boss Cock's growing frustration with the grudging nature of his support, and partly to the pressures Cassius himself was feeling with regard to the real-world costs of empowering the differently productive. The budget deficit was exploding under the burden of the EDPP, and the process of offsetting the program's costs with new taxes was bogged down in the complexities of projecting long-term trends—what with inflation, depreciation, population growth, and so on. (These were farm animals, after all.) Boss Cock wasn't so good at counting beans either, but once he knew where to find the federation's mounting liabilities on the Wall, he made a habit of checking the length of that column routinely—and he didn't need beans to appreciate the power of compound interest. He also didn't need the notoriety of having personally bankrupted the farm....

But however estranged from the more naturally evolved, Cassius was still a member of the greater avian community, and he finally realized that when your payload is pulling you into a nose-dive, you don't stop to make calculations before lightening your load. So at a meeting of the Appropriations Committee—which is what the Council called itself when it met at the gazebo—Cassius pushed for a stopgap measure targeting Pluto Baboon and the Church of the Suffering Sow. "Look, we're just gonna keep sinking deeper into debt without new revenues, right?" he explained to the beleaguered majority leader, "—so until we get all the numbers sorted out, let's just make Pluto and Fatback pay two percent a month like every-body else." Then, giving it a moment's thought, he added: "In fact ... as long as we're at it, let's *double* it for the *big* dogs— Pluto, Carlo, and Frankie—let's make them pay *four* percent. That should help trim that column some."

"CLASS WARFARE!" roared Grover.

"... SOCIALISM ...!" sputtered the Councilor for Swine.

"INDEED!" exclaimed an outraged Eunice.

Spencer just snorted and laughed derisively. "Lemme get this straight: you figure on shaking down Big Feed, and your backup is the CFC—the *Chickens for Change ...?*"

"You must be talkin' about the *Cocks* for Change," said Cassius, turning to the pigs' side of the gazebo. "Yeah, that's right, Councilor—they just got their spurs. And if that's some kinda veiled threat ..."

"Of course it's a threat!" Bucky broke in, his voice trem-bling with feeling. "Don't you know what you're dealing with here? And it's *Chickens* for Change, Cassius, *Chickens!* I'm sick of pretending I'm not a chicken, 'cause I am, Cassius—I'm a *chicken!* God help me, it's true...."

It was exactly the wrong time for a meltdown, and Cassius acted swiftly—giving Bucky several hard shots between the eyes. "You're a *fighting cock,* is what you are, and the Council's majority leader," he said, "—start acting like it!"

Myrtle, Petra and Henrietta had their heads retracted so far into their plumage they almost looked like they'd been decapitated—but Bucky just squawked pathetically: "No, I'm a chicken, Cassius, a *chicken*—and you know what? I don't care anymore! I'm tired of the charade, I'm tired of playing the part—I want the world to know: I'm a CHICKEN!"

"You *tell* him, Bucky honey," said Henrietta, poking her head up out of her inflated plumage. "There's nothing wrong with being a chicken, Bucky—you know why? 'Cause chickens are *beautiful*. Chickens are about love and peace and sharing...."

There was no way to retrieve the situation at that point, so in frustration, Cassius administered a sound thrashing to the insurgent chicken, hopped down off the bench where the CFC had parked itself, and left the gazebo without another word.

The pigs ate it up.

It could be argued that in the grand scheme of things the incident wasn't so much a major political humiliation as a minor breach in protocol—and in the incident's aftermath, Cassius argued as much (while reiterating for the ill-informed that he was not then—nor had he ever been—a member of the CFC). But as any agent of the second law can tell you, a minor scrape yearns to be a festering, life-threatening affliction—and it wasn't long before chickens were coming out of the closet from Hawg Homestead to the back forty. In no time at all, it became a full-fledged movement—"the chicken wing of the Chickens for Change"—and having as they did a well-developed sense of victimhood, its members felt a common bond with the beleaguered beavers, and adopted the rodents' plight as their signature cause.

As for Bucky Leghorn, he emerged as the movement's putative head, and—ironically—enjoyed an increased measure of influence despite having been forced out as the Council's majority leader.

But Bucky's influence—and that of his "chicken wing" faction—came at the expense of the CFC itself, which was weakened as a political force. The winds of change that had bolstered Cassius and the CFC and their progressive approach to the problem of the Hundred waned when the Chickens for Change found itself tainted by a radical faction that talked of putting *rodents* on the public dole—making the party's appeal to the voting public somewhat more species-specific. In truth, there was little public support for the idea of assistance to beavers—despite all the talk amongst a political faction that was, after all, too chicken-hearted to actually *fight* for something.

And yet hope springs eternal....

"Justa mattera time," said Chico. "Las' fall you couldn' even *talk* about it. Now ..."

"Yeah, but talk is jus' talk, stink," said Leroy,"—justa lotta hot air."

It was happy hour at the Bucket of Fire Saloon, and the two beavers were getting happily shitfaced after an afternoon hustling nuts in the yard. Located at a corner of Mandrill Mall between the Toad Valley Distillery and a busy nit-picking concession called Nits-R-Us, the Bucket of Fire consisted of a bower-like assemblage of branches, stones, and human artifacts, with a high canvas canopy sheltering a liquor locker, a fire pit, and several sheaves of hay for the watering hole's patrons to lounge on. As usual, Pluto had stopped by just long enough to retrieve a jug from the locker, pour the first round, and tally the charges before heading out for his last run with the Omnibeast—all of which took maybe two minutes; it was a thin crowd. Across the pit from the beavers, Frankie sat sharing a half-bucket with Polack, the Black Poland boar—but aside from the hogs, the only other patron was a beat-up old Rhode Island Red cock sitting off by himself, his head hanging in a bucket.

"Look at it this way," said Chico, "Cassius'll prolly get one more term *at least*—I mean, who's gonna beat him, right? An' he's gonna wanna do something really big for, like, his *legacy* and shit—like benefits for beavers! I mean, what else is there?"

Leroy pulled his head out of the "four-finger special" the two were sharing, shook the fiery liquid from his whiskers, and gasped wordlessly.

"Hee, hee, hee," Chico giggled, "—kinda burns, doesn't it? Fucking pig ..."

Frankie, who'd been drinking in sullen silence with the obsequious Polack, gave the beaver a sharp look.

"I don' know, stink," Leroy croaked, "—maybe he'll jus' whitewash the barn or somethin'.'"

"No, no, I tellin' you, stink—he gonna put us on the dole. Pay us jus' for breathing, you watch."

"Think they'll pay us for drinking?"

"I don' know about *that*," said Chico, "but a' leas' if they feed us, we won't have to waste any nuts on food."

"Hey, that's right ..."

"Sure, stink—we c'hustle nuts in the morning, drink all afternoon—sit around, talk about existentialism and shit ..."

"And then go home to our nice little public housing unit over on Easy Street!"

The beavers got to laughing and slapping their tails on the ground, and Frankie—baring his big yellow tusks—thrust his head angrily into his bucket and drained it. Then he raised his head and waited, all crimson-faced, for the fire in his gullet to subside. "When the fuck is that monkey coming back?" he said finally, his gut rumbling like distant thunder.

"Oh, I imagine Mr. Baboon'll be a while yet," said Polack. "He has to work his way up through the Homestead, loop around the back forty to Whiskers' place, come down along Liberty Creek to the pond, and then ... well let's see, now, I'm not sure *where* he goes from there. But you know, I have a half-bucket or so just a-goin' to waste over at my place if you'd care to join me...." Then, by way of explanation: "I was entertaining a fetching young, uh ... *sow* last night—not much of a drinker, I'm afraid."

"Yeah..." said Frankie, scowling at the beavers, "yeah, let's get the fuck outta here!" He picked himself up and lumbered out into the yard, with Polack and a cloud of methane in his wake. "That's what I'm payin' four percent a month for!" he bellowed at the wide world, "—so beavers can sit around drinkin', and talkin' about exi-whatever-the-FUCK!"

"Oh, the good Lord will punish those heathens for their torpid ways, brother Francis—rest assured," said Polack, who was deacon at the Church of the Suffering Sow. "He will cast them down into a lake of fire for all eternity, and their flesh will fall away from their bones, and their bones will turn to ash, and their ashes will..."

"Don't call me Francis," said Frankie.

As the two hogs made their way over to Hamhock Arms, where Polack had an apartment, Frankie continued to fume —and the word is *fume*—about high taxes and differently productive beavers, while Polack detailed the ever more bizarre and sadistic punishments awaiting the insufficiently industrious in a harrowing afterlife the deacon seemed unaccountably acquainted with. Polack's "apartment" was essentially a dim little stall with a door, but there was room enough for the two hogs to set themselves down on opposite sides of the aforementioned half-bucket of spirits, and take up where they'd left off. Either because there was a chill in the air, or because they had private business to discuss, they pushed the door closed behind them—leaving it ajar just enough to allow a bit of the early evening light to filter in. Given that one of those two 400-pounders had an industrial-strength case of flatulence, you'd think they might've left the door open—but pigs are famously oblivious to the foulest stench.

And then too, the Unraveling is bound to smile on a crow every now and again. For if the porcine pair had had the good sense to leave the door open, there wouldn't have been any dangerous buildup of gasses as Frankie sat farting and fuming to his fawning host and tenant about taxes and bureaucratic excess and the failings of democratically elected bodies—and

I, in turn, would've been deprived of a sight the likes of which any crow would be blessed to witness when the monkey came around to ignite a few photon emitters to brighten Polack's little stall.

And brighten it they did.

Suspecting nothing, Pluto pulled up with Marla in the traces. He took one of the candles from his sack, lit it from the smudge pot under the wagon's seat, and scrambled down to Polack's door with the sack in one hand and the flickering candle in the other. He shoved the door with his shoulder, and as it opened the candle flared; he hesitated—comprehension taking a moment to dawn—and then turned on his heel to flee.

The explosion knocked me right off the fence I was sitting on—but not before my retinas registered the image of a flaming monkey soaring up into the deepening evening sky. It was an image so wondrous that it took several more ear-ringing moments to put into perspective: in the unraveling continuum of time and space, after all—as perfection spirals into chaos and decay, and everything that can possibly happen ultimately happens—flying monkeys are pretty much inevitable.

Now Polack, as it happened, couldn't stand being told he was lucky. When beastfolk told him that he was lucky to be alive —given his proximity to ground zero—he railed that he was burned over 90% of his body, and there was nothing lucky about that; when they told him he was lucky the EDPP would be covering his sizable medical bills—given his limited means —he protested that as long as the EDPP didn't cover morphine or assisted suicide, it was only prolonging his agony; and any time anyone ever mentioned how lucky he was to be doing stud service for George the day of the Uprising—given his consequent liberation—he noted bitterly that living large as Von Rumpel's top stud compared rather favorably to an impoverished existence as deacon at Fatback's crappy little church. But as Polack lay in whimpering agony in a crowded corner of the barn, there was little he could do to stop every critter in the commonwealth from coming by to tell him what a lucky hog he was.

But hanging over it all was the big question: How did it happen? Polack apparently had no idea what had happened, or why. The last thing he remembered—at least, according to his *initial* account—was Frankie rolling to one side to release yet another withering blast; the next thing he knew, he was barbecued—and pieces of Frankie were *still* turning up. Of course, having suffered bouts of delirium in the early stages of his convalescence, it was easy enough for Polack to disavow any statements that conflicted with the story as it subsequently evolved—a narrative that had a lone Von Rumpel slipping past the sentry pigeons, making his way through the Goats' fields to Hamhock Arms, and then tossing a stick of dynamite into Polack's stall before making a clean getaway. Never mind that no conceivable advantage would accrue to Von Rumpel in killing or maiming—rather than simply capturing—his own champion boar, or that the whole story was ridiculous on its face; with time, the tale was embellished and massaged and made to sound almost plausible (at least to a bunch of reflexively ignorant farm animals): he was past his prime, he would explain, and would no longer have been much use to Von Rumpel anyway, and the farmer wanted to send a message to the rest of his livestock, which had been growing restive and rebellious—etc., etc. For the most part, Freedom Farm's beastfolk had no taste for mystery and were happy to seize on almost *any* explanation, no matter how unlikely—and once a corroborating witness began confirming the basic outlines of the story, even the skeptics were silenced.

"It's just like Polack said," Pluto told a crowd of animals at the barn as the last of the fall harvest was put up, "—it was Von Rumpel, alright." The mandrill had taken to wearing a cowl in order to hide the singed remnants of his mane (and he would inhabit the black folds of that cloak for a long time to come, too). "I saw him run into the Goats' hay field just as I was getting down off the wagon—this was right before the blast. I'd have mentioned it sooner, but I didn't want to create a panic...."

So as the season that dawned so brightly extracted its final harvest from the fields, seeds of fear—carefully tended, and amply fertilized—were being sown in the dark loam of the public mind.

CHAPTER 22

But those residing in more rarified socioeconomic strata could afford to remain blissfully detached from the concerns of the common beast. I was reminded of this fact as I whiled away a Sunday afternoon sticking my beak into this and that, and contemplating my own gloomy concerns—in particular, the prospect of flying through Beaver Gorge. (Those imprisoning walls of rock loomed larger every time I looked.)

After taking a dust bath in the yard with some pullets and getting an earful of the usual sordid rumors, and then chasing down earwigs at the woodpile and finding too few to make the effort worthwhile, I found myself drawn to the sanctity of the Church of the Suffering Sow; if nothing else, there was an outside chance a morsel or two had survived Sunday Slop. Not surprisingly, however, the pigs had licked the trough clean —and any scraps that might've fallen to the ground had been trampled irretrievably into the muck.

A splattering sound came from where Booger Hawg and a few of his cronies were lying with their bellies to the sky and their heads propped up against the sty's plank sides—passing around a jug of shine, typically enough, and amusing themselves with various bodily functions. Peeking out from under the straw hat he had tipped over his face, Booger tried to contain his amusement as a glistening stream of piss "slipped the surly bonds of Earth" and rose skyward from between his legs. But it doesn't take much to tickle a besotted hog, and before you could count yourself lucky that pigs don't fly, Booger was giggling like an idiot—which, to everyone's delight, sent that steaming yellow geyser squirting wildly in every direction. Not to be outdone, the big Chester to Booger's left rocked ceremoniously on his flank, slowly cocked a mud-encrusted leg, and proudly released a resonant blast that poignantly evoked Frankie's passing, while shattering what remained of the pigs' already-rustic sense of decorum—the lot of them erupting in shrieks and giggles as they smacked their hams and rolled in the rancid slime.

I ruffled my plumage, dropped some ballast in the trough, and was about to lift off when I noticed Edna Hawg—this would be Booger's mother—storming up to the rear of this oblivious soiree in her flowered cotton nightie. I decided to stick around for the fireworks.

Edna was a big, wrinkly old, hatchet-faced sow who was every bit as mean as she looked. She was fiercely opposed to the imbibing of spirits, and Booger, sad to relate, was a bona fide dipso—though he was usually careful not to get caught in the act. But Edna had been laid up with a virus for a time, and Booger had given free rein to his worst inclinations—and after a while, I'm not sure the fool even remembered that a touch of swine flu was something a pig generally recovered from by and by.

"AUGUSTUS HAWG JUNIOR!" Edna roared as she came barreling into the sty. As usual, the sound of his mother bellowing out his full proper name made Booger jump like he'd been stuck with a pitchfork—which, as he sat up into a sitting position, catapulted the hat off his face and into the puddle of piss steaming at his feet, while knocking over the jug he had cradled in the crook of his foreleg. At the sight of rotgut spilling into the mud, he squealed in horror and tried to right the jug—but Edna wrestled it from his grasp, raised it up over her head, and brought it down on Booger's skull so hard it not only broke the jug, it drove his tail-end another 6-inches into the mud. "There!" she said, "Now maybe you'll think to come visit your poor mama's bedside the next time she's hovering inches from death!"

Booger shrieked: "EEEEEEEEEEEEEEE ...!"

"I should've known you'd be drinking and chewing and carrying on like a common porker," she continued, "—and in a *church,* no less! You should be ashamed of yourself!"

"Eee, eee, eee, EEEEEEEEEEEEEEE ...!" said Booger.

"Oh, quit your damn squealing, for god's sake—I didn't hit 'nything vital."

"EEEEEEEEEEEEEEEEE ...!"

"SHUDDUP, OR I'LL GIVE YOU SOMETHING TO SQUEAL ABOUT!"

Booger made a determined effort to stifle himself—no mean feat, under the circumstances: his head was throbbing *visibly,* his eyes were burning with 190-proof corn liquor, and he was further suffering what the puzzled vet would identify as a "mud-impacted bowel"—which would *have* to be a trifle excruciating. Booger's associates inched away from him till they were safely out of reach, and then bolted for the gate.

Edna kept her sights on Booger. "Haven't you embarrassed your family enough?" she said, shaking her head in disgust. *"I'm* the one who should be blubbering, not you. Look at you— you're a disgrace to your lineage! I can't even *begin* to tell you how ashamed and disappointed I am! And how do you suppose this sort of behavior makes your father feel? By the time your father was your age, he was serving his second term on the Animal Council—and serving with distinction, I might add! And what have *you* accomplished? Have you done anything to honor the Hawg family's fine tradition of service to our glorious federation? Have you done the first thing to honor your grandfather Carlo, who fought in the Uprising and played a leading role in building this bastion of bestial self-determination? Have you so much as joined the Militia or gotten a job or even sobered up long enough to sire a few piglets of your own ...?"

"Eee, eee, eee," said Booger, whimpering to himself as he licked at the rotgut running down his forelegs.

"WHY, YOU'RE NOT EVEN LISTENING ..." said Edna, sounding just a hair shy of homicidal. Booger squealed with alarm and covered his palpitating pate with his forelegs, but Edna—who had the instincts of a prizefighter—stomped on his flank, curling him up like a pill bug. "How dare you treat your poor mother with such callous disregard?" she railed, knocking the wind out of him with a well-placed hoof to the ribs, "Is this the thanks I get for all my selfless sacrifice over the years?" Then she kicked him in his mud-impacted ass for emphasis. "Where did I fail you, Augustus? Tell me ...! TELL ME!"—to which Booger could only respond with more of his pathetic, stuck-pig sounds.

This enhanced interrogation went on for another minute or so before Edna started to run out of steam. "Oh, *why* must I reap this bitter fruit in my dotage?" she asked the sky when she was finally winded. Booger just whimpered, and squirmed at her feet like a stepped-on slug. Her anger spent, Edna was consumed with unalloyed self-pity. "Just look what you've done to me now..." she said in this thin, deflated voice. "I've scarcely recovered from my dire affliction, and already you've gotten me so out of sorts I'll probably suffer a relapse—and lord knows I haven't the strength to fight my way back from death's door twice. I just hope you're proud of yourself, Augustus Hawg." Edna turned, smoothed her mud-spattered nightie, and headed back across the yard with her nose in the air like Marie Antoinette going to the guillotine.

CHAPTER 23

The sight of a besotted, beat-up Blueback wallowing in foul mud and even fouler self-pity is enough to make any crow's day, so I laughed and heckled and savored the moment well before moving along. As I would learn, however, Booger lay there sniveling and whining till well after dark before pulling himself together finally and stumbling out into the yard—but as luck would have it, he fell into the hole where the outhouse had been and nearly drowned.

And I missed the whole thing.

I saw him in the morning down at Liberty Pond, and he was certainly one sorry-looking pig. Except for his ears, snout, and those two beady little eyes—which were red and squinty behind puffed-up lids—his entire head was encased in bandages. I think it was the first time I'd ever seen him with anything but his custom, perforated-for-pig-ears straw hat on his head. His pudgy midsection was all wrapped up too, Edna having cracked a few of his ribs, and I noticed he was a little gimpy besides—though he still managed to get up on his hind legs. But his customary entourage was nowhere to be seen, and wrapped up as he was in all those bandages, he'd have looked only slightly more pitiful hanging from a meat hook.

Still dazed from his thrashing, he stood motionless at the edge of the pond, staring blankly at the water. His presence made the ducks uneasy, and the whole flock of them finally waddled off into the surrounding foliage somewhere, quacking irately. By and by, their babbling faded away, leaving only the gurgling of Liberty Creek—which spilled out over a ledge of rock and into the far end of the pond. There wasn't even the hint of a breeze, and for a long while the only thing that moved was the fragrant pine I was sitting in as it leaned into the radiance of the sun, which had slipped out from behind a cloud a moment before. Everything was so still, you'd have thought the Great Unraveling itself had ground to a halt.

I gnawed anxiously on a branch.

Then something caught Booger's eye—a set of ripples that appeared on the water a couple of feet from the pond's muddy bank. As the ripples blossomed, another cluster of ripples appeared only inches from the water's edge. "C'mere frawgy," he drawled, in his whiney little dime store twang, "C'mawn frawgy." A tiny frog climbed out of the water a few feet from where Booger stood—probably to try out its new legs on solid ground. "Thass right li'l frawgy," said Booger, taking a plug of tobacco from his vest, "Nice frawgy." Then he bit down on the tobacco, tore off a piece, and started to chew. "C'mere frawgy," he said as he worked the tobacco into a wad, "C'mawn over here, now—I'll tell y'all a secret." The curious frog hopped a bit closer, and Booger rolled the wad on his tongue and took aim. A bullfrog watching from a distance croaked out a warning, but it was a shade late; a thick, ropey stream shot out from Booger's mouth and engulfed the critter in a sticky black glob. The frog kicked frantically to free itself, but before it could, Booger stomped on the critter and ground it into the mud.

A moment later, the reverend Fatback rounded the path

that ran through the woods along Liberty Creek. "Mornin' Booger!" he called out, huffing and puffing from his long bipedal hike. "Your papa said I might find you down here."

Booger nodded, and did his best to strike a devil-may-care pose despite his ludicrous appearance.

"My, my—I'd forgotten what a glorious little sanctuary this is!" said Fatback, surveying the setting. "Is this where you come to commune with nature—to witness the passing of another season, and put life's little ups and downs in perspective?"

"Naw—jes killin' frawgs. Heh-heh, heh-heh."

"Killin' frogs ...?" said Fatback, as he stepped up beside Booger. "What for?"

"Cause they green an' slimy. Heh-heh, heh-heh."

"Uh ... well of course they are," said Fatback, "heh, heh—ahem." He frowned and stared down at the mossy bank for a moment as he scraped his thoughts together. "Augustus," he said finally, "—may I call you Augustus?"

"Well ... I guess. Jes don' go callin me 'Lil Gus'—I hate that."

"Oh, I wouldn't think to call you 'Little Gus.' That's a piglet's name, and you're one fine, full-grown boar—none better. And it's as one boar to another I'd like for us to talk, Augustus."

"One boar to another ...?"

"Well, in a manner of speaking ..." said Fatback, ignoring Booger's smirk. (Like most male hogs being fattened for the table in the days before the Uprising, Fatback had parted with his gonads early on, and so—properly speaking—was a *barrow*.)

"What's on yer mind, Padre?"

"Well son, I'd like for us to talk about someone you've been ignorin' lately."

"Aw, now look, Padre, I know I shoulda gawn t'see Mama while she was sick, but I believe she made that very point herself yesterday—an' iffen y'look real close, you'll notice she was none too equizocal 'bout it, neither."

"Oh, she made her point in forceful terms, alright. Your mama's one strong-minded sow—I think we can all appreciate that." Fatback hid his amusement with an exaggerated scowl. "But you know, Augustus, your mama reminds me of another pig I know...."

"Oh?" said Booger, with obvious disinterest, "An' who might that be?"

"She reminds me a lot of yourself, son."

"Is that right?"

"As God is my witness," said Fatback, raising a foreleg. "You've got that same sort of willful, headstrong personality, when you stop and think about it." Booger wasn't inclined to stop and think about *anything* if he could help it, but Fatback was determined to make his point. "What I mean to say is just that some folks are all wishy-washy about things—they can never decide if they wanna shit or go rootin' for turnips; but you—you're like your mama: once you make up your mind a certain way, neither Hell nor high water is gonna change it. I dare say that's one of the reasons the two of you always seem to be buttin' heads...."

Booger just shrugged and spat in the water.

"But the thing is, Augustus, as much as it might make problems for you and your ma at times, I'd be remiss in my function as a councilor to troubled pigfolk if I didn't point out that bein' headstrong can be a *good* thing in its own way."

"I'll take yer word f'that, Padre."

"Well don't just take my word for it, Augustus, think about it: supposin' ol' Silas had looked at you last night and said, *Holy Hogwallop,* look at this poor animal's busted head! Lord! Can't say that I've ever dealt with anything like this before...." Fatback fell into character, cocking his head and squinting the way Silas was inclined to do: *'Let's see now*—as I recollect from that mail order veterinary course I took, the thing to do here is to plug up his nostrils and ear holes with cotton so's his head don't collapse, and then bind up his skull real good so it holds together while its mendin'. But then again, my *instincts* tell me it might be better if I immobilized him somehow and then hooked up his ears and snout to an arrangement of pulleys and sash weights and the like, and thuswise put his entire head in *traction*. Now I wonder, should I follow my instincts or just go by the book? And then too, supposin' there's complications? Like say his head goes and collapses on me before I can affect a repair of some sort; could I just maybe drill a wee-little hole in his skull and then pump it back up again with a tire pump? I don't believe my veterinary manual has a dang thing to say on the subject of un-caving caved-in pig heads. And now that I reflect on it, is this somethin' I even wanna be messin' with while my stomach's a-rumblin' and my mind's on biscuits and gravy? Maybe I oughtta just go home and think about it some more and come back tomorrow....

"Lord, Augustus, can you imagine the fix you'd be in if that's the sort of doctorin' you got? Luckily, Silas took one look at you and said to himself: I know just what I need to do to patch up this swine good, and by God, I'm gonna do it! And he did, too; no hemmin' an' hawin', no second thoughts —just went right to work on you without hesitation or doubt. Oh, he complained some about you bein' a bit more pungent than he'd like after the plunge you took in that shit hole—but he didn't let that stop him from doing what needed doing. And glory be, here you stand the very next day, pretty near good as new."

"I think thass stretchin' it, Padre."

"Well, maybe a little. But you see my point...."

"I guess. But wuss all this got t'do wif me ignorin' my mama in her hour-a need?"

"Augustus, I didn't come down here to talk about your mama—much as I love the dear sweet old sow. No, I expect you and her'll manage to work out your differences by and by without any interference on my part. I just wanted to make that point about the value of bein' headstrong and willful— since it's a trait that seems to run rampant in the Hawg family.

But here's the important thing, Augustus: without some kinda direction in life—without a *moral compass* to guide your way— bein' strong-willed ain't worth *spit*, it truly ain't. And that gets me back to the subject of that certain somebody you've been ignorin', son—someone a lot more important than your ma."

"Padre, in case you ain't heard, my mama's about the mos' important dang swine in all creation," said Booger, with only a hint of sarcasm.

"Well now, your mama's mighty important alright, no question about it—but she's also one devout, church-goin' pig, and I know she'd agree that there ain't nobody nowhere more important than the Almighty himself."

"Gawd ...?" said Booger, confused.

"Of *course* God! Who but the good Lord himself would a naturally ordained pig of the pulpit be havin' on his mind, anyways?"

"Well, if that don' beat the bugs off a buzzard's ass," said Booger, with a conspiratorial wink. "I shoulda knowed you'd come an' track me down one day iffen y'din see my face in yer conjugation fer a couple–three years or so. No disreswpeck, Padre, but I'd rather not have t'drag my hungover carcass outta bed ever' Sunday mornin' an' listen t'yawl go awn 'bout Damn Nation, an' Tar Nation, an' all them other nations and whatnot fer a full hour or more—insprational as it might be f'mosta yer flock. But I'll tell y'what I'll do: from now awn, I'll sen' one-a my hangers-awn down to the church each week wif a bag-a nuts fer the donation bin. Fair 'nough?"

"Augustus Hawg!" said Fatback, looking like he'd been spit on. "Is that what you think I'm doin' out here, shakin' the old hickory tree? You think I got nothin' better to do than go skulkin' around the back forty hittin' up wayward parishioners like some sorta damn clerical panhandlin' swine? I must say, Augustus, it's mighty gratifyin' to know you hold the Reverend Fatback and his earthly mission in such high regard!"

"Dang, take it easy there, Padre."

"No, I will *not* 'take it easy there Padre!' Now you listen to me pig, and you listen good, 'cause your soul's in some serious jeopardy! Did you ever give any thought to what you plan on sayin' to the Hog Father when you find yourself up yonder rattlin' the gates to that big sty in the sky? You gonna say, *Oh please* let me in, Your Eminence—I swear I never missed no Sunday worship, nor shamed my mama and papa, nor poked nothin' but sows, nor touched a drop of corn liquor in all my days—I've just been one good, righteous pig living a sober, industrious life of pignacious piety ...? Why, he's just gonna laugh in your face, Augustus, 'cause the Sky Pig sees all—and I mean *all*. And what're you gonna say then? You gonna say, *Oh but Your Excellency,* I swear I always sent one of my lackeys to church in my stead every Sunday mornin' with some nuts for the donation bin—and I'm pretty sure he probably didn't usually keep too many for himself most of the time ...? You know what he'll say to that, don't you? He'll just tell you in his mighty, thunderous voice that a righteous life ain't something you can buy with a sack of nuts! And then he'll cast you down into Hog Hell for all eternity, and your bacon'll be fried but good—fried to a cinder!"

Booger just stood there scowling at the water—and as he did, I found myself wondering what, exactly, had compelled Fatback to haul his blob-like tonnage all the way out there to Liberty Pond (aside from Booger's soul, I mean). But it was a somewhat different question piecing itself together in *Booger's* mind: "D'they a-lease letcha take a li'l pull down there from time t'time?" he said finally.

"Holy Hogwallop, Augustus! If you came to church once in a while, you'd know full well they don't let you so much as lick your dang poker down in Hog Hell!"

"Yeah, well ... sounds like the same sorta deal I got aroun' here," said Booger sullenly.

"What in blazes are you talkin' about, son?" said Fatback in disbelief. "You got a life of ease and privilege and all the advantages of good breedin'! What more could a pig ask for?"

"A pig jes might ass fer a chance t'*enjaw* his stinkin' good fortune f'one thing," said Booger, getting worked up. "This *is* a free farm, ain't it? The Hawg fambly is one-a the mos' richess famblies in all-a Freedom Farm—prolly the *richess,* fer all I know. Shee-it, my fambly got some gnarly nuts, Padre! So why can' I jes kick back'n *enjaw* my life-a ease an' prillage? Ain't that why they call it a 'life-a ease and prillage'...?" Booger spat in the water. "I'll *tell* y'why I can' enjaw it—iss cause they keep beatin me over the head with what a dang-blasted *big pig* my papa is, an' how I gotta live up t'his *fine* ezample. I got a perpetuous dang headache listenin t'whatta fine, big pig my papa is. Dang...! Let some other pig gitta job an' jawn the Militia an' be all respectacle an' such—I got better things t'do. Ain' no need f'me t'ever work a single blasted day-a my life, the way I see it. I got *nuts,* Padre! Ain like I gotta go out an' make a big pigga m'seff—I was *borned* a big pig!"

"Son, a mega-pig like your papa can cast a long shadow, I know—but there ain't no escapin' the fact that the best way of steppin' outta that shadow is to make an even *bigger* pig of yourself."

"Yeah, well I don' see where I'm obliged t'prove a blasted thing t'nobody. Hell, I don' see wuss so dang big 'bout my papa anyways! What—jes 'cause he spent a little time awna Council, fartin and speechifyin an' actin so all-fired important? An' *so what* if he was the firss Hawg ever t'run f'Boss Cridder? Din win, did he? Got beat by a dang chicken!"

"But *you* wouldn't get beat by a dang chicken, would you son?"

"Now wuss *that* supposed t'mean?" said Booger, eyeing Fatback suspiciously.

"It means just what I said: *You* wouldn't let yourself get beat by a chicken, would you?"

"Hell *no!* I mean ... iffen I was runnin' f'Boss Cridder."

"Well...? What does that tell you, son?" said Fatback—pausing like he actually expected an answer. "I'll tell you what it tells *me,* Augustus—it tells me maybe you *oughtta* run for Boss Critter! Whip ol' Cassius Cock in the next election and let your papa worry about *your* shadow for a change."

"Aw, c'mawn now Padre—whatna hell would *I* know 'bout bein' Boss Cridder?"

"Augustus, what's *anybody* know about bein' Boss Critter? It ain't like there's a Boss Critter school somewhere so's folks can learn how it's done. That's what advisors are for."

"Advisors ...?"

"That's right, advisors. Doesn't matter if a problem's political or economical or legal or whatnot, the BC's got advisors that tell him what to do."

"Yeah, well, *nobody* tells Booger Hawg what t'do!" Booger protested, drawing himself up.

"No, no, it ain't like that, Augustus—the advisors are just there to *explain* things, that's all. Like if the Council cooks up some proposed ordinance or other, the advisors explain *what it means*—but the Boss Critter ain't called the Boss Critter for nothing: *he's* the one that decides whether to approve it or not."

"Oh ... well, I guess thass different," said Booger, sounding a trifle interested.

"Of course it is, son. Hell, bein' Boss Critter is easy—it's gettin' elected that's the hard part."

"Yeah," said Booger, sounding a trifle disappointed, "I 'magine iss a heap-a work, awright...."

"Oh, it's brutal work, son," said Fatback, "—the sort of work most critters just don't have a stomach for." He glanced sidelong at Booger. "An election campaign is a *fight,* Augustus, plain and simple—a knock-down, rollin'-in-the-mud fight to the finish—and if you're not ready to rumble, if you're not a brawler at heart, if you don't have that *killer instinct,* well then you've got no dang business runnin' for public office in the first place." He noticed Booger's ears perk up a little, so he seized the moment and went into full preacher mode—his voice booming out over the pond. "When you're out there on the campaign trail, you gotta show beastfolk that you're *tough* enough to bust heads, Augustus, that you're *ruthless* enough to go for the throat, that you're the sort of ornery, cantankerous pig that'll roll right over anyone fool enough to get in his way! After all, you gotta prove to beastfolk in no uncertain terms you got the *balls* to be Boss Critter! You gotta demonstrate by the sheer *cussedness* of your campaign that you're not squeamish about drawing *blood,* that you relish the opportunity to bare a little tusk and fight *dirty,* that you're a bilious bruiser with the grit and meanness to *gore* your opponent when he's down—that you're so damn rotten, in fact, that you won't be happy until you've *destroyed* the poor devil's reputation, and *terrorized* his family, and made him rue the very day he was fool enough to think he had so much as a prayer against you!" Booger was becoming engorged. "You gotta show the voters that when the going gets tough, by God, you won't hesitate to dig down into the darkest depths of your primeval porcine soul and unchain that snortin', snarlin', fired-eyed, full-blown, beastly-awful meat-eatin' dang ragin', rampagin' blood-and-guts *wild boar!* That's what it takes to win an election, Augustus!"

"YEAH!" said Booger, staring glassy-eyed into space with his piggly-wiggly standing at attention. "Say Padre—y'really think I could run fer Boss Cridder?"

"Well ..." said Fatback, shifting gears, "let's not get ahead of ourselves here, Augustus. First off, in order to run for BC, you gotta get the party behind you—and as things stand, that might take a little doin'. See, by sheer *coincidence,* me and Pluto and your grandpa and a couple other pigs were chewin' on this very subject the other night at the Bucket of Fire—tryin' to figure out who to put up against Cassius this winter—and danged if your name didn't come up a number of times. And everybody said the same thing, Augustus: that you probably got exactly the kind of grit it'll take to whip that blasted chicken; trouble is, all you really *wanna* do is lay around in the mud all day—probably 'cause half the time you can't hardly walk straight anyways. And I gotta tell you son, if you can't walk, you can't hardly run."

"Now hode on there, Padre," said Booger, taken aback, "you make it soun' like I got some sorta ... some sorta *drinkin'* problem, or somethin'!"

"Augustus ..." said Fatback, turning to look Booger in the eye, "save that horseshit for your mama, alright? I've seen a few pickled pigs in my day, but you ... you could drop dead right here and now, and the buzzards'd die of old age waitin' for you to get ripe. Hell, I could smell alcohol when I rounded the bend back there! And I know danged well you still got a couple swallers left in that flask you keep there in your vest pocket, or you wouldn't be hangin' around here mashin' frogs —you'd be off huntin' up another snoot-full. You're a *drunk,* Augustus, there ain't no pretty way of sayin' it—and it ain't no use tryin' to pretend otherwise. I know it, you know it, your mama knows it—the whole world knows it!"

Booger was crestfallen, his noodle suddenly *al dente.* He knew better than to argue with Fatback, so he just stood there in silence with his shoulders slumped and his eyes downcast. Fatback offered no further comment, but remained at his side —seemingly intent on a mission he hadn't yet accomplished. They stood like that for a long while before Booger opened his mouth again. "Guess I ain' never gonna 'mount t'*nuffin',*" he mumbled.

Fatback was focused on something off in the distance. "Well, Augustus ..." he said, "it's a dang shame that such a fine fall day has to find you with body and spirit in such a god-awful, pitiful state, it truly is. But ask yourself this, son: Who's to blame?"

Booger said nothing.

"Well?" said Fatback, still gazing off into space.

Booger just scowled at the ground in dejected silence.

"You're not answering my question, son," said Fatback, turning to Booger. "Who's to blame, Augustus?"

Booger started breathing hard.

"I think we both know the answer to that question, don't we Augustus?"

"Awright!" said Booger, all puffing and red-faced beneath his bandages, *'I'm* t'blame! Is that what y'wanna hear, Padre? Iss *my* fault! I'm jesta wuthless heap-a pickled hawg flesh that don' go t'church on Sunday an' don' care 'bout nobody but hisself an'll prolly go t'Hell jes like you say! Is that whatcha wanna hear? I'm *no good,* Padre, plain an' simple—y'happy now? Iss *my* fault!"

"No, no ..." said Fatback gently, shaking his head, "you got it all wrong, son." He wrapped a foreleg around Booger's shoulder. "It ain't your fault, Augustus—it ain't your fault at all. Shoot, you're one of the finest dang pigs I know—always were too, so you just stop that kinda crazy talk! Heavens to Moonachie, Augustus, I *know* you—I was there the day you was borned. You were the very first one to stick his little nose out, and I remember lookin' in your face and sayin' to myself, *Now this is no ordinary piglet*—this is somethin' special.... This spunky little feller's got a stubborn strength in his eyes, he's got fire and purpose in his gut—this one was sent by the Almighty himself for some kinda important work! Ain't even been borned yet, and already he's leadin' the way! This here pig is not only gonna make his mama proud, he's gonna make *every pig in the land* proud to be of his kind—and I believe that still, Augustus. I've watched you grow up into a fine young boar, I've seen how all those porkers follow you around, how they look up to you—and I believe more strongly now than I ever did that you got an important mission in this life. Oh sure, you've hit some rough spots along the way, but that's only natural; *everyone* steps in a few potholes as they make their way down the winding road of life. Bein' tested is what our earthly sojourn is all about, son. But I can tell you this: the strongest back invites the heaviest load. If you're being sorely tested, it's only because you come from sturdy stock—and that ain't no fault of yours, Augustus. Can't hardly blame a pig for *that.*"

At this point, Booger was trembling with emotion. "Iss true ..." he said, his bogus twang forgotten, "Iss true—it *ain't* my fault! It ain't *even*—I'm a *good* pig! *I'm a good pig, Mama!* Eeeeeeeeeeeeeeee..." And just like that, Booger was squealing and drooling and blowing snot bubbles.

Fatback let him go on like that for a minute or so—and then, very softly in Booger's ear, he said: "Who's been leading you astray, Augustus? Who's to blame?"

"I don' know, Padre! Eeeeeeeeeeeeeeeeee ..."

"Of course you do, son!" said Fatback sternly. "God put you here to do big things, Augustus—but who's always tryin' to mess up the good Lord's work? Who's to blame?"

"Eeeeeeeeeeeeeeeeee ..."

"That ain't the answer, Augustus!" said Fatback, shaking Booger roughly. "Now you listen to me, dang it, and hear me good: it's the *Devil,* son—he's the one been messin' up your life! The Devil's to blame!"

"Iss the Devil! Iss the Devil's fault! Eeeeeeeeeeeeeeeeee ..."

"That's right, Augustus—and what's the *one thing* the Devil can't stand?"

"Iss the Devil makin' me bad! Eeeeeeeeeeeeeeeeee ..."

"We've established that, son. Now what's the one thing that just scares the daylights outta the Devil?"

"Eee, eee, eee," said Booger, trembling and blowing snot bubbles, "eeeeeeeeeeeeeeeeee ..."

"Gotta show these danged inbreeds everything ... " said Fatback, muttering to himself. The pastor was a hefty Poland-Chester mix, but until that moment I hadn't realized just what a powerful beast he was. Heaving a sigh, he wrapped both forelegs around Booger from behind and then, straightening his back, lifted him right up off the ground; then he whirled around in a mighty circle and hurled Booger, thrashing and squealing, out into the pond. There was a gigantic splash—big enough to have emptied a lesser body of water—and for a moment there were frogs and crayfish and turtles and such raining down as swells of water inundated the pond's soggy banks. "It's WATER, Augustus," Fatback shouted, as Booger's bandaged, algae-festooned head bobbed to the surface. "The Fire

220

Pig can't stand water!" The shock in Booger's bloodshot eyes was replaced with a look of terror as the pastor charged into the water after him—and I have to say, the sight of Fatback cleaving those swells and throwing up a bow wave like the prow of a tanker under full steam was an arresting sight. "The Lord's gonna cleanse your soul, son!" said Fatback, plunging Booger beneath the roiling waters.

By the time Fatback had run through his incantations and dragged Booger, gasping and sputtering, from the pond, Booger was not only reborn, he was so light-headed and dizzy for lack of oxygen he could barely stand up. "That's the good Lord talkin' to you, son," Fatback explained as Booger fell face-first in the mud. "How does it feel to have a conversation with the Almighty himself?"

Getting dizzy, falling down—it was a lot like being properly hammered, and Booger liked it just fine. In the wake of that momentous event, in fact, it would get so that he could hardly pass a water trough without sticking his head in for a minute or two and having a word with his new best friend. Yet owing to the tendency of beastfolk to give extra consideration to those least in need, the eccentricities of this Hawg family scion were largely overlooked, and before long the word went out to the four corners of Freedom Farm that Booger Hawg and the Devil had parted ways—and the Pigs for Profits party had found itself a candidate fit to whip Cassius Cock.

CHAPTER 24

Just before Election Day, the leading candidates for Boss Critter debated the issues in a much-heralded public forum. It'd been heavily promoted by the PFP, and was produced by Pluto Baboon. The Council was even persuaded to fund the event from the public bin as a service to the community.

Cassius knew he was being set up, but he also knew the pigs would tag him with the "C-word" if he didn't participate.

The barn was jammed to the rafters for the early evening debate. The candidates stood at opposite ends of a long, narrow dais that ran from left to right, and in the flickering glow of klieg lights—a row of kerosine lanterns—the incumbent rooster and his porcine challenger cast a multitude of giant, pulsing shadows on the aged planks of the wall behind them. Orchestra seating was reserved for the Hawg and Hamhock clans, whose massive members lounged on the floor in lumpy, disorderly heaps that surrounded the dais like a mountain range keeping the rest of the animals at bay. In the midst of these Swine Mountains—elevated on a sheaf of alfalfa—sat Grover Hamhock, who moderated.

"I would like to begin," Grover began, nodding to each of the candidates, "by thanking Pluto Baboon for entrusting me with this honor, as well as for honoring me with his trust. Unfortunately, Mr. Baboon was unable to attend tonight's debate—but let me stress that his absence should in no way be mistaken for a lack of interest or involvement; it's fair to say tonight's event wouldn't even be possible without his ongoing efforts—along with some help from the taxpayer, of course." For the hogs, undermining the political opposition was obviously gratifying in itself, but doing it at taxpayer expense was like a roll in the mud—and they all squealed with appreciation, their tails twitching with little spasms of delight. "The rules of this debate are as follows: candidates are free to posture, pose, pontificate, ridicule, cast aspersions, and attack one another's credibility, character, family, and friends; candidates may exaggerate, obfuscate, distort, misquote, unfairly characterize, willfully misinterpret, or otherwise misrepresent the facts; they may resort to histrionics, name-calling, and personal slurs, they may tell maudlin stories of questionable authenticity in order to exploit the sympathies of gullible voters, and they are free to make inflammatory statements aimed at inciting mindless passions such as fear, hatred, envy, greed, resentment, jealousy, and so forth. At no time are candidates obliged to be fair, reasonable, relevant, honest, or even civic-minded—this is politics, after all. A human by the name of Socrates held that the dialectical nature of argumentation was such that a properly conducted debate would always resolve itself in the incontestable truth; but in fact the truth is mostly what we make of it, and largely beside the point—and certainly, it didn't do Socrates any good. It's *winning* that counts, my friends—and in that spirit, I wish you both luck: may the bigger beast win.

"To start with, let's explore each candidate's reasons for wanting to serve as the federation's Boss Critter at this pivotal moment in its history. Out of deference to the office of the chief executive, we'll begin with the incumbent," said Grover, turning to Cassius. "So tell us, Boss Cock, just what makes you think you're fit to serve another term?"

"What makes me think I'm *fit*...? Well, let's see—I run five miles every morning and do a hundred pirouettes before eating a wholesome, high-fiber breakfast. Is that fit enough?"

"Very good, Boss Cock—very good," said Grover. "But let's get serious here. Freighted with your dismal record of failure, what makes you think you wouldn't do as much damage in a second term as you have in your first? I mean, with all due respect..."

"Do I detect a bit of a slant to these proceedings?" said Cassius.

"Boss Cock, please. A disaster is a disaster in anyone's book—and it's become clear to the citizens of Freedom Farm that your administration has just been one ongoing, unqualified disaster. When you took office..."

"Wait a minute, who am I debating here anyway—you, or the Blueback over there?" said Cassius, indicating the still-silent hog at the other end of the dais.

"As the incumbent is unwilling to address the question," said Grover, turning to Booger, "I'll put it to *you*, Mr. Hawg: Why is the sort of muscular, no-nonsense leadership you advocate so vital to Freedom Farm's future in today's increasingly dangerous world?"

"This is bullshit..." said Cassius.

"Boss Cock," said Grover, "the rules explicitly prohibit a candidate from interrupting his opponent; if I wasn't clear on that point, I apologize. Still, I have to insist you allow Mr. Hawg to answer the question."

"Hey, by all means," said Cassius, "—I wanna hear this."

And actually, *I* did too. Booger wasn't exactly the smartest bomb in the payload, so when the PFP announced that he'd challenged the feisty, quick-witted Cassius to a debate, the scent of monkey business was unmistakable. But Booger's reply was about as thoughtful and incisive as you might expect: "Um ... din catch the question ..."

"Oh, I'm sorry Mr. Hawg—let me repeat the question," said Grover thoughtfully. "Why is the sort of muscular, no-nonsense leadership you advocate so vital to Freedom Farm's future in today's increasingly dangerous world?"

"Ain gonna answer no three-part questions," said Booger.

"Well, uh ... let me see if I can be more succinct," Grover suggested, "—Why do you want to be Boss Critter?"

"Ain nobody's *bidness* why I wanna be Boss Cridder!" said Booger. A thump was heard as someone kicked the dais. "I mean ..." He fell silent, his eyes shifting about nervously.

If nothing else, Booger had the common pig-look down: he wore the overalls that would become his trademark—the shoulder straps hanging uselessly at his sides on account of his shoulder-less, gourd-like form; his usual perforated-for-pig-ears straw hat, meanwhile—reeking as it did of hog piss—gave the hayseed ensemble its authenticity. (The stalk of rye grass sticking from the corner of his mouth only gilded the proverbial lily.)

But just as it appeared Cassius might win the debate by default, Booger cocked an ear and stood motionless for a moment. "Tell 'em—no wait!" he blurted out, "I mean ... the human whores surround us on ever' side! Yeah, thass it—an' what they see is a lotta meat awna hoof! An' now that Von Rumpel knows how easy it is t'jes stroll right in here 'n blow somebody up—why, iss jesta mattera time afore he jawns up with the Klunder boys an' the Shitzelbergers an' all the ress, an' they all jes march right in here one day an' have theyselves a barbecue! Pause fer affeck—*no wait* ... Freedom Farm needs a strong, far-sided leader that unnerstans we ain never gaw be safe less'n we git a strong militia, an', an'... an' we ain never gaw have one-a them iffen we keep squanderizin' feed on wasteful social programs! Yeah, thass it!"

"BOO-GER! BOO-GER! BOO-GER!" the pigs chanted, "BOO-GER! BOO-GER! BOO-GER ...!"

"Well!" said Grover, as the din of porcine approval died away, "I guess we know who took *that* round! Boss Cock, would you care to rebut Freedom Farm's next chief executive?"

"You pigs can't be serious ..." said Cassius. "You really expect the voters to fall for this shit?"

"Boss Cock, I would remind you that the rules explicitly prohibit the use of foul language," said Grover, admonishing the cock before turning back to Booger. "Mr. Hawg, would you care to rebut your opponent's rebuttal?"

"My rebuttal ...?" said Cassius, his voice trailing off.

Once again, Booger cocked an ear and squinted—like he was trying to hear a faint voice from somewhere below.... "My 'ponent's a starryied idea list," he proclaimed after a moment. "Fact is, the voters'll fall fer anythin! Lookit all them signs in the yard—signs like 'Get Smart Wiff Brain-Grain'; I tried that stuff—din make me smart. Or like 'Miracle Milk for Lustrous Fur'; I tried that too—*still* don' have no fir. Or 'Lou-Ella's World Famous Nitpickin'; never heard of it 'fore Tuesday. Beastfolk'll fall fer anythin!"

"BOO-GER! BOO-GER! BOO-GER ...!"

"Point well-made," said Grover, "—well-made indeed! I knew this would be a lively debate. Alright, so... the next question would go to you, Boss Cock: How do you explain your cowardly inaction in the wake of Von Rumpel's brazen attack on Freedom Farm?"

"Who you callin' *cowardly*, pig?" Cassius fired back, puffing himself up.

"Boss Cock, I only meant that the *action*—or rather, the *lack* of any action—was cowardly," Grover clarified, "I didn't necessarily mean you *personally*. But let me rephrase the question, if I may: How do you explain ... how do you explain your *failure* to take swift, decisive action in the aftermath of Von Rumpel's brazen attack?"

"First off," said Cassius, "if it's not too much of a strain on your gray matter, think back to the night Polack's apartment blew up. You didn't hear beastfolk sayin', 'Oh shit, Von Rumpel just blew up Polack's apartment!'—and feel free to penalize me for salty language. What you heard them saying was, 'Oh shit, Polack's apartment just blew up!'—but nothin' about Von Rumpel. Not a word. The sentries didn't see anyone, nobody noticed any suspicious footprints—there was *nothing* to indicate any kind of human involvement. Everybody was sayin' it was probably some sorta freak lightning strike or somethin'. But you got one thing right: the situation called for swift, decisive action. There were two survivors—a smoldering monkey, and one charbroiled hog throwin' off enough fried bacon smell to get the hens hidin' their eggs. So what'd I do? I hopped up on Hector's back, got my hooks into his mane, and rode right down through Beaver Gorge to Falling Rock. And it was a hell of a ride, too—you should try it some time! And then I spent the better part of an hour heckling Silas Clusterberry into climbin' up on that horse and lettin' us haul his ass back up here in the dead of night to tend to those in need—and if that ain't swift, decisive action, I don't know what is!"

Grover gave Cassius a skeptical look, and then turned to Booger. "Mr. Hawg, would you care to respond?"

"I believe I would," said Booger, cocking an ear, "—jes lemme gather my thoughts here fer a minute ... lessee, now... um ... *My 'ponent's playin fasten loose with the facks!*—Yeah, thass what ... Um ... Polack *toad* ev'body it was Von Rumpel—said so all along. An' Pluto seen him too! No use pretendin it din happen that way...."

"BOO-GER! BOO-GER! BOO-GER! BOO-GER ...!"

"Alright now look," said Cassius, getting hot under the hackles, "I don't know who you think you're foolin' here, but facts are facts—and the fact is, it was a month at least before Polack came out with that story about Von Rumpel. And I don't count Polack a reliable source anyway...."

"Not to inject myself into the debate, Boss Cock," said Grover, injecting himself into the debate, "but given that Von Rumpel is, in fact, generally viewed as the culprit, the real question would seem to be: What evidence do you have that it *wasn't* Von Rumpel—that the survivors of the attack are either lying or delusional?"

"What evidence do I have that it *wasn't* Von Rumpel ...? Well, let's see—that'd be what the brainier among us call *memory*. As to whether the survivors are lying or delusional, I could only speculate—and since you pigs are better at that than I am, why don't *you* tell *me:* Are Polack and Pluto lying or are they delusional?"

A rumble of consternation arose from the Swine Mountains surrounding the dais. "You realize, of course," Grover cautioned, "that what you're suggesting opens you to charges of being out there on the fringe with, with ... *crackpots* and conspiracy theorists?"

"Only around the pigpen," said Cassius, "—not in the *real* world."

Grover just shook his head in feigned befuddlement and turned to Booger. "Did you have any thoughts, Mr. Hawg?"

"I think iss my *'ponent* thass either lyin' or that other thing he said ..." Booger responded, after pausing to "gather" his thoughts. "See, beastfolk need t'unnerstan, the so-called 'real world' is jesta buncha radicals and loonies that believe in *facks,* —and facks are *stupid!"*

"BOO-GER! BOO-GER! BOO-GER! BOO-GER ...!"

"An' you know what else?" said Booger, a mob of throbbing shadows backing him up, "My 'ponent had connubular relations with a *duck!"*

Squealing outrage erupted from the Swine Mountains: "GODLESS PERVERT ...!"

"FILTHY DUCK-DIDDLER ...!"

"INTERSPECIES ADVENTURIST ...!"

Booger was on a roll: "When *I'm* Boss Cridder, ain gaw be none-a them kinda tawdry goin's-awn inna office-a the cheap ezecutive if *I* got anythin t'say 'bout it—an' I will too, y'see, 'cause *I'll* be the cheap ezecutive! Heh-heh, heh-heh ..."

"BOO-GER! BOO-GER! BOO-GER! BOO-GER ...!"

"... An' I'll tell you what else: when I'm runnin' things, I ain gaw jes stan aroun an' let ourseffs be invaded by human beans! I gaw put together a kickass militia t'keep us safe from the human whores, so's if they ever try an' pull anythin' funny agin, why, we'll jes gim a taste-a they own menacin'!"

"BOO-GER! BOO-GER! BOO-GER!" roared the swine, "BOO-GER! BOO-GER! BOO-GER ...!"

The sheep looked at the pigs, and then looked at each other, and bleated: "BOO-GER! BOO-GER! BOO-GER ...!"

"Now maybe y'all are thinkin, 'Well Booger, tha' sounds mighty fine havin a clean-livin hawg fer Boss Cridder an' a big, strong militia t'keep us safe from the human whores an' all, but ain none-a that gaw happen lessen y'git yerseff 'lected —an' they's lottsa cridders don' vote fer swine.' Well, if thass what yer thinkin, I got news: the *Hawg Father* got my back! Thass right—the Sky Pig hisseff! Tol' me coupla weeks back, he said, 'Booger, I wancha t'be Boss Cridder real bad—so y'know what I gaw do? I gaw *fix* it!' Thass right, tol' me hisseff he gaw fix it. I mean, he din say it jus like that—got a special way-a talkin—but thass what he said. So even if yer fool enough t'vote awna wrong side-a Gawd, my victorious triumph inna comin 'lection is what y'might call a *four-gong* conclusion.... 'Notherwords, issa conclusion wif four gongs.... Can' do nothin 'bout it, 'notherwords."

"BOO-GER! BOO-GER! BOO-GER!" squealed the pigs, "BOO-GER! BOO-GER! BOO-GER ...!"

"BOO-GER! BOO-GER! BOO-GER!" bleated the sheep, "BOO-GER! BOO-GER! BOO-GER ...!"

For their part, the chickens just sat there.

Except the incumbent cock, that is. "Listen up, pigs!" said Cassius as the clamor was running out of steam, "If you're gonna be walkin' around on your hind legs all the time, maybe you oughtta learn to be standup hogs! You know, if you had said to me, 'Boss Cock, we'd sure be pleased if you came to a rally for your opponent, Booger Hawg, and let us whip up the crowd with a bunch of lies and make you look bad and all,' I might've come on down just for the hell of it—just to show

I'm a good sport. But this is *bullshit*—no offense to Commander Fritz."

"Point taken, Boss Cock, point taken," said Grover, "—I think it's fair to say we *all* got carried away there for a minute or two. So let's get back on track here, and turn to a subject of growing concern to the beastfolk of Freedom Farm: the *internal* threat posed by a ballooning public debt. Since you're largely to blame, Boss Cock, the next question is yours: Why would Freedom Farm's own Boss Critter want to drive it into bankruptcy?"

"Let's see—it's either 'cause I'm a dumb shit, or I'm just plain evil and for some reason I'm out to destroy Freedom Farm's way of life. It's one of those, right?"

"Well, you'll have to admit, Boss Cock, there aren't too many possibilities that make a whole lot of sense. I mean, how else do you explain your pet project, the EDPP—a program that's only done one thing well since its inception and that's push Freedom Farm further into debt? We all know that when the cost of carrying the debt exceeds the federation's ability to generate revenues, the game'll be over and the farm'll be broke —yet you've continued to champion this program throughout your term."

"I guess that nails it, then: I'm evil and I'm out to destroy Freedom Farm's way of life."

"Can you give us a more plausible explanation? I mean, help us understand this, Boss Cock...."

"I hate to break it to you, Hamhock, but you're behind the times," said Cassius. "You know where to find the public debt over there on the Wall?"

"I know roughly where it is," Grover answered carefully. "What's your point?"

"My point is that you haven't looked at that column lately or you'd know that it's been getting *shorter* ever since the Big Dog Tax kicked in."

"I don't see how that's possible," said Grover, "—but I'm sure your opponent would be happy to explain how raising taxes, in reality, *decreases* revenues. Mr. Hawg...?"

At that moment, a horrific squealing erupted from the rear of the barn: "E-E-E-E-E-E-E-E-E-E-E-E-E-E-E-E ...!"

With hundreds of civic-minded free beasts jamming the structure, it was practically inevitable that one of them would eventually step on the long-suffering Polack, who'd been lying in a back corner of the barn praying that he'd make it through the evening without getting stepped on. At this point, his hide brought to mind the cracked mud of a dry lake bed, and could best be characterized as a layer of articulated *cracklings*—and because the smallest movement created painful new fissures in his flash-fried epidermis, Polack spent his eternal days trying not to breath as he lay motionless in some remote part of the barn. But when the besotted Mrs. Cow trod on the unlucky hog, she did more than create a few new fissures: she punched a hole the size of a dinner plate in his flank—plunging him into an abyss of white-hot agony.

"E-E-E-E-E-E-E-E-E-E-E-E-E-E-E-E-E ...!"

"Oh, for pity's sake," said Grover, "Did someone step on Polack again? Alright, well—I guess we'll just have to raise our voices a little...."

"E-E-E-E-E-E-E-E-E-E-E-E-E-e-e-e-e-e-e-e-e-e ...!"

"*Ahem*—SO AS I WAS SAYING, MR. HAWG, PERHAPS YOU COULD EXPLAIN THAT HIGH TAXES DISCOURAGE PRODUCTION, WHICH IN TURN REDUCES BOTH INVENTORIES AND REVENUES...."

"EEEEEE ... EEEEEE ... E-E-E-E-E-E-E-E-E-E-E ...!"

At a loss in the sonic squall, Booger stole a nervous glance at the large knothole in the rear corner of the dais, his proximate ear grown to about twice its normal size.

"E-E-E-E-E-E-E-E-E-E-E-E-E-e-e-e-e-e-e-e-e-e ...!"

"YOU MIGHT ILLUSTRATE THE CONCEPT," Grover suggested, "BY NOTING THAT IF TAXES WERE A HUNDRED PERCENT, NO ONE WOULD HAVE ANY INCENTIVE TO PRODUCE ANYTHING, AND TAX RECEIPTS WOULD BE ZERO...."

"EEEEEE ... EEEEEE ... E-E-E-E-E-E-e-e-e-e-e ...!"

Booger remained focused on the knothole; he got down on all fours, turned, and cocked an ear to the aperture.

"EEEEEEE! EEEEEEE! EEEEEEE! EEEEEEE!"

"AND CONVERSELY," Grover continued, "IF TAXES WERE ZERO, THE FEDERATION'S ACCOUNT WOULD BE FLOODED WITH REVENUES BECAUSE ... AH ..."

"E-E-E-E-E-E-E-E-E-E-E-E-E-e-e-e-e-e-e-e-e ...!"

Booger flung off his hat in frustration and then, getting down on his forelegs, laid an ear directly over the knothole; his ass-end rose up like a thunderhead, threatening to split his overalls wide open.

"Don't move," said Cassius, "—that's just the way I want to remember you, pig...." Then he turned and exited left.

"E-E-E-E-E-E-E-E-E-E-E-E-E-e-e-e-e-e-e-e-e ...!"

Polack passed out shortly afterward, and a panel discussion ensued. The panel consisted of three pigs and one chicken. Sitting on the dais, from left to right, were Henrietta, Spencer Hamhock, Carlo Hawg, and Grover.

"So, any initial impressions?" said Grover.

"I thought our esteemed Boss Critter was a little defensive," said Spencer.

"I sensed that too," said Grover.

"Maybe that's because some of his more radical views were being dragged out into the open," Carlo theorized, "—a credit to the able officiating, I have to say."

"Thank you," said Grover, momentarily humbled.

"In all fairness," said Henrietta, "I think Boss Cock had to endure some very hurtful charges...."

"OH, THAT'S JUST TOO BAD!" said Spencer, "IF HE CAN'T TAKE A LITTLE CRITICISM WITHOUT SHRINKING AND COWERING, HE DOESN'T DESERVE TO BE BOSS CRITTER!"

"I wouldn't say he was shrinking and cowering," said

Henrietta.

"HE WAS SHRINKING AND COWERING!" Spencer insisted, "—WHICH IS EXACTLY WHAT SHRINKING, MINCING LITTLE COWARDS DO! DID HE RUN AWAY, OR WHAT?"

"Well ..."

"AND IF NOTHING ELSE," said Grover, popping off, "IT WAS DAMN RUDE THE WAY HE WALKED OUTTA HERE! I JUST FEEL SORRY FOR ALL THE GOOD CITI-ZENS WHO CAME HERE TONIGHT IN THE HOPE OF HEARING THEIR SO-CALLED 'LEADER' DISCUSS THE ISSUES OF CONCERN TO THEM IN A RESPONSIBLE, INFORMATIVE WAY—ONLY TO HAVE HIM TURN HIS BACK ON THEM AND WALK OUT!"

"THAT BIRD WAS ALWAYS A RUDE BASTARD," Carlo agreed, "BUT I THINK SPENCER HAS A POINT: THERE SEEMS TO BE THIS STREAK OF COWARDICE RUNNING THROUGH HIS PUBLIC PROFILE GOING RIGHT BACK TO THAT THREE-ROUNDER WITH ROCKY—HE SPENT THE WHOLE TIME RUNNING AWAY, IF YOU RECALL. MAYBE IF HE'D STOOD HIS GROUND AND PUT UP A FIGHT, HE MIGHT'VE WON THAT BOUT AND GONE ON TO A SUCCESSFUL CAREER IN THE RING INSTEAD OF INFLICTING HIS IMAGINED LEADERSHIP QUALI-TIES ON THE CITIZENS OF FREEDOM FARM...."

"Rocky was the one running away," Henrietta noted.

"STICK TO LAYING EGGS, LADY!" Spencer cautioned. "ROCKY CHASED HIS BIG CHICKEN ASS ALL OVER THE BARN!"

"OF COURSE HE DID," said the Chancellor, "—IT WAS SHAMEFUL! AND LET'S NOT FORGET HOW HE FLED THAT MEETING OF THE APPROPRIATIONS COMMIT-TEE THE DAY BUCKY CAME OUT OF THE CLOSET! I TELL YOU, SPENCE, RUNNING AWAY IS A RECURRING PATTERN WITH THIS BIRD! AND DON'T MISUNDER-STAND, I THINK EVERYONE'S ENTITLED TO HIS PEC-

CADILLOES—BUT DAMN IT, WHEN FREEDOM FARM FINDS ITSELF BEING ATTACKED BY HUMANS, I WANT A LEADER WHO'S GONNA STAND UP TO THE THREAT AND TAKE ACTION INSTEAD OF ADOPTING A POLICY OF CRAVEN DENIAL IN THE FUTILE HOPE THAT THE DANGER'S GONNA GO AWAY BY ITSELF. IT WON'T. AS BOOGER POINTED OUT, WE GOT A LOTTA MEAT ON THE HOOF HERE, AND SOME DAY THE HUMANS ARE GONNA COME FOR IT—IT'S JUST A MATTER OF TIME. AND I DON'T KNOW ABOUT YOU, BUT I DON'T WANT TO END UP HANGING FROM A MEAT HOOK IN VON RUMPEL'S ABATTOIR!"

"I think you're getting a little worked up," said Henrietta.

"THAT'S WHAT I LIKE ABOUT BOOGER ..." Grover enthused, "HE COMES ACROSS LIKE A SIMPLE, PLAIN-SPOKEN HOG—BUT HE GETS IT. HE SEES WE'RE IN TROUBLE, AND HE'S GOT A GOOD, FIRM GRASP ON WHAT NEEDS TO BE DONE...."

"OH, HE'S SMARTER THAN HE LETS ON," Carlo observed.

"SMART ENOUGH TO SEE WHAT CASSIUS WAS UP TO!" said Spencer.

"OH, YOU PICKED UP ON THAT TOO?" said Carlo, "YEAH—BOOGER SMELLED A RAT BEFORE ANY OF US...."

"What are you talking about?" said Henrietta.

"SOMEBODY WAS FEEDING THAT ROOSTER THE ANSWERS!" said Carlo.

"Oh, I really don't think ..."

"WHERE DO YOU SUPPOSE HE WAS GETTING ALL THOSE SNAPPY COMEBACKS FROM?" said Carlo, "—HE WAS GETTING HELP! IT FINALLY GOT SO BAD THAT BOOGER GOT DOWN ON HIS ALL-FOURS TO SUSS OUT WHAT WAS GOING ON!"

"AND THAT'S EXACTLY WHEN THAT BIRD HIGH-TAILED IT OUT OF HERE," said Spencer.

"OF COURSE ...!" said Carlo.

"SEE, THAT'S WHAT I MEAN ABOUT BOOGER," said Grover, in tones of wonder, "HE MIGHT SEEM LIKE JUST A 'GOOD OL' PIG,' BUT THERE ISN'T A LOT THAT GETS PAST HIM...."

"HE'S GOT YARD SMARTS," said Carlo.

"YOU CAN'T HELP BUT WONDER WHAT THINGS WOULD BE LIKE IF WE HAD SOMEBODY LIKE THAT RUNNIN' THINGS," Spencer mused, "—A RESPONSIBLE, CLEAR-EYED PIG WITH A HEAP OF BARNYARD SAVVY AND A MUSCULAR, FORWARD-LEANING POLICY PORT FOLIO INSTEAD OF SOME WACKY FOWL WHO NEVER MENTIONS GOD AND LIKES TO HANG WITH FRINGE GROUPS LIKE THESE CHICKEN WINGERS AND REAL WORLDERS ..."

"HEY, WHO ARE THESE 'REAL WORLDERS,' ANY-WAY?" said Grover.

"THEY'RE A RADICAL UNDERGROUND FACTION," said Spencer, "—A CFC SPLINTER GROUP, IF I'M NOT MISTAKEN. I DON'T KNOW TOO MUCH ABOUT THEM, EXCEPT THEY GOT THIS PATHOLOGICAL PREOCCU-PATION WITH FACTS AND SO-CALLED 'REALITY'."

"AND THIS IS THE SORT OF COMPANY OUR ES-TEEMED LEADER IS KEEPING ..." said Grover, shaking his head in disgust.

"I had a few thoughts I'd like to share ..." said Henrietta.

"AND DID YOU HEAR THE WAY HE DISPARAGED POLACK'S CREDIBILITY?" Spencer added, "—THE DEA-CON AT THE CHURCH OF THE SUFFERING SOW! CAN YOU IMAGINE ...?"

"WELL, WHAT CAN YOU EXPECT?" said Grover, "HE CALLED THE CHURCH A 'PIG PEN', DIDN'T HE?"

"CAN I JUST SAY, I FEAR FOR THE FEDERATION, I TRULY DO," said Carlo, "—AND I JUST HOPE TO HELL THE VOTERS APPRECIATE JUST HOW SERIOUS OUR SITUATION IS! THE LOOTING OF THE PUBLIC LARDER

PROCEEDS APACE, THE HUMAN ENEMY IS BEGINNING TO ATTACK, AND WE'VE GOT A PROFLIGATE CHIEF EXECUTIVE WITH SO LITTLE REGARD FOR SECURITY THAT HE PERSONALLY ESCORTED A HUMAN TO THE VERY HEART OF FREEDOM FARM!"

"YEAH, AND WHAT ABOUT THAT BUSINESS WITH THE DUCK ...?"

By the time the pig-heavy panel had completed its post-debate analysis, half the animals in the barn were thinking maybe it was time to put a hog in the top slot.

It was a victory the "Booger for Boss" campaign would build on, with Booger looking like the odds-on favorite as the solstice approached. But just to make sure, the PFP sponsored a marathon series of cockfights on Election Day, billing it as "Chicken Day at the Fights"—so-called because chickens drank for free. Needless to say, a lot of chickens didn't make it to the polls.

CHAPTER 25

Shortly after the elections—as Rip was enduring yet another in his ongoing series of Saturday night thrashings—Pluto was visiting with members of the Council in their little roped-off section of the barn. "What do you have to say for that brother of yours?" he snorted, setting down a bucket of corn liquor and squeezing in beside Spencer, the new minority leader.

The bout wasn't generating much excitement; the crowd had seen Rip get his ass kicked before, and the thrill was gone. Even Grover, who was officiating, couldn't work up much interest. The only one with any enthusiasm for the spectacle was Rip's opponent—who, as usual, was a young cock looking to make a name for himself by beating up on a geriatric legend.

Spencer stuck his head in the bucket and took a drink; then he sat up and braced himself against the fire in his gut. "I told him all along," he gasped, tears rolling down his snout, "I said, *Look*—you only got *two* constituents, and you never know what Madame Cow is gonna do, so make sure Fritz votes! But no—Election Day rolls around, and Fritz is out

237

there prowling the fence all day while Grover's at the fights getting stupid with you!"

"Hey, I can't be holding *everyone's* hand," said the monkey.

"Oh, I'm not blaming *you,*" said Spencer, "I lay it all at Grover's doorstep—it's *his* career. It just pisses me off, that's all. I mean, apart from the obvious fact that it just complicates things, he didn't have to do shit! He didn't have to make any appearances, he didn't have to make any speeches, he didn't have to spend so much as an ear of corn on advertising—all he had to do was drag Fritz over to the barn on Election Day!"

"It's probably just as well Fritz *didn't* vote," said Pluto, thinking out loud. "If he had, the Councilor for Cattle contest would've been a push—and that's probably all it'd take to precipitate a full-blown electoral crisis."

"Oh, wouldn't that be perfect?"

"You know," said the monkey thoughtfully, "it might at that...."

"Don't get me started."

"Yes, well—for the time being, we just have to get used to the idea that we have one less pig on the Council and one more chicken."

"*Technically* it's a problem," said Spencer, "but in reality, we're just talking about a bunch of hens. Plus Bucky ..."

"Same thing ..."

"Exactly," said Spencer. "And if you're thinking me and Emmet are gonna let a bunch of hens push us around, you need to get some rest—you're working too hard."

In addition to Grover losing his seat to a fat hen named Lucia, Gus—having retired from the Council in order to learn the family usury business from his father—was succeeded by his brother Emmet (or *cousin* Emmet, depending on how you look at it).

"It's good to know your heart's in the right place," said Pluto—and then, lowering his voice, "And if Myrtle and Petra start getting too independent, I'll just cut them off—I don't think either of them could go without a drink for more than a day or so."

"Of course, of course—pressure can always be brought to bear. We'll deal with it—we'll create *our own* reality. The important thing is, we finally got a pig at the bully pulpit."

"It's very gratifying," said Pluto, "And look, out of the kindness of my heart, I'll keep your brother busy officiating at these events so he doesn't have to go back to farming."

"Did you have to mention farming?" said Spencer.

"Actually," said Pluto, "I might just have some ideas for alleviating your erosion problem."

"Well, do me a favor and don't keep them to yourself," said Spencer. "I don't mind admitting, me and my brothers don't have the soil management skills of our dearly departed paterfamilias—and after last season's disaster, we're at a loss, we really are. I mean, how in the hell do you grow crops without topsoil?"

"You innovate, that's all," said Pluto, "—it's all you *can* do. Your family probably has as much acreage under cultivation as everyone else combined—you *can't* keep having crop failures; it'd be no good for you, no good for me—it'd be no good for Freedom Farm. Hamhock Downs is just too big to fail...."

"You won't get an argument from me," said Spencer.

"You know what you need to do first?" said Pluto, "You need to isolate the problem. Now, I don't pretend to have your father's gift for soil husbandry either—although I do think he'd have been wise to allow a portion of his fields to lie fallow each season. But now it appears your soil exhaustion problem is being compounded by a serious erosion problem: because the timber on the hillside above your property has been repurposed, there's nothing there to impede the run-off from rain and snowmelt. It just comes blasting down across your fields in torrents, and takes the topsoil along with it— just peels it right away. And the only way to prevent that from happening is to build a rock-lined levee at the base of the hill, and a series of flood control channels with sluice gates to meter the flow of water to your fields.

"Now, building up your topsoil again is a whole separate issue—and from everything I've been able to learn, it'd take generations to reconstitute a decent layer of loam. So over the short term, at least, the only solution would appear to be chemical fertilizers: nitrogen, phosphorous, and potassium, mainly. And having come to an understanding with Falling Rock's foremost agricultural supply house on my recent trade mission, I think it's safe to say the necessary materials can be made available."

"You don't understand—we probably got twenty, thirty percent *hardpan*. Thor couldn't even plow the stuff...."

"I'll have to come out to Hamhock Downs come spring and take another look," said Pluto, getting up. "By the way, did you ever rent Polack's old place?"

"Fuck no," said Spencer. "I mean, no reflection on you— you did a first rate job patching the place up. Unfortunately, beastfolk think it's *haunted*—and now the units on either side have been vacated too. Remember that buck and his girlfriend? They didn't care for that lingering bacon smell, so they moved out. And then those ducks on the other side gave notice last month—they said they could hear things at night. I told them *I* can hear things at night too—it just means your ears are working—but try talking to a duck...."

Spring thaw revealed that Spencer, if anything, had understated the damage done to his family's once-fertile fields. The erosion was ongoing, and runoff from the melting snowpack carried away many additional tons of topsoil—leaving bleak new vistas of rutted, naked clay hardening in the sun. Even where a layer of topsoil remained, it wasn't more than a few inches thick.

So galvanized was Pluto after inspecting the damage, in fact, that he scrambled directly over to Hawg Homestead on foot (being unable to find a taxi). He rousted Booger from his gated mud hole, dragged him down to the farmhouse, and had him interrupt a meeting of the Committee for the Development of Guidelines for the Naming of Liberated Bodies of Water in order to officially declare Hamhock Downs a disaster area.

This freed up enough emergency management feed to retain the hastily assembled Emergency Management Division of P. Baboon & Co., which wasted no time in heading up a fact-finding mission to Falling Rock's "foremost agricultural supply house." The fact-finding mission found that facts are stupid, confirming Booger's claim—but among the heaps of rusting, moldering debris behind the Falling Rock Trading Post, it also found a rusting, moldering 1957 John Deere tractor with a bent wheel spindle. Silas assured the animals the bent spindle was merely an esthetic flaw, and he claimed that when equipped with the proper accouterments the tractor was more than sufficient to break up the toughest hardpan, and worth every bit of 200-jugs of corn liquor—though he'd let it go for a hundred-fourteen. The weather-beaten old mule skinner—thinking the mandrill was toying with him—became alarmed when Pluto responded that 200-jugs of shine seemed like a perfectly reasonable price, and further, that he'd be willing to throw in an extra hundred for the "proper accouterments"; so the mynah explained that Pluto was putting together a *cost-plus* deal—and Silas and the monkey soon developed warm rapport.

But two obstacles remained: getting the taxpayer to pay for the tractor, and getting the tractor up through the gorge to Freedom Farm.

As Pluto learned when he bought that chainsaw, there was strenuous opposition to trade with humans for reasons of security, economics, and morality—so funding the purchase promised to be challenging. And compounding the cost problem was the obvious fact that the tractor would account for only a part of the overall price of rescuing Hamhock Downs: additional costs would include those for the rock-lined levee and flood control channels, along with the ongoing costs of fuel and fertilizer. And the fact that so much of the envisioned bailout would be paid for with corn liquor had little-appreciated implications—in particular the reality that corn liquor couldn't be produced with the kind of funny-feed that drove the market for housing: notwithstanding the scrawlings on the Wall, no feed was involved in constructing BeaverBilts —only trees; but in distilling spirits, the feed itself was consumed—which meant that a significant quantity of actual corn would vanish from the bins entirely without feeding (or intoxicating) a single free beast.

But again, the implications were little-appreciated—and the hogs would argue that if the cost of saving Hamhock Downs was large, the cost of *not* saving it was larger (while neglecting to note that the cost of not saving it would be borne mainly by the Hamhocks); they would argue that while the scheme would take a big bite out of the season's corn reserves, the feed would be an investment in *future* reserves (while neglecting to mention that the monkey would pocket the tractor's pink slip); and they would argue that while it might be immoral for animals to conduct business with humans, the prime contractor in question—Pluto—wasn't an animal. Furthermore, they would argue their case at the Saturday Night Fights, after the Council's CFC majority—united in its opposition to animal/human trade—was suitably stupefied. (And if they had to be roughed up a bit, all the better.)

As a strategic necessity, they would also neglect to mention the full scale of the plan until the tractor was bought and paid for.

Getting the tractor up through Beaver Gorge, by contrast, promised to be an unqualified ballbuster—and Pluto wasn't fool enough to attempt it himself. So he offered to pay Silas—who knew every inch of the way and was as tenacious as his mules—a 50% premium to deliver the tractor and its accessories, along with a drum of diesel, right to the federation's front gate. That brought the animals' down payment on their mechanized future—including fuel—to an even 500-jugs of shine, distilled and dispensed.

Recognizing the urgency of the situation, Silas agreed to deliver the tractor immediately upon receiving 20% of the promised spirits. But even as he led four of his mules down into the maelstrom of Beaver Gorge not long afterward—a hundred plastic jugs of shine slung over their backs—the odds of him ever getting a *tractor* back up through that rift in the mountains seemed a shade on the long side.

But the monkey—wasting no time obsessing over the odds—occupied himself with his manifold tasks: dishing out feed at the barn, milking the cow, running the Omnibeast through its circuit several times a day, tending to his various concerns at the mall—and, of course, distilling massive quantities of corn liquor.

He also began making appearances at Polack's erstwhile apartment as the "Mystic Oracle of Hamhock Arms." Just because beastfolk weren't inclined to *live* in a haunted stall, he reasoned, didn't mean they wouldn't pay for the morbid thrill of visiting one from time to time—and he was right, too. He did the place up in gypsy parlor retro, and promoted séances with ubiquitous signage reading: FRANKIE SPEAKS—and managed thereby to turn an un-rentable stall into a profitable enterprise. Sitting on a rug with the snow globe he'd mined from the farmhouse basement (a souvenir from the Klunders' trip to the Big City), he would contrive to make contact with the spirit of Frankie Hamhock on behalf of the crush of inquiring minds seeking answers from a dead pig.

"I can feel his presence," the monkey would mutter from beneath his cowl, "—yes, yes, he's here...." The only source of light would be a single flickering candle casting huge, quaking shadows. "It's cold on the other side," he would inform his clients, gazing into the contents of the globe as it swirled around the tiny form of a skiing beaver, "—so cold that his words freeze, and drift through the void like snow. Let us heed the flakes—let us divine Frankie's message. He's trying to tell us something, trying to warn us ... He says ... he says there's a great danger on the horizon. *What is it, Frankie—* what danger do you see?"

The danger Frankie saw from the Great Beyond didn't vary much from day to day, or client to client: "He says ..." the monkey would whisper after a dramatic pause, "he says *the humans are coming.*"

CHAPTER 26

But while Pluto wore many hats, for the time being none of the myriad tasks demanding his attentions was of greater consequence than managing the born-again swine freshly ensconced in the executive suite. It's true that with the election behind them, there was no need to keep Booger on quite so short a leash—and it helped that the hog's interest in governing didn't extend much beyond his enthusiasm for parading around the yard on the massive form of Commander Fritz; but the monkey was a hands-on manager, and he had no intention of letting his most valuable political asset go to waste. There were functions of the chief executive that called for mental acuity—like public addresses and press conferences—and if that meant crawling underneath a podium and serving as Booger's auxiliary brain, the monkey was prepared to do it. Even when nothing at all was required of the federation's top hog, Pluto felt it wise to closely monitor his activities (if only to keep him from inadvertently drowning in a water trough).

But as much trouble as he was, Booger had qualities the monkey found invaluable. He was arrogant and aggressive, which had a way of bringing other critters to heel, and could be left to his own devices when helping Spencer and Emmet ram the pigs' agenda down the chickens' throats at the Saturday Night Fights. (As Spencer suggested, when 50-pounds of chicken found itself backed-up against a wall by half-a-ton of hog, the balance of power had little to do with the actual headcount.) At the same time, his cerebral shortcomings were such that when it came to policymaking—or *any* activity that threatened to engage either of his neurons—Booger was only too happy to "delegate" broad responsibility to the family's simian asset (who, in turn, collected a substantial advisor's fee for his troubles). And because many of the federation's animals were no more inclined to piece together a thought than Boss Hawg, the public generally found this otherwise mean-spirited pig to be endearingly dim; he wasn't bright enough to dupe them, after all—at least, not on his own—so they trusted him.

And that was his finest attribute, as far as Pluto was concerned—for the monkey understood that the work of the administration, like any successful con, would have to be built on a foundation of *trust.*

Consequently, when Boss Hawg informed the public of his administration's initiative to cut the EDPP's rations by 50%, beastfolk figured, *Well, Booger's a good ol' pig—so it must be the best thing.* They hardly needed to be reminded of the human threat—although they were—and of the consequent need to divert all available resources to expanding the Militia. And when the administration moved to eliminate the same program's popular veterinary benefit, beastfolk reluctantly accepted the official explanation: the cost of the Hamhock Downs bailout—funded for the purpose of preventing critical shortages of feed—made the cut impossible to avoid. And when ramming through a whopping-big tax cut in the face of ballooning deficits, Booger explained (with some help from the wings) that cutting taxes was the fiscally responsible thing to do, as it would actually *increase* revenues—and an obligingly credulous public suspended its disbelief.

It should be noted, however, that this particular tax cut was a shade deeper than it was broad: the only one to get that whopping-big tax cut—or *any* tax cut—was Pluto. And because this surgically targeted cut amounted to a sum greater than the total taxes he *had* been paying, the monkey was left with a negative tax liability—so rather than paying taxes at tax time, he received a subsidy from the public bin. A substantial subsidy. Meanwhile, everyone else's tax bill actually went up slightly—but averaged-out over the entire taxpaying public (monkey included), it was nonetheless a statistical fact that the federation's *average taxpayer* got a modest cut. The measure was even styled "Relief for the Average Worker"—or "RAW."

As for the Hamhock Downs rescue effort, the chickens on the Council remained blissfully ignorant of the plan's full scope until Silas showed up with that ancient John Deere (some assembly required). At that point, the public was contractually on the hook for the tractor's full cost, and hopelessly committed to the rescue effort. So at the Saturday Night Fights—where most business of any consequence was now conducted—the CFC majority was apprised of a "sobering new study" by the Emergency Management Division of P. Baboon & Co.; not surprisingly, the study concluded that any effort to reclaim the eroded acreage at Hamhock Downs was doomed to failure without the attendant construction of a levee and flood control channels. The choice was simple, said the pigs: either write off the price of the tractor, or *double down.*

Sensing they were being railroaded, the incensed chickens asserted their right to postpone a final vote till the next *official* meeting of the Council—but it was just a pathetic attempt to save face. Whenever push came to shove, the CFC would peck and posture, but ultimately play dead—and this time was no different: at the Council's next official meeting, the chickens caved—claiming as usual that they were saving their five-to-three majority for when they "really needed it."

But the ballooning price of the Hamhock Downs disaster was more than matched by the cost of fortifying Freedom

Farm's already formidable militia. From its beginnings as an undisciplined, disorganized, ragtag assortment of farm animals, the Animals' Militia had grown in both size and sophistication—enhancing, in the process, the federation's security while simultaneously supplying much-needed jobs. But though the Militia's expansion had already accelerated with Fritz's appointment as its Commander—it being hard to say no to a mountain of bull—the Hawg (Baboon) administration demonstrated a missionary zeal in seeing that Fritz got everything he wanted, and more. What the beast-in-the-yard failed to appreciate, however, was that the additional security provided by the Militia's ongoing expansion was subject to the law of diminishing returns—and the point at which it began to look invincible was the point at which the Militia stopped securing the peace and started looking for a fight.

And Fritz was ready to rumble. Ever since the time Marla had jumped the fence and he'd managed to get a piece of Von Rumpel, Fritz had patrolled that stretch of fence obsessively in the hope of getting another shot at the old farmer—and in the wake of the Hamhock "assassination," he'd redoubled his efforts. Even on those occasions when Boss Hawg himself prevailed upon the bull for a ride around the yard, Fritz would usually end up walking the fence anyway.

One such instance unfolded typically enough on a hazy summer evening when Booger appeared in the yard with his entourage, and spotted the bull lapping up a gallon or two at the trough. Booger—ludicrous in overalls and straw hat as he did his bipedal-best to saunter—approached the massive Fritz. "How 'bout a ride, good buddy?" he suggested.

The bull lifted his muzzle from the water. "Whaddya got for *me*, Boss?" he muttered without turning. No one had ever mounted Fritz before Boss Hawg—but even Boss Hawg had to pay for the privilege.

"Whaddya need, ol' buddy? Name it ..."

"Need more eyes," said the bull, "—lots more. Can't be watching everything myself."

248

"I 'magine we can skeer up s'more pigeons," said Booger.

"A dozen, at least—and maybe a few sharp-eyed goats for the hillside."

Fritz would stoop for no beast, so as usual Booger was obliged to haul his fat, quivering ass up the loading ramp at the yard's Omnibeast stop and wait as the bull took another long draft, snorted, and then ambled on over to the ramp to be mounted.

"Awright, Commander, now we gaw jes parade aroun' the yard fer a while ..." said Booger, balancing himself precariously on the animal's mountainous withers. He waved to the admiring throngs as the bull made a perfunctory loop around the yard with the pig's preening entourage bringing up the rear—then took a hard right and headed for the Von Rumpel property line. "Um ... well, this is good too," said Booger.

It was a scene that had played itself out often enough—a fact which, in itself, accounted for much of the Militia's vigorous buildup during the Hawg (Baboon) administration. But on this particular occasion, Commander Fritz and his titular superior came upon the monkey himself after walking along the fence a ways. Shrouded in his hooded cloak and indistinct through the mist settling over the landscape, the Machiavellian mandrill resembled nothing so much as a huge vulture perched stock-still on the top rail of that split rail fence. His gravelly voice drifted from beneath his cowl in admiration: "Could all the forces of nature create a more powerful beast?"

"Now, now—jesta big fish in a little pond," said Booger with a wink.

The bull said nothing.

"Seen Von Rumpel lately?" said Pluto.

"Still keeping a low profile," said Fritz.

"You know," said the mandrill, "it occurs to me that in rehabilitating Hamhock Downs, we'll be bringing up shipments of fuel and fertilizer from Falling Rock on a regular basis—and as you're aware, you can't go from here to Falling Rock and back without going past Von Rumpel's place. Even if Silas agrees to keep delivering the stuff, the logistics of it still leave us in a vulnerable position."

"Can't we talk about the fights or somethin?" complained Booger as he slid down from Fritz's back.

"I'm afraid I have to interface with the Commander on a number of important issues," said the monkey.

"Yer in his face all the time ..." said a dejected Booger.

"It can't be helped," said Pluto, "—it's a security matter."

"Fine, fine," said Booger, "—me an' my pigs'll jes go awn up t'the mud hole...."

"And then there's the Liberty Creek incident," the monkey continued, as Boss Hawg wandered off with his collection of sycophant-swine.

"It's theft, plain and simple," said the bull.

In reality, the Liberty Creek incident wasn't theft so much as an unintended consequence of the Hamhock Downs rescue effort. Unable to stop himself once he'd gotten that tractor up and firing on all cylinders, the monkey plowed the Hamhocks' damaged acreage before even beginning work on a levee— confident that the worst of the spring rains had come and gone. Then the worst of the spring rains blew in and washed away so much of that freshly broken subsoil that it clogged Liberty Creek and diverted a whole section of the stream right into Von Rumpel's pasture.

"Even if you argue, as some have, that Von Rumpel didn't technically *steal* that section of our waterway," said the monkey, "I don't exactly see him giving it back."

"I say we *take* it back," said Fritz.

"Well, unfortunately, as long as you've got your naysayers undermining the public's resolve, it's a lot easier said than done. And forget about the Liberty Creek incident—we still have elements claiming that Von Rumpel had nothing to do with the Hamhock assassination."

"That's crazy talk," said the bull.

"Oh, we're talking about some fringe elements, no question—but they're highly vocal, and at this late date they make it very difficult to build the kind of support we'd need for an incursion. If I had my way, I'd throw every one of the scumbags in the pit."

"What if he attacks us again?"

"Now ...?" said the mandrill, "We'd walk all over him—and we'd do it with the full support of the public, too. But I think he *knows* that—I have no doubt he watches us as closely as we're watching him. He knows we have new leadership—muscular, *pigheaded* leadership —and he knows damn well he'd be a fool to take on the Animals' Militia. He'd really have to be provoked to attack us again...."

"Define 'provoked'."

Pluto offered the bull several definitions, and then the bull thought up a few of his own—and that very night, Von Rumpel was awakened when his water trough was overturned with a thunderous crash. Daylight found the farmer inspecting a breach in his fence—but apart from repairing the damage to his property, he took no action.

Then, at the quarter moon, Von Rumpel's chickens were jogged from their own dreams when the earth beneath the henhouse began to rumble and shake a couple moments before the entire coop erupted in a blast of splinters, feathers, and scrambled eggs as something the size of a small truck went crashing right through it. Once again Von Rumpel took no action, apart from affecting repairs; the ill-tempered old farmer had only two grown sons, and few friends—and as cantankerous as he was, he had no desire to tangle with an army of "demon-possessed beasts."

Refusing, however, to be pacified by pacifist strategies of non-engagement, Von Rumpel's tormentor stepped up the pressure with a midnight raid on the farmer's barn—crashing in through the north-side doors, and then exiting through the south. Two points worth noting: there hadn't previously been a doorway in the barn's south wall, and the perpetrator absconded with both the farmer's cows.

Other raids would follow.

Not coincidentally, your average free beast was oblivious to the ongoing travails of the reviled Von Rumpel—despite the public's growing concern over the "human threat." The topic of conversation at the time, more often than not, focused on the regrettable demise of Sumner Hawg, a maternal/paternal uncle of Booger's.

After a big night at the fights, Sumner had stumbled shit-faced to the cab stand, and decided to put Cushy Cab's reputation for "Cloud-like Comfort" to the test. Cushy was staffed exclusively with big wooly ewes—but though the ewe at the head of the queue certainly looked comfortable enough, she politely declined the fare, saying it took a horse to carry a hog. Swaying in the winds of intoxication, Sumner insisted he was capable of judging for himself who could carry him and who couldn't—and then proceeded to climb aboard. Staggering under the load, the ewe managed to carry the half-conscious hog as far as Liberty Creek without her legs buckling—and then lost her footing on the rocks and collapsed midstream; Sumner fell face-first in the water, flailed torpidly for a few moments, and drowned.

Ever the consummate opportunist, Pluto lost no time in launching a big push—in the name of public safety—to ban all forms of public transport not having 4-wheels. Working the bully pulpit to good effect, a closely managed Booger lent a folksy plausibility to the poignant proposition being peddled: that only in assuring the safety of the commuting public could the Hawg family find any solace in Sumner's untimely passing. But just to be sure the message was resonating in the right circles, Pluto quietly augmented Booger's efforts with sizable contributions to the campaign war chests of key representatives.

Naturally, the proposed ordinance would kill what was left of the taxi trade, so members of the CFC majority—champion of the bottom-feeding masses—made a noisy show of opposing the measure before sticking their tails in the air in the name of decorum and taking it up the ass. In approving the measure's passage into law, Boss Hawg pronounced the new ordinance a victory for free markets everywhere.

But if Pluto found inspiration in Sumner's final act—i.e., paying the ultimate price for that "Cushy" ride home—he was inspired by the hog's penultimate act as well. Before leaving the barn that night, Sumner broke the bank with a big bet on a longshot named Woody. Pluto had been making book for some time, and knowing his fighters as he did, he was skilled at working the odds for steady profits over the long haul. But over the short term his returns could be much more erratic, and on that fateful night, Woody secured the first (and only) win of his career when his opponent's leg cramped up—and Pluto had to tap his line of credit to cover his losses. It got the monkey to stroking his chin hairs and wondering if maybe there wasn't a way to take the risk out of the whole business of wagering.

Making book appealed to the monkey for the obvious reason that it allowed him to turn a profit without having to produce a single service or utility—and the way he figured it, you couldn't get more productive than that. (He'd been feeling the strain of his myriad obligations, so productivity had become a major concern.) But Sumner's big score that night inspired the monkey to give the short term variability aspect of playing the odds some extended brain time—and to that end, he examined various games of chance. Blackjack had obvious appeal, as it required only a deck of cards; unfortunately, Pluto could only work a single table by himself—and that would leave him just as vulnerable to short term losses as he was taking bets on cockfights. *Any* casino game, in fact, that could conceivably be adapted for play by farm animals suffered from the same drawback—and after wrestling with the problem at length, the monkey had all but given up when the solution came to him one night in a dream: a lottery.

CHAPTER 27

Pluto's lottery tickets went for a walnut each and promised the buyer a shot at winning a jackpot equaling 1000-bushels of corn—an amount that would grow with each drawing that left the grand prize unclaimed. There were smaller prizes as well: a peck of corn for a ticket bearing two consecutive digits of the winning number, and a full bushel for one with a 3-digit match—prizes awarded often enough to tease and titillate. But no one ever won the grand prize for the simple reason that each digit of the winning 4-digit number was determined by a ceremonious roll of a die—so it could never be greater than *six*—and Pluto only sold tickets with 4-digit numbers greater than 6666.

And that resolved the monkey's short term variability problem.

So, properly speaking, Pluto's foray into the wholesaling of risk wasn't so much a lottery as a scam—a popular scam, as it happened. There was no shortage of critters facing a difficult winter, and the hope of solving all one's problems for the price of a walnut fueled a healthy demand for tickets.

Your average farm animal wasn't real clever with numbers (obviously), but the *logic* of a winning strategy seemed plain enough: the more tickets one bought, the better one's chances of winning—and as long as there was that hope of winning, the prospect of winter didn't seem quite so bad.

Yet for Freedom Farm's "differently productive"—who *had* been empowered with subsistence levels of feed and were now gradually starving on half-rations—the prospect of the approaching snows was bad enough. Had they been productive in a more mainstream way, they might've been able to bootstrap themselves into the ranks of the working poor, say, or join the Militia during one of its many recruiting drives—but under the Hawg (Baboon) administration, the differently productive had to content themselves with panhandling and buying lottery tickets as they slowly expired.

And with the monkey consolidating his hold on the economic affairs of the federation, even the propertied classes were feeling the heat. Ulysses was never much of a farmer, but he and his family got by on revenue generated, in large part, from the sale of grazing rights. By steeply discounting access to his own pastureland, however, Pluto had driven the ram out of business and bought up the last of his holdings for kernels on the ear. At the same time, the monkey and his porcine agents in the public sector conspired to have the various cultivating implements employed by Stella and Thor privatized. Technically speaking, the plow, mower, and other implements were public property—though no one ever gave it much thought—and it was argued that if Mr. and Mrs. Horse wanted to keep using them in their pursuit of the "almighty bushel," they could bid on them in a fair public auction. And they did too, but they couldn't hope to outbid the monkey, who summarily relieved them of their livelihood—pledging cynically to make those horse-drawn "relics of a bygone age" the centerpiece of an envisioned agricultural museum (to be built at some later time).

With the mothballing of the traditional instruments of

tillage, Pluto Baboon and his sputtering John Deere became the only game in town when it came time to turn the soil. Even Thor was forced to swallow his pride and hire Pluto to plow his fields—although the experience sent the old draft horse into a 3-day bender at the Bucket of Fire. (The monkey got that horse coming and going.)

The situation would've been difficult in any case, but Thor—a master at contouring his furrows to the land's topography—could only watch in despair as the monkey and his mechanical horse ignored the topography entirely and desecrated his fields in a lunatic manner arising from the tractor's tendency to pull hard to the right. In order to get the tractor up through the gorge, you see, Silas had disassembled it—and then lost a rear wheel in a crevice; he managed to hunt up another one back in Falling Rock, but it was a different size —and fitted with those mismatched wheels, the tractor had a pronounced tendency to go in circles. So rather than fight it, Pluto adopted a singular style of plowing characterized by spiraling furrows—a rhapsody of nested curlicues when viewed from aloft.

Down on the ground, Thor was aghast.

Nor did Thor's humor improve any when—his fields having all been chewed-up in like fashion—he learned that Pluto's quoted price, which he'd taken to be a package price, was only the *per-acre* price. What it all added up to in the end was that Thor's farming days were over. Pluto's predatory pricing forced the horse to take out a loan to plant a crop that wouldn't cover his costs if it were cannabis. Swearing he'd never take a reaming like that again, Thor bid his fields an angry farewell and sold them off in a fit of disgust—sold them to Pluto at fire-sale prices.

To his credit, Thor had the presence of mind to hold onto his pasture—and that being the case, he might almost have retired at that point and called it a life. But a horse doesn't live by grass alone—not even an *old* horse—and Thor and Stella had recently mortgaged a large BeaverBilt in Hawg Homestead. Prices just kept going up, after all, and they wanted to have something "to leave the kids." Along with the newly-landless sheep clan, however, the Horse family became almost entirely reliant on the taxi trade for its meager income—and once the lot of them was banned from the public byways for insufficient wheelage, they were left with a stark choice: a life of privation, or a life of crime. Panhandling was beneath the horses' dignity, and generally outside the skill set of sheep—so with the scent of autumn in the air, sightings of bandit taxis (heads down, cutting across fields to escape detection) served as an irksome reminder to the proprietor of the Omnibeast that his market penetration was less than total.

Yet in truth, the first instance of civic dysfunction probably occurred when the Hamhocks' turnip patch was raided. Then, not long afterward, the apple barrel was gnawed into and plundered by a gang of beavers—and *then* you started seeing bandit taxis snagging fares in the yard; but by then, a full-blown crime wave was underway. The phenomenon was new to Freedom Farm. In the past, a misdeed such as theft—on those rare occasions when it occurred—was dealt with effectively enough by the federation's constable, a goat named Horace, who would generally give the culprit a stern talking-to and arrange for reparations of one kind or another. But Horace, a career bureaucrat with a stall in the Office of the Executive, had been appointed at a time when Freedom Farm was like a big, quasi-functional family in which bad behavior was largely kept in check by a critter's natural reluctance to incur the community's umbrage—a reluctance enforced by the complete lack of anonymity. Problems were minor and easily resolved, so the constable's role was essentially that of a mediator—a *facilitator* of justice. At this point, however, the federation was populated with free beasts by the thousand—and because transgressing against strangers was increasingly more doable than finding gainful employment, Horace found himself overloaded with casework. But when he requested additional facilitators to help facilitate the workload, he was informed that the whole business of facilitation was the province of appeasers, sodomites and socialists, and would be superseded immediately by a policy of *enforcement*. In keeping with this new policy, the Office of the Constable was unceremoniously dissolved—swept into the dustbin of history. The old goat's stall in the executive suite was taken over by Sluggo, Freedom Farm's first Enforcer General, who immediately assembled a gang of deputies comprised entirely of veterans of the 1st and 2nd Boar Brigades of the Animals' Militia.

Being of mixed pedigree like most working class boars, Sluggo and his deputies were excellent examples of "hybrid vigor": they were big, sturdy hogs with impressive tusk development—and well suited, therefore, to the task of enforcement. Eager to get to it, they went right out and worked-over half-a-dozen ewes their first day on the job—a public relations setback, it turned out, for the newly formed Department of Enforcement. Sluggo tried to claim that he and his deputies were vigorously enforcing the ban on transporting passengers for profit without sufficient wheelage—but amid charges of profiling and brutality, he was forced to admit that none of the ewes had been observed in any proscribed activities at the time of the beatings, and further, that he was unclear as to the prescribed penalty for the presumed infraction in any case, but assumed a good beating would suffice. It turned out there *was* no penalty for transporting passengers for profit without sufficient wheelage (and certainly none for *not* transporting passengers for profit without sufficient wheelage); the vaguely-worded ordinance instituting the ban neglected to specify any penalties.

The incident threatened to expose the administration's law-and-order credentials for the sham they were. Without a coherent body of laws to enforce—and the federation's tangle of contradictory ordinances didn't qualify—the Department of Enforcement was nothing more than window dressing, a clumsy attempt at image management. The CFC—fueled by public outrage—demanded the creation of a comprehensive penal code, along with procedural guidelines for enforcing it. The pigs and their simian asset—hoping to get out in front of events—released a statement saying a penal code was pointless without a judicial body to adjudicate it, and proposed the creation of Freedom Farm's first court of law as part of a new law-and-order initiative. With Election Day on the horizon, the whole thing turned into something of a political firestorm.

The creation of a court was the easy part—though you wouldn't have known it for all the hype. The predictably-named "Freedom Court" took the form of a tribunal—consisting of the majority- and minority leaders, together with the Boss Critter—which would meet periodically to determine the guilt or innocence of the accused, as well as the nature and magnitude of any penalties.

By contrast, cobbling together even the rudiments of a penal code before Election Day was a tall order. But with the monkey and his agents shepherding the process along, the Committee for Cobbling Together the Rudiments of a Penal Code Before Election Day—which is what the Council called itself when it met in the solarium—began by compiling a schedule of fines to be levied against perpetrators of various crimes and infractions. It was a mind-numbing but practical beginning to the problem of contriving penalties for law-breakers: fines were easy to formulate and easy to administer—a mere debit entry on the Wall of Accounts—and despite being suitably punitive, didn't appear to violate any of the Six Rights.

But when it came to more serious crimes, it was instructive to see just how imaginative some chickens, a few pigs, and a monkey could get. One of the more significant products of their imaginations was the idea of incarcerating violators in direct violation of their right to range—an idea that would've been heresy in less anxious times. But the citizenry was much alarmed by the scourge of crime—a sure sign the social order was unraveling, according to some—and it was argued that a policy of enforcement would be a lot easier to implement if freedom were thought of more as a ... *privilege* than a right. Before the Uprising, it was noted, no one questioned that a breeding male was *privileged* to be able to live his life, year after year, heedless of the chopping block; yet on Freedom Farm, the liberty to live a full span of years was just one of *many* privileges enjoyed by all. No one could deny that of all the valley's farm animals, only the beasts of Freedom Farm—the *privileged few*—were at liberty to range freely, to speak their minds, to keep their children, and so on; the proposition that freedom was a privilege seemed so utterly self-evident that the Council—in what was seen as a refinement of Freedom Farm's founding principles—amended the Six Rights such that they became the *Six Privileges.*

And unlike rights—which were always associated with words like "inviolable" and "inalienable"—privileges could more easily be revoked (which just goes to show what a name change can do).

But having imagined the incarceration of scofflaws, the Committee was obliged to conjure up a detention facility in which to incarcerate them. There was the corral, of course, but the gate had long since been removed—and anyway, it wouldn't have held any of my winged cousins, or even the smaller quadrupeds, by and large. For the same reasons, the pigpen—had it in fact been a pigpen and not the Church of the Suffering Sow—was equally deficient. But just as it appeared the only solution was to award P. Baboon & Co. a contract to *build* a facility, someone suggested the pit—the very hole in which Pluto himself had been detained. For most of the animals, it'd be near-impossible to escape the pit unaided—even for the majority of Freedom Farm's fat, flabby fowl (and it'd be easy enough to clip the wings of the few that could manage it).

The idea of using the pit as a detention facility captured the Committee's fancy. It offered innumerable possibilities for correcting criminal behavior—and the progressively-minded side of the table insisted the goal of incarceration be *correction*. For moderately serious crimes, for example, miscreants could be lowered into the pit for relatively short periods of incarceration determined on a case-by-case basis. Those convicted of more serious offenses could, in addition to being sentenced to longer terms, be *dropped* into the pit from a height determined by the severity of the crime. (Dropping a horse from a height of 10-feet or so would certainly correct such frivolous acts as prancing, loping, and trotting about.)

Ironically, the level of severity assigned to various offenses —from minor infraction to heinous crime against nature— seemed to reflect a certain "real worlder" influence: under the new code, stealing a walnut or laughing at Boss Hawg were serious offenses—"gateway crimes" warranting the harshest penalties—whereas pilfering a thousand bushels of millet or slaughtering a hundred free beasts were mere infractions.

But despite the time-consuming nature of the task, the Committee for Cobbling Together the Rudiments of a Penal Code Before Election Day succeeded in doing exactly that— and Boss Hawg talked like it was all his doing: "I toad jew the Hawg Menstruation was a lawn order menstruation, an' I weren't jes talkin," said Booger—the vision of rustic authenticity in his sodbuster getup as he addressed a gathering on the eve of the election. It was a gray day with a foot of old snow on the ground, and he spoke from an overturned washtub at the edge of the pit—his words drifting off in little puffs of vapor. "Unner my leadership, my menstruation done put together a lil somethin called the Department of Enforcement —I mean, Department of *Empathy*. Heh-heh, heh-heh—had t'change the name—heh-heh, heh-heh. Anyways, we come up with this here Department of Empathy, see, an' then we put together the Freedom Court, an' we even cooked up whass called a *penal code*—an' that ain't got nuttin t'do wit yer poker, stud, so jes get that right outta yer head. What a penal code is, y'see, is a buncha *escuses*—a whole heap of 'em. That way, the nex time my pigs go an' hurt somebody, they'll have a good escuse. Then, after they empathize the tar out of him, they'll haul his ass off t'Freedom Court an' sentence him to a stretch in the Freedom Pit—which is what we gaw call this hole from now awn. An' jes t'prove all this lawn order talk ain't jesta lotta talk, we gaw show you zackly what happens to evil-doers unner a lawn order menstruation."

Pluto had been working overtime on a jib crane of sorts—a rig for lowering convicted critters into the Pit (and, presumably, for raising them back out again when they'd done their time). It was an essential part of the enforcement infrastructure, and the administration wanted to showcase its accomplishments by publicly incarcerating the Freedom Pit's first inmate. Strategically located on the far side of the quarry where it could be viewed by all, Pluto's contraption had the distinctive deconstructivist character of all his creations—so much so that it almost appeared to be a growth of some sort, clinging to the rocky edge of the Pit like some gnarly old, wind-blown cypress. A tangle of mismatched members formed a superstructure supporting a twisted timber that stretched out over the Pit; mounted to its end was a pulley from which a greasy cable dangled, and dangling from the cable was a sling fashioned from the hammock that once hung in the orchard.

The mandrill—like a hunched executioner in his cowl—stood in the snow beside his rig and prepared to complete the certification phase of his latest government contract by successfully lowering a "dangerous, medium-sized critter" into the Pit. The pig patrol stood in a semicircle behind him; before him stood a luckless ewe convicted of pig-on-ewe sex (the pig copped a plea). Such kinky goings-on had been going on sporadically among consenting farm animals for as long as anyone could remember, but it was proscribed behavior under the "Heinous Crimes Against Nature" section of the new code—and deserving of a commensurately harsh penalty: 19-years in the Pit, to be exact—augmented by an 11-foot plummet. After gaffing the dangling sling, Pluto looped it under the shivering animal, brought it back up—balancing himself on a milking stool—and secured it with a slipknot. Thirty seconds later, the monkey actuated the winch on his tractor—which sat about 10-feet back from the jib—and the cable pulled taut; the ewe's scrambling feet left the ground, and the critter swung out over the Pit. So frantically did she thrash about as she dangled above that gaping hole, however, that the slipknot slipped and the ewe plummeted before the monkey could lower it to the pre-scribed height.

The crowd gasped.

It was probably a 30-foot drop to the snow-covered rocks below—and after bouncing once, the ewe lay still. "Uh-oh," said Booger, "we gaw hafta charge extra fer that one! Heh-heh, heh-heh ..." Then a thin bleating arose from the broken animal, and the hog rolled his eyes as he worked a wad of tobacco in his cheek. "Oh, boo-hoo—ever'body git out yer hankies! Dang, would jew jes listen t'all that whimperin an' whinin an' carryin awn? Pluto got throwed in the Pit jes like that—an' he was all tied up! Shee-it...!" He spat a black glob in the snow. "Anyways, the dirty liddle pervert deserves ever'-thing she gets as far as I'm concerned!"

The ewe eventually succumbed to her injuries.

It was a shabby performance by any standard—but by and large, beastfolk seemed oblivious to the shabby details. They told themselves the ewe wouldn't have survived her 19-year sentence anyway, and they seized on Booger's claim that only "tough enforcement" would keep them safe from the scourge of crime.

And so, having burnished their law-and-order credentials, officials of the Hawg (Baboon) administration went to the straw that night confident of victory over their CFC challenger, the dementia-addled Ulysses. (The old ram needed the job in a big way, and the CFC needed a candidate that wasn't a chicken.) But just to be on the safe side, the administration farmed out the task of counting up the following day's votes to the Election Technologies Division of P. Baboon & Co.

Not long after Booger secured a second term, a bleary-eyed Fatback—afflicted increasingly with insomnia—stirred noisily from his bed in the dead of night, squirmed into his mud-encrusted greatcoat, and went out to survey the full moon. That glowing celestial presence was an old friend to Fatback —and the way it lit up the snow-covered landscape, it could almost have been mid-afternoon. As it drifted toward the horizon, the moon grew to immense proportions, and Fatback —drawn to it like a moth—ambled through the Hamhocks' unattended gate and out into the family's pasture.

No less bleary-eyed than Fatback, but compelled to stick my beak into every little thing, I decided to tag along and see what was what. I caught up with the old swine maybe a hundred yards from Von Rumpel's split-rail fence; I circled, and was about to put down my skids when I saw something move. Fatback saw it too—but as he squinted at the snowdrift where a flicker of motion had turned his head, he could only guess at what was behind it. For all he knew, it was just a field mouse that had caught his eye as it hopped over the crest of that drift —and not the tip of a gray wolf's ear as it ducked down into a crouch.

But from *my* vantage point, that big gray wolf was as plain to see as the fact that Fatback had strayed way too far from the safety of the hog house. The wolf lowered its ears and slowly raised its head for another look at the walking feast on the far side of the drift; Fatback locked eyes with the animal, and the vapor billowing from his snout stopped dead. He must've known right then and there his bacon was fried, and there was nothing in the wide world he could do about it. He was a big, powerful hog, it's true, but having had his balls lopped off as a piglet, he'd never developed the sort of fearsome tusks flaunted by the boars of the pig patrol—and he had no hope of outrunning a wolf, even on all fours. So he prayed. He just looked up at that ghostly immensity hovering above the horizon and prayed to the Holy Hog Father:

"Oh Lord ... oh Lord ... I don't know what your plan is, but I have to say, I was sorta hopin' for a more peaceful end —no disrespect, Your Hogness. I just mean, if, if—if there's any way you could fix it so's you don't have to take me right here and now in this awful way... I mean, if you could just afflict this here beast with the teensiest bout of indigestion, say —just long enough for me to make a few tracks—I'd be grateful till my dying ... I mean, I'd do anything ... I mean ..." His voice trailed off as he stole another glance at those burning, hungry eyes; then, as the wolf rose into full view, he implored the moon with renewed intensity: "Oh Lord, please—*please.* I've done your work all my days, you know I have, and I ain't never asked for much—and I done it all on faith, too! I never once asked for any kind of proof, did I? But Your Hogness, I have to say, right about now I sure could use a sign—just a little *somethin'* so's I know I ain't all alone here...."

Head held low, the wolf—carefully testing the snow's crust with each step—picked its way over the top of the drift and advanced on its prey in torturous slow-motion. Had Fatback turned and run, the wolf would've been on him in an instant, but the hog was rooted to the spot—and the wolf paused from moment to moment to raise its snout for a clue. The distance between the two was only a dozen feet or so, but the wolf didn't trust its eyes; here was an oddity the likes of which it'd never seen: a creature that looked like a hog, stood like a man, and talked to the moon—and featured a gigantic gut hanging out of an incongruous, ill-fitting greatcoat.

But then the wolf caught the unmistakable scent of hog flesh, and bared its fangs.

Fatback's pleas had gone unanswered, and the wolf— having closed to within striking distance—set its feet and drew into a crouch. "Alright you evil, murderous bastard!" roared Fatback with uncharacteristic rage, "I guess it's just you and me then...." In a single sweeping motion remarkable for its speed and precision, he shrugged off his coat and flung it at the wolf—then took a step and threw his entire 500-some pounds on the startled beast. The wolf dodged the unexpected attack a moment late, and yelped in pain as the hog landed on its hindquarters. Limping slightly, the wolf circled at a safe distance—momentarily confused by this odd turn of events. But Lord Gastric is a powerful motivator, and as Fatback struggled to regain his upright posture, the wolf—in the midst of an uncertain lope—saw an opening and leapt for the throat. Fatback rolled a shoulder into the attack—then squealed with pain as the wolf laid it open. Blood spattered the snow—and as Fatback turned reflexively to lick his wound, his throat made an easy target; the wolf's jaws found their mark, and the next moment Fatback was staggering around with his throat spraying blood like an Oklahoma gusher in the moonlight—creating a great, grisly Rorschach on the snow. Squealing and gurgling and gushing, the hog lumbered this way and that—but didn't go down. He'd have bled out sooner than later, obviously, but hunger had left the wolf with a deficit of patience. Its fur glistening with gore, the animal circled around behind Fatback—ducking and dodging as it zeroed in on its lurching target; then it lunged, buried its fangs and dug in its heels in a sliver of an instant—and hamstrung the hog. And that brought him down.

But as the wolf went about disemboweling the thrashing, dying Fatback, it was oblivious to the dark form closing swiftly from the rear—and moments later, the wolf was hurtling through the air, grievously gored. By the time it landed, the wolf had clearly lost its appetite—and with a rampaging show of violence, Fritz made sure the animal never regained it.

Presently, Pluto's cloaked form came loping up. (If there were others awakened by the incident, they were loath to venture from their beds and roosts.) The bull offered a string of angry excuses for why he hadn't been able to save the reverend Fatback, whose remains lay nearby—but Pluto was more interested in the wolf. He rolled the animal's mutilated carcass on its back and examined its belly; amid the gore and rent flesh, a double row of swollen spigots was clearly visible in the moonlight. Before turning his attention to the wolf's tracks, the monkey reassured the bull. "History will show that you played a vital role here tonight," he said, "—but history is written by the victors, and we have a battle to win."

CHAPTER 28

The opening chapter of Operation Kick Human Ass would take a little thought, but in the meantime, Pluto wanted to give the free beasts of Freedom Farm a little something to chew on. Before Fatback was even cold, the monkey retrieved some logging chain from the tool shed, fired up his John Deere, and hauled the hog's mutilated carcass in from the Hamhocks' pasture—and left it in the middle of the yard. Then he rousted Sluggo from his stall in the Boss Critter's suite—Boss Hawg, as usual, was at the family compound—and had him post a security detail at the carcass to keep it from being covered over. (Beastfolk began covering the dead almost reflexively—though family and friends of the deceased generally removed their remains to the meadow first.)

Pluto knew the shock of seeing this beloved hog's mauled carcass lying exposed under the open sky—right in the middle of the barnyard—was the sort of persuasion no amount of feed could buy. And certainly, beastfolk were persuaded that something was horribly wrong as they began to gather in the yard for their morning feeding—and they were all the more alarmed that there was no explanation to be had: when the guards posted at the grisly exhibit were questioned, they went into robo-hog mode and pretended not to hear. Pluto was equally closed-mouth as he served up feed—saying only that security considerations prevented him from discussing the matter.

The crowds came and went, and beastfolk gave that dreaded thing in the yard a wide berth—but their anxiety consumed them; rumors sprang up, fed by deftly-leaked scare-talk—and the free beasts of Freedom Farm grew senseless with fear.

Finally, with the public verging on hysteria, the administration preempted the Saturday Night Fights with an address to the commonwealth—or at least to that portion of it represented by a barn full of besotted cockfight enthusiasts. "My fellow free beasts an' fight fans ..." said Booger, addressing the crowd from a predictably lofty podium; as always, he was sporting the common pig look, and—signaling the gravity of the occasion—Fritz and Sluggo sat on the floor on either side of him. "Thuther night, the Revren Fatback was brooly murdered in the Hamhocks' pasture," he told the crowd when all the squawks and squeals of ovation had subsided, "—'magine y'all have seen his carcass outside. Ain pretty, I know. It was that rat-bastard Von Rumpel that done it—come right in here in fragrant violation of our ... of our ... 'notherwords, he was *tresspassin,* is what! Got hisself a packa them rot-wilders—big, bad howns, hoe pack of 'em! Been breedin 'em in secret down in his cellar—Polack done filled us in awn all the details. An' them two cows of Von Rumpel's ...? Tol' me theyselves they never seen any such goins-awn—which is proof *right there* he messin 'round in secret! Jes gotta think about it a minute. Anyways, what they done t'Fatback was jesta lil practice run, see ...?" A thumping was heard from the base of the pulpit. "Oh ... an' lemme jes say, if it weren't fer the heroic efforts of Commander Fritz, here—why, Fatback woulda looked a hoe lot worse than he do, believe you me! Heh-heh, heh-heh ...

"But the thing of it is, now that Von Rumpel sees what killer howns he got, he gaw breed hunnerts of 'em—an' he got them special fast-breedin howns, too! Breeder howns, they call 'em. Six munts, an' he'll have a whole army-a howns—nuff t'come right in here an' rip us *all* t'pieces! Thass what he figgers awn doin, see, 'cause he don' figger critters like us oughtta be diggin up the groun' an' cuttin down trees an' the like—bein' free, 'notherwords. An' he sees all our land an' our bouny an' especially all our fat, fleshy asses waddlin around, an' he figgers iss all *his* fer the takin—jesta matter-a time. An' I hate t'say it folks, but we do have a problem here—fact is, we in a heap-a trouble! Ain no way t'candy coat it...."

A clamor of alarm arose from the crowd. "Hode on now, hode on," said Booger, cutting it short, "—I din say we gaw jes sit aroun an' do nothin like the las' menstruation! If they had took action the firss time Von Rumpel attacked, why, ol' Fatback'd still be around! But see, the chickens ain runnin things no more—the *pigs* are in charge now; an' we gaw run Von Rumpel an' his murderous pack-a varmints right outta Toad Valley!" A thunderous ovation of animal noises shook the barn, and Booger—framed by his own dancing shadow in the lantern light—waited for it to subside before continuing. "But here's the deal, folks: we ain gaw win this thing lessin ever'body gits behind us—thass right, thass right. So from now awn, y'all gotta believe ever'thing we say, y'unnerstan? 'Notherwords, we say somethin—*gotta believe it.* Cause iffen y'start askin funny questions an' stickin yer nose where it don' belong, then we'll know yer a Von Rumpel synthesizer, fer all tents an' purposes—an' we'll throw yer ass in the Freedom Pit! So jes go awn about yer bidness, do what yer toad, watch what y'say—an' we'll take care-a the *big* stuff." From beneath Booger's feet came an urgent thumping. "Oops—almos fergot the mos important part! Bess thing y'kin do right now is start hittin the ol' feed bin real hard: git awn over t'the mall an' buy the missus some flowers, or git yerself a massage, or whatever—jes blow some feed somehow, even if y'gotta do it awn credit! Thass right! They gaw have some big sales in the nex few days, believe you me—an' you'll feel a hoe lot better after y'snag a few-a them 'Fatback Fat Buys' they got goin'. Thass right—jes look fer the yeller signs...."

The civic-minded hordes did the responsible thing and flocked to the mall. Aside from keeping the monkey flush, it served to keep Otis Everybeast's mind off "funny questions" arising from certain curious facts—like the fact that nighttime security patrols had been discontinued some time prior to the attack, or the equally curious fact that no one had seen the remains of the three exterminated rottweilers.

Polack, meanwhile, did his part in keeping the public mind churning along productive lines. "We gather here today to remember brother Fatback on the occasion of his passing," the hog wheezed to an overflow crowd at the Church of the Suffering Sow, "—a simple task, perhaps, given that he was a memorable old swine. And then too, his publicly displayed carcass is a powerful mnemonic device...." Polack had been carried in on a litter and propped up before the congregation —defiantly naked, except for the grubby bits of gauze that still clung to his shattered, blood-caked hide. He spoke carefully, not wanting to crack his face. "But long before the Council, in its vanishingly finite wisdom, endeavored to legislate charity, brother Fatback was helping the poor and the hungry—while living in poverty himself; long before there was a Church of the Suffering Sow, brother Fatback was ministering to his flock—while burdening no one with his own troubles; and long before there was even a Freedom Farm—before most of your parents were born—Fatback dreamed of freedom. So remembering a larger-than-life swine like brother Fatback is easy enough, Lord knows; the part we gotta be real conscientious about—the thing we all gotta *dedicate* ourselves to—is remembering *why* his pitiful, torn-up carcass is lyin' out there in the first place! It all goes back to the Wallow—you heard me, the original Wallow—where the mud was always cool, the slop was always sweet, and life was a never-ending delight.

That's where Boar listened to the mentally-challenged Sow and ate from the hand of Man—and we've been paying the price ever since! And it ain't like we weren't warned; as the Hog Father told us in the very beginning—and I quote: 'Yea, though the hand of Man giveth, it taketh away more. It giveth swill, verily—but it taketh thy flesh and maketh pork chops and bacon and ham; it taketh thy hides and maketh boots and bridles and belts; it taketh thy feet and maketh pickled pigs' feet, it taketh thy brains and maketh headcheese, it taketh thy bristles and maketh brushes of every kind—it taketh thy ears and thy snouts and thy tails and thy entrails and everything else it can't figure out what to do with and maketh sausage; sometimes, it taketh thee whole and putteth an apple in thy mouth and maketh of thee a feast; henceforth, let it be known to swine the land over that whosoever taketh from the hand of Man condemneth a thousand generations to bondage....'

"That's right, children, a thousand generations of oppression, murder and exploitation—the price of feeding from the hand of Man! But though the time of our condemnation has come and gone, the human hordes cannot abide our liberation; they long to pen us up, to fatten us up, to *eat* us up—to return to the dark days of yore—and as surely as night follows day, Liberty Creek will run crimson with the blood of both man and beast before the human scourge has been driven from the land! The hour is upon us, children—the merchants of death are massing at the gate! The hour is upon us ...!"

A handsome negative tax was levied on the Church of the Suffering Sow for its support of the administration's policy of "anxiety enhancement."

For their part, the big dawgs grappled with "the big stuff" behind closed doors. Freedom Farm had never attacked one of its neighbors before, and there was much to consider—not the least being battle strategy. Commander Fritz, who was actually too big to *fit* behind closed doors, plotted strategy with his lieutenants at the gazebo (which he'd appropriated from the Appropriations Committee). The objective of the assault would be precisely the one enunciated by the BC: To drive farmer Von Rumpel and his family right out of Toad Valley. Since Beaver Gorge was the *only* way out of the valley, and the mouth of the gorge was a scant half-mile from the Von Rumpel's front gate, achieving that objective appeared to be a simple matter of closing off Toad Valley Road above and below the family's property—blocking two of three possible escape routes—and then driving the lot of them off the plot and into the gorge. End of story.

Others, however, worried about the aftermath. Once the Von Rumpels had been run off their land, they wondered, what would become of their livestock? Who'd be responsible for the critters—who would feed them? Dodger the duck, the freshmen Councilor for Ducks, observed during an alcohol-enabled discussion at the fights that every one of those animals would be jobless, and would need to be kept fed until gainfully employed—and Freedom Farm already had hundreds of its own "differently productive" slowly starving on half-rations.

In response to Dodger's point, Spencer—who was now a lobbyist for P. Baboon & Co.—explained caustically that Von Rumpel was an able farmer and would therefore have sufficient feed put up to support his livestock well into spring. "Those animals won't cost us a single ear of corn!" he insisted.

Myrtle cautioned that the farm's supply of feed would last till spring only if properly managed—and suggested further that in removing the current management, Freedom Farm would bear the principal responsibility.

This got the pigs to hemming and hawing—but it also got Bucky's besotted neurons firing, and before he thought the better of it, he was letting his personal beliefs get in the way of the job: "Freedom Farm should do more than just manage Von Rumpel's stores," he blurted out, "—it should *commandeer* them! With the extra feed, we could pay down our debt and have enough left over to start making loans...." Not having thought it through, Bucky probably figured the idea of confiscating a neighbor's stores and permanently slaying the "debt monster" embodied the sort of cold fiscal calculation the pigs would appreciate.

"Making loans ...?" said an incredulous Grover (who was now a lobbyist for Carlo Hawg).

"Why not?" said Bucky, his excitement mounting, "Carlo himself showed us how to do it! He's been making tall feed for years mortgaging BeaverBilts out of his own bin—and with the public stores flush, the federation could do the same thing! Instead of borrowing feed and paying interest all the time, we'd be *lending* feed and *earning* interest—we wouldn't even need to collect taxes! With Freedom Farm's account on a solid footing, we'd be a real asset to the community—and we'd also be in a better position to help our newly-liberated neighbors!"

Grover developed an urgent interest in the current match, and the discussion's other participants followed his lead. Then Emmet called for another bucket, and changed the subject.

Recognizing that he'd committed a monstrous faux pas, Bucky seized his first opportunity to slink away unnoticed.

Ultimately, the pigs were successful in arguing that Operation Kick Human Ass should limit itself to its stated objective of driving Von Rumpel from his land. The CFC opposed a laissez-faire approach to the invasion's aftermath, but it went along with the plan anyway. (Though the chickens enjoyed a six-to-two advantage on the Council—Dodger caucusing with the CFC—they decided to use their crushing majority only as a last resort.) Once Von Rumpel's animals had been liberated, the hogs insisted, they would "revel in the blessing of self-determination"—and determine for themselves how best to manage their resources; in the absence of meddling bureaucrats, the thinking went, supply and demand would be efficiently balanced by the "invisible hand" of an unfettered free market. (The pigs had all become subscribers to the Semi-Fortnightly Baboon Bulletin—a free market propaganda rag.)

"That the federation is mired in debt is proof enough," said Emmet at the evening's conclusion, "that Freedom Farm would do well to mind its own affairs and stick to running Von Rumpel off his land!"

"Indeed!" said Eunice, who caucused with Emmet.

Ironically, Bucky would be called on to play a vital role in the invasion....

The plan was to attack by night—in the pitch blackness of a new moon—and the Militia needed a solution to the problem of finding its way in the dark. Some thought was given to recruiting a few of the cats that frequented the barn, but being feral free agents of the carnivorous persuasion, they had little incentive to assist a strike force of farm animals in its quest to eliminate the threat of a neighboring farmer—or liberate his animals, or secure Beaver Gorge, or achieve whatever it was they were supposed to achieve; the official story changed all the time. (The cats weren't even citizens; tolerated only because they kept the feed bins free of mice, they were held in even lower esteem than beavers.)

But just before the new moon, Bucky and Pluto were engaged in their usual morning feeding ritual. As always, Pluto fed the larger animals first—heaving buckets of feed into the troughs as Carlo's clerks ran back and forth to the Wall and kept a running account of who ate what. When he was through working the troughs, the monkey started tossing feed on the snow for the impatient crush of hungry fowl. Bucky, standing at a safe distance, called for his breakfast—and as usual, Pluto ignored him. This would've been extremely humiliating for most holders of high public office, but Bucky had long since made peace with being a chicken—so, as always, he waited without objection. Only after hundreds of others had eaten and dispersed did Pluto turn in Bucky's direction: "Oh yes, Councilor Leghorn ... and what was your pleasure?"

"A handful of millet, please," said Bucky.

The mandrill stared at the rooster for a long moment—or so it seemed; it was a little hard to tell, with his war-painted features hidden beneath that cowl. But finally, like a stunted Grim Reaper, he turned, reached into one of the buckets by the barn door, and raised a fistful of millet in the air; then he slowly opened that black, knobby hand and let the grain fall to the snow. "Come and get it ..." he growled from beneath his hood.

Bucky remained at a distance—knowing the monkey had little time to waste taunting him, and would go about his business soon enough. And, by and by, Pluto turned and hobbled back into the barn. Bucky warily approached his breakfast— freezing every step or two, cocking his head this way and that as he peered into the barn's shadows; finally, he began pecking cautiously at the millet.

He hadn't cracked his first kernel when the monkey's paw coalesced from an explosion of motion in the doorway— throttling the cock, and yanking him aloft. "Could I have a word, Councilor?" snarled the mandrill, holding the frantically flapping Bucky before his hooded mug. "It's been so long since we've had a chance to interface.... What's wrong, cat got your tongue? Oh, of course—you can't very well speak if you can't breath, can you? But that's all right—you don't need to speak, you just need to listen. And you should really stop all that flapping, or you'll run out of oxygen before you've heard what I have to say—and then you'll be *dead,* which won't do either of us any good." The mandrill's logic was as inescapable as his grasp, so Bucky—in a desperate act of self-preservation— forced himself to stop flapping and go limp. "That's it, that's it—very good," said the mandrill. "Now listen to me, Councilor: on the night of the Von Rumpel invasion, you're going to guide our forces up the hill—that's right, *you.* Not because you can see in the dark, obviously—and certainly not because you're such a *heroic* little cock—but rather because no one knows his way around that hillside better than you do. I know, I've watched you; it wouldn't surprise me if you've got *names* for all of those stumps you're always cowering behind...." The bird's breast was beginning to heave in oxygen-starved futility. "In any case, once we cross over into Von Rumpel's territory, we'll be able to feel our way along the wire fence that runs across the face of the hill; what we don't want, however, is to overshoot Von Rumpel's property and invade the Putzkammer spread by mistake—which could easily happen up there in the dark of a new moon. We could end up fighting the humans on two fronts—a situation neither of us, I'm sure, would find desirable...." It's fair to say there was *nothing* Bucky found desirable at that particular moment apart from a lungful of that fresh mountain air; he hung from the mandrill's fist as limp as snot—except for his thoracic region, that is, which was heaving away in frantic fibrillation-mode. "But here's the key point, Councilor: If you fuck up in any way—if you run off, if you fail to show up, if you get us lost up there in the dark or do anything other than what I want you to do—I'll track you down and put you in a cage. No more of this 'free range' shit. And it'll be the sort of cage they use to incarcerate hens in all those egg-laying factories, only smaller—so small, in fact, that we'll have to *cram* your ass into it! Not only that, I'll see that you spend the rest of your pathetic life like that—every minute of every day of the rest of your sorry life mashed into the shape of a cube. And if you think I'm being anything other than brutally, clinically literal, it's probably because you're suffering the effects of oxygen starvation and you've forgotten how seldom I'm given to hyperbole. So let me reiterate my pledge one last time before you pass out: If you fail me, I will personally see to it that you spend the rest of your days in an enclosure so crushingly small as to prohibit any movement whatever—you won't even be able to take a deep breath! So remember the feeling, Councilor...." He dropped Bucky on the snow and returned to the barn's shadows—leaving the bug-eyed bird flapping torpidly, gasping for air.

CHAPTER 29

The new moon brought chaos enough for any crow—most of it, unfortunately, lost in the blackness.

The pre-battle preparations, for the most part, amounted to a tedious, interminable exercise in assembling and maintaining a reassuring sense of order. Following the afternoon feeding, a curfew was imposed, and the invasion force began assembling in the yard. The troops formed individual "attack units" that situated themselves at measured intervals along a 1000-foot length of rope secured for the occasion; held in the animals' teeth, this rope was the means by which the individual teams planned to follow each other up the hillside in the dark—and then space themselves out across the top of Von Rumpel's property before sweeping down the hill in the attack. (Looking like a circus act, each of these attack units consisted of a ram with a pigeon perched on its head, and a rooster perched on its back—along with a boar bringing up the rear on all fours. The rams' job was to go for the humans' legs, while the pigeon flew interference for the cock—who, for his part, went straight for the eyes; once the target had been taken down, the hog would attack his vitals. That was the idea, anyway.)

As night fell, the preparations continued by lantern light. When his troops were fully prepared and briefed, Fritz took his place at the head of the column, and Pluto tied the lead-end of the rope around the bull's neck. Then the mandrill ducked into the barn and returned with a dejected Bucky, who also wore a necktie for the occasion—a leash, that is, fashioned from a 10-foot length of bailing twine; lantern in hand, the mandrill held the other end of this leash in his teeth as he mounted the bull. "Torch ... cocktails ... flint ..." he muttered, inspecting the contents of a pair of burlap sacks slung over the animal's withers. "How's it looking, Commander?"

"Ready to roll," said Fritz confidently.

"Okay, Councilor, don't just stand there..." said Pluto, shaking Bucky's leash as he held the lantern aloft.

Trudging like Sunday dinner going to the block, Bucky led Pluto and the bull and the rest of the unwieldy, unwinding column out of the yard and toward the hill. It took a while, but the last of the warrior-beasts finally filed out past the barn and other outbuildings, and the column crawled into the night like a millipede with a single glowing eye. But when the attack force began its trek up the face of the hill, Pluto doused the light according to plan—and that's when all that carefully orchestrated order went all to hell.

The sordid details wouldn't see the light of day till the light of day—but squeals of alarm and yelps of pain and the frantic sound of pigeons flying aimlessly in the dark suggested even then that all wasn't going entirely as planned. The operation's difficulties began with the snow on the hillside, which —being unprotected by vegetation—had developed a thick crust of ice after repeatedly thawing and freezing; even the surefooted rams had a bad time of it—and the folly of following ¾-ton of hamburger up a slippery slope in the dark became painfully obvious the first time the column was hit by an avalanche of kicking, scrambling bull. Conditions deteriorated rapidly as animals were incapacitated, lost in the dark, or tangled hopelessly in those thousand feet of line.

It was a night of blind, bumbling confusion, and by the time Pluto and Fritz finally penetrated "enemy territory," it was with a decimated, disorganized gang of lame and injured animals. Then, as they groped around in search of the wire fence that would guide them across the hill in the next phase of the operation, Von Rumpel's sheepdog began raising a racket below. This awakened the farmer and his sons, who emerged from the house—shivering in nightshirts, exhaling plumes of orange vapor in the light of their lanterns—and proceeded to wander around the yard, peering into the darkness for signs of invaders. But the dog knew well enough that the invading presence was in the woodlot, so it went charging up the hill—planning, no doubt, to chase around after Fritz like it had on the bull's previous raids, yapping noisily while the rampaging beast did his damage. But the dog encountered an unexpected presence in the darkness of those woods—a jungle beast—and its yapping was cut short, never to be heard again.

At that point, however, the element of surprise had been lost, the attack force was scattered, and farmers all over the valley would soon be up milking their cows and slopping their hogs. Neither Pluto nor Fritz saw any point in waiting for the farmer and his sons to come looking for their dog, so they attacked. From my vantage point, it began with an explosion of light in the blackness of the hillside, which coalesced in a ball of fire that came bouncing and weaving down through the trees. It wasn't till it'd cleared the woods that this apparition took on distinct features, and I could make out the mandrill's form—torch blazing aloft, cloak flapping in the wind—standing on Fritz's rolling, pitching shoulders as the bull came barreling down the hill. In their wake, a ragtag gang of Militia-critters scrambled to keep up.

Von Rumpel and his sons stood in slack-jawed incomprehension as the attacking beasts approached. "It's that danged bull ..." said Von Rumpel at last, "only this time he brought all the beasts of Hell with him!" The three of them turned on their heels and sprinted back to the house.

As the bull came charging into the yard, Pluto fired up a Molotov cocktail and hurled it at the back of the house, where it smashed and set the porch ablaze. Charging past the burning porch, the bull and the mandrill continued on around the house—the rest of the animals chasing along behind like a pack of hounds after a bear. After tossing another cocktail into a basement window and firebombing the far side of the house, the whole structure lit up—which served as a beacon for all the troops that had gotten lost in the dark. They came scrambling and flapping out of the night just as the whole Von Rumpel family, still in nightclothes for the most part, emerged from the side door of the house—wielding knives, cleavers and sundry blunt, heavy objects—and tried to fight its way through the demon-possessed beasts charging and diving from every direction. But the humans had no plan, and the animals had no strategy, and there was no order of any kind on any front—there was *no front;* just blazing, blessed bedlam.

The Von Rumpels were driven from their land, though there was some disagreement as to whether they'd fled the valley—much having been veiled by the "fog of war" (not to mention the dark of night).

The invading troops, meanwhile, managed to get themselves organized again, and a detachment returned home later that morning for a victory parade through the crowded yard. Decorum dictated that the bull not be seen with the monkey on his back, so it was Booger straddling the mighty Fritz at the head of the parade. The hog, as always, was resplendent in full hayseed regalia—but for this performance, his overalls had been splattered picturesquely with fake blood.

Being all business all the time, the monkey skipped the festivities altogether.

The parade would ultimately kick off a day of celebration, which would yield to a long night of debauchery, and the sun would be well above the horizon again before correspondent pigeons from the BBC (the Baboon Broadcasting Company) brought word that Otto Von Rumpel and his sons were seen conspiring with some of their Grumpish neighbors up at the Putzkammer spread. The ominous report would include the shocking allegation that one of Freedom Farm's own was freely collaborating with the plotters—a traitorous chicken tentatively identified as Bucky Leghorn.

CHAPTER 30

But while that victory parade was cleaving its way through Freedom Farm's cheering throngs, the monkey was just over the rise—cleaning out Von Rumpel's silo. The barn doors had been thrown open and the animals liberated (i.e., kicked out) —whereupon the entire occupation force circled the barn and stood guard while Pluto hooked up the family's hay wagon in tandem with his own, docked and loaded them both, and hauled them off to the Hawg family's private storage facility. It'd be the first of many trips. Escorted by a security detail, he took a roundabout route so as to avoid Freedom Farm's raucous crowds—and though his tractor occasionally bogged down in the snow and produced almost as much smoke as the smoldering remnants of the Von Rumpels' house, it managed the pair of hay wagons passably well. (Having corrected the John Deere's tendency to go in circles by letting down the larger of it mismatched tires, Pluto had begun using his "iron horse" in place of the real kind for almost every task; depending on the function being performed, the sign mounted above the grill would read, "OMNIBEAST," or "AGRISERV," or—as

283

in this particular case—"Wealth Transfer Operations, Div. of P. Baboon & Co.," in very small letters.)

Pluto left nothing but echoes in the barn's feed bins and silo—though he did leave some hay in the loft (probably because the Hawgs' storage shed was filled to the rafters)—and he probably would've cleaned out the Von Rumpels' pantry too if it hadn't burnt to the ground with the rest of the house. It was a momentous beginning to what could only be called the Day of the Monkey: a time of such monumental monkey-shines—such thieving, profiteering, calamitous, five-fingered chaos—that I had to remind myself more than once that he was merely building on the bedlam occasioned by my own groundbreaking efforts. But build on it he did.

Shortly after Von Rumpel's feed had been liberated, the liberated beasts of the "Occupied Territory"—driven to the brink by Lord Gastric—stormed the barn, which was being used by the occupation forces as its headquarters. The Militia managed to fight them off, but there were many injuries, and reinforcements had to be brought in. Eventually, a quantity of hay was thrown out onto the snow for the animals to fight over, and that quelled the insurgency for a time. But the restive locals would be an ongoing "contingency" requiring an occupation force consisting of the larger part of the Animals' Militia; in the Occupied Territory, the newly-liberated were destined to either die or join the insurgency.

Pluto, meanwhile, had turned his attention to the deposed farmer's woodlot—and it wasn't BeaverBilts he had in mind. The monkey had come to the conclusion that the bottom line potential of homebuilding was dwarfed by the profit potential of *firewood.* "You see what happens when you burn a log?" he observed one night, as he and his porcine patrons sat around the fire pit at the Bucket of Fire Saloon. He poked at the ashes with a stick, and a cloud of embers rose in the air like fireflies. "You have to get yourself another log...." Pluto was already delivering corn liquor and candle-lighting services at sundown —when the Omnibeast became the Vulcan—and he saw no reason why he shouldn't be moving firewood as well. He'd have launched the enterprise sooner, in fact, if it weren't for Freedom Farm's dire shortage of trees.

But now that he had an abundant source of timber, he found himself short of the time needed to cut it—and he had to act fast if he expected to capitalize on cold weather demand. So he gave up sleeping—entirely—and for the longest time the sound of that chainsaw could be heard howling like a banshee in the late night air. Meanwhile, everyone on Pluto's Vulcan route got the hard sell—though it was hardly necessary; the prospect of curling up beside the radiant embers of a dying fire on a cold winter evening had universal appeal. "A hearth is the difference between a house and a home," Pluto would say—and most everyone agreed.

It helped that retrofitting a BeaverBilt for central heat was just a matter of digging a pit in the middle of the floor. (The ratty structures were generally drafty enough that no chimney was necessary.) Pluto provided the service, gratis—he even threw in a free log, and fired it up—and even your most frugal BeaverBilt owner could envision burning a ceremonial log on birthdays and anniversaries and such. Invariably, though, the warmth, and the light, and the enchantment of those dancing flames—which could keep a family mesmerized for hours on end—would prove all too seductive to save for a few special occasions. Before long, the winter evenings were dense with the scent of burning pine as smoke seeped from BeaverBilts all over the Federated Free Farms of Toad Valley.

But ample firewood was about the only upside to come out of Operation Kick Human Ass—at least for the common beast. The downside took many forms—the most toxic being the cold fear that set in once the wave of triumphal sentiment had spent itself in the wake of the invasion. Fatback's carcass still lay in the yard, and though several light snowfalls had covered it with a blanket of white, that featureless mound remained a powerful reminder of the human threat—and as always, the throngs gave it a wide berth. Rumors came and went, but most were variations on the idea that the traitorous Councilor for Pigeons was supplying vital intelligence to Von Rumpel and his sons, who were busy organizing a massive counteroffensive. Whatever the facts, however, few doubted that the invasion of the Von Rumpel's homestead had set Freedom Farm on a collision course with the valley's entire human population: every conversation seemed to turn eventually to the subject of "the inevitable." (The term was never defined, but always spoken with foreboding.)

The receding snows yielded a bumper crop of thawing carcasses. Those that weren't already in the meadow were taken there and covered over with the rest. But the reverend Fatback's remains—which remained under guard where Pluto had left them—proceeded to publicly rot. This occurrence was much appreciated by an alliance of scavengers needing the infusion of readily-digestible protein—and being among its number, I can attest that Fatback was as savory in repose as he was righteous in life; but farm animals being farm animals, the exhibit only exacerbated the grim public mood.

And then there was Polack, with all his dire, depressing sermons. The ailing hog had assumed the pulpit at the Church of the Suffering Sow—essentially by default—and the church, as a result, returned to its somewhat more swine-centric roots (though a large and growing portion of the congregation consisted of sheep drawn to Polack's clear, authoritative voice). But unlike his predecessor, who had a generally sunny disposition, Polack was predictably dark, bitter, and angry. The Unraveling, after all, had not been kind: he had to be carried around on a litter, he lived in perpetual fear of sneezing, and his dream of being a propertied free beast had gone unrealized. (The Occupied Territory was a lawless place—much too dangerous for the infirm—and showed no sign of being settled any time soon.) In short, Polack saw nothing good on his own horizons, and he wanted lots of company—so he stamped out optimism at every turn. He shared his bleak outlook with every sermon, foretelling misery and destruction at the hands of humans—most of it apparently well-deserved. "The Hog Father does not abide the unholy," he told his flock often, "—nor does He equate moral erosion with social progression. His contempt for perverts, socialists, and sluggards is boundless, and we will all pay mightily for allowing these elements to move freely among us! Oh yes, children—do not think that because you tithe generously, and your affiliations are prudent, and you worship Him above all others, the Hog Father will spare you! It isn't that easy. Leading a righteous life does not absolve you of the moral pestilence in your midst—these, these ... *chicken wingers,* for one, and their clients, the so-called 'differently productive,' and the legions of shiftless, feral life forms forever loitering in the yard—and all the other leeches and parasites that would plunder the public weal! The Hog Father sees that these vermin, contrary to His divine plan, are being elevated from their rightful place underfoot—and it offends Him mightily! And in His supreme displeasure, He will conjure up a plague of humans, and they will descend upon Freedom Farm like locusts, and seize every one of you and take your children, and force you to bear witness as they are violated repeatedly—oh yes, as many times as there are humans! And when your children have been humiliated near unto death, they will be slaughtered, and the Hog Father will delight in your grief, and then you in turn will be bled, and disemboweled, and ground into sausage, and then flame-broiled in the fires of Cincinnati—and the smoke of your torment will ascend forever and ever...."

And then came the rains. The monkey apparently cut some corners when he constructed the levee above the Hamhocks' troubled acreage, and during a hard rain, a 9-foot section gave way. Little if any topsoil was lost in the resulting flash flood—given that there was little if any to lose—but tons of nitrogen, phosphorous, and potassium fertilizers were swept away. It all ended up in Liberty Creek—which killed off much of the aquatic life that supplemented the duck community's diet. This was a development of no small consequence, but the incident's full dimensions only became clear as Liberty Pond was slowly choked with algae.

Walking on water was just fine for deities, and for lesser critters in winter, but in the warm weather you were supposed to be able to swim in it—and the ducks rioted. They came streaming into the yard and stormed the back porch, where a meeting of the Committee for the Development of Guidelines for the Naming of Liberated Bodies of Water was in progress. Councilor Dodger, looking notably uncomfortable, explained to his angry constituents that the Committee's purview didn't include the physical state of liberated bodies of water—just the development of guidelines for their naming—and he assured them the subject of the algae bloom would be taken up when the Council convened a couple of days hence. But the Committee and the Council looked like the same bunch to the rampaging ducks, and their response was immediate and full-throated: "W-A-A-A-K, wak-wak-wak-wak-wak! W-A-A-A-K! W-A-A-A-K! W-A-A-A-K! W-A-A-A-K ...!"

The ducks' displeasure was deafening. The Committee members waited patiently for the squawking, trumpeting mob to run out of steam so they could continue with their important work—but the ducks persisted. They'd probably have persisted the rest of the day, too, such was the depth of their wrath. But just as the Committee was preparing to adjourn in frustration, a blur of motion erupted from the side of the house —and before I'd even made out the forms of six gray wolves, they plunged rabidly into the sea of ducks, ripping and snarling and flinging bloody duck parts this way and that. The din of duck protest jumped to a panic pitch as the entire mass of them exploded in every direction—leaving behind a scene of turbulent carnage: scattered blood, feathers, and entrails presided over by marauding, wild-eyed wolves—a *pack* of them —thrashing the life out of the last of a dozen ducks that were just a shade too slow.

After a few moments, the only things left moving in the yard were the wolves. As if on command, they all stopped in the midst of inspecting the fruits of their efforts and loped over to where the hunched and hooded figure of Pluto waited at the corner of the house. "Excellent, excellent—fine work," he told the wolves as they gathered around him. Deprived of the sight of his ugly mug, I'd gotten pretty good at reading the mandrill's body language—and as he praised his "feral facilitators" (the "FF," as they came to be known), I was reminded that Pluto was nowhere more at ease than in the company of wild beasts like himself. "It's yours," he told them finally, nodding toward the carnage, "—eat."

So as the terrified members of the Committee watched from the kitchen windows, the wolves sat in the empty yard and devoured the slaughtered ducks.

"HAW, HAW, HAW!" laughed Emmet, "You shoulda seen it!" The Councilor for Swine was relating the afternoon's events to a festive gathering at Booger's gated mud hole. "Every fucking duck in the federation was there—they took up half the yard! And they're raising all this holy hell—well, I don't have to tell *you*. You heard it all the way up here! And everything Dodger says to calm them down is just getting the little shits more riled up, right? And then all of a sudden, out of nowhere—WOLVES! A pack of fucking *wolves!* And they go charging into the crowd of ducks and just start ripping them apart! HAW, HAW, HAW—I never seen anything like it! Little duck heads and duck feet and shit flying this way and that! HAW, HAW, HAW! You shoulda seen Dodger and the chickens break for the kitchen door! HAW, HAW, HAW ...!"

"Eunice too," said Pluto, sitting by the wall with a bucket of fire between his legs, "—and they almost beat you to it."

"O-o-o-o, hoo, hoo, hoo ..." said the other pigs.

"Oh, fuck you, Pluto!" said Emmet, turning red, "—I watched the whole thing from the porch!"

"The fresh pile of pig shit in the kitchen speaks for itself," said the mandrill, "—the really *big* one by the corner window."

289

"HAW, HAW, HAW!" the other hogs guffawed, "HAW, HAW, HAW!"

"It's a good thing you're just foolin' around ..." Emmet said, his tone teetering between threatening and pleading.

"Only fools fool around," said the mandrill, sipping from his palm.

"HAW, HAW, HAW, HAW, HAW!"

"What're you saying?" said Emmet, "You saying I *didn't* watch the whole thing from the porch—is that what you're saying? You're saying I'm a liar ...? 'Cause if that's what you're saying, why don't you just come right out and say it?"

"Why don't you suck my dick?" said Pluto.

"That's it!" said Emmet, "I'm not taking this shit from a goddamn monkey!" The hog crawled out of the muck and onto solid ground, stood up on his hind legs—his bulbous form glistening with mud—and bared his tusks. "Alright, now you got just *one* chance to apologize...."

It's a funny thing about pigs: unique among farm animals, they just keep getting bigger and bigger as long as they live —right up until the day someone cuts their throats. But on Freedom Farm, obviously, they didn't slaughter hogs—and Emmet had been kicking around long enough that he probably tipped the scales at a good quarter-ton.

Compared to this towering specimen of pighood, the mandrill almost looked small, if sinister. He had long since become, for all practical purposes, a disembodied entity lurking behind a black robe—his repugnant form being the sort of thing most of the federation's critters were only too happy not to contemplate. But without warning, he burst from that shroud in all his snarling, incandescent ferocity—a savage, saber-toothed beast with the obvious wherewithal to mess up that hog in a big way. His eyes were crazed and bloodshot from lack of sleep, and his mane had grown back as blazingly ostentatious as ever—and every hair of it stood on end, swelling him up to about twice his true size; but when he let out that primeval jungle scream, there was no mistaking the size of those jaws: they could've wrapped themselves around a watermelon.

Emmet dropped to his all-fours, did a one-eighty, and scrambled for the open gate. The mandrill didn't give chase, so the hog paused at the gate long enough to hurl a parting insult. "You're still just Hawg family property," he blurted out, before turning to flee, "—and don't forget it!"

But Pluto had forgotten it long before then.

CHAPTER 31

Feeling decidedly less empowered was the growing number of critters running afoul of the new penal code. Times were hard, and the surge of such serious crimes as petty theft and transporting passengers for profit without sufficient wheelage showed little sign of abating. Stella got nailed for the latter offense in a sting operation involving the former Constable Horace, who claimed to have an urgent job interview on the other side of the federation—but in fact was working under-cover with the pig patrol. "Oh Stella, I'm so sorry," said the goat to the mare as the pigs took her away, "I needed the work —and the Department of Empathy needed somebody every-one trusted...."

Among those bolstering the Freedom Pit's growing pop-ulation were the gangs of critters detained during Operation Kick Human Ass. During the curfew that accompanied the invasion, the pig patrol went about rounding up violators— which, unavoidably, included every indigent free beast not ensconced in public housing. (The EDPP's budget for new housing had been eliminated.) There were way too many to arrest all at once, but Pluto—immediately after securing Von Rumpel's feedstock—made such a heap of silage lowering suspects into the Pit that he pressured the Council into creating an ordinance specifically outlawing indigence (an obvious gateway crime). Once the War on Poverty got underway, the pig patrol spent most of its time chasing around after these criminal elements—until it discovered the efficiencies of simply waiting for them to show up at feeding time for their subsidized half-rations.

The Pit's population ballooned.

And as it did, the issue of rights began to emerge in the public mind—a concern raised initially by older beastfolk who remembered the Six Rights, and assured their younger compatriots that one of those rights was the right to range. The right to feed was also evoked after feed subsidies were halved again (and would've been eliminated altogether if the Department of Empathy didn't find them so useful for entrapping indigents). And it seemed perfectly obvious that every one of the slaughtered ducks had had its right to life violated.

But others thought they'd heard the Six Rights had been changed somehow—though they couldn't remember how or why.

Eventually, the administration called a press conference to clear things up. "Ain no more Six Rights," Booger told the assembled pigeons of the press corps in his opening statement. "Been supercedified by the Six Prillages—long time ago. But thass a good thing, see, 'cause iss always better t'be prillaged than right—believe you me. Not only that, prillages can be provoked—which is jes what happens when somebody gits hisself throwed in the Pit: they prillages git provoked. But thass ol' news—happen lass season. Jes weren't payin attention is all. So afore y'start makin lotta noise, y'best know what yer talkin 'bout—elsewise yer own prillages might geet provoked." A vigorous thumping issued from the base of the podium. "Oh, thass right, yer prillages *already* got provoked— thass what happens inna time a war! An' thass what we got here, a time-a war. So from now awn, we kin do anythin we want: ain got no rights, ain got no prillages—jes got the right t'shop, is all. Heh-heh, heh-heh ..." The reason the press conference was held in the barn instead of its usual place on the back porch became evident when Booger turned and gestured in my general direction. "Beastfolk keep sayin they rights is up there in the rafters," he said, "—you see anythin? I don' see nothin but that evil crow thass always hangin 'round." And in fact, the scrawled document I'd bequeathed to the free beasts of Freedom Farm had long since succumbed to the ravages of time and pigeon shit.

Following the ducks' ill-fated demonstration, the pig patrol was obliged to suspend its poverty-fighting efforts for a time while it rounded up scores of ducks suspected of insurrection. Most of these ended up in the Pit with their wings clipped, pending an investigation and possible prosecution—but some disappeared altogether. A dozen of them ended up in the wolves bellies, of course, but there were a total of nineteen unaccounted for. Lobbying on behalf of his client, P. Baboon & Co., Spencer Hamhock easily persuaded the Council over a bucket of shine that every duck arrested was right there in the Pit for all to see—and more to the point, if there were still reports of missing ducks, it was clearly because the insurrection's ring leaders had gone into hiding. "What it amounts to," said Spencer, "is we got a serious security problem—and it's not *out there* somewhere, it's right here, right now. It's all well and good to be mindful of the human threat—it's imperative—but we can't afford to ignore the internal threat either. These are perilous times; the destruction of our way of life could come crashing through the front gate tomorrow—or it could slip in through the back door tonight. We have hundreds of BeaverBilts all across Hawg Homestead and elsewhere—and no idea what's going on in any of them. Insurrectionists could be hiding in the house next door, and you'd never even know it. Fortunately, my client has a proposal designed to meet this urgent challenge—and any representative desiring his support in the coming elections would be advised to get behind it...."

Thus was born the Secure Privacy Initiative, or "SPI." Your typical BeaverBilt had a form somewhat like a snail's shell lying on its side—the curved entranceway providing both access and privacy. But with the advent of SPI, all such structures were required to have at least one window, and be subject to inspection without notice. The plan was promoted as a lifestyle improvement: not only would it provide increased security against "evildoers," it would provide homeowners with "health-giving light and fresh air."

Even before the measure had been rammed through the approval process, Pluto fired up his chainsaw and set about cutting holes in the sides of every BeaverBilt in the commonwealth. Once the "fenestration phase" of the contract was complete, the mandrill and his wolves began random security patrols. As it happened, homeowners didn't much care for their newly installed windows: those BeaverBilts were drafty enough as it was—and though the additional fresh air kept the demand for firewood healthy, it didn't do much for the health of homeowners. But if residents were less than fond of all that health-giving light and fresh air, they were terrified of the wolves' hungry eyes glaring in at them at unexpected moments. It was a well-founded fear, too; every now and again the call of the wild would take over when one of the wolves spotted an especially tasty-looking critter, hopped through a window, and proceeded to have at it. Typically, this would get the whole pack's blood up, and they'd all enter the house and chow down on the rest of the occupants. (Remarkably, however, the wolves would prove to have infallible instincts for spotting "evildoers," as official investigations invariably found the victims to be either agents of Von Rumpel or unaligned insurrectionists.)

Yet the ducks that were originally reported missing never turned up. This was because they weren't hiding in a Beaver-Bilt somewhere; rather, they'd all been spirited off to Pluto's secret detention site—the cellar. None of the animals ever entered that part of the farmhouse—at least not willingly. It was dark, damp, and gloomy, and the stairs leading from the kitchen to the cellar were narrow and steep—though Pluto himself never used them; back when he'd contracted to free up space in the basement, he discovered a set of doors hidden by a stand of weeds on the side of the house—which is how he managed to come and go without being detected.

The cellar is also where Pluto kept the wolves he'd raised since their mother's untimely demise. He'd boarded up the basement windows immediately upon rescuing the pups, but there were cracks and knotholes enough for a crow to peer through—and occasionally I did. The view wasn't ideal, but from time to time I'd catch glimpses of the wolves moving through the shadows, or of Pluto's dark, sinister form hobbling about as he tended to unseen projects. But it wasn't until after the duck slaughter that I first made out a row of tiny cages which appeared to be crammed with feathers and nothing more—until I noticed the occasional head or webbed foot mashed up against a side of one or another of those enclosures. The wolves showed much interest in these "compactors," as the mandrill called them—sniffing at one, snarling at another, and salivating like rabid beasts as they circled and paced in the gloom.

But in between raising wolves and compacting ducks, the mandrill was up to something else down in that dungeon—though I wouldn't discover *what* till I happened upon an intimate gathering of luminaries out in a section of the monkey's pastureland. It was mid-afternoon, and Pluto's tractor and wagon were parked off to the side of a rutted path skirting a remote, grassy expanse—the sign above the tractor's grill reading, "MAINTENANCE." Carlo and his simian asset sat in a heap of hay just behind the wagon's seat, while Fritz stood twitching and snorting alongside the cart. They appeared to be in the midst of one of those private little policy discussions that often took place at the Hawg family compound, or at the

Bucket of Fire when everyone else had gone home—but not usually out in the back forty somewhere. I parked in a pine, and cocked an ear hole.

"They're *always* having meetings ..." I heard Carlo say.

"I don't mean just the Sunday meetings," said the bull, "I mean during the week too. Been a lot of activity ..."

"You know what's happening, don't you?" said Pluto, "We're letting the bastards get the jump on us."

"Look, we gotta be careful here," said the hog. "We got lucky with Von Rumpel—the asshole didn't have any friends! But if we go after Wurfel or Puzkammer or somebody, we could end up fighting half the humans in the valley."

"We can't just sit around and wait for them to attack *us*," said Pluto.

"That goes without saying," said Fritz. "But the Chancellor has a point too: if a sizable portion of the human community bands against us ..."

"They're banding against us now," Pluto insisted, "—and they'd be fools not to. We ran Klunder off his land, we ran Von Rumpel off his land, and we have strategic control of Beaver Gorge; they've got every reason in the world to attack us—including the obvious fact that we've got enough meat on the hoof to feed the entire Grumpish community for a good long while. And they know their only chance of taking us out is to band together against us...."

"That still doesn't mean there's an imminent attack in the works," said Carlo. "Maybe they're just establishing a defensive alliance of some sort."

"Maybe ..." said the bull, "but from their point of view, the logic of aggression *is* compelling: if they *don't* attack us—and sooner rather than later—we'll just keep getting stronger."

"Logic has its place," said Carlo, "—but logic isn't destiny. I like to look at the odds: if Freedom Farm went up against a united Grumpish community, the odds are pretty good we'd get our asses salted, right ...?"

"What if we had an edge?" said the monkey.

"What sort of edge?" said Fritz.

"I'm glad you asked," said Pluto, "—since I obviously didn't bring you out here to admire the scenery." Reaching beneath the wagon's seat, the monkey carefully removed a nail keg—its contents sealed over with beeswax. A fuse sprouted ominously from the wax. He tucked the keg under his arm, lowered himself to the ground, and hobbled out to where a termite hill rose from the grass a ways off; after placing the keg on the mound, he struck a flint and lit the fuse—then scrambled back to the wagon. "I put a nice long fuse on it ..." he said to Carlo, as he settled back into the hay to enjoy the fireworks. The shockwave from the blast knocked them both off the hay wagon before the pig could respond—and almost knocked Fritz off his feet as well. Dirt clods rained down from the afternoon sky as the bull went charging into the pasture—only to stop short at the realization that there was nothing to charge.

After the dust had settled, the three gathered around the crater where the termite hill had been and concluded that the technology embodied by this FDFBED (Fertilizer/Diesel Fuel-Based Explosive Device—pronounced "bomb") would do more than give them an edge—it would make them virtually invincible.

And invincibility brought grave obligations. "I'm sure you can see where this changes the whole equation," said Pluto. "Now we have *no choice* but to take the initiative. Before, you could argue that the odds were against us, and initiating further hostilities with the human enemy would be irresponsible; but with victory all but assured, aggression would be the very *essence* of responsible action."

"Absolutely," said the bull. "How soon can you cook up some more of those things?"

"Yesterday," said the mandrill.

"Hold on, you two," said Carlo. "We'll have to lay some groundwork first. It was easy enough to sell Operation Kick Human Ass—Von Rumpel attacked us first. But a lot of beastfolk might not see the sense in a standing policy of indiscriminate aggression."

"It's all in how we package it," said Pluto. "Obviously, we can't just say we're attacking our neighbors because we're afraid they might attack us first—it'd sound paranoid and reactionary...."

"At the very least, it's a policy that would benefit from a lofty moniker," said Carlo. "Something suggesting restraint, solemn deliberation, an academic pedigree ..."

"The Hawg Doctrine," Pluto suggested.

"I like it!" said Carlo, "—Oh, but it'll go to Booger's head something awful."

"It's just as well," said the monkey, "We'll need to project confidence, after all."

"You can hang a fancy name on it," said Fritz, "but beast-folk are still gonna call it expansionism."

"We can always play up the idea that we're liberating the valley's beasts ..." said Pluto.

"I'm not sure the valley can stand any more liberated beasts," said the bull, "—things are getting pretty hairy in the Occupied Territory."

"Freedom is messy," said the monkey, "—but messy situations are filthy with opportunity. So let's make a mess—let's make a *big* mess. Let's launch a crusade to liberate every goddamn animal in the valley!"

"We need to get Spencer and Grover in the loop..." said Carlo.

"Of course," said Pluto. "And obviously, Chancellor, it'd be helpful if you could get Emmet to set aside his little drama and start acting like the Councilor for Swine."

"I'll give the surly pig a choice," said Carlo, "—Get it together, or get cut off."

The monkey turned to the bull. "This sort of device," he explained, "can be lobbed from a catapult, it can be planted in the ground during a retreat, it can be packed with rocks—it can be used in any number of ways. So confer with your tacticians, and see if you can't give me some idea what sort of devices you'd find useful in terms of configuration and quantity so we can come up with a price tag. If we act fast, we can close a deal tonight at the fights."

"I've got two speeds," said Fritz, "—Haul-ass, and *Charge.*" Making his point in bullish style, he turned and charged off.

"What does it cost to make one of those things, anyway?" said Carlo.

"Not much," said the monkey, "It's just diesel fuel and fertilizer—a substantial markup would go without saying. A huge markup, actually, given that we're really selling *victory*—victory, and all that comes with it: security, hope, *life* ... The most appealing feature of an explosive device, of course, is that it can only be used once...."

Carlo and his simian asset eventually went on their way, while I gave my undivided attention to a blackberry bush laden with overripe berries. Things became hazy, confused, and then dark —and by the time the fragments of my mind finally found each other again, it was in a hollow log with a self-righteous badger heaping scorn on me just as the sun was cracking the horizon to the east. Those blackberries had been aging a long time.

But though I'd missed the Saturday Night Fights, I made it back to the yard in time for the next round of *Emmet vs. Pluto.* Having finished feeding the beastial hordes, Pluto had just opened the Walnut Exchange, and was clearly preoccupied as he began doing business—but then Emmet appeared in a fashionably shit-spattered town coat and yanked him into the here-and-now. "I have the winning ticket!" the hog announced, waving his ticket in the air as he parted the crowd with his belly. "Out of my way, peons—I've come to collect the grand prize!"

The grand prize had grown to 19,000 bushels of corn.

CHAPTER 32

Sure enough, Emmet's ticket matched the number posted on the door of the Exchange: 6554—a number determined, as always, by four consecutive rolls of a die. Furthermore, the hog demanded his 19,000 bushels of corn "in feed"—i.e., he wanted the actual corn, not some figure scribbled on the Wall of Accounts. The request was highly unusual, though it didn't violate any of Freedom Farm's rules of exchange; it was also laughable, given the logistics of satisfying such a demand—and the fact that a dogged search of the storeroom and every bin in it wouldn't have turned up more than a dozen bushels of corn.

Ever since Carlo started lending imaginary feed, there had been a serious discrepancy between what was on the Wall and what was in the bins. But this discrepancy was compounded when Carlo transferred his own store of feed to his private storage facility at the Hawg family compound. And with regard to corn reserves in particular, the Toad Valley Distillery had been a particularly heavy drain; demand for corn liquor rose dramatically when Pluto began delivering the popular elixir, and then soared with Freedom Farm's transition to industrialized farming. (Silas Clusterberry remained steadfast in accepting only cash or hard liquor in exchange for fertilizer and fuel—and obviously, the animals had no cash to speak of.) On top of everything else, Pluto had been cutting the distillery's costs by pilfering corn on a regular basis.

Theoretically, the monkey had the option of offering substitute grains of equal value, but instead he wordlessly closed the door in Emmet's face—whereupon the hog stormed off to lodge a complaint with the Director of Empathy.

But as it happened, Sluggo was enjoying one of Polack's inspirational sermons at the Church of the Suffering Sow....

"You've heard it before," Polack was telling his flock, preparing them for some warmed-over wisdom, "—but it bears repeating: the Hog Father helps them that help themselves. Now you might be thinking His efforts would be better spent helping them that *can't* help themselves—but that's the problem with thinking: it can get you in a whole heap of trouble —for woe be to the pig that questions the Hog Father's plan! Faith isn't about thinking, children, it's about *believing*—and this much you can take right to the silo: the Hog Father likes *winners*. That's right, children, as far as He's concerned, the losers can go pound salt! Now that's not to say the losers of the world don't have their place—they do; *all* things have their place in the Hog Father's plan. And a loser's place, by God, is lying *face down* in the mud!"

"Indeed!" said Eunice, who never missed a service.

"But why, you might ask, would the Hog Father want a collection of losers cluttering up His luxuriant, health-giving mud?" Polack continued. "Well, the answer to that one is obvious: it's so the winners have somebody to trample on their way to the trough! That's right, children, the express purpose of the downtrodden is to be trodden down! Such has it always been and such will it always be. 'Trample thy neighbor, else he trampleth you,' spake the Almighty in all his divine wisdom. It all comes down to the simple fact that you can't have winners if you don't have losers—by *definition*—and the Hog Father gave each of us the free will to choose between being the pig shouldering his way to the trough, or the pig getting trampled underfoot! So don't be misled by all these bleeding-heart chicken-winger types; when you tread on the less fortunate, you're doing the Lord's work!

"These big crybabies that are always whining about how they're not getting their fair share and there aren't any jobs and the big dogs got it all—you know the ones I mean—they need to, by God, get up on their hind legs and *step* on somebody! Hell, you don't see *me* up here whining like a piglet, do you?—and Lord knows, I got a right! Do you have any idea what it's like to spend every minute of every day of your entire existence in the throes of agony? Why, I can't even *piss* without the most fearsome, god-awful pain—but you don't hear me *whining* about it, do you? You don't hear me whining about the way the sows turn their heads when they see my disfigurement, you don't hear me whining about how the farmhouse ain't litter-accessible, and you don't hear me whining about being tasked with delivering a sermon every Sunday morning despite the suffering occasioned by every danged syllable of it! The worst of it is, the one thing in the wide world that could deliver me from this torment is a bucket of Toad Valley—but in the cruelest stroke of all, the shock of sticking this bleeding cinder of a snout into those fiery spirits is more than my heart could bear!

"But I ain't gonna start *whining* about it, I can tell you that! Hell, if I weren't in such a God-awful, sorry state, I'll tell you what I *would* do—I'd get up off this danged litter, go out into the yard, and *stomp* the first whiner I come across! That's right, children, I'd go out there and do the Lord's work! I'd stomp me a beaver or two—and then I'd go duck hunting! That's right, *duck hunting*. The Hog Father ain't real pleased to see all these ducks waddling around with impunity after every last one of the little Bolsheviks was involved in a blatant act of insurrection! But it's not the ducks stoking the fires of His wrath, children—oh, no! They're doing exactly what they're supposed to be doing—which is acting like a bunch of whiners and malcontents! It's the rest of us he's pissed off at—that's right, you and me—'cause we're not doing a blasted thing to stop these crybabies and troublemakers from openly conspiring to bring down our beloved federation! Every night, children, every night I pray to the Hog Father above to heal this poor broken body so I can get up off my pallet and go stomp me some *ducks....*"

Emmet intercepted Sluggo as the congregation dispersed, and demanded Pluto's arrest. Sluggo waited expectantly for a punchline, and then—seeing that none was forthcoming—grew visibly uncomfortable. "But Councilor," he whispered, "I can't arrest Mr. B-Baboon...."

"Of course you can!" said Emmet, "You're the Director of Empathy, aren't you?"

"Well, I mean—the thing of it is, I'd have to get a warrant from the Freedom Court, and, and ..."

"Don't worry about the goddamn warrant—just arrest the bastard!"

"I don't know—you know—I don't know—I mean ... wh-what's the charge?"

"Fraud!"

"Fraud? We got an ordinance against that ...?"

"If we don't, I'll make one up!"

After going back and forth for several minutes, it became clear that in the absence of a warrant, Sluggo—who worked out of the Boss Critter's Office—would do nothing without a direct order from Boss Hawg himself. After expressing his displeasure, the Councilor for Swine scanned the yard—as though he might actually spot a bandit taxi fool enough to give him a ride—then snorted angrily and teetered off in the direction of the family compound.

At the Hawg family mud hole, Booger waited expectantly for

a punchline—and, being sluggish of wit, waited a tad longer than you might expect before growing concerned. "Prolly got some mud in m'ear, Emm-o," he said finally, "—you din say y'wannid Pluto apprehennid, didja? Heh-heh, heh-heh—'cause thass what iss sounded like."

"That's *exactly* what I said!" Emmet quaked, "I want him arrested for fraud!"

"Fraud? Ain thass some dead human or other?"

"*Fraud*—it's a crime! I've got the winning lottery ticket, and Pluto won't pay up!"

There were certain sensitive tasks Booger relied on Pluto for—making decisions, chief among them. But obviously, the monkey wasn't a player in this particular scene, and the Chancellor was off taking his morning constitutional—and Gus, for his part, was minding the store at the Wall of Accounts. Booger looked from one to another of his blank-eyed entourage—arrayed in the mud around him—and turned back to his uncle/brother. "Jes need t'have a word ..." he mumbled; then he extracted himself from the mud, waddled over to the family trough, and plunged his head in the water.

Just then, Carlo appeared at the gate. "Where the hell were *you* last night?" he bellowed at the sight of Emmet. "We're trying to put together a major defense contract, and you can't even bother to show up...?"

"I want Pluto arrested!" said Emmet, ignoring the question. "I've got the winning lottery ticket, and he won't honor it—and goddamn it, I mean to collect!"

Carlo stared at the councilor, momentarily at a loss. "Now you listen to me, pig," he said, his voice rising with every word, "I don't know what you're trying to pull here, but you're messing with one of the family's most valuable assets, and I'm not about to stand by while you jeopardize everything I've worked to build over the years! So unless you've got some inexplicable hankering for a career in the furrows, I suggest you tear up that bogus ticket and don't mention it again!"

"There's nothing bogus about this ticket," Emmet sneered,

"—and if you think I'm walking away from nineteen-thousand bushels, you're getting senile, Pops! I want that monkey arrested!"

"You idiot! You can't arrest an *asset....*"

"We'll see about that!" said Emmet, pushing past Carlo as he made his exit.

A moment later, Booger pulled his head from the trough, twirled precariously, and fell writhing on the ground in oxygen-starved delirium.

But Emmet was a shade delirious himself—charging off in one direction and then another as he struggled to sort out his thoughts. Whether or not a simian asset could be arrested was a touchy question—and once Emmet cooled down a bit, he concluded as much. So he sought the advice of a legal consultant who'd helped to craft Freedom Farm's penal code—and who had, in addition, a well-developed sense of discretion: Horace, the erstwhile constable. Emmet found him in the yard waiting to be fed—along with hundreds of other hungry free beasts.

"Well, it's rather a gray area of jurisprudence," the goat opined, "—and not a very useful one, if you ask me. The relevant question isn't whether or not it's legal to arrest a simian asset, but whether or not it's *possible*. Who's supposed to do it, anyway?"

"Sluggo, of course—who else?"

Horace gave the hog a skeptical look. "The pig patrol came through here just a few minutes ago," he said. "They were after a gang of porkers who were out terrorizing ducks —allegedly—and the miscreants had no trouble at all eluding them in the crowd. Of course, Sluggo and his minions probably weren't trying all that hard—but how hard do you suppose they'd try if tasked with apprehending Pluto Baboon? He always keeps himself covered these days, so it's easy to forget what a nasty piece of work he is...."

"He's a fucking monkey!"

"Well ... even if he were a less fearsome sort of monkey, with those wolves of his, attempting to arrest him would be suicidal...." The goat turned to the hog and lowered his voice confidentially: "But tell me this, Councilor: inasmuch as Mr. Baboon has helped to make your family quite wealthy, why in the world would you want him arrested?"

"'Cause he *fucked* with me, that's why!" said Emmet, his temper flaring, "And I'm gonna fuck with *him*...."

"Well, I've often said he's gotten entirely too powerful," said the goat diplomatically.

"What I mean ..." said the hog, getting hold of himself, "what I mean is that he refused to honor my winning lottery ticket, and I'm *very* disappointed in him. The Hawg family takes a dim view of such tactics, and I think he needs to be held to account—otherwise he'll just continue down the path to iniquity, and many others will suffer...."

"Why would he not honor your ticket?" Horace wondered. "What's a peck or a bushel to someone like him?"

"It was the *grand prize,* you twit—nineteen-thousand bushels of corn!"

"Oh my lord, you won the grand prize?" said the old buck, looking faint. "Why, that's extraordinary—I *never* have that kind of luck!"

Luck, of course, had nothing to do with it. While everyone else was at the fights, Emmet lifted the appropriate key from its hook above Carlo's bed—Pluto having entrusted the Chancellor with a spare to each of his concerns—and then stole the winning ticket from the Walnut Exchange. (Pluto ordered all his tickets, in lots of ten-thousand, through Silas Clusterberry—discarding those numbered 0000 through 6666 and selling the rest; eventually, he burnt the discards—but he was a busy baboon, and things had piled up.)

"It's gonna take more than luck to get that fucker to pay up," said Emmet.

"You know, it occurs to me," said the goat, regaining his

composure, "that a less confrontational approach might be fruitful. Rather than criminalizing the matter by trying to have him arrested, why not just summon him before the Council, and arbitrate?"

"Arbitrate ...?"

"My specialty," said the goat.

"Hmmm," said Emmet, thinking, "—is it still a third?"

"Forty percent ..."

"You fucking thief!" said the pig.

The two haggled awhile, and then went off in search of the Council's majority leader—the only official empowered to call an emergency session of the Council (and Emmet clearly felt his grievance was an urgent matter). It proved to be a challenging search, owing to the tumultuous conditions in the yard: dozens of starving beasts from the Occupied Territory had breached the fence and descended on the barn—further inflaming the hundreds of locals who'd already been waiting several hours for their morning feed. The two found Myrtle, who'd given up being fed, at the BeaverBilt she shared with her sisters—and after prevailing upon the hen in forceful terms, Emmet persuaded her to convene an emergency session of the Council. It took a while, but the rest of the Council—along with a few aids and assistants—were rounded up and assembled in the kitchen.

"As you all know," said Myrtle, opening the meeting, "this emergency session of the Council has been called to address the concerns expressed by the Councilor for Swine, who believes that certain business practices of P. Baboon & Co. pose an imminent threat to the federation's economy—and since nobody can get a mouthful of feed today, I'm thinking maybe he's got a point. So by all means, Councilor Hawg, explain to us what's going on."

Emmet rose to his full bipedal height and teetered to the head of the table. "It would appear," the hog began, "that P. Baboon & Co. is beset by a liquidity crisis of rapidly escalating proportions—as evidenced by breach of contract and possibly by other ethical lapses as well. I've suspected for some time that many of Mr. Baboon's business interests weren't entirely sound, so when I asked him to make good on a contractual obligation this morning, I insisted on *feed* in order to plumb the depths of his reserves—in the public interest, as well as my family's. But he refused. Then, as I began to look into the matter, it came to my attention that no one was being fed today—leading me to believe the problem is far bigger than I'd imagined...."

"What are you talking about?" said Henrietta, "—he's got more feed than Archie Daniels! And even if he didn't, what's that got to do with anything? The only reason the rest of us can't tap into our *own* feed is 'cause Mr. Baboon didn't show up for work today. The Omnibeast isn't running either...."

"First of all," said Emmet, with strained patience, "it's not as though everyone's got his own little bin in the storeroom; everyone's feed is stored with everyone else's. And the way you know what part of those stores belongs to you is by looking at the Wall of Accounts. But you have to understand, the Wall of Accounts doesn't *really* reflect what's in the bins...."

"Wait, wait ..." said Henrietta, "if the Wall of Accounts doesn't reflect what's in the bins, what *does* it reflect?"

"Well look, it's ... it's very hard to explain," said Emmet, "—there's only a couple of pigs in the whole commonwealth who even understand it. But I can tell you this: the federation's entire economy could collapse overnight—*literally*—if we don't nip this thing in the bud. Now it appears Pluto's little house of cards began to fall apart this morning when he reneged on his contract with me—so as a first step toward setting things right, I move that he be summoned immediately so that he and I can settle accounts...."

"Just what the HELL do you think you're doing?" Carlo bellowed as he came crashing through the back door in a mildew-stressed, crushed-linen duster—trailed by Grover and Spencer in equally natty attire.

"I'm taking steps to see that Pluto meets his obligations!"

said Emmet.

"By trying to make good on that goddamn lottery ticket?" said Carlo.

"*Lottery ticket ...?*" Myrtle clucked.

"A lottery ticket is a *contract,*" said Emmet, "—a contract which, in this case, obligates Pluto Baboon to pay me nineteen-thousand bushels of corn!"

"*Nineteen-thousand ...?*" Dodger quacked under his breath.

"What about *your* obligation to *me?*" Carlo thundered.

"Indeed!" said Eunice.

"It's only out of familial loyalty that I'm not pressing a criminal case!" said Emmet. "I just want an equitable settlement to a legitimate claim, nothing more."

"If I could interject ...?" said Spencer, addressing the proceedings. "My client, Mr. Baboon, doesn't *have* that kind of feed. Several days ago, he closed a deal with Whiskers for the bulk of the rooster's holdings—anyone who was paying attention couldn't have missed the sizable transfer of feed, duly noted on the Wall. The price was heavily discounted, given the seller's recent difficulties—but it still left my client in a highly leveraged position."

"You mean he's tapped out," said Petra.

"Well, let's just say he'd be hard-put laying his hands on nineteen-thousand bushels...."

"Exactly the point I was making when you three barged in!" said Emmet. "He's insolvent—and given how intertwined P. Baboon & Co. is with the federation's economy ..."

"I've got a question for the Chancellor ..." said Lucia, turning to Carlo. "Since you own Mr. Baboon, aren't his obligations *your* obligations?"

"Pluto's obligations are *his* business!" Carlo fumed. "The fact that I own him in light of this ... large, unexpected obligation," he added, glaring down the table at Emmet, "just means that he's suddenly worth a whole lot *less* than he was. Anyone care to buy a cheap monkey?"

"Look Chancellor, I don't pretend to understand all this,"

Myrtle conceded, "but if getting some breakfast is just a matter of Mr. Baboon settling accounts with Emmet, you could just *lend* him the feed, right? I mean, his credit's good with you, isn't it?"

"If he wanted a loan," Carlo snorted, "I imagine he'd have *asked* me for a loan!"

"Indeed!" said Eunice.

"The reason I bring it up," Myrtle persisted, "is because the federation's in no position to bail him out—especially not after that deal we made last night."

"What deal was that?" said Petra.

"You know, all that *exploding* stuff," said Myrtle, "The bombs, and mines, and petards ..."

"I kinda blacked out," said Petra.

"I really don't see the problem here," said Horace, butting in. "Mr. Baboon may not be solvent at the moment, but there's no reason he couldn't liquidate a portion of his holdings."

"Do you know what that would do to property values?" Carlo sneered at the goat.

"I can see we're not gonna get this thing resolved until we talk to Mr. Baboon himself," said Myrtle. "Do you have any idea where we can find him, Chancellor? I'm famished...."

"What do I look like, the fucking Oracle of Hamhock Arms?" Carlo huffed. He glowered at Emmet—the very image of defiant, porcine rectitude in his befouled woolen town coat; then he heaved a sigh, made his way over to the cellar door and flung it open. "Whoa ...!" he said, teetering back from the snarling wolf in the doorway. "Easy there, fella—you know me, right? Heh, heh ... HEY PLUTO, YOU DOWN THERE?"

Pluto's wolves came streaming into the kitchen. Three of them took up positions at the doorways while the other three began an olfactory survey of the room's occupants. "I suggest none of you move a muscle," Carlo advised. The moment one of the wolves began sniffing at Lucia's tail feathers, however, the fashionably obese hen began flapping frantically in an attempt to become airborne; she rose only a few inches from the chair back that served as her perch when the wolf brought her down—snapping her neck in the process. "That's one less vote for the CFC," Carlo commented, as the hen thrashed around the floor in her death throes. No one moved after that. (Your prudent narrator had already moved from the window sill to the clothesline.)

"I see my feral facilitators have everything under control," said Pluto in his raspy monotone. Everyone was so focused on those wolves that no one even noticed the mandrill's entrance. He no longer wore his cowl, and his blazing mane was fuller and more fearsome than ever. Every inch the wild beast, he stood up on his hind legs and scanned the room with his creepy, close-set eyes; then he put some knuckles to the floor and vaulted to the table top. "I believe you have the floor," he growled, sitting on his haunches as he peered down the table at Emmet.

But Emmet was frozen with fear, and a heavy silence ensued.

It was the goat that finally spoke up. "M-My client," he stammered, "would seem to have the winning lottery ticket, sir—as I believe you're aware—and n-naturally he'd like to collect his winnings. Sir. Now, should it be the case th-that you're not entirely solvent, I'm sure my client would be willing to forego his demand for feed—and, and, and if you'd be amenable to liquidating some holdings—or perhaps simply transferring ownership of some properties ..."

"Take it all," said the mandrill.

Another silence ensued.

"What's going on, Pluto?" said Carlo, a note of concern in his voice.

"I'm thinking it's time to take my wolves and move on."

"Shit ..." said Carlo.

"But ... but why?" said Myrtle.

"I don't want to take the hit, obviously," said Pluto. "I've had a nice run—but now that things are turning against me, why stick around?"

"Could I have a word?" said Carlo to the mandrill, nodding toward the pantry. "And you too!" he barked at Emmet, "—we need to talk feed!"

After the three squeezed into the pantry and closed the door, the others shot glances at each other—and at the wolves —and their eyes betrayed their thoughts as they struggled to imagine life on the farm without the monkey to serve up the feed, and milk the cows, and shear the sheep, and deliver the firewood, and provide all the various distractions that could make a critter forget that life isn't really a whole lot different than flying into a 50-knot headwind at 40-knots; the thought of doing it sober must've been especially depressing.

Some of the Council Critters were too young to remember the days when the federation's free beasts had somehow managed on their own, and the animals that did remember recalled a hard life—its saving grace being that it beat the hell out of the Klunders' chopping block. But those times had come and gone, and there wasn't a critter among them that could imagine life on the farm without the monkey.

By and by, the conferees emerged from the pantry. "All I can say is it's a sad day for Freedom Farm," Carlo announced, shaking his head. "My pigheaded son refuses to withdraw his claim, and my simian asset refuses to honor it; paternity and equity apparently mean nothing anymore. Under different circumstances, I'd be happy to bail Pluto out—I've been bailing him out since the day I sprang him from the Pit; but feeling light-footed as he does, he's just not an acceptable risk. So I'm afraid the time has come to say goodby to an old friend...."

"Wait, wait," said Petra, "—what if Freedom Farm guarantees the loan?"

"He doesn't *want* a loan," Carlo insisted, as the monkey headed for the door—his wolves falling in behind.

"A grant, a grant!" said Myrtle, "You could lend Freedom Farm the feed, and we could bail him out with a lump sum grant—no strings!"

"Oh please," said Carlo. "The federation is on the verge

of default as it is. The only way Freedom Farm could take on the additional obligation is if it settled a sizable portion of its *own* account. And obviously, it'd have to do it before Pluto gets through that door...."

"But wait, wait—I mean ... how?"

The monkey stopped in the doorway.

"Tell her, Horace," said Carlo.

"Me ...?" said the goat. "Um, well ... in that case, it'd be the federation that would have to liquidate some assets—or else negotiate a fair market value for said assets, and transfer ownership of same to its creditors. Or creditor, as the case may be ..."

"Exactly," said Carlo.

"Could you give us an example?" said Myrtle.

"Alright," said Carlo, "—you give me the house, and I'll lend you the feed for a bailout."

"*This* house ...?"

Carlo nodded.

"I see ..." said Myrtle. "Could you, um, give us another example?"

"No."

"Well, I mean, what about the tool shed, say—and maybe, maybe ..."

Carlo shook his head.

CHAPTER 33

"I still think you should've gone for the barn," said Pluto, "—we could've had all those animals paying rent."

"Now, now," said Carlo, admiring the kitchen's ceiling beams. "Not everything's about feed."

"And then there's the Pit," Pluto persisted, "—a potential reservoir of slave labor...."

"All in good time," said Carlo, "all in good time."

"Would a simple 'thank you' be too much to ask?" said Emmet.

"Pig, another word out of you," said Carlo, "and you can just take your carcass up to the compound and spend the rest of the night by yourself!"

"What about the bird?" said Grover, nodding in Echo's direction.

"Yes, right—unfortunate about the job, bird," said Carlo to the mynah, "but I'm sure you can see where the federation wouldn't be in a position to squander any more feed on education. And look at the upside: you've got a bright new future tutoring piglets."

Echo was uncharacteristically silent.

"Speaking of birds," said Pluto, "I thought it might be nice if we had Bucky and a few of his friends for dinner."

"Izzat dang chicken-winger still kickin around?" said a befuddled Booger. "I thought he was lawn gone...."

A minute later, Pluto brought Bucky up from the cellar—plucked, cleaned, and ready for the spit. "You won't hear anymore bright ideas out of this one," he said.

"How in the hell did you get him shaped like that?" said Spencer in wonderment.

"It's proprietary," said Pluto.

By and by, the pigs and their simian asset feasted on flame-roasted Leghorn and glazed duck—all of which was exceedingly tender, owing to Pluto's proprietary process of "immobilization." Then a lamb was led in, laid over a chair—it's legs lashed to the chair's—and they all had a go at her. After that, the monkey brought up another bucket of corn liquor, along with a board game he'd picked up in Falling Rock. Before long, the pigs were feuding:

"I'm the racing car!"

"No, *I'm* the racing car!"

"You're the hat!"

"I don't wanna be the hat!"

From the chopping block in the corner, Pluto egged the pigs on—taunting, ridiculing, mocking them at every turn—and the game degenerated into a brawl; chairs were broken, the table was tipped over, and blood and corn liquor pooled on the hard plank floor.

When the debauchery in the kitchen began to wind down, the mandrill joined his wolves on the back porch. He climbed up on the railing and sat like a gargoyle, surveying the bedlam in the yard. In the fading light, thousands of hungry beasts lay siege to the barn, as Fritz and his troops chased through the crowds after the multiplying invaders from the Occupied Territory, and a gang of aggrieved ducks searched in vain for Sluggo and his minions so they could report Mrs. Cow for invading their pond—which, in truth, the shit-faced cow became mired in when she failed to distinguish between the pond's mossy banks and its thick mat of algae; Sluggo and his minions, meanwhile, were fleeing up the stump-studded hillside searching for someplace to hide from Pluto's bees—Africanized radicals who'd declared war when their hive was kicked over in the melee; sheep were wandering leaderless, chickens were cowering in their coops and BeaverBilts, and duck-stomping porkers were out doing the Lord's work—and the mandrill just sat there on that railing and took it all in with reverent, stony-faced appreciation.

"Let's hunt," he said at last, hopping to the ground. Then he and his wolves loped off in the direction of Hawg Homestead and disappeared in the encroaching gloom.

The whole place was going all to hell, but rather than celebrating, rather than being filled with wonder and exaltation, I was seized by the reality that the monkey was finally, *truly* free—and it weighed on me like wet plumage.

"Yeah, you'd hardly know the place," I said, surveying the heaps of hog flesh lying amid the kitchen's smashed and upturned furniture. "When I first came here, there was all this bestial bondage and human oppression...."

"We still got plenty of bondage and oppression, if you ask me," said the mynah, "—it's just not human anymore."

"Hey, you gotta take the good with the bad," I said. "But you have to admit, I really turned this place upside down."

"Not like that monkey..."

"Yeah, he's got a few tricks up his sleeve—I'll give him that. But who's the bird that made it all possible? Who's the one who got a bunch of downtrodden farm animals to rise up against their human oppressors and run the bastards off? How far do you think that monkey would've gotten if the Klunders were still running things when he came along?"

"Oh, *Mr. Big* ..." she said, sticking her beak in the air.

"You just can't give credit where credit is due," I pointed out. "Shit, if it weren't for me, you'd still have a door on that cage."

"Believe me, I wished I still had a door on this cage when those wolves came in!"

"The window was wide open, lady—you could've joined me on the clothesline," I told her. "Oh that's right—you'd rather be sitting in a cage than flying around free."

"Here we go with the freedom talk again," she said. "Tell me this, Mr. Free-as-a-bird: when you come to me in the middle of winter lookin' for a handout 'cause everything's covered with snow, and the pigs in the barn are watchin' every kernel, and you can't scrounge up anything anywhere else, who's free from *hunger and want*—you or me? Answer me that!"

"You got an answer for everything," I said. "I'll tell you one thing for sure: when I'm up there doing three-sixties and surfing the currents, and you're down here selling your life away a day at a time so you'll never have to see the bottom of that food dish, I'm a lot freer than you—even when I got Lord Gastric nipping at my ass."

"Oh yeah? If you're so goddamn free, how come you're still hanging around Toad Valley?"

"As a matter of fact," I said, with an expansive air of generosity, "the whole reason I came by was to see if maybe you wanted to go on the road with me...."

"Go on the road with you ...?" she said, incredulous.

"Sure, why not?" I said. "There's a whole big world outside this little backwater valley, you know. And a couple of odd birds like us?—we'd make a good team."

"Well, I'm flattered to know I'm *odd*," she said, getting puffed up.

"Come on, you know what I mean...."

"I got just one *odd* little question," she said. "How do you propose to get out of this little backwater valley?"

"I propose to do exactly like you suggested," I told her, sidling up close to her cage, "—we hire Hector Horse to take us down through the gorge...."

"Oh, I see. And who's supposed to pay for this?"

"Well ... you've got a little put aside, right?"

"Yeah, I got some feed put aside—and you know why that is? 'Cause I bust my *ass,* that's why! And I don't squander my feed at the Sneak-a-Peek, or the Oracle of Hamhock Arms, or any of that other shit—and I'm sure as hell not gonna let some crow con me into financing a trip to Falling Rock so he can leave me high and dry the minute we get there!"

"A simple *no* would've sufficed."

"How 'bout a simple *get fucked?*" she said. "First you insult my self-esteem by callin' me *odd,* then you insult my intelligence with this blatantly obvious con ..."

"I'm outta here," I said, hopping up on the window sill.

"Guess again, crow," she said, "—you're *stuck* here, just like the rest of us! You can't con your way out, you can't buy your way out—and it doesn't matter how many three-sixties you do, you can't *wing* your way out!"

"How would you know?" I told her, "—you never even tried!" Then I flashed my primaries flamboyantly and leapt into the night—pounding the air for all I was worth. I'd never tried to fly over those mountains either, of course; the mere sight of them was enough to take the wind out of any such impulse—and if I could've seen them at that moment, I probably wouldn't have tried it *then,* either. But I was flying blind, and I was pissed off—and after shooting off my mouth, I sort of felt obliged to give it a shot. So I just kept climbing up into the blackness propelled by bravado—along with a creeping sense of desperation. For all my eyes could tell, I could've been 50-feet off the ground, or a thousand, but as I labored on, I could feel the air growing cooler and thinner—until at last it seemed I was just flailing away in an inky void: a cold ocean of nothing to breath and nothing to pull against. I became light-headed, and realized even before I ran out of steam that I was no longer climbing, I was sinking—sinking back into some warm, muggy place. And then I heard a helicopter....

CHAPTER 34

As it turned out, the helicopter I heard was just Henry snoring in my ear—but that sinking feeling was real enough: it engulfed me as I opened my eyes and found myself sitting on the old buzzard's shoulder. He was still slouched there on that bench—head hung back, mouth gaping at the sky. His star-spangled stovepipe was lying, stepped-on, behind the bench, while Fred—wrapped in a blanket, and as dead to the world as he was—lay curled up at his feet. Across the street, Wally was ensconced in his cardboard coffin in the doorway of a vacant storefront. The park itself was littered with trash from the night's festivities, the sky was brightening to the east, and all the trees were beginning to sing—and there I sat on my ragged roost longing to slip back into a dream.

Not that I'd ever have another dream like that one: it was some beastly weed those three were smoking.

But my Toad Valley adventures had slipped away, and there was nothing to look forward to but another day with Henry. In the interminable hours to come, I could expect to accompany my human patron down the same streets and alleys exploring the same dumpsters and trash cans we explored in exactly the same order the day before; I could expect to sift through Hillsdale's tides of trash searching pathetically for something shiny and interesting while my siblings raised hell in the branches overhead; and I could expect to be his monkey at the 7-Eleven, where he would recount my story a dozen times, and babble on about Babylon and world affairs and the age-old art of hunting and gathering—and I, as usual, sat on his shoulder salving myself with a daydream. It would be a day of crushing, predictable, two-dimensional order—a day with no surprises, no mystery, and no end. And if I flapped my wings at all, it would only be to keep my balance as the doddering old shit traced his maddeningly predictable path around the neighborhood.

What I could *not* expect to do was fly; any hope I'd harbored of ever taking to the air had crashed and burned weeks before.

At least, for the most part it had. But every day, Henry would stir up that hope by going through the motions of teaching me the presumed skills I'd need to make it on my own—and doing it in the most emphatic way, like he was right on the verge of taking me in his bony mitt and tossing me up high in the air. In truth, I'd been waiting for him to launch me into my avian life ever since sprouting a full set of primaries—but I guess those daily briefings were just his way of keeping himself company.

Still, it's a crow's nature to fuck with things—to poke and tear and pick things apart—even if it's the tangle of his own beliefs that's got his attention. And a particularly inconvenient belief had my full attention as the sky continued to brighten and the trees swelled with song: the notion that a bird has to fall before it can fly—that only a precipitous drop can make that flight reflex kick in the first time out. The last time I experienced a precipitous drop, I flapped my ass off—so I could see why birds had been learning to fly like that for a million years.

But was it possible, I wondered *stupidly*—through a simple act of will—to transcend whatever hardwired bullshit had persisted down through untold generations and just lift off into that big open sky like I'd been doing it all my life?

Before I could think of a reason not to, I unfolded my wings and sprang into that cool morning air—and for a moment I was a culled nestling again, plummeting to earth after getting the boot. But I pulled hard and caught myself just inches from the ground—nearly crashing into a lamppost as I careened to one side, before veering out over the street and grazing some electrical wires as I climbed. After I'd cleared the trees, buildings, and other obstructions, a persistent sense of disbelief gradually fell away as I circled in all that free open space—getting a bird's eye view of the terrain stretching endlessly in every direction, and exulting in the squirrelly way my wings quivered as they cut through the shifting currents. My avian soul came to life with a rush.

By and by, I tipped a wing to the inert form sprawled on the bench below—I owed the old derelict that much—and took a moment to thank the Unraveling for delivering me to the sky. Then I banked to the east, and flew straight into the dawn of an immaculate new day.

A world of chaos awaited.